MARMADUKE WYVIL

AN

HISTORICAL ROMANCE OF 1651

BY

HENRY WILLIAM HERBERT

AUTHOR OF "THE CAVALIERS OF ENGLAND," "KNIGHTS OF ENGLAND, FRANCE," ETC.,
"CHEVALIERS OF FRANCE," "THE PURITANS OF NEW ENGLAND," "CROMWELL," ETC.

"Vengeance is mine; I will repay, saith the Lord."

FOURTEENTH EDITION—REVISED AND CORRECTED.

REDFIELD,
110 AND 112 NASSAU STREET, NEW YORK.
1853.

STEREOTYPED BY C. C. SAVAGE,
13 Chambers Street, N. Y.

PREFACE.

THIS historical romance, which was originally issued from the "New World" press by Messrs. Winchester and Benjamin, in the days of cheap publication, has never been offered to the world in any shape fit to be preserved in a library, or to lie upon a drawing-room table. It was infamously printed, during the absence of the author from the city, and teems with the most absurd errors of the press, never having undergone any real or careful correction.

In spite of these drawbacks, it was so fortunate as to meet general favor; fourteen editions, the first of three thousand copies, the others of a thousand each, having been sold in a few years. It is hoped that no further apology will be needed for offering it to the public, thoroughly revised and corrected by the author, and printed in Mr. Redfield's elegant style, as one of a series, which, it is intended, shall ultimately combine all the romances and fugitive writings of his friends' and the public's

Grateful and obedient servant,

HENRY WILLIAM HERBERT.

THE CEDARS, *March* 31, 1853.

MARMADUKE WYVIL.

CHAPTER I.

In a sequestered vale of merry England, not many miles from the county town of Worcester, there stands, in excellent preservation, even to the present day, one of those many mansions scattered through the land, which—formerly the manor-houses of a race, now, like their dwellings, becoming rapidly extinct, the good old English squires—have, for the most part, been converted into farm-houses; since their old-time proprietors have, simultaneously with the growth of vaster fortunes, and the rise of loftier dignities, declined into an humbler sphere. In the days of which we write, however, Woolverton Hall was in the hands of the same family, which had dwelt there, father and son, for ages. It was a tall, irregular edifice, of bright red brick, composed of two long buildings, with steep flagged roofs and pointed gables, meeting exactly at right angles so as to form a letter L; the longer limb running due east and west, the shorter abutting on the eastern end, pointing with its gable southerly. In this south gable, near the top, was a tall, Gothic, lanceolated window, its mullions and casings wrought of a yellowish sand-stone, to match the corner-stones of all the angles, which were faced with the same material. Beneath this window, which, as seen from without, appeared to reach nearly from the floor to the ceiling of the second story, was the date, 1559—the numerals, several feet in length, composed of rusty iron; and above it, on the summit of the gable, a tall weathercock, surmounted by a vane, shaped like a dolphin, which had once been fairly gilded, but now was all dim and tarnished by long exposure to the seasons. To this part of the house there were no chimneys, which was the more remarkable, that the rest of the building was somewhat superfluously adorned with these appendages, rising like columns, quaintly wrought of brick-work in the old Elizabethan style. Corresponding to the Gothic window in position, though by no means so lofty, a range of five large square-topped latticed windows, divided each into four compartments by a cross-shaped stone transom, ran all along that front of the other wing, which, with the abutting chapel—for such it seemed to be—formed the interior angle of the L. From the point of the western roof, to match, as it were, the weathercock which crowned the other gable, projected a long beam, or horn of stone, at an angle of about ninety degrees, curiously wreathed with a deep spiral groove, not much unlike the tusk of that singular animal, the sword-fish.

This was all that could be seen of the main building from without, by a spectator looking at its southern front—for it stood in a court surrounded by a heavy wall of brick, with a projecting parapet and battlement of stone, flanked by short towers, with roofs shaped like extinguishers, and having its base washed by a broad rapid rivulet, which, rushing through a narrow artificial channel, along the eastern wall, expanded in front of the house into a wider bed; and after falling over a steep dam, swept off down the lone valley to the left, in a southwesterly direction. In the outer wall, close to the base of a flanking tower, crenelled and looped for musketry and ordnance, was a low water-gate, well-closed with a portcullis of stout iron bars, and, some ten feet within, by a strong second door of oak, studded with massive nails. Toward the west, the courtyard wall rose higher, for there a smooth and velvet lawn, with no impediment of fosse or ditch, swept, with a light ascent, up to its very foot; and in the centre of its length, seen, in perspective, by one standing as above, was an embattled gatehouse. It should be added that from within this wall, the tops of many ornamental trees might be discovered, now slightly tinged by the first hues of autumn. The northern and eastern faces of the houses, which could not, of course, be seen from the position indicated, displayed no entrances, nor aught save narrow loops and shot-holes on the ground floor, while, even on the upper stories, the apertures for air and light were small, and guarded against escalade by heavy iron gratings.

The whole had evidently been originally meant, no less for a defensible position than for a peaceful dwelling, in those stern days, when every man's house was, in truth, his castle; but easier times had followed, and many of the sterner points had been concealed, and that not casually, by graces and embellishments of milder nature. Fruit-trees, and many flowering creepers, were trained along the landward fronts of the main building; a mass of dense and tangled ivy covered the turrets of the gate-house, and on the moat—little designed for such use by its makers—floated two stately swans, their graceful necks and snow-white plumage reflected to the life, on its transparent bosom, with a whole host of smaller waterfowl, teal, widgeon, golden-eyes, and others of rare foreign species, diving and revelling, half-reclaimed, in pursuit of their prey or pleasure.

Such was the aspect of the hall, on the day following the desperate fight of Worcester, the sounds of which—the dull, deep bellowing of the cannon, blent with the harsh, discordant rattle of the volleying musketry—had been distinctly heard by its dismayed inhabitants. Some symptoms of fresh preparation were there, though, for the most part, slight and ineffective—the creepers had been cut away in places where they had entirely obscured the crenelles; fresh loopholes had been broken in the western wall; a few small cannon, falcons, and culverins, were mounted on the parapet; and from an embrasure, which flanked the water-gate, the muzzle of a heavy gun was run out, grinning its stern defiance. There was no flag, however, displayed from the walls; no show of any garrison, not so much even as a solitary sentinel—so that there was no reason to believe the inmates partisans of either of those factions which had so long disturbed the country; or to suppose them capable of any more prolonged defence, than might suffice to beat off the marauders, who, ever profiting by times of civil discord, levied their contributions equally on friend or foe or neutral.

South of the moat, the bank of which was fringed with a low shrubby coppice, mostly of ornamental plants and bushes, a park-like meadow dotted with clumps of trees, and full of sunny slopes and cool, deep hollows, extended, half a mile perhaps in width, to the high road, from which it was divided by a broad, sunk fence and ragged paling; and was flanked by the stream, which, strong, and deep, and rapid, had cut itself a deep gorge through the rich alluvial soil, the sides thickset with broom, and furze, and brachens, and many a polished holly-bush, and many an ash and alder, forming a dense and seemingly impervious brake. Beyond the river, which the road traversed on an old one-arched bridge of brick, lay a wide tract of low and swampy woodland; and at the angle of the park, formed by the meeting of the highway and the brook, stood a small fishing-house, much overgrown with ivy, but kept in good repair; as might be seen by the neat painted lattices, one of which, standing open, showed a white muslin curtain gracefully looped up, and a small table with a vase of flowers arranged there, evidently by a woman's hand.

This scene, with all its details, has not been thus particularly and closely drawn, from the mere wish of laying a picture before the eyes of the reader—although it is a picture, and a true one—but from a desire of impressing on the mind localities, without a full and distinct perception of which much of the variegated tale to be related would be obscure, to such a degree, as to lose one half of its interest.

It was, as has been said, on the day following Worcester fight—the crowning mercy of that remarkable man who swayed so skilfully the destinies of the great kingdom, which he so strangely won—that Woolverton Hall looked, in the level rays of the declining sun, as it is here described. The morning had been raw and gusty, and though toward sunset the chilly clouds had opened, and let out a few faint beams to gild the melancholy hues of autumn, which were encroaching fast upon the cheerful greenery of the woods, it was but a gray and gloomy evening. A few small birds had, indeed, mustered courage to chirrup some short notes to the brief sunbeams, and a single throstle was pouring out his liquid song from the thick foliage on the river bank; but the wind whistled dolefully, although not high, among the tree-tops, whirling away the sere leaves with its every breath; and a thin, ghostly mist seethed upward from the surface of the brook, like the steam of a caldron, and through its smoky wreathes flapped the broad pinions of that aquatic hermit, the gray heronshaw, meet habitant of such a spot.

Sadly, however, as the scene, beautiful in ordinary aspects, and romantically wild, showed, under such a sky, it was yet gazed upon by soft and lovely eyes; for, from the open lattice of the fishing-house, nearest to the highway, a young girl, surely not past her twentieth summer, looking forth half listlessly, half-mournfully, over the bridge, and up the sandy road, which, skirting the dank woodlands wound over a small hill, the verge of which cut clear against the ruddy sky at a mile's distance. She was a genuine English beauty, with a fair and oval face, a bright, delicate complexion, shaded by a profusion of rich nut-brown hair, falling in ample curls from off her lustrous brow, and sweeping, in thick clusters, down her neck. Her eyes were of a full, bright blue, with long, dark lashes; and they, and all her features, spoke volumes of soft, gentle, girlish feelings—of tenderness and pity; and of love, latent—but ready to leap forth a giant from his birth. Her figure was below, rather than above, the middle height of woman; but exquisitely shaped, and far more full and rounded, although her waist was very slender, than usual at her years. Her arm, which was a good deal displayed by the open falling sleeve of the period, was symmetry itself; and her whole person, and its every movement, full of that graceful ease, which goes yet farther to win hearts than the most regal beauty. A book or two lay scattered on the table at her side, and an old-fashioned lute; while at her feet, stretched out at his full length, was an enormous bloodhound, his lithe and sinewy limbs now all relaxed and easy, his huge black-muzzled head quietly couched between his paws, and his smooth, tawny hide glancing like copper in the last lurid sunbeam. But now that sunbeam vanished; a deeper shade sank down over the landscape, a dull, gray hue swallowed up all the glimmering tints that gemmed the fleecy clouds with light, and all was dim and dark — woodland, and mead, and sky, and river, except one pale, bright streak far in the west, against which the brow of the hill, with the road winding over it, stood out in clear relief

The girl, who had been gazing so long on the darkening scene, evidently half unconscious that she did so, suddenly seemed to recollect herself, and gathering her cloak about her, drew its hood over her rich tresses, and rose as if to go — the bloodhound, wakened from his dose by her light tread, lifted his head, yawned lazily, and stretched himself; and then arising to his full height, looked wistfully into her face, as if he were aware of the importance of his trust.

But at that very moment a dull, flat report, as of a distant gunshot, broke the silence; and the dog pricked his pendulous ears, and stalked with a low growl to the doorway, while the lady turned her head quickly toward the window whence she had just withdrawn. Her first glance was toward the road; and, where it crossed the hill-top, she saw clearly the head of a man, and then his whole figure, with his horse, rise rapidly against the brilliant gleam of the western sky — so instantaneous was his transit, however, that she would almost have distrusted her eyesight, had not the clatter of hoofs, dashing fiercely down the hill-side, assured her of its accuracy — for now the slope and base of the hill were all in misty and uncertain shadow. Before she had well thought on what she had scarce seen, another, and another, and another head topped the steep vèrge; and, as they crossed it, were discovered, by the bright glitter, to be covered with steel caps, the well-known head-dress of the puritan troopers — another second sufficed to bring into full view a party of some twenty horse, who halted for a moment on the summit — a dozen of quick flashes ran along the front, and the sharp rattle of a volley followed—again, a minute—and they, too, had galloped down the slope, and were enveloped in thick gloom. All this passed in less time than it has taken to describe it, but still the lady marked and understood it all; and acted on the instant, as a kind heart, instigated by woman's natural sympathy with the oppressed, dictated. With a quick step she left the fishing-house, and stood upon a little flight of steps which ran down from a platform level with the bridge, to the stream's brink. And scarcely had she reached her stand, before the single horseman wheeled round the angle of the wood, and crossed the bridge at as fast a rate as his drooping steed could compass. The pursuers, scarcely five hundred yards behind him, were still beyond the woodland, which alone hindered them from seeing him.

"Hist!" she cried—"hist! Sir Cavalier!" in clear, low tones, which made themselves distinctly audible to him whom she addressed, though they could scarcely have been heard at three yards' distance. "Halt, as you love your life! Halt, for Godsake!"

Almost instinctively the rider drew his rein; and the wearied horse obeyed so readily, that he stood statue-like upon the instant. The horseman was a tall, slight figure, with a slouched hat and drooping feather, a cuirass of bright steel, crossed by a broad blue baldric, and all his buff coat slashed with satin, and fringed with Flanders' lace—thus much she saw at half a glance, and it confirmed all she supposed and dreaded.

"You have but one chance for your life!" she said—"but one! but one! There is another troop of Cromwell's horse not half a league before you. 'Light down! 'light down! for Godsake, while yet they are behind the wood—nay! speak not, but 'light down," she continued, even more vehemently, seeing him now about to answer. "Do it with the speed of light—cross the bridge back again, fasten your horse there in the wood, and join me instantly—I can—and *I will* save you, so you delay not!"

The tramp of galloping horses came nearer, and the shouts of the pursuers — he paused, he doubted, but as if to accelerate his resolve, a distant trumpet-tone, and the long hollow boom of a kettle-drum came down the road from the direction he was following, and proved the hopelessness of flight. He turned his horse's head—

"Lady," he said, "I trust you, I obey!" — he retraced his steps quickly, and had just reached the friendly covert, when, at the top of their speed, the Puritans drove round the corner —a second sooner, and he had perished at their feet.

With instant readiness of mind, she hurried down the steps, bidding the hound, in a low voice, be still, and from the last low stair, sprang lightly to a small abutment under the bridge's arch, just level with the water; and scarcely was she there, before, with clash of harness, and jingling of spur and scabbard, and all the thundering din of charging horse, the troopers drove above her head. The solid masonry appeared to quake beneath the fury of their speed. Her heart stood still with awe — then, as the tumult passed, and died away in the distance, bounded as though it would have burst her bosom. Timidly, cautiously she crept up the damp, mossy steps, and reached the causeway — and hardly was she there, when a dim shape came crouching toward her from the woodland.

"Heaven be praised!" she exclaimed — "oh, Heaven be praised!" as he stood safely by her side. "Follow me swift and silently. Life! life is on our speed!"

Descending once more to the margin of the water, she drew aside the tangled branches, and entered a small winding footpath, worn by the devious tread of the wild deer, and widened by the steps of village urchins, nutting or birdnesting among the matted dingle. So narrow was the track, however, and so abruptly did it twist and turn round many a doddered ivy-bush and stunted oak, now covered, for a few steps, by the shallow ripples of the stream, now scaling the ravine by sudden zigzags, that none but a well-practised eye could have discovered it by that glimmering twilight. Though well aware that life was on his speed — that the avenger of blood was but a little way behind — the stranger scarcely could keep up, though muscular, and swift of foot, and active, with the deer-like speed of his fair guide. At length, after a rapid walk of perhaps ten minutes, they reached the dam at the moat-head — where was a low-arched boat-house, with a small light skiff moored beneath it — and stood quietly facing the south side of the mansion. From the two windows, farthest of the five in the upper range, a steady light was shining into the quiet night; and from a loop, beside the water-gate, a long, red ray streamed out, casting a wavering line of radiance over the rippling water. With these exceptions, all was profoundly dark and silent. By the boat-house she paused a moment, as if in deep reflection.

"They will come here anon!" she said — "they will come here anon, and search the house from battlement to cellar, before we can bestow you where I would. And I must blind the servants, and speak, too, with my father. Meanwhile, here must you tarry — here they will never dream of searching."

And as she spoke she stooped under the low-browed arch, and tripped along a little rib of stone-work, scarcely a foot in width, to the extreme end of the boat-house, where was a narrow paved landing, with three steps downward to the water, and a slight wooden ladder upward, leading to a small hole beside the keystone of the arch.

"Up there," she cried — "up there," laying her hand upon the ladder, which they could just distinguish by the reflection of the windows from the moat. "It is a little sail-loft, not two feet high, under the slated roof, full of old sails and oars. Up there, and draw the ladder after you, and should they come to search there, which they will *not*, I think, roll yourself in the canvass, and lie still. And now attend to me. There is a little air-hole in the front, toward the house, whence you can see the windows. Can you swim, sir — you can, I warrant me!" and as she heard his brief affirmative, she went on rapidly — "well, when you see that red light thrice extinguished, and thrice re-lighted, with such a pause that you may reckon ten between, come down, swim boldly to the water-gate, and I will be there to admit you. Farewell — God keep you," and she stepped into the light boat, unmoored, and pushed it out, while the young cavalier ascended, and drew up the ladder obedient to her bidding.

The distance was but short, and the light paddle, wielded by her fairy hands, scarcely had cut the surface six times, ere the boat floated by the portcullis of the water-gate ; and a voice somewhat tremulous from age, hailed from the lighted shot-hole, inquiring who was there.

"'Tis I—'tis I, good Jeremy," she answered. "Open to me, quickly, for it is somewhat late and cold for the season."

The aged servitor required no second bidding ; the grating was drawn up, and the inner doors thrown open, and — while the old man held his link on high, casting a smoky light over the steps, and the black water, and several boats moored there of various sizes — two younger grooms, with badges on the sleeves of their jerkins, ran out along the platforms on each side, and drew the boat, with its fair freight, up to the inner landing. The gates were again barred, and the portcullis lowered — the cresset in the ward-room was extinguished, and Jeremy preceding with the torch, and the grooms following cap in hand, the lady passed out from the water-tower into the court-yard of the hall.

The upper portion of the building, as viewed from without the wall, has been described already ; but a new prospect was now shown — the court, from the walls of the chapel, to the gate-house at its western end, would have measured not less than a hundred yards, one half of which, toward the gate, was laid out in a formal parterre, divided from the rest by a stone balustrade, with richly-carved stone vases, and planted thickly with yew and box and holly, clipped into all fantastic shapes of peacocks, centaurs, dragons, and the like, according to the taste of that old day, with two time-honored giants — vast pines — presiding over them, like Samsons, in all the majesty of unshorn strength and beauty. The remaining space was open, paved with small pebbles, divided by long rows of granite curb-stones, diverging from a common centre, where, in an ornamental basin, played a small fountain. The door of the mansion, under a low stone arch, bearing upon its keystone the same date, 1559, was placed exactly at the extremity of the main building, where the abutting chapel formed a right angle, and was flanked by several long crenelles for musketry, which, it would seem, with similar apertures, had, formerly, been the only means of giving light to the ground floor of the edifice. Of these, however, only five remained flanking the doorway, while, for the others, had been substituted good, honest, latticed casements, four in the front, under the windows of the upper story, the portal corresponding to the fifth, and six in the basement of the chapel.

From all of these now shone a bright and cheerful radiance through the transparent medium of snow-white curtains, against which many a shadow of male and female forms were cast, as persons hurried to and fro between them and the lights; while ever and anon the hum of merry voices and light laughter rang out into the night, suggesting many an image of fireside English comfort. Not long, however, did the lady pause to note a scene which she had looked upon many times daily from her childhood, but passed across an angle of the garden, and through the middle of the court, directly to the door. It was a formidable massy-looking remnant of antiquity—a piece of hard black oak, six inches thick, all clenched with great nail-heads, and crossed with iron bars—yet it stood on the latch, which gave way readily to the light touch of the lady, and admitted her to a small neat square hall, with two doors, to the right and left, and a huge staircase at the back—the steps, and balustrades, and wainscoting, and floor, all made of beautiful and highly-polished oak. A Gothic window, with stained glass, in the second story—for the hall was the whole height of the building, with a gallery above—lighted it in the day; but now a brazen lamp, with several blazing branches, swung by a crimson cord from the roof. Two or three portraits hung upon the wall, grim-visaged warriors cap-a-pie in steel, with brandished truncheons—and long-waisted ladies, looking unutterable sweetness at huge nosegays. Upon a large slab table, under the first turn of the staircase, lay several gloves, a broad-leafed hat and feather, and a sad-colored riding-cloak of camlet; while, in the corner, stood a miscellaneous assortment of hand-guns, fishing-rods, crossbows, and hunting-poles—weapons of rural sport—as on the walls above hung suits of bright plate armor, with arquebus and petronel and pike, and every implement of veritable warfare.

"There—that will do, Jeremy. I trow I shall find my father in the library above: that will do—go your way to supper," said the fair girl, waving her hand to her attendants, eager to get away from the restraint imposed on her by their presence; and as they disappeared through the door to the right—whence, as they opened it, proceeded a most savory smell of supper, and a loud buzz of merriment—bounded with a light foot but anxious heart, up the broad staircase; hurried through several spacious rooms, illuminated only by the dim glimmering of the new-risen moon, and entering the library, stood in a broad glare of light before her father's chair.

CHAPTER II.

The apartment which the lady entered, was a small room, furnished on every side with book-cases and presses of some dark foreign wood, which, indeed, covered all the wall, with the exception of the panel immediately above the mantelpiece, and this was filled by a large and exquisitely-painted portrait. There needed not two glances before pronouncing it a masterpiece of Antony Vandyck; it was a lady, in the pride and prime of youthful beauty, and the calm melancholy features and dark glossy curls told, beyond doubt, the place which she had occupied in that old house, and the relationship she bore to the fair girl who stood below, younger and fresher and more gay, but still the breathing counterpart of the old picture. The only inmate of the room, when the girl cast the door abruptly open, was a man very far advanced in years, but yet of stately presence—time, which had covered his fine classic head with the thin snows of nearly fourscore winters, and ploughed deep lines of care and thought on his expansive brow, had not curtailed his upright stature by one inch, nor dimmed at all the lustre of his dark brilliant eye. He had been, it would seem, employed in writing; for the pen was yet in his fingers, and paper lay before him with many books—folios, and ponderous tomes of reference—scattered around him on the table. But the unwonted speed of his daughter's tread had excited him—for those were days when each new hour brought a new tale of terror, and men not naturally observant, were forced to become so, by the immediate pressure of events. He had arisen, therefore, from his cushioned chair, which he had pushed back toward the ruddy hearth, and even taken a step or two toward the door—when it flew open, and with cheeks paler than usual, and a slight air of anxiety, but, nevertheless, all calm and passionless and tranquil, she stood before him.

"Why, how now, Alice," he exclaimed; "what has gone wrong now—what is amiss, my darling, and wherefore so late?"

"Oh, nothing, nothing is amiss, dear father," she replied, forcing a smile, which, nevertheless, failed to deceive his fears or calm his apprehension. "Nothing has gone wrong, I assure you, but I have much to tell you, and brief space wherein to do so; and, above all, I fear me much, we shall, ere long, have most unwelcome visiters."

"Sit down, then—sit down, Alice, and tell me all about it—if there be brief space, so much the more need for good haste;" and he pulled forward, as he spoke, a settee from the corner of the chimney, and placed himself in his own seat in attitude of deep attention.

"Well, father, to begin," she said; "I took the little skiff, when you came up to write, and crossed the moat, and walked down with old Talbot to the fishing-house by the high road to Worcester; and there I got engaged with a book till my attention was called from it by sounds of martial music, sounding away beyond the top of Longmire Hill; and then I looked out in surprise, for we had heard, you know, that the troops had all moved away southward, and saw first one, and then a second troop of horsemen file down the slope; and, as I did not fear at all, having no cause to do so, I waited there to see them pass, and they were men of Cromwell's own regiment of Ironsides, with scarlet cassocks, and bright corslets, and steel caps, and large boots, and no feathers. There were above a hundred of them, and they rode by quite leisurely, laughing and chatting, and some smoking. And when they passed by, I fell into a sort of revery, which must have lasted a long time, for when I recollected myself it had become quite gray and dark; and there was no light in the sky except one yellow gleam along the summit of the hill, where the road crosses it. And then I rose to go away, and had put on my cloak, when a sound like the shot of a hand-gun or pistolet, attracted me, and I looked out again and saw one horseman cross the ridge at a full gallop, and half a minute after, the top was covered by a whole troop of Puritans, for I could see the glitter of their helmets; and they halted and fired a volley, and charged down hill after him. So then I went out on the platform by the bridge, and waited till he came up—a tall young gentleman, with long light hair, and a slouched hat and feather, and a steel breast-plate, with a broad blue scarf across it; and I called out to him to stop, and told him how there was another company of horse before, and bade him turn back, and tie up his own beast—sorely jaded it was, too, though a noble charger—down in the heronry wood, and to join me while his pursuers were hid behind the tall trees of the beech clump, and he went back—and was just out of sight, when the whole party turned the corner, and drove down, shouting and brandishing their swords at a fierce gallop. Then I ran down the steps, and hid beneath the arch of the brick bridge, while they dashed on overhead. Not one of them saw me or Talbot, I'm quite certain, and the dog never growled nor showed his teeth, but seemed to know what he was to do, as well as I did. When they had all gone by again, I ran up to the top once more, and there he joined me; and I brought him home along the little patn through the dark dingle; and when we reached the boat-house I showed him the sail-loft, and made him mount the ladder, and draw it up after him; and then I crossed the moat alone, and came directly home to tell you all that I had done. And I *have* done right—have not I, my father?"

"Right! right, of course, my girl; you could not see the fair youth slain. Yet 'tis an awkward chance. None of the serving-men nor foresters saw him with you, you are certain?"

"Certain—most certain!"

"So far well—these troopers, as you say, will be here anon, and will search all the house; but they know me, that I have not borne arms nor taken any part in these sad broils, and our cousin Chaloner has drawn his sword for the Commonwealth; so that if we can hide him from this first search, I fear little but that we may preserve him. He must stay where he is at present, and until they be here and the search over—then will we have him in when it's quite late, and hide him in the priest's hole. Did any of the first party of troopers see you?"

"One did, and pointed me to his next comrade, and I heard them laugh and whisper."

"Then this must be your tale; you saw the first two companies go by, and tarried at the fishing-house yet longer; but when you heard the shots, you were afraid, and fled across the park to the boat-house, and came here by the skiff."

"Were it not better, father," she replied, "to make no mention of the boat-house, lest they should search and—"

"No! no!" he answered—"oh, no no! They will interrogate the servants, and learn where the boat lay, and so will suspect what you would conceal, even from your own omission."

"I see," she replied, thoughtfully. "Yet 'tis a fearful risk."

"It is so, Alice," answered the old man—"it is so; yet fearful as it is, it must be run; and now away—go to your bower, and call your tirewoman, and dress as is your wont; and then to supper; all must go on as usual; we must leave them no hint whereon to hang suspicion."

She left the library, and in a little while returned with her rich hair combed back from her fair brow, and neatly braided, and all her dress chastely arranged as for the evening meal. The pair descended to the hall, where, as was customary in those unsophisticated days, the household was assembled to partake, at the same board, of the same meal which was prepared for their superiors. With easy dignity, but naught of stern pride or cold presumption, the aged gentleman presided with his sweet child beside him; but ere the meal was ended, the interruption—by two at least of the party fully expected—occurred to break it short. A trumpet was blown clamorously at the gate-house, and before it could by any possibility have been answered, a second and a third blast followed.

"Go, some of you, and see," exclaimed the master of the house, with an air of the most perfect unconcern—"go see who calls so rudely—bestir you, or the man will blow the gate down."

Two or three of the badged green-coated serving men, of whom the hall was full, ran off at speed to perform his bidding; but ere they reached the gates the porter had discharged his duty, and forty or fifty of the Ironsides dismounted, and marched in, their long steel scabbards and huge boots clanking and clattering over the paved courtyard, while thrice as many of their comrades were drawn up round the house on horseback, so as to form a cordon, rendering escape impossible except by the moat, which, of course, could not be included in the chain of sentries.

"Ten men, with Sergeant Goodenough, straight to the water-gate," shouted a loud authoritative voice; "cut down or shoot all who attempt to pass without the word."

"Ha! here is something more than common," cried the old man; "nay, fear not, gentle daughter, I will go see to it;" and he arose as if to put his words into effect, when the doors were thrown violently open, and two officers—one a rough-looking veteran, well seamed with scars of ancient honorable wars, the other a sleek, hypocritical-looking youth, with a head of close-cropped foxy hair, and an evil downcast eye—both clad in the full uniform of Cromwell's Ironsides, and with their swords drawn, entered; while about the door clustered a group of privates, with their musquetoons all unslung, and their slow matches lighted.

"Let no one quit the room, who would not die the death;" exclaimed the first who entered.

"What means this outrage, gentlemen, if gentlemen ye be, who violently thus intrude upon a lady's presence, with your war-weapons and rude tongues? What makes ye in my peaceful dwelling at this untimely hour?"

"It means, Mark Selby," replied the second, in a low nasal strain—"it means that thou, despite our noble general's proclamation, hast traitorously harbored and secreted one of those rakehell cavaliers, whom, yesterday, the Lord delivered into our hands, to slay them. Wherefore, surrender him at once, so shalt thou 'scape the penalty this time on strength of thy relationship with stout and trusty Henry Chaloner."

"What cavalier? or of whom speak ye? I know not whom ye mean. My household, save the porter and the scullions, are all here. Save we ourselves, there are none else in all the house."

"Lie not!" replied the young man, violently; "lie not, lest the Lord deal with thee, as he dealt in old time with Ananias and Sapphira."

"I thank thee for thy courtesy, and shall make thee no answer any more. Search the house if ye will—ye will find no one here!"

"We will search—and search thoroughly—yea! very thoroughly! for though thou thinkest it not, we know your secret corners, your priest's holes, and your jesuit's hidings—yea! we shall search them, and finding what we shall find—ill will it go with thee. Keep guard thou, lancepesade, over all here till we return;" and with the word they left the hall in which all the household was collected, and for two hours or more they were heard searching every room, and stair, and landing-place of the large rambling edifice—sounding the panels with their musket butts, thrusting their broadswords into every crevice, but evidently finding nothing to justify their violent intrusion. At length re-entering, they strictly questioned the old servants, from whom, however, nothing was elicited, except that their mistress had gone forth with the boat alone, some hour or so after the dinner, and had returned alone by the water-gate two hours since.

Then came the lady's turn, and, though with something more of delicacy and restraint, she, too, was very narrowly examined. The story she told, being the literal truth, except that she omitted to say anything about the cavalier, and corresponding exactly with the narrative of the servants, produced a very visible effect upon the hearers, who, having searched all the out-houses and stables, and every nook and corner in the house, without finding anything, and having, in the first instance, intruded only upon a vague suspicion, began to fear that they had got into a troublesome scrape. After a pause, however—

"The boat-house," exclaimed one; "the boat-house—we have not searched the boat-house! Bring all of them along; or, stay, bring Master Selby down, and his fair daughter, to the water-gate, and we will boat it over, they guiding us. Without there, sergeant—move a guard round by the dam on the moat, to the boat-house."

The words were not well uttered before they were obeyed, and in ten minutes the whole party, consisting of the officers, with six stout troopers, were floating in the barge toward the boat-house. The face of the old man was stern and dark, and save of anger and resentment, showed no emotion; nor did his daughter, though inwardly her whole frame shook with bitter and heart-rending anguish, suffer a single tremor to betray her feminine terrors. The boat shot into the little cove, the torches threw their broad glare through the whole building, and there was naught to see.

"Here is a platform and a landing," cried the same youth who had proposed to search the boat-house, and who, with a strange pertinacity, persisted still—"let us ashore, for I doubt much we have him here:" and landing on the narrow rib whereon the little feet of Alice had trodden but a short while before, he strode with echoing tramp to the far end, and waving his torch round, discovered the entrance of the sail-loft.

"Ha! said I not so?" he exclaimed, exultingly; "said I not so? What have we up this trap, sweet Master Selby?"

"A sail-loft," answered he, very quietly; "a little place about a foot or two high, with some old oars in it; best search it, sir—best search it; there may be a whole troop of cavaliers therein for aught I know against it."

Poor Alice set her teeth and drew her breath hard, and with a tremulous grasp clung to her father's arm as he replied, "I will."

"Tush, man," his comrade interposed, "thou carriest caution to sheer folly; seest thou, there is no ladder? how should a man have mounted—or, having mounted, how in God's name should he lie there?"

"They may have cut the ladder down, lest it should leave a clew. Be it as it may, I will essay it. Here, jump ashore you, Martin and John Burney, hoist me into this trap, and pass me up a torch."

And in a moment, by their aid, he caught the edge of the trap with his hands, drawing his head and shoulders in till he could hold himself up by his elbows; the torch was then passed up to him, and he thrust it forward into the loft a little way up.

"Well, Despard, what see you?" cried his comrade.

"Four old oars, and a roll of canvass," answered the disappointed soldier, tossing his torch into the water, and leaping down.

"I thought so," was the answer; and a loud burst of laughter from the Ironsides, who were tired out by the fruitless search, and eager to get back to quarters, drowned the convulsive sob which Alice could not master.

With brief and blunt excuse the troopers mounted and departed—the hall was again quiet, and when they were again left to themselves in the old library, Alice fell suddenly into her father's arms, and burst into a flood of weeping.

CHAPTER III.

It was long after the departure of the Ironsides, before the excited feelings of the fair girl were in the least degree composed; but gradually, when the harsh clank of their march, and the shrill clangor of their trumpet, had subsided into absolute stillness, or rather into that soft and soothing mixture of natural and accustomed sounds, which, after the home ear has grown acquainted with their never-ending murmur, pass for entire silence—the violent fits of half-convulsive sobbing which had at first shaken her whole frame ceased, and the tears flowed in a quiet and unpainful stream. These, too, by slow degrees, diminished, and at last flowed no longer. It was not grief, however, nor even sorrow, that had called forth so strange and passionate emotions from that calm bosom; for the whole heart was full of deep and tranquil gratitude to Him, by whose good providence the stranger had been preserved from his bloodthirsty enemies—much less was it all joy, for though there was a sense of happiness, or of relief at least from terrible anxiety, springing up from the depths of her pure soul, yet there was nothing strong or passionate, nothing tumultuous in the character of that pure, stilly pleasure. No, it was merely the reaction of a mind over-tensely strung during the late dread scenes. It had been only by an exertion almost too great for female powers, that she had crushed down into her inmost soul all semblance of anxiety or interest during the search of the rude Puritans; yet so completely had she crushed it down while in the presence of those stern inquisitors, that not only had she compelled her steps to be equal, and her hand steady, but she had actually forced her cheek and lip to retain their wonted color—her eye its quiet undisturbed expression. And well was it for that young stranger that she did so. For it was even less, the grave unmoved demeanor of the aged gentleman—less, the unconsciousness of the alarmed domestics—than the perfect tranquillity of that sweet and lovely maiden, which had convinced them that their searching longer would be but a vain labor.

It had been some suspicion—vague, indeed, and indefinite—that she might have concealed the cavalier, without the knowledge of the household, by which the leaders of the party had been induced to search the boat-house; and therefore had they caused her to accompany them; that, if their doubts were true, some terror or expression of alarm might, as they judged, inevitably betray the secret of his hiding-place. And so far were they right, that it had only been by dint of almost superhuman fortitude that she forebore to scream aloud in the intensity of her excitement, when they persisted in examining the sail-loft, wherein, scarcely six inches from the torch of his pursuer, the object of her care lay hidden.

Excitement, such as this, must end in a revulsion; and it was fortunate that there was cause enough apparent, to have disturbed the equilibrium of her mind, in the events which had transpired in the full sight of all—so that the outbreak of hysterical passion called forth no more alarm, than a mere fit of feminine terror, from the assiduous attendants who crowded round their beloved mistress, with all the remedies of essences, strong waters and the like, which their ignorant but kindly zeal could dictate.

Gradually, as we have said, however, her tears ceased to flow; and, as her mind regained its usual serene and balanced tenor, she recollected that there was yet much more to do, and much more cause than ever to avoid wakening suspicion. With her, to see the right, and to perform it, were scarcely the results of a two-fold operation; and bidding her tirewoman await her coming in her own chamber, she dismissed all the rest; her father adding his injunction, that as the hour of bedtime was long passed, they should not linger in the hall with idle gossipings, else there would be late rising in the morn., No more was said; but in those good old days, and in that orderly and peaceful household, there was no doubt that his words would be obeyed even to the letter. In a few moments

2

the old gray-headed porter brought in the keys of the great gate and water-port, and laid them on the table by his master's hand; and before half an hour, except in old Mark's library, and in the chamber of his sweet child, there was not a light burning, nor an eye unclosed, through the whole building.

Hours were early in those days, so that the clock had barely stricken ten when all the fires were quenched and the lights extinguished. Eleven—twelve—one, followed—the deep sounds of the stable clock-house, solemnly booming through the lonely night; and still the lamp burned steadily in the small library; and the two lighted windows might be seen above the courtyard wall, and through the foliage of the park plantations, even as far as the high road, had any one been watching them.

And one *was* watching them. The younger of the Puritan officers, wrapped in his scarlet watch-cloak, was standing on the platform of the fish-house, with a neighboring farmer, dressed in his usual toil-worn garb, beside him, and a stout trooper holding some five or six saddled chargers on the bridge.

Just as the clock struck one, the soldier stamped impatiently. "Doth the old hoary dotard keep watch thus always till 'tis morning?" he exclaimed, turning toward the rustic.

"Ay, ay, sir," he replied, "I'll warrant him. Master Mark's a great scholar, I've heard tell, and speaks all sorts of untold old-time tongues. And so you see he keeps poring over a sight o' musty books night after night. Many's the time and often, when I've been kept from home past common, at Worcester market or the like, I've seen yon light in yon two selfsame windows, till three o'clock o' the morning. And yet the old man's astir with the cock, too—that's what does bother me like—"

"See! see!" the other interrupted him, "it has gone out."

"Ay, ay. Now we shall see it cross the next three windows to the right, then if any one were watching the west end, he might see it a little while in the west gable. The old man's chamber there, next to young mistress's bower."

While he yet spoke, the light, as of a candle or a lamp in motion, flitted across the three tall casements to the right, and disappearing, the southern front of the old Hall was left in absolute darkness.

"Well! there it does go, of a surety," replied the Puritan, "and there *is* one to watch on the west end. Do they burn tapers all night through in their bed-chambers?"

"No, not a light is burnt in all the house, when the old master's lamp is out; that's the last always, ever since I was a boy!"

"Peradventure, then, we shall know more anon," returned the other, and then relapsed into silence, awaiting the arrival of his subordinate watchers. Nor had he very long to wait; for scarcely half an hour had gone by since the removal of the lamp, when nearly simultaneously three came up, though from different directions, and made their several reports all to the same effect, that not a mouse had stirred about the Hall for three hours, and that now every candle was extinguished, and every soul abed for certain.

"Well, then, we have but lost our time, and they know naught about this same malignant, who 'scaped us here so strangely," muttered the officer between his clenched teeth. "Mount, men, mount and away; we'll beat these woods for many a mile to-morrow."

"Had you known the folks at the Hall as I do, master," the farmer interposed, "you never would have dreamed o' thinking that they did. Lord! sir, they are the scariest, timidest, ease-lovingest people—they never trouble their heads with no politics, nor parties!"

"Well, well, good friend, it is no harm to be assured, and so good night to thee," the soldier answered, striking his spurs into his horse's flank, and galloping off, followed by his men, at a rate that soon left the quiet woods of Woolverton many a mile behind him."

"Good devil go with thee!" muttered the countryman, as they rode off, "and with all like to thee, thou cheat and hypocrite! I trow now, thou mayest be mistaken yet, for all thy cunning! If Mistress Alice had fallen in with the poor youth, I warrant me she would a hid him somewhere, in spite all danger! So I'll away up to the Hall to-morrow, and see about it; for if so be there be aught i' the wind, I'll have a finger in't, or my name is not John Sherlock."

Times of great peril and emergency have not unfrequently been known to impart a species of instinctive and instantaneous shrewdness to minds not previously remarkable for any such quality. Bookmen, and grave secluded scholars, intuitively, as it were, under the pressure of great present peril or necessity, have been known to attain the skill of practised generals, the craftiness of the most subtle partisans. So in this instance was it with Mark Selby. Born of an old and honorable family, a second son, he had been educated many long years before with a view to taking orders: and the grave tastes and habits which he had then acquired, clung to him afterward, when by his brother's death—who fell at Zutphen, fighting by Philip Sidney's side—he became heir of Woolverton; and, of course, with his altered fortunes, abandoned the profession to which he had before been destined. Never, during his earliest and gayest youth, had he been a frequenter of courts, or even an associate in the daring field-sports or jovial festivities of the neighboring gentry. Long after his succession to the family estates, when he was far advanced already in the vale of years, he had taken to wife the daughter of a baronet, whose estates paired with Woolverton—a fair and lovely creature, whose living type we have beheld in Alice. Her he lost young, after having followed to the grave two sons, his first born; the infant Alice being left alone to his paternal care. Thus situate, more gloomy every day had waxed the aged widower's abode —more ineradicably were those bookworm habits fixed—till Alice, from a sweet prattling child, the licensed interrupter of her father's musings, had grown up to be the pure and lovely thing she was, when the occurrences fell out which it is our's to narrate. Rarely was old Mark Selby seen abroad by any—rarely at home, save by the members of his own quiet household—no scenes of broil, or riot, or warfare, had ever been beheld by him, much less had he been an actor in any such. Yet had he read, and mused, and dreamed, that he could have performed the deeds, and undergone the woes, and braved the terrors which his loved heroes of historic lore had done, and borne, and braved undaunted; and now, in his old age, was he tried—tried, and not then found wanting.

After his daughter had retired to rest, he had conceived it very likely that some—as, indeed, was the case—of the Puritans might yet linger on the watch without, and that any deviation from the wonted customs of his household would certainly create suspicion. Before she went, he had promised Alice himself to rouse her from her slumbers, if any slumber she might take, when the time should arrive for admitting the young royalist to a more safe retreat than that which he now occupied; and after she was gone, though anxious and excited, he sat down to his books, not at the first without an effort; but after he had sat some time, he returned to his ordinary frame of mind, and read, and pondered, and made notes, until the period should arrive, apparently, and indeed *really*, as fully engrossed in his subject, as though no graver matter than the full force of the particle τέ had occupied his meditations.

It would, however, have been worthy of remark—to those who make the human mind their study—that while his understanding was devoted altogether to the unravelling of an obscure passage in one of Pindar's darkest Pythian odes, to which he had turned in the hopes of gleaning thence some light whereby to see into the depths of some yet deeper classic mystery, he was still quite awake to all the exigencies, and the perils of his immediate position. Had he not been indeed fully aware of the necessity of being tranquil, it had not, perhaps, been within his power so calmly to have followed his accustomed studies. Had he not been a student, it would, perhaps, have frustrated his utmost coolness so to have waited the event. Yet was the result of the strange mixture, the blending of the feelings of the scholar and the man, simple although they were untaught and natural—the most complete and perfect skill, and craft, and subtlety, that ever graced the wariest and most wily partisan.

When the lamp was extinguished in the library, and the hand-taper cast its flickering light, as witnessed by the wakeful Puritan, across the lattices of the less-frequented apartments, the old man, indeed, retired to his chamber; and when there, had at once cast himself into a large arm-chair, where he reclined for many minutes absorbed in the deepest mental meditation.

After a while he started up, and for a moment it was in his thoughts to pass directly to his daughter's chamber, but in an instant, and he scarcely knew why, his mind was altered; for he had little thought that any were still in ambuscade without, watching his every movement; and he stood quietly before the casements, with the bright lamp behind him, casting his shadow on the wide illuminated panes. He threw his dress aside, put out the light, and cast himself down heavily upon the bed. And there were those upon the watch who saw all this, albeit he knew it not, and testified thereto in after-days; and it was well for him he did so.

After a space of deep and painful meditation, he once again arose. The moon was shining clearly, as she waded with uncertain gleams among the scattered clouds, through the tall latticed casements; and there was light enough, that the old man could find his scattered garments, and attire himself without the need of kindling any lamp. Once dressed, he opened his door carefully, but without any fear, for the domestic slept far from the inhabited apartments of the hall, and took his way through the old well-known passages, directly to his daughter's chamber. The rays fell misty and dim through the stained windows as he passed, and many an indistinct and fleeting shadow wavered across his path, as he went onward; but in too deep a school of philosophic thought had he been trained, to cast a single thought to superstitious tremors; and student though he was, he had too deeply proved life's stern realities to blench for any shadow.

He reached the fair girl's chamber, and entered all unsummoned—and the same bright, pure lustre, which had enabled him to don his dress without the aid of lamp or taper, was pouring upon her virgin couch, as she lay all disrobed and tranquil, but thoughtful, and awake, and full of her high purpose, as she awaited the appointed time.

"Father!" she whispered, in soft but untrembling accents, as his hand touched the latch. "Father! is't thou? then tarry but for a little moment's space without, and I will join thee." and with the words, she too arose. And hastily, but yet completely, she attired herself in plain dark garments of simple country fashion; and ere ten minutes had elapsed she stood beside him, silent, in the dark corridor.

"Now to the library!" he whispered, and with slow, faltering steps they groped their way through the large, vacant, lonely rooms, and reached it at last, breathless and panting, not from the speed at which they had advanced, but that they had scarce drawn a full breath since they left her chamber. Once there, a feeble glimmering light shone in, transversely and reflected—for the moon's rays touched not the southern front—and they were able to distinguish things, though indistinctly.

"So far," the old man whispered, "so far all's well; no living ear has heard that we are stirring, and if you lack not courage to finish out what you have well begun, there is no more of danger. But look you, we have need of caution. No door must be unlocked, no foot must tread the staircase. I have a silken ladder here, framed long ago against emergency of fire; it will I let down from this casement under the shadow of yon pine; by it you must descend—creep through the garden greens, avoiding the bright court—enter the water-tower, and making there your signal, admit your guest with your own hands. By the same path you must return together; I will await you here; hence opens, as you know, the passage. Have you the courage, girl?"

"Lower the ladder, father," she answered in a whisper, "lower the ladder, and give me the keys!"

"So brave," he said, half musingly, "so brave, and yet so young!" and he paused long, and shook his hoary head, and seemed to hesitate; but then, "Well! well!" he said. "Well! well! God's hand, I trow, is in it, and on it be his benison;" and without farther words, after a little groping in the dark, he drew out the rope-ladder he had mentioned, and lowered it from the extreme west window, across which fell the broad and massy shadow cast by the largest of the giant pines which we have named above. He handed her the key, pressed her with a long lingering pressure to his bosom, and printed one kiss on her brow.

"The God of mercy go with thee," he said, "my child, for that thine errand is of mercy."

Another moment and she had passed the window-sill, and with a firm step, and untrembling though delicate hold, she trod the shaking rungs, and stood in safety at the bottom. For one short second more, the old man's eye could follow her threading the mazes of the labyrinthine shrubs; then she was lost, and in a moment more had entered the untenanted and lonely water-tower. It was all as dark as a wolf's mouth, save where one faint and broken ray fell through the embrasure, half intercepted by the breech of the huge gun; yet cool in every movement, and collected, she felt her way down the rude steps, unlocked the inner gate, and half raised the portcullis by aid of the complicated winch, which moved it in the groove of stone wherein it traversed. Retracing instantly her steps, after some minutes spent in search, she found the porter's tinder-box and link. She struck a light, and for a second's space the red glare shot out through the lattice; yet so low did it strike, that a spectator, standing ten yards beyond the moat's south bank, could have seen naught of it. She blew it out, and counted ten, and lit it once again, and so on till the third time; and as she blew it out, a slight splash reached her ears, and in a moment after a waving movement of the water, and a deep panting breath, and she received him at the steps, and led him upward to the embrasure, and lowered the portcullis once again, and locked the gate, and thrust the key into her girdle.

"Be silent for your life," she whispered, as speedily she led him through the low postern gate; but when she reached the open air, it flashed upon her mind that she had not replaced the half-burned flambeau, with its appropriate flint and steel, in the same niche where it lay when she found it; and laying her finger on her lip, as they two stood in the half shadow of the twilight garden, she tripped back, and placed it rightly, so to avoid suspicion. Quickly they traced the shrubbery paths, and reached the pendent ladder; one signal and he climbed it, and scarcely was he well landed in the library, before she too was in the room.

"Not a word, sir, not a word," exclaimed Mark Selby, in one of those sharp whispers which fill the ear far more than the deep roar of ordnance. "Not a word, if you would not betray your rescuer."

And they three stood there silent, in the pervading hush of deep awe, and yet deeper feeling; while the old man drew in the ladder, and laid it by in its accustomed place, and closed the latticed window. Then, after searching about yet another while, he drew forth from a drawer in an old cabinet a small, old-fashioned lamp, with flint and steel and matches—a flask of wine or cordial, and a strangely-shaped brazen key. Giving all these to the young cavalier, he turned to a compartment of the library wall, covered by shelves well stored with ponderous books; drew out one folio volume, and turned an iron button, replaced it, pressed a spring this way, and turned a screw-head that, and the whole bookcase, with its load, from floor to ceiling, revolved upon a pivot, disclosing the bare plastered wall, with a low-browed arch, descending, as it seemed, into the outer wall, and full of black impenetrable darkness.

"Alice," the old man said, "to bed; we will speak more to-morrow. Pass in, sir;" and the girl left the room, and hurried to her chamber with a glad but quick-throbbing heart; and the stranger entered the dark passage, and old Mark Selby followed him, and drew the concealed door, masked by the ponderous book-shelves, after him; and the old library was tenantless again, and not a soul could have suspected, though he had searched it for a month, that private passage. But when they stood within it, the old man struck a light, and lit the lamp, and raised it to the face of his new guest, and gazed into his features as though he would have read his soul.

"Ha!" he said; "ha!" and paused again a little while, and then—"be it so; I will trust you;" and no word passed between them more, for the old man almost angrily imposed strict silence when the stranger would have spoken. And far he led him, by long and winding corridors, delved through the thickness of the wall, up stairs and down, till he had brought him to a low dark vault, scarce six feet perpendicular height, by twelve in circuit, in which there stood a table of dark oak, an old armed chair, two or three stools of the same plain material, and a low pallet bed heaped high with blankets, and soft coverlets, and sheets of snowy whiteness. Besides these articles of furniture, the gloomy chamber contained nothing but a few shelves in one corner, whereon were piled two or three pewter platters, an earthen bowl and pitcher, a salt-cellar, a knife-case, a cruise of oil, and four tall Venice wine-glasses. There was no carpet on the floor, nor any hangings on the bare plastered walls; nor was there any window or even shot-hole, whereat a single ray of blessed daylight could pass in to cheer the sad soul of the inmate. As if to compensate, however, for this want, there was no less than three doors besides that which had admitted them, massy and steel-clenched, and secured by bolts of singular device, and bars, and chains of iron.

"This is a poor abode, young sir," said Selby, as he set down the lamp upon the table; "but it is safe at least, and that to one in your condition is always something. No person now alive, save Alice and myself, knows the existence of this hiding-place, much less the ways which lead to it; and you, before you quit it, must swear by all that men hold holy, never by word or deed, by sign or hint or writing, to reveal it. Meantime, here will we shelter you, until such time as we may send you forth in safety. Food shall be brought you daily, and lights, and change of raiment, and, if you wish it, books; but on society you must not count—not even on ours—for carefully we must eschew suspicion. Before I leave you to repose, one other secret of your abode I must disclose to you." He opened, as he spoke, another door, and showed a narrow stairway, winding, as it seemed, downward into interminable gloom.

"At the foot of those steps," he said, pointing through the opening, "you will find what appears a square well of water, and by it a trap-door; the first will furnish you the means of cleanliness and comfort, and by the latter you may cast into the moat nightly the remnants of your food, and aught else that, if discovered here in case of any search, might cause suspicion. On no account, however, enter the well to bathe, for *it were certain death*, unless you knew the secret. Be careful, when you pass these stairs, to do so very silently; here you can not be heard, though you should sing or whistle—there it were perilous, indeed! The other doors lead elsewhere, and are locked. Let me know now, who is my guest; and pledge me, as a soldier and a gentleman, your word of honor not to leave this apartment, except by the door I have shown you leading to the water; you would risk all our lives by wandering about the corridors."

"My name is Wyvil—Marmaduke Wyvil, of Allerton Mauleverer, in Yorkshire, serving till yesterday as captain in my good friend and kinsman Sir Philip Musgrave's regiment of horse, not ten of whom now hold together—not fifty of whom now are numbered with the living. Alas! for thee, my friend, my more than brother—good, gallant, murdered Musgrave! Alas! for the good cause, that is a cause no longer!" and as he said the words, he wrung his hands till the blood started from the finger-nails, and burst into a paroxysm of violent sobs and weeping. In a few minutes, however, he recovered himself somewhat, and mastering his passion, as it seemed, by a strong effort, "Pardon me," he said; "this is unmanly, very weak and trivial; but I *am* weak from weariness and watching, and from the want of food; pardon me, I beseech you, my kind friend and preserver."

"That can I not do, my young friend," returned the other,

"seeing that there is naught to pardon. The cause you speak of, I respect and love; and had there been less years upon my head, should have armed for it. Your feelings for your lost friend I honor; we will talk more to-morrow! meantime throw off your dripping garments, drink a cup or two of this sovereign cordial, stretch yourself on your humble bed, and after one night's safe and peaceful sleep, I warrant me I find you a new man in the morning." He had already trimmed and lighted a brazen lamp which stood upon the board, and now reached down two glasses, filling them to the brim from the long-necked flask he had brought with him. "I drink," he then said—"I drink, Captain Wyvil, to your good repose, and leave you to it straightway. Lock the door after me when I go forth, and open it not, save for my voice or that of Alice; no thanks, my friend, no thanks! Now, God be with you, and farewell!" and without suffering him to answer, he shook his young guest warmly by the hand, and left him.

CHAPTER IV.

At little more than a mile's distance from Woolverton Hall, not situated, however, on the Worcester turnpike, but on another road passing the principal entrance of the Park, and forming its northern boundary, stood a small wayside inn, deeply embosomed in the woodlands which at the period of our narrative overspread many a mile of that fair country. This road, which entered the main turnpike some three miles to the eastward of the Hall, was one of those innumerable country tracks which traverse all the agricultural parts of England, winding about with no regard whatever to the space occupied, or the needless miles included in their sinuosities; wandering "like rivers at their own sweet will," and affording the only means of communication to the inhabitants of many a sequesered hamlet, many a lowly grange ; devious indeed and long, but all-sufficient to the simple wants of the people, and full in themselves of picturesque and rural beauty. Its narrow wheel-track was bordered on each hand by many yards of deep, rich greensward, pied everywhere in the early spring-time with tufts of the soft saffron primrose, and perfumed by the rich scent of unnumbered violets ; tall, straggling hawthorn hedges, overrun in summer by the bee-haunted tendrils of the honey-suckles, and the flaunting streamers of the dog-rose, shaded it from the morning and the evening sunbeams ; while overhead, it was so thickly canopied by elm and ash and many a giant oak, that scarce a ray could penetrate the shadowy foliage at high noon. So seldom, too, did this road run any distance in a direct straight line, that spots were rare indeed where the eye of a traveller could see a hundred yards before him. It was upon this winding lane, in preference to the broad and dusty turnpike, that the gates of the Hall, consisting of a low massive arch of antique brickwork between two short and stubborn-looking towers, now so completely mantled with dark ivy that the very outlines of their form were lost, had been placed by the original founder; and it was at about a mile's distance from these, toward the west, and consequently so much the farther from the highway, that the "Stag's Head," for such was the well-known sign of the little hostelrie, invited passers-by to taste its humming ale and stores of rustic cheer.

It was a quaint and curious building, that old inn, consisting of a long front of a single story, with three projecting gables, one in the centre and one at either end, protruding some six feet into the road, and having the upper stories, which were in each entirely occupied by a large latticed window of four or five compartments, again thrust forward about the same distance in advance of their bases. Below the window in the central gable was a wide low-browed doorway, or porch rather, of black oak, with the weather-bleached skull and broad-branched antlers of a huge red deer nailed above it, and a long bench on either side within. The two end gables and the flat fronts between them, showed several lattices, but of irregular heights and sizes, all neatly curtained with white dimity, and decked with pots of lavender, balm, rosemary, and other savory herbs, to gratify the smell or tempt the dainty palate. A thick thatched roof, all green with moss and lichens and masses of the yellow flowering stonecrop, with far-projecting eaves, whence hung in clusters the clay-built cradles of the summer-loving martlet, covered the whole of this hospitable mansion—which was built of vast beams of jet-black oak, curiously interlaced one with another, the interstices being filled up with neatly whitewashed plaster—and afforded a pleasant haunt to a score or two of plump-necked pigeons, strutting to and fro from morning till night on the ridge-pole, filling the whole air with their hoarse love-making, or wheeling in short flights about their happy home.

In front of this truly rustic inn the road expanded into a little bay or circle, with a small meadow, of three or four acres at the utmost, fenced all around by deep plantations, facing the windows; while at the back the building actually abutted on the park wall, and was securely sheltered by the tall ranks of its immemorial elm-trees. Along the palings of the meadow, moss-grown and old and weather-beaten like all about them, ran a long horse-trough, fed constantly and full from a rude aqueduct of hollow trunks by a bright and crystal rill, which, keeping it still brimming over in the hottest seasons, danced out with a fresh gurgling sound at the lower end in a mimic waterfall, and was soon lost to sight among the rich tall herbage which it supplied with its perennial moisture. But the chief boast and ornament of the Stag's Head was the enormous aged oak—so aged that, as wise men said, it was recorded for a bound-mark in the pages of the Doomsday book—which stood exactly in the middle of the little circle, its gnarled gray arms completely sheltering the space below, and its leaves rustling on the one extremity against the diamond-shaped panes of the chamber windows, and on the other covering the horse-trough with their cool, cave-like umbrage.

Around the trunk of this vegetable giant was built a range of comfortable seats, with a high back and arms dividing it, as it were, into separate compartments, like the boxes of a modern coffeehouse, all framed of tortuous roots and unbarked branches, and each compartment having a round table in the middle, for the benefit of the rustic banqueters who here were wont to solace themselves every evening after the heat and burden of the day's toils were over. It must not be omitted, that on a low artificial mound in the meadow there stood a lofty Maypole, round which in those blithe days, before the sullen and morose Puritans had clogged fair England with the curse of their black creed — before the happy peasantry were changed by the loud lies of artful demagogues into a horde of bitter discontented politicians — the young folks of the parish would meet on many a spring or summer evening, with merriment and music, to twine their May-wreaths from the abundant wild flowers, and at the sound of pipe and tabor present to the great Architect of nature an offering most grateful to divine beneficence — the offering of innocent, rejoicing, and grateful hearts.

Alas! where are they now, those festive meetings? where is the frolic mirth, the innocence so cheaply pleased with trifles, the love of music, the affection — most natural affection, and most indicative of pure and graceful spirits — for the sweet perfumes of the dewy flowers, the dance upon the greensward under the mellow eye of evening, the cheerful congregation in the old village-church on every Sunday morn, including every inmate of the village, from the blind frail octogenarian to the wee toddling prattler that sat grave-eyed and hushed in decent awe by its young comely mother? Where is the veneration for old age? the grateful reverence to the kind superiors? the love for the frank, free-spoken, learned churchman, who preached not one iota the less wisely, nor prayed one tittle the less fervently, that he could chat with the old gossips by the fireside, and jest with the young lasses on the green, and wing an arrow to the clout with the featest yeoman in the ring? Where are they now, those once characteristics of the people of the *once* merry England? Gone, one and all — gone, to return no more. Surrendered, bartered, contemptuously cast aside, for what? for a dream! a vain, fitful, feverish dream—a dream of liberty! of freedom! free trade, free institutions, free religion! a dream which fills the prisons and the pot-houses of that once happy realm with desperate criminals, with brawling, vicious plotters! a dream which has converted pure green fields into huge prisons of red brick, dungeons of toiling artisans, reeking with blasphemy, sedition, and licentiousness; day-schools of all impiety, rife with the agonies of tortured infancy, the woes of premature old age! a dream which has torn, literally torn, the church asunder, and swelled with worshippers the shrine of every loathsome creed, of every mad fanaticism, hard by the half-deserted doors of God's time-honored temples.

Not then, however, had these things come to pass, although the events were even then in progress which sowed the seeds of what should be thereafter; and though throughout the land, full many a furious fanatic had fulminated the dread wrath to come over the guilty dancers—licentious worshippers of Baal, circling like Moabitish women with flutes and timbrels round the high places of false gods—the Maypoles were not yet entirely abandoned; and smiles were sometimes seen upon the faces, and songs heard from the lips of youths and maidens. Drunkenness was not *then* the only authorized amusement; the only licensed relaxation of the *free* British peasant.

At a very early hour of the morning following the events narrated heretofore, almost indeed as soon as the sun was up, the Stag's Head saw collected under the old oak-tree a group of people, some two or three of whom were waiting, as it would seem, for the first meal of their day; while the rest were for the most part countrymen, pausing a moment on their way a-field, to take their morning draught of ale, and hear the gossip of the times; or servants of the inn bustling about their hospitable duties.

The country people soon passed onward, and the company, when they were gone, appeared to consist of four persons. One was an old gray-headed man, spare-made, and tall and bony, but hale, fresh-colored, comely, and retaining still many signs of strength which in his younger days must have been more than usually great. He was dressed in a much worn long coat of forest green, with buckskin breeches, soiled and glazed at the knees, and long calf gaiters. A rabbit embroiddered in tarnished silver on the sleeve of his coat, and a brace of rough wire-haired terriers, long-backed and short-legged—one of which was sleeping at his feet, while the other was making demonstrations most decidedly hostile against a comfortable-looking tabby cat inside the kitchen window—seemed to designate his profession as that of warrener to some neighboring gentleman; and this was confirmed more fully by the appearance of an old gray pony dozing in the shade, to whose wooden pack-saddle were attached a bundle of nets, a spade, a bag which from its constant and eccentric agitations seemed to contain a ferret, and a dozen or more of fine wild rabbits hanging by their heels across his withers, with the blood dripping (so freshly had they been killed) from their long silvery ears.

The second of the group, who sat by the old warrener, talking to him and laughing with a familiarity which showed as if they had been old acquaintances, was a man something past the middle age, dressed like an ordinary yeoman, though perhaps something better, in a suit of dark-colored fustian, with a high broad-brimmed hat. His face, without being actually good, was marked and striking. There was a keen quick twinkle of intelligence in his sharp, black eyes, and an expression of sly cunning humor about the same feature, with a queer, half-pleasant, half-cynical smile constantly fluttering around his mouth. His complexion was much tanned and sun-burnt, as were his hands likewise; on one of which, the right, there was a long seamed scar, as of a broadsword cut, which having slightly grazed his fore and middle fingers, had completely severed the two others from the knuckles, and terminated only at the wrist. His garments and his shoes were all powdered over with thick dust, as if he had travelled many miles; but there was nothing about him to indicate his business, unless it were a pedlar's pack, an ell wand of stout oak rendered available as a weapon by a steel spear-head screwed into one end, and a flat wooden box with a broad belt of leather; all of which lay on the table of the box next to that in which he and the warrener were sitting, and which might, or might not, have been his property. The third, and only remaining occupant of the seat beneath the tree, was an athletic bronzed young fellow, with somewhat of a dare-devil expression in his bright hazel eye, but a frank, cheerful, and good-humored smile, clad as a forester or game-keeper, with a bucktail in the silver band of his black velvet cap, and a badge on the sleeve of his green jerkin. A short rifle-gun or musketoon stood in the corner of the settle at his elbow, with its appurtenances of powder-horn and bullet-pouch lying upon the seat beside it; a long broad two-edged knife, with a handsome buckhorn handle, thrust into his belt at the left side, completed his equipment.

There was yet a fourth person present, but he was not one of that party, nor was he one who had much part at all in the companionship of men; he sat a little way aloof from the rest in a low wicker chair, placed where the morning sun fell full upon it; but he saw not, or at least noticed not, the glorious sunlight with the innumerable living atoms wheeling and circling in its golden radiance; he only felt its warmth, and dozed, scarce conscious of the comfort it poured down upon him—a large, well-formed, and powerful lad of seventeen years or better, his muscular and shapely limbs giving the promise of vast strength, to be developed ere he should have attained to the full years of manhood. One glance, however, at his features told in an instant his whole melancholy tale; the low receding brow—the beadlike and unmeaning eye—the prominent mouth, thick-lipped, with teeth as white and strong as those of a wild beast, which had scarred all the lips around in the dread seizure of his convulsive paroxysms! He was an idiot of the worst and lowest grade, scarcely endowed with speech, so inarticulate were the sounds which alone his defective organs could produce; with instincts scarcely equal to those of the inferior brutes, and amounting to little more than a sense and memory of wrongs or kindnesses, with an occasional gleam of desperate animal ferocity, and now and then, at rare—most rare and distant intervals—a burst of tender and affectionate feeling, blended as it were with a partial revelation of deeper and more human thoughts within than anything in his external bearing could be held to indicate. During these partially lucid intervals, it was remarkable, moreover, that all his powers seemed to expand proportionably; eye, tongue, expression, all aiding the development of thoughts which, if they were at work continually in the depths of his shrouded mind, left at the least no token of their workings upon the stagnant surface. A large, gaunt, mastiff bitch, now nearly toothless and grizzled over all her face, slept close beside his feet, keeping, nevertheless, as it would seem, a strict guard over her witless master, for ever—though she seemed to sleep—if he but moved a limb, or drew a heavier breath than common, she would unclose one eye, and watch him for a moment with an expression almost superhuman, and with a quick nervons quiver of her thin pendulous ears, till, as she saw him settle down again into his soulless musings, she, too, would relapse into her daylong slumbers.

"Holloa! my pretty Cicely; what ails thee, lass, this morning?" cried the young forester, as the last of the peasants moved off; "canst give us naught to break our fasts withal? Here 's old John Brent 's been out since four of the clock, and Master Bartram has walked all the way from Barrington—and that 's ten miles—since daybreak, and here am I, Frank Norman, not like to walk a mile—though I've got all my rounds before me, and that 's *twenty* good—till I've got cake and ale!"

"Coming! oh! coming, Master Frank," cried the smart country lass, running across the green, with her short petticoats displaying her clean ankle and neat foot as they fluttered in the wind, and the bright ribands in her cap paling beside the blush of her soft peach-like cheek, "you mustn't flurry one so, there you've just been, and taken all my breath away, there! there's your ale, double ale, too, six quarts of it, stirred with a sprig of rosemary, and a nice roasted crab in it, and there's your glasses, and here's hot cakes and sweet fresh butter, and here comes Jenny with the rasher and the eggs, and I'll away to fetch the trenchers. Marry! will that do for you, Frank?"

"So nicely, Ciss, that I'll e'en pay thee with a kiss when thou hast brought them."

"I won't go after them then, saucebox. Welsh Jenny here may fetch them you, and serve your table, too! Marry come up! green jackets and bucktails must needs be scarcer sights than they be now in these parts, when pretty girls like me buy kisses of such chaps as thee for service."

And tossing her pretty little head coquettishly, she tripped off into the porch, while with a loud and cheery laugh John Brent rallied his young comrade.

"Hey! Norman, lad, she hit thee as clean as ever thou struckst heart of geese—"

"With headless shaft at roving distance!" the young man interrupted him, for he had caught a sly glance, and a wicked smile, cast over her shoulder as she disappeared, which contradicted quite the import of her words, "but come, let's try the ale!"

For some minutes' space after this, they were so well employed over the eggs and bacon that few words passed between them. While they were thus engaged, however, a fifth personage was added to their number. It was no other than John Sherlock, the stout yeoman whom the Puritans had stopped the preceding night, upon the herony bridge, while keeping watch over the inmates of the hall. He was a right good specimen of a fine blunt English farmer of the olden time, full six feet high, and with a breadth of shoulder and a volume of muscle amply proportionate to his inches, clad in his snugly-fitting doublet of gray broadcloth, buff breeches and blue woollen hose, with heavy silver buckles in his strong ankle shoes, and a clasp of the same metal to the band of his slouched beaver hat.

He came upon them suddenly, so much so, that although on horseback, the others neither heard nor saw him till he was close beside them; for he came down the road behind them from the westward, as they sat looking down it toward the park gates, so that the body of the oak-tree was interposed between the new-comer and the party; and it was not, therefore, until he had well nigh passed by, that he perceived them. When he did so, however, the recognition was simultaneous.

"Ho! is it thou, John Sherlock? Best stop and take a horn."

"What, Norman, lad, how be you? and how be you, John Brent! Good, morrow, Master Bartram."

"Come, 'light down, John, 'light down, wilt not?" said the forester, "but what's i' the wind now?" he continued in accents that denoted no small wonder, as he looked more steadily at the good yeoman. "Where, i' the fiend's name, didst get that beast thou straddlest so gallantly?"

And well indeed might he ask and admire, for in sooth it was no sober cart-pad that bore the jolly farmer, nor yet was it his own high-bred and powerful hunter, for he was well to do in the world, and turned out now and then with the earl's stag-hounds, and followed them as close as squire, or knight, or baron; but a tall, jet-black barb of Dongola, clean-limbed, with a coat bright and soft as satin, and a broad, flashing eye, and a full nostril. The head-stall of his bridle was all adorned and studded, as were the bits, the poitrel, and the crupper, with knobs and bosses of chased gold; the housings and padding of his demipique were of rich velvet, laid down with gold embroideries of full three inches depth, while to match the color of the saddle-cloth, his flowing mane was gathered up and plaited with blue ribands.

"By George, but that's a baron's charger, at the least on't," exclaimed old Brent. "'Light down, 'light thee down, Master Sherlock, and tell us all about it."

"Nay! I've got naught to tell," returned the farmer, alighting, however, as he was requested, and given the rein to an old half-palsied hostler, who had tottered out at the sound of the horse tramp. "Nay! I've got naught to tell you much. I found t'nag down i' the heronry wood, tied to a young ash sapling. I was a passing by like, when I heard him nickering and neighing a mile off or better; and there he 'd been all night for certain, for t' dew was thick on t' saddle, and all quite white on his long mane and tail. I took him up to my own stable, and made the lads sort him down. Some gentleman on the king's side has owned him, that got off from Worcester fight, I reckon."

"Ay, ay!" responded all the listeners, "I warrant me."

But John Brent went on speaking: "Ay, ay! *He 's* owned him, I 'll be bail, as the red-coated roundheads was a looking arter, down at the Hall last night."

"What 's that—what 's that? Tell us, John Brent, tell us man? what i' the fiend's name are you thinking on, to tell us naught about it before this?" cried the young forester, starting to his feet, and snatching up his musketoon. "Did they trouble Master Selby? did they *dare* harm fair Mistress Alice?"

"No, no! no wrong, Frank Norman; thou needst not be so hot upon 't, lad," answered the old warrener. "They did *scare* Mistress Alice woundily, but no harm done. You see they'd chased some gentleman clear down from Worcester field, and fired at him from the top of Longmire hill, and lost all track of him, as it was growing dark, down in the bottom by the bridge; so they came and searched the old Hall from the garret down; but, Lord! he wasn't there, not he! Old Master 'd been in 's study, Jeremy says, all day, and Mistress Alice came in from the park, about an hour or so afore supper, and no one with her any how, for Jeremy he let her in at the water-gate, and Charles and Launcelot were with him; and they say nobody came with her, no Christian, anyways, except the old Talbot; and so they went their ways, arter they 'd got done searching."

"The devil's luck go with them," added young Norman, playing with the trigger of his gun-lock; "there 'll be no peace in England any more till the rogue-roundheads are put down, and our good king enjoys his own again!"

"Ay, ay! that's right, chimed in the pedlar Bartram. "Heaven send the rogues well down! A yard or two of Holland's linen, and a commodity of Scottish serge-cloth, and old calf-leather, is all the merchandise they need. Their very wenches won't ware a tester on a top-knot. Heaven send them down, and we'll have jolly times again. But now naught's doing, and for fine Flanders' lace, and Genoa velvets, and Cypress lawns, and soft French taffetas, I'm fain to sell old sermons and stale psalm-tunes, and such rubbish! But that has been a noble's horse, I warrant him. Why, that's all solid gold upon the trappings, and that gold lace is worth ten crowns the Flemish ell, and all that velvet 's prime Genoa. He 's a lord's horse, at least! What do you mean to make with him, hey, Master Sherlock ?"

" Why, you see, lads," said Sherlock, " the soldiers stopped me on the bridge last night, of this same party that searched Woolverton. They watched about the house till it was nigh-hand two o'clock, and all the lights was out, and they asked me a sight of questions; but nothing seemed a-stirring, and they couldn't scent out anything, and so they went off to their quarters. But I had heard them talk, you see, and guessed by what they told that he had took to the woods; and I went off betimes this morning to see if I could find the gentleman, and show him where to hide away. By what they talked, he 'd been a prime one! fought to the very last by the king's side at Worcester; and when their picquets came upon him in a barnyard, somewhere nigh-hand the field, where he had hid himself the first night, he shot two of them with his pistols—they 're discharged sure enough"—and as he spoke he drew two large gold-mounted pistols from the holsters, with the hammers down, and the pans black with smoke—" and charged clean through their troop, cutting down one, and wounding two more badly. And so I found his horse, but couldn't hit upon no track of him at all; and then I thought I'd best go down to the Hall, and talk with Master Selby, and he 'd be telling me what I should do with him."

" That's right, John; that's right," said the warrener. " I'm going home myself now with these rabbits; Andrew, cook, wants them for a pie, I reckon. Bartram, you'd best step up, man, with your packs; young mistress will buy, like enow."

"Well, I don't know but what I had," returned the pedlar, shouldering as he spoke his box and bales, and grasping his ell-wand; "but we must pay the reckoning first."

"No, no; that's mine," said Norman. "The score's mine this time, anyhow; when we next meet, you'll stand the treat for us, Bartram. I'll in and pay it up now; and then I've got to tramp clean round by Reardon Forest, and Low Moor, and down by the Hagard-mere to Hazel-woods and Burford Old-lane-end, and so home by the Ring-woods and the Goshawk dingle. I would I might fall in with the young cavalier. Well, good den, boys;" and throwing his pouch and horn across his shoulders, he caught up his gun and was turning to the house, when the arrival of a mounted party, making itself heard a minute at least before it came into sight by its clang and clatter, arrested all their plans in a moment.

CHAPTER V.

The new-comers, as it appeared in a few moments, were no less than a patrolling party of the Ironsides, consisting of eight privates with their lancepesade or corporal, and a subaltern officer; a lieutenant, or cornet more probably, commanding them. Like all the splendid corps of which these soldiers formed a part, they were picked men, and nothing could be more solder-like or perfect in its way than their whole bearing and appointment. There was nothing superfluous; nothing tawdry or tinselly; nothing defective, much less mean, about them. The strong high-bred black horses which they rode were accurately groomed and in superior condition, while all their furniture of plain black leather, mounted with polished steel, showed the severe and rigorous discipline of the regiment by its exact unsullied brightness.

The men were uniformly clad in scarlet doublets, with low pot-helmets of brightly-burnished steel—the most efficient and least cumbrous head-piece, by the way, that has been yet invented—and musket-proof cuirasses; the taslets on their thighs being of lighter substance, though of the same clear and highly-tempered material. Heavy jackboots with glittering spurs, buff breeches, and stout leather gauntlets extending almost to the elbow, completed their uniform; while for offensive arms each soldier carried a long, straight, two-edged broadsword, a brace of pistols at his holsters nearly two feet in length, and a short, heavy musketoon slung over his left shoulder, and crossed by the bandoleers containing his ammunition. There was not a particle of embroidery or lace upon the doublets of the men, nor any distinctive mark in the uniform of the lancepesade or of the cornet, except that the former had a short scarlet tuft, and the latter a red feather, in his morion. They came up at a brisk hand-gallop in double file, the non-commissioned officer leading them, and the subaltern in the rear; but as they entered the little green before the door of the Stag's Head, the cornet set spurs to his horse, and coming up to the head of the column wheeled them into a single line, closing in on both sides the tree, and surrounding the litle group between the inn door and the semicircle of his troopers.

"Halt, ho!" he shouted; "and you, sirs, stand all, and show your names and business, if ye be honest men. Ha!" he continued in a harsher and more insolent tone, as his eye fell upon Sherlock and the noble charger, which he had but that moment remounted; "Ha! what sort of knave have we here? what do you with this war-horse? Verily I do believe, Elisha Burnet, the dog is leading him out even now to mount that same malignant, who 'scaped so strangely from us yester even. Doubtless he is even now within. Unsling your firelocks—prime, load, and make ready! and now, thou most base knave and dog," he went on addressing Sherlock, when his orders had been complied with by the party he commanded, "why dost thou not speak out?"

"I've had no chance to speak," responded Sherlock doggedly enough, for he was not well pleased by the tone or manner of his questioner; "I've had no chance to speak, unless I interrupted you; and in the next place, for that matter, I've yet to learn what you would have me tell you."

"Who are you, dog, that bandy words with me?"

"No dog, sir," answered the other, "but an independent English yeoman—a peaceful and a loyal subject, troubling no man, and living on mine own land, which lies in this same parish; my name is John Sherlock, pretty well known in these parts, ay, and in Worcester too."

"Ha! thou art he I did speak with last night upon the bridge? Verily, John, verily, I misdoubt thee grievously; my mind misgivés me that thou didst lie unto us this past night, and that thou art in league with this malignant. Speak out, where is the traitor? See that thou answer truly, else, as my soul liveth in the fear of the Lord always, so surely shalt thou die the death."

"Of the owner of the horse," answered the honest yeoman, whose face had flushed exceedingly red at the imputation of the lie, "I know no more than thou dost, nor so much as thou dost neither, for thou hast seen him, which I never have, I trow. The horse I found tied to a ground ash in what we call the heronry wood, within a gunshot of the bridge where you were on the watch last night."

"Oh! thou did, didst thou; and what makest thou with him here, on this by-lane? Mark his words, corporal; whither wert taking him?"

"To Master Selby's, at the Hall, to ask him what I had best to do with him," was the immediate answer; "and I am on this lane, because it happens to be the nighest road to the Hall gates."

"And why to Master Selby's, knave? see that thou palter not."

"Because he is my landlord, and my right good friend and kind master, and the wisest man, too, and the best scholar, for miles round. Why, all the plain folks hereaway go for good counsel to Master Selby, when they need it."

"A very palpable lie," replied the Puritan; "but now thou didst tell me that thou didst dwell on thine own land, and now thou dost avouch this dreaming dotard to be thy landlord and thy master. Down from the charger, dog! down with thee in quick time; pitch him off if he loiter, lancepesade."

"There 'd go two words or more to that same bargain," answered John, dismounting slowly, "if you were alone, my gay lad! For, 'spite your toasting-fork and pop-guns, I'd find you work with a stout arm and a good crab-tree staff, and make your tin pot there ring, that it should fancy itself i' the tinker's hand again. A man can't own one farm, I trow, and rent another of his landlord—hey, master officer. I'd not get down now neither, but that the nag is none of mine, nor I don't want him."

"Ha! ha! well said, John Sherlock—well said, mine old friend. And if thou needst a backer, count upon me for one," exclaimed Frank Norman, the forester, with a hearty laugh, who had listened with much disgust to the insolence of the Puritan soldier.

"Ha! lancepesade, link bridles, and dismount your men, and seize me these malignants." A momentary bustle followed, during which Norman coolly loosened his whittle in its sheath, and very deliberately cocking his musketoon, levelled it full at the head of the speaker.

"The first man of you," he said, speaking through his set teeth with extreme firmness, "that stirs one step to lay a hand on me, an ounce ball 's in your leader's brain-pan."

"Who art thou that darest thus resist lawful superiors?" asked the cornet, not, to do him justice, apparently alarmed by the threat, which the other stood evidently prepared to execute.

"Frank Norman," was the ready answer, "head-forester and wood-ranger to the Lord Ferdinando Fairfax, on his estate and manor here of Oaklands; so put that in your pipe and smoke it, master cornet, after you have laid the strong hand on the lord-general's servitor!"

"Hold your hands, lancepesade," cried he, turning very pale

at the announcement; "this is an error all. He is an honest fellow, doubtless, though somewhat malapert. Hold your hands all! Is the Lord Fairfax at the manor now—how call you it —on his lands in Yorkshire?"

"He is at Oaklands," answered the forester, lowering his rifle as he saw that no violence would now be offered to him; "he came from the north three weeks since, if it concerns you anything to know."

"Well, well! good fellow, be not, I prithee, sullen; no evil has been done, nor any meant, I trow. Thou mayest go hence, I have no call with thee."

"But I have a call here," muttered Frank, "and so I'll even tarry."

"Well, be it so then. Lancepesade, look to that fellow Sherlock, that he escape not; guard him, but harm him not; while I look to these others." And as he finished speaking, he leaped down from his horse, and strode up to the old warrener.

"Now, sir, whose knave art thou? and what dost thou here?"

"No one's knave," answered old Brent, "but Squire Mark Selby's warrener, for these last score of years."

"Ha! and thou; marry, thou art a pestilent-looking thief, a spy of the malignants, I'll be sworn;" addressing the pedlar, on whose full bags the Ironsides had been for some time casting greedy glances.

"Not so, most noble sir," replied that worthy; "not so, most valiant captain"—in a strange, sanctimonious snuffle, widely at variance with his quick keen eye and somewhat roving air; "a poor but honest pedlar, licensed by the most worshipful house of parliament—trafficking in a poor way, fair sir—a very small, poor way; and judging it a gain always, I do profess it in the sight of Heaven—a gain not carnal, nor pertaining to mere worldly lucre, but a great gain to the immortal soul, if I can spoil somewhat in the way of trade those overproud Egyptians, the malignants, even as excellent Moses despoiled Pharaoh and his court. Verily, yea! indeed, if it be but a few poor pennies on the ell measure, it is still somewhat."

A grim smile curled the lips of one or two of the soldiers at this outburst; but nothing could exceed the entertainment of the young forester, manifested by a stentorian roar of laughter, which burst as it were irrepressibly from his lungs, till the tears fairly rolled down his sunburnt cheeks, at the pedlar's ludicrous and somewhat overstrained imitation of the puritanic snuffle. With no friendly eye did the officer regard his mirth, nor was he in the least persuaded by the pedlar's eloquence.

"Show me thy license, sirrah! I do misdoubt thee yet, for all thy seeming honesty. Surely 'tis no rare thing for the wolves now-a-days to don the sheep's clothing. Show me thy license. Well, it is right, I see," he added, after a pause; "but I shall search thy pack before I let thee go, I promise thee. Now, lancepesade, take three of your best men, bring all the women folk together into one place, and set a sentry over them, but see they take no harm. Then search the hostelry from the cellar upward, and if ye find *him*, as well I wot ye will, tarry not to ask questions or make prisoners, but shoot him dead upon the instant, and hew his head off from his shoulders—there is a price set on it that will pay the labor. Thou, Anderson, picket the horses there beside the horse-trough. You, sirs, stand to your firelocks, and see that none of these stir hence, unless it be that fellow of Lord Fairfax's following. Ha! who is this? I saw him not before," he continued, stepping out as he spoke toward the idiot boy; "who art thou?"

"He is an idiot lad," said Sherlock, speaking very quickly; "witless, and almost speechless, from his cradle, he cannot answer thee if he would; vex him not if thou art a man."

"Keep your breath, my good fellow, I advise you," retorted the other, "for your own porridge, which you'll find hot enough anon, I deem it very probable; and you, sir, answer me straightway, if you would avoid the strapado;" and with these words he laid his hand roughly on the poor idiot's shoulder, who glared upon into his face with an unmeaning vacant stare, but answered not a word.

"Speak, sirrah fool!" continued the other brutally, giving him at the same time a slight shake; but at that moment the old mastiff bitch, which had slept without moving during all that had passed heretofore, but had roused herself up as the soldier drew near her hapless trust, uttered a savage yell, and flew at his tormentor. But he, seeing at half a glance that she was toothless, and quite impotent to do him any harm, drew back a little, so as to give the utmost impetus to the blow, and kicked her in the chest with the full swing of his heavy boot: her furious yell was changed into a dolorous howl, as she rolled over and over, sprawling and struggling, close to the feet of one of the privates, who, following up his officer's brutality by a piece of his own, instantly knocked her brains out with the iron-plated butt of his heavy carbine.

A deep red flush crossed the bold features of the forester, and again left them pale as death; but he saw that it was useless to interfere, and that to do so might, in fact, only produce worse usage. Not so John Sherlock, who struggled so violently with the two Ironsides who held him, swearing and calling them by every vituperative and contemptuous term the cavaliers had applied to their party, that one of them gave him to understand that he should share the same fate as the mastiff if he did not hold himself still on the instant.

But in a moment, in the twinkling of an eye, the whole expression of the idiot's face was changed. The unmeaning, bead-like eyes, glared with a strange unnatural fire; he champed his strong white teeth, till the foam flew from them like the froth churned from the angry tushes of a hunted boar; he sprang upon his feet, uttering a long-protracted howl, more like the cry of some fierce and terrible wild beast than any voice of man, and brandishing his hands, contorted into the semblance of an eagle's talons, he seized the strong man by the throat, and, nerved by the supernatural force of madness, throttled him till his face grew purple, and his breath rattled in his throat, and shook him to and fro as if he was the merest stripling in the hug of a practised athlete. For a few seconds' space the men stood mute and motionless in consternation, but roused to a perception of their officer's danger—for the boy still clung to him like an enraged tiger, giving vent to his fury all the while by the most appalling sounds that can be conceived to issue from a human throat—sounds terribly chorused by the deep sobs and inarticulate ejaculations of the half-strangled soldier, and by the thrilling shrieks of the imprisoned women from within—three almost simultaneously sprang forward. But, as the foremost stretched forth his hand to grasp the idiot, Norman advanced one pace with a swift stride, and shifting his rifle rapidly into his left hand, struck him a flush hit in the face with all the strength and quickness of a skilful boxer. Between the actual force of the blow, and the impetus with which the Puritan rushed to meet it, the effect was tremendous. Headlong was the wretch hurled, as if he had been shot from some engine, with the blood spouting from nose, eyes, and mouth; and when he struck the ground, with all his steel accoutrements clanging about him as he fell, he lay there prostrate and motionless, as if he had been killed upon the spot. Almost at the same point of time in which Norman struck that hearty blow in his defence, the paroxysm of the idiot's attack was over. Relaxing his hold on the half-strangled Puritan, he staggered backward, and sunk into his wicker chair in the rigid seizure of an epileptic fit, slavering fearfully through his grinded teeth, rolling his eyes upward till the whites alone were visible, and clenching his hands till the blood started from his palms under the pressure of his nails. As he did so, the other two privates, who had sprung forth in the first instance to release their officer, seeing him now freed from his assailant, rushed on the forester, and taking him entirely by surprise, disarmed him ere he could use his rifle, and bound his hands behind him with a sword belt. At the same moment the corporal, with the three privates who had accompanied him, returned from their search, and announced it fruitless, for that there was no person in the house except its usual inmates, and farther, that they had found no signs of any recent visiter; while, freed from the restraint of the sentry, the women ran out to the assistance of the wretched idiot, and carried him in, still altogether senseless and inanimate. It was a little while before the cornet, by whose brutality the whole disturbance had been caused, recovered from the confusion into which the assault of the witless boy had thrown him; but when he did so, his face livid with all bad passions, and his cool malignant eye, proclaimed him dangerous, no less surely than did the first words which he uttered.

"Lancepesade, draw up instantly three file, tie the dog forester to yonder horse-post, and shoot him in two minutes, for an example to all treasonable brawlers. I'll teach him, that to serve a lord is no excuse for treason!"

Not a shade paler did the cheek of the stout-hearted Norman grow, as he heard the fell sentence, and saw the minions of his enemy clustering around him, and preparing to carry into effect the atrocious mandate; nor did one muscle tremble in his sinewy frame, although he saw that no mere threat or mockery was intended, but that it was cold and stern reality, without one hope of rescue. He did not speak a word, but his lips moved as he prayed fervently in silence.

"By God!" exclaimed John Sherlock, almost in a shout, as he looked on in impotent but furious indignation, at the preparations for the murder of his friend: "By God! to see this, a man would think there was no law in England, no justice under heaven."

"Then would a man think most unwisely," answered a clear, harmonious, and well-pitched voice from behind the group, all of whose faces were turned either toward the house, or down the lane to the eastward; "then would a man, I say, John Sherlock, think most unwisely; for there are laws in England, and while I am a magistrate, there shall be justice too!"

The eyes of all were directed in an instant to the sound; and there, just at the western entrance of the lane into the little green, upon a fine bay hunter, which he had just pulled up as he came suddenly and most unexpectedly upon the scene of so foul violence, sat the speaker. He was a fine-looking young man, of eight or nine-and-twenty years, with a broad ample forehead, from which a profusion of dark chestnut-colored hair fell off in loose and natural curls over the collar of his doubtlet; large clear gray eyes, and a set of features not in themselves so eminently handsome, as they were remarkable for their intellectual cast, and for the stamp of worth and calm unaffected majesty which they wore, as if it were their every-day accustomed garment—not a disguise assumed to suit occasions, and thrust at other times aside, lest it should mar the the aims or clash with the pursuits of the wearer. In person he was broad-shouldered, and deep-chested, and long-limbed, and sat his horse with that easy grace acquired only by long practice, and with something of a military air.

His dress was a complete riding-suit of fine pearl-colored cloth, slightly but tastefully embroidered with silk of the same color, high cavalry boots carefully polished, and a broad-leafed hat of gray beaver, with a silk hat-band fastened by a broad silver buckle, but without any feather or cockade. His sword, a handsome silver-hilted rapier in a steel scabbard, was girt about his waist by a rich scarf of silvery satin, presenting, with the aid of the snow-white linen and lace border of his Heemskirke cravat, a picture of the most graceful and finished neatness that can be imagined; although from the soberness of its colors, and the absence of all tawdry ornament, it was evident that the wearer belonged to the parliamentarian party, which was generally—and for the most part, it must be admitted, justly—stigmatized by the cavaliers as careless and ill-appointed, if not actually sordid, in appearance. There were holsters at his saddle-bow, and a pair of handsomely-mounted pistols showed they were not there for mere show.

When he had spoken those few words, in a voice and manner that accorded perfectly with the calm dignity of his demeanor, he rode slowly forward toward the house, followed by no less than six servant men dressed in plain liveries of dark drab cloth, superbly mounted on bay horses, and all well armed with sword and pistol, who drew out from the lane and quietly fell into line without any word given, but with a regular and business-like method, that showed very clearly that both men and horses had been accustomed to military manœuvres, and had performed them not only on the holiday fields of practice, but under the hot fire of squadrons.

A bright smile played across the face of Norman the moment that he heard the voice of the young gentleman, chasing away the shadows that had gathered there, even as the summer sunshine dispels the mist that shrouds some striking landscape; and a still broader expression of delight gleamed out upon the sturdy lineaments of good John Sherlock. The others appeared, indeed, somewhat confused and disappointed at the interruption; but their commanding officer, seeing that his force was still superior to that of the new-comers, hastily ordering his men to fall in and look well to their carbines, walked forward a few steps, and said—addressing himself to the leader of the party, with something more of respect than he had hitherto displayed to any person present, but still abruptly, and almost rudely:—

"And pray, sir, who may you be who talk so loudly about justice? I am Cornet Despard, at your service, of his excellency the Lord-General Cromwell's own regiment of Ironsides; and if, as your words seem to show, you be in truth an admirer of justice, and you think well to tarry here some six or seven minutes, then you are like to see it done upon as sturdy a knot of malignants as an honest man need light upon in one September day."

"I thank you for your information, Cornet Despard," returned the other, in the same cool, sonorous voice which he had used before—"I thank you for your information, sir; and have the honor to reply to you, that I am Major-General Henry Chaloner, colonel of the fifth regiment of horse, and commander-in-chief of this district here of Worcester. And now, to speak of justice, sir, I trust that on looking somewhat more narrowly into these matters, it may not appear that you have overstepped the limits of its more accurate construction."

CHAPTER VI.

It can be very readily conceived what was the effect produced by this announcement of the name and rank of the gentleman who had come in so opportunely to interrupt the summary proceedings of the Ironsides—a name which had been rendered honorably notorious by the gallantry and conduct of its owner throughout the long and bloody war which had so fiercely devastated England—a rank which placed him in the immediate command of all the military parties within the limits of his district. The men immediately presented arms, and with an aspect singularly meek and crest-fallen, the cornet commenced stammering out a justification of his barbarous proceedings. But Chaloner scarce heard him through four sentences—wherein, though laboring hard to show some case against Frank Norman, he had entirely failed to do so—before he interrupted him.

"No, sir, no cause at all," he said; "no cause at all, even to arrest the young man. If he did strike the soldier, he was in execution of no duty. I do assure you, Cornet Despard, that it is very well for you I came up, ere you had gone further. As it is, sir, give me your sword; return straightways to your quarters, and report yourself under arrest. I will see your colonel, and confer with him to-morrow. How now, Master Sherlock," he continued, "what have you been about, to bring yourself within the pale of martial law?"

"Lord love you, General Henry," returned the jolly farmer, "nothing! unless it be a crime in the calendar to find a horse. And if it be, it is a very new one. But I don't know, mayhap the young man thought I stole it."

"Fie! fie! thou steal, John Sherlock! That scarcely will pass muster, even for a suspicion. Here is another very palpable straining of authority, which trust me, Cornet Despard, I am not the man to pass over or forget. Setting aside the gross injustice, the petty pelting tyranny of these proceedings, sir, the mere report of such things, done by an officer of the parliament, will work more evil to the cause than a defeat on a pitched field of battle. We shall have all the country crying out on us, and that too very justly; for of a truth this is the very wantonness of petty persecution. What were the further duties, sir, enjoined upon this patrol, besides the bullying of idiot boys and plundering of pedlar's packs? What were your orders?"

"To scour the country roads, searching such places as I should deem suspicious, and making prisoners all armed malignants, with an especial view to the arrest of Captain Wyvil, who escaped somewhere in this quarter from Gettes' brigade last night. When I had finished here, I did propose to make further search at Woolverton."

"To what end, sir? The Hall was searched last night, as I have learned this morning by a despatch from my worshipful friend, Master Selby, and no one found therein, nor any shade of reason for suspicion. There was some rudeness, too, on that occasion, and his fair daughter was entreated but discourteously. Strange! that men, calling themselves soldiers, and wearing honorable swords, should stoop unto so base actions. Enough, sir, for the present, you know my pleasure; this sword shall be restored to you only upon the verdict of your officers. Lancepesade, Cornet Despard is your prisoner; march him at once on to headquarters, and give my service, Major-General Chaloner's service, and fair greeting to Colonel Keating, or to Major Gettes, and I have ordered him under arrest for a court martial! And for yourself, sir, and your men, I bid you to beware. I have heard complaints erewhile of much misconduct toward the people of the country. See that ye bear yourselves henceforth soberly, at the least, modestly, or it shall be the worse for ye. It hath pleased," he continued, reverentially touching the brim of his hat as he spoke—"It hath pleased the Great Dispenser of the universe to put an end to the bloody and infuriate strife which hath now for so many years laid waste our native land! The power of the parliament is firmly established throughout all England! There are no enemies in arms throughout the island! And you must learn to know, that although soldiers, ye are citizens also; and as citizens, amenable to the English laws, to which, in my district at least, I will take care that ye shall be obedient. Remember, men, what I now say to you, so shall ye 'scape, it may be, worse censure in the time to come; and, above all, remember that while I rule in Worcestershire, all men of all opinions, of all parties, so they obey the laws, and keep the peace of the land, shall be protected harmless, as our countrymen and brothers. Now, lancepesade, release your prisoners, draw off your men, and mount them, and make no tarrying on the way. See that you do report yourself at Barnsley Moor ere noon! Begone, sir."

Within five minutes the horses were unpicketed, the musketoons reslung. The corporal gave the word—" Prepare to mount—mount! Fall in! By files ma-arch! Steady, men! Trot!" and with their late commander riding crest-fallen, dark, and sullen, as a disarmed and disgraced prisoner in the centre of the detachment, they swept off at a hard trot, that soon caused the jingling of their spurs and scabbards, and all the noisy clatter of their harness, to be lost in the distance down the green windings of the lane.

The Ironsides were scarcely out of hearing when Henry Chaloner dismounted from his horse, and casting the bridle to the oldest of his servants, who had sprung to the ground as soon as he saw his master alighting, desired him to bait the beasts with a good feed of oats, and then to get his breakfast with his fellows; instructions which were attended to forthwith with a degree of alacrity that seemed to prove them by no means unwelcome. After having given these directions, he turned to John Sherlock, and begged that he would proceed no farther on his way till they should have some minutes of discourse together; and receiving his assurance that he would wait his pleasure, if it should be till midnight, he stooped his head to pass into the low-browed porch, and entered the little hostelrie in silence.

"There now," exclaimed the farmer, as he disappeared—"there goes as brave a soldier, and as good a gentleman, as any one in all England."

"Ay, that he is," replied young Norman, "be the other who he may. If all the Puritans were such as Henry Chaloner, many a kingsman hereaway would join with them."

"Puritan! Tush; he's no more a Puritan than thou be," Sherlock answered. "He always went to church, while church there was, i' the old abbaye, and never was seen at conventicle; and he rides well with the staghounds; ay, and I've seen him shoot at the butts, and dance around the Maypole, many's the summer evening. *He* is no Puritan."

"Why, man, he was against the king from the beginning," retorted the other; "he spoke against him always in the parliament-houses; and when the people armed, he was among the first, and fought in every battle through the war from Edgehill down to Worcester; and if he was opposed to them that cut the king's head off at Whitehall, when it was done and over, he helped to keep the son out of the father's throne. If he be not a Puritan, then I don't know what is one."

"Well, well! he is n't what I call one," persisted honest John, "for he is n't a preaching and a praying always, in season and out of season; and he do n't snuffle through his nose, like a hog in a high wind, nor whine like a whipped spaniel. He is n't a fanatic, nor a hypocrite, nor a canter—not a fawner on the great, nor a grinder of the poor and helpless. He has an honest, kind heart, and an open eye that looks a man i' the face, and a frank smile on his lips, and a ready and bold answer on his tongue. And so I say he is not a Puritan; and what I say, that I'll uphold, Frank Norman."

"That's right," answered Norman, laughing; "that's right, John, always. But you'll find no one here to contend with; for he is a good gentleman, and well liked through the country, Puritan or no! But it won't do, my standing chattering here, with all my rounds to go, and the morn growing late already, I must be moving, and that briskly; there's an outlying buck somewhere nigh Reardon forest, that I've been after these three days, and for the life of me I can not get on's slot." And with the words he took his rifle up again, looked at the priming and the flint, and whistling a lively air, vaulted over the fence at the horse-trough, and traversing the meadow with a light springy step, was lost to sight in the plantations at the farther side. His example was immediately followed by John Brent and the pedlar, who went off, the former leading his white pony, and the latter sturdily shouldering his pack, in the direction of the Hall; while the bold farmer, after watching the grooms for a few minutes busied about the horses, tied the black charger to a staple in the shade, and stretching himself out at full length on a settle in the sunshine, to wait the officer's leisure, was soon snoring in as sound a morning's sleep as ever sealed an eyelid.

In the meanwhile the subject of their conversation, quietly lifting the latch of the old oaken door, entered the kitchen; which was, as usual in those days, the principal apartment of the inn. It was a large, long room, with wainscoted wall and a low ceiling of black oak, from which were suspended hams, flitches of bacon, and huge pieces of hung-beef, sufficient to have maintained an army for a twelvemonth. The whole farther end of the room was occupied by an enormous fireplace, with a high-backed wooden settle on each side of it, and a tall mantelpiece grotesquely carved and blackened with the smoke of ages. Along the front, looking out upon the little green and the old oak-tree, were no less than three latticed casements, their ample sills bedecked with pots of flowers and sweet herbs; and under these was a huge oaken dresser, so brightly polished that it might well have served for a mirror to the bright-cheeked damsels of the inn. The greater part of the wall facing the windows was covered by a rack filled with long rows of splendid pewter trenchers hardly less clear than silver, a tall old eight-day clock, surmounted with a glorious canopy of peacock's feathers, two corner beauflets well stored with silver tankards, long Venice drinking-glasses, pieces of antique porcelain, a japan-box or two of knives and spoons, and a gilded salt-cellar—the glory of the whole collection, and an heirloom of the family—with sundry short-legged, high-backed chairs, completed the furniture of the quiet, hospitable room. It should be added, that everything was most minutely and fastidiously clean; from the neatly-sanded floor to the polished platters, and gleaming copper candlesticks and skillets, arranged so orderly upon the walls. There was not a cobweb in the darkest nook—not a grain of dust on the panes of the corner cupboards—not a cloud of moisture on the drinking-glasses—not a speck of tarnish on the cups and tankards; the white dimity curtains were not merely spotless, but glossy with the traces of the recent iron; the very flytraps of paper, quaintly fashioned by the scissors, which hung from the low beams, seemed to be but just placed there, so free were they from any stain or blemish.

It must not be supposed, however, that these particulars were all, or indeed any of them, now observed by the young soldier. His eye did indeed run over them as he entered; but if he noted them at all, it was merely as things which he had seen a hundred times before, and of which the absence alone would have surprised him. Had it, however, all been unusual and new, as on the contrary it was familiar to his eyes, he would at that moment have disregarded it, for there were two groups in the room, either of which, from their distressful and interesting aspect, would have monopolized the thoughts of any one. The first was composed of the unhappy idiot, or "innocent," as he was delicately termed by the country-folks, who had not recovered from his seizure, although the violence of his paroxysm was even now abating, surrounded by several females of the house, bathing his sallow brow with simple essences, laving the acrid slaver from his quivering lips, and using such mild remedies to soothe him as their experience had taught them to apply.

Among these, most conspicuous was the girl Cicely, with another pippin-cheeked dark-eyed handmaid, and a thin, gaunt old woman, with snow-white hair neatly arranged below her checkered kerchief; but superintending all, and observing with a deep anxious eye the long-drawn sobs and convulsive twitches of the boy, was a young woman, whose appearance could scarce fail to create an immediate interest in the eyes of the most casual observer. She was a pale, fair creature, with a singularly intellectual expression on her features, which were moulded in the most exact lines of Grecian symmetry. There was not, however, one shade of color on her pure pale cheek, not one tint of the blood showing through the transparent skin; all was as colorless, and seemingly as cold, as statuary marble, except the mouth, which, with a singular contrast, was of the ripest, richest crimson; her eyes were very large and bright, of a deep liquid blue; but they, too, had a strangely cold and chilling aspect—a clearness, like that of the cloudless frosty sky of a December day, which, although quite as deep and liquid and transparent in its hue, could never be mistaken for the warm azure of a midsummer's evening. Her hair, which was exceedingly profuse, even to redundance, was strained tight across the shapely temples, and rolled up into a knot of the smallest possible dimension low down on the neck, as might be seen through the thin lawn of her unornamented cap. In person she was below the middle size, slightly and delicately made, with small neat feet and hands, so white and slender that many a court lady might have envied them. Her dress was a high-necked close-fitting gown of some black stuff, and a white apron, worn without any ornament at all, except a wedding-ring of plain gold, which perhaps might explain both the black garments and the melancholy air; for no words can describe the fixed and settled sadness which was visible, not in her tranquil features only and her unsmiling lip, but in every sound of her voice, in every movement of her body, in every look of her clear, unimpassioned eye. She spoke, and moved, and looked, like one who, although in the world, is yet not of it—who with duties to perform, and cares to undergo, has neither pleasure in the present nor hope in the future. And, alas! how sad, how unspeakably sad and pitiful, that one so young, so gentle, and so fair, should have been so bereaved as to make all the laughing earth, with all its sounds and sights of beauty, one wide illimitable tomb for ever!

The second group, which had an interest little if at all inferior to the first, consisted of three persons only—an old, old woman, so old that she seemed indeed to have lived far beyond the space allotted to man's sojourn here below, seated erect in a large easy chair before the fire, and two little children. A single glance showed that the ancient dame was confined to her seat by some paralysis, or other ailment, which crippling her lower limbs, had left the upper portion of her body unaffected, and her mind unimpaired; she was stone-blind, moreover, with that uncommon species of blindness, which, while it entirely destroys the vision, yet spares the appearance of the eyeball; so that it is but by the wandering unspeculative glare of the clear orbs that a stranger can pronounce them sightless. A terrible expression of anxiety and grief and fear was now distorting the serene lineaments, and filling the blind eyes of the helpless woman with bitter scalding tears, as with a querulous and lamentable cry she would now wail, and now ask hurried questions, which no one could find time to answer, concerning "her boy, her poor boy—her poor, witless, innocent boy, Martin!"

The little children, two bright-haired, blue-eyed, fairy-looking girls, of six and eight years old, clinging to the grandmother's apron, had tried at first to comfort her with their small artless prattle, assuring her that cousin Martin would soon be better, and the like; but now, seeing that the old woman's tears and terrors but increased, they too were sympathetically frightened, and were both weeping, as fast as their little eyes could weep, they knew not wherefore.

Such was the scene that met the kind eye of Henry Chaloner, as he entered: and he immediately advanced to the first group, as being that where he most probably might render some assistance; but seeing immediately that those about poor Martin, long since habituated to his malady, were managing him as well, or better, than he could have advised himself, and that his seizure was fast yielding to their soothing applications, he turned away gently without asking any question, and walked across the room with a light step toward the old lady.

"Don't be alarmed," he said, in the lowest tones of his deep measured voice; "don't be alarmed I beg of you, dear dame, for there is no occasion, I assure you."

"Dear Lord!" cried the old woman, starting at the unexpected sounds, for the bustle about the sick youth, and the quietness of his own movements, had prevented her discovering the entrance of the young soldier. "Dear Lord! if that be not General Henry;" for with the instinctive quickness of the blind she had easily recognised his accents, which were, indeed, sufficiently remarkable.

"It is, indeed, Dame Rainsford," he replied, taking her hand gently as he spoke, and sitting down upon the wooden settle near her; "it is indeed I, and sorry I am, too, to find you thus grieved and terrified; but I assure you there is no occasion for alarm, much less for grief, at all. And you well know I would not say that if it were not true, even to set your poor heart at rest; but truly there is none. Some rude men here a little time since alarmed poor Martin, it would seem, and he has had one of his wonted fits—no more, I do assure you—and it is yielding fast, I see, even now to your fair daughter-in-law's kind tendance; he will be better, I dare promise you, anon!"

"Ay, sir, I'll warrant it," responded the old woman, reassured instantly by the calm voice and characteristic consolations of Henry Chaloner; "I'll warrant it, if that be all. Marian knows how to care for him well. Heigho! poor Marian. I was afraid that it was something worse, for I heard Martin cry out fearfully a while since, and they have had no time to answer a poor, helpless, castaway old thing, such as I am; but I don't find any fault, for they 're good children all of them, heigho! but since I lost my poor boy Roger, in that sad fight there at Long Marston, it's all dull somehow—dull and dreary, and no head to the house like, though Marian be a wonder! Well, well, it's all for the best—all for the best, thank God—and his good time will come!"

"Ay, indeed, is it," answered Chaloner. "HE never burdens any beyond their power to bear, and never casts a snare before the feet of any, but that therewith he frames a path whereby to make escape from it! And, lo! here in good season, Martin is on his feet again, and doing bravely."

"Bring him this way—bring my poor child this way—will you not, Marian; where are you taking him, my girl?"

"To lie down, mother, for a while," replied the young, pale widow, obeying her words, nevertheless, and guiding the helpless being across the sanded floor; "he always needs sleep, you know, after the fit leaves him!"

A melancholy scene, but one of surpassing interest and beauty, followed, as the poor idiot, led up by his widowed aunt, approached his bereaved sightless parent, on whom his meaningless and stolid eye dwelt with a feeble glimmering of expression, as if his veiled imperfect memory partially recognised the venerable being who years ago had soothed his anguished infancy. A faint sick smile played over his pale lips, as by the force of habit he bowed his head to meet the pressure of her thin shrivelled tremulous fingers, and felt her kiss upon his sallow forehead, and the warm tears which fell like summer rain upon his matted locks.

"Bless thee, my boy—my poor, poor boy! God bless thee, for thou art very dear to me; oh, very, very! Although thou be not comely to the sight, nor gifted with the light of heavenly reason, very dear art thou to my soul, child of affliction, being of suffering and sorrow, sole relic and last gift of my fair firstborn; God's goodness be about thy lifelong darkness, to guide and comfort and protect thee."

The heavy tears dropped fast and frequent from the kind eyes of Chaloner at this heart-touching prayer; and as he saw that aged woman, deprived of all the wonted blessings of this life, crippled, and blind, and reft of all her children, bending in grateful prayer over that idiot boy, his soul was so full that he could not frame an "Amen," as she ended.

They led the poor youth to a chamber, and gradually the comely and serene tranquillity, which was its usual expression, resumed its reign over the face of the blind woman; and the tears of the little girls were lost, like April showers, in light sunny laughter, as they played with the fringe of Henry's scarf, and wondered at his glittering sword-hilt; and Marian and her maidens returned from their labor of love, and all things again wore their wonted aspect.

A thoughtful, quiet gladness, was perceptible on the wan features of the youthful widow, as she greeted her kind guest, and apologized briefly and simply for the neglect he had experienced, and the confused state of the household.

"Oh, speak not of it," he said, much more quickly than it was his custom to reply; "speak not, I pray you, of it, if you would not grieve me. I saw, and was very sorry for the cause, and if I could I would have prevented it in time; you will believe me when I say I would; as it is, I will take care no such abuse occur again within my district. But now, my good Marian, I must put you to some trouble. I have ridden nearly a score of miles this morning, and have not broken my fast yet; and I have with me six hungry knaves besides. Will you prepare some food for us, and show me to your summer parlor, where I may write a letter, and commune with my own thoughts a little while in private?"

"Surely, sir, surely!" she replied; "would it were in my power to show by greater services my gratitude for all your goodness. Walk this way, General Henry;" and as she spoke she opened a small door in the chimney corner, behind the oaken settle, which gave access to a narrow winding staircase, up which she led him into a pleasant lofty chamber, occupying one of the gables, and overlooking from its large latticed window the smooth green meadows, and the dark quiet woodlands in the distance. The floor was strewn with clear white sand, the fireplace filled with the varnished leaves and bright red berries of the holly—the walls were wainscoted with highly-polished oak—there was a round table, with a standish, pens and paper, and two vast old-fashioned arm-chairs in the recess of the window; and, in short, all was so cool and clean and tranquil, and the mild air of the radiant autumn morning came in so balmily through the leaves of the old oak, and caught such pleasant perfumes from the flower-pots on the window-seat, that a more fitting place could hardly have been found wherein to fix the mind in meditation, And so thought Henry Chaloner as he threw himself into the chair, and wrote, and pondered on his writing; while servants went and came, and spread a larger board behind him with all appliances for the morning meal, unheard by him, or at the least unheeded. At last, his task concluded, he raised his head, and asking for a taper and some wax to secure his letters, desired that his head-groom might come to him; and, by the time he had fastened up the two notes he had written, the man stood before him.

"Andrew," he said, "let James Warr take the Peacock gelding, and ride with all speed to Colonel Hastings' quarters at Low Barnsley; he must be contented with a crust of bread and a draught of ale, till his errand is done, for it is all important. Then he may feed his horse, and dine and breakfast both in one, and ride home at his leisure; there is no reply to wait for. And do thou take this note thyself to Woolverton, to Master Selby's, and tarry for an answer. It will not hold thee long, and thou must e'en make up for it when thou get'st back. I warrant me thou 'rt hungry now, but there 's no help for it, good Andrew. The meat will tarry, but not so the matter."

"I'm not so hungry, sir, but I can ride all day, and all night too, and that gladly, fasting, if it were on your service," answered the old groom, who had long served, and well loved his young master.

"I thank you, Andrew, and believe you," he replied, "but shall not have, I hope, so far to tax your willingness. Meanwhile, as you go down, ask them to serve my breakfast."

CHAPTER VII.

The mind of Henry Chaloner was one of those unquestionably, which are so well and accurately balanced by nature in the first instance, and so well schooled in the second, by experience and Christian philosophy, that of all they are the least likely to be thrown into violent perturbation by the pressure of any external circumstances. He had, moreover, that fixed and tranquil self-reliance, common to men of great parts who have seen much, and suffered much in the world, which enables its possessors to meet the most difficult contingencies with a quiet resolute front; and, better yet, he had that immovable faith and confidence in God's power, and mercy, which supports the Christian, dauntless and invincible, through all extremities of toil and trial. Still, there is no combination of natural and acquired parts, no innate hardihood of heart, no practice in the world's warfare, no sternness of philosophy, no support of Christianity, nothing, indeed, short of apathetic dullness, and deadness of the soul, that can at all times master grief, and bid the foul fiends, doubt, despondency, and anxious penetrating care, avaunt in the first moment of their onslaught; and in the present instance, well-regulated as was the mind of the young officer, and well-disciplined to suppress its feelings in consideration to the necessities of others, it were useless to deny that for some cause or other he was exceedingly restless and uneasy. The meal which was set before him remained almost untasted, although it consisted of every delicacy that the time and place could furnish. Though the red-spotted trout were fresh from the neigboring brooklet; though the eggs, which accompanied the bubbling rasher, were new-laid that morning; though the buttock of cold powdered beef was of the fattest, and the mustard genuine Tewksbury—and though all was served with that appetizing and rare cleanliness which will do more to tempt a fastidious palate, than the most luxurious dishes, still there was something at work within, which would not suffer him to swallow a mouthful; he made, indeed, several efforts to conquer his reluctance, but still the meat would not go down; and he gave up the point, after a second long draught from the spiced tankard, which the fever and heat of his mind rendered very grateful.

Throwing himself back in the arm-chair, he remained for some time in deep thought, with his hand tightly pressed upon his eyes; then he rose up restlessly, and leaning out of the window, seemed to listen whether he might hear anything of his man's return, although there had scarcely elapsed time enough for him to reach the Hall; and then, as if recollecting himself, turned away from the casement, and began walking to and fro the room with slow and measured paces, which showed that if he was disturbed, it was the disturbance of a regular self-governing spirit, not the headlong rashness of a violent and passionate nature, excited beyond all control by any casual irritation.

"I much fear, I very much fear that it is so," he at length muttered to himself, thinking as it were aloud; "and if so, it will be in truth a difficult bad business. I know not what will come of it."

The fact was, that holding a situation of vast importance in the country—the office of major-general of a district under the parliament being tantamount to that which which is now termed lord-lieutenant of a county—he had received despatches which gave him no slight uneasiness, and imposed on him duties, the propriety of which he half doubted, and the performance of which could not but be most painful to all his better feelings. After the attempt of the cavaliers, seconded by a great part of the Scottish people, to elevate Charles the Second to the throne of the Martyr, as they fondly persisted in calling the weak man who had fallen a victim to his own obstinate and selfish insincerity—after this attempt, checked by the daring energy of Cromwell in the battle of Dunbar of the preceding year, and now completely overthrown and prostrated by the crowning mercy of Worcester fight, a spirit of persecution broke out, or at least manifested itself far more generally than at any previous period of the war, among the Presbyterians and Independents, toward the scattered fugitives of the defeated party. The king himself was hunted with a vindictive pertinacity, from which men augured easily that his capture would lead to a repetition of the tragedy of the thirtieth of January, while his adherents were cut down, or shot like dogs, wherever they were taken, many days after the entire dispersion, and, as it might almost be termed, dissolution of the party.

The fears, however, or the hatred of the parliament remained unsatisfied; and instructions were issued throughout all the country, to all the major-generals in command, to omit no precautions for the preventing the assemblage of small armed bodies, which might serve as the *nuclei* of future risings, and to spare no pains for the apprehension of sundry, the most eminent leaders of the late rebellion, whom they were directed, as fast as captured, to send up to London, where it was intended that they should be left for trial on indictments of high treason. A general amnesty was indeed talked of; but unquestionably, if any such measure were in contemplation, so many exceptions would be made as would render it such in name only, and this was rendered evident by the long list of persons forwarded to the governors of districts for immediate proclamation, whom men were forbidden on pain of forfeiture, imprisonment, and in some cases death, from "resetting, harboring, or comforting with food, or fire, or raiment."

All this tended to render Henry Chaloner uneasy; for though he had, as we have seen, systematically opposed the usurpations of the king, from the first to the last—though he had considered Charles the First unfit to reign, and his son even more unqualified to succeed him—though he had exerted all his powers of mind and body to banish the obnoxious issue from the throne and the country—and though he was prepared to resist to the utmost all efforts to reinstate them—he had yet nothing in his nature of the bigot or persecutor; and he would now have instantly extended, not only full indemnity from any personal harm, but all political and civil privileges to all men, of all parties and opinions, who should thereafter be contented to keep the sword at rest within its scabbard, and vex the land no longer.

But this was not all that troubled him, nor would this have sufficed to trouble him so far, had there been no more reason for anxiety; since, in the first place, by virtue of his office, he possessed some discretionary power; and so great was the attention which had been ever paid to his opinions by the great man who swayed the destinies of England, that he had little fear of winning from his calmer judgment a sanction to more merciful proceedings than were at present contemplated.

At a late hour of the preceding night he had been roused from sleep by the arrival of an orderly, bearing to him from the colonel of the Ironsides quartered at Barnsley Moor, a full narrative of the pursuit by a patrolling party of the proclaimed malignant, Captain Wyvil—of his extraordinary escape, when escape seemed impossible—of the fruitless search of Woolverton Hall, and of the strong grounds which still existed for believing him to be harbored on those premises. The narrative was drawn up with technical nicety, and therein it was certified that several of the brigade which had first passed the place, both officers and privates, had seen a young and beautiful woman at the window of the fish-house. It was shown further, that when the second party came up, scarce twenty minutes later, and actually searched the place, it was vacant! Again, it was proved that during that brief interval, the fugitive must have passed within a gunshot of the window where she sat; and that there was not any lane or by-road between the angle of the road leading directly to the bridge—which he had been seen to turn by his pursuers—and the spot where the patrol had overtaken Gettes' brigade, by which he could have turned off to the right or left, and so eluded the close chase.

The effect of this evidence, although by no means really conclusive, went far to convince Henry Chaloner, who well knew the secret predilections of his cousin Selby, and the romantic high-minded generosity of his lovely daughter, that by some means or other one or both were concerned in the escape of Wyvil. In this opinion he was confirmed yet further by a note which he had received before he left his chamber in the morning from Mark Selby, informing him of the search which had been instituted on his premises, complaining of the rudeness of the soldiery, and requesting to see him at his early leisure on business of some import. The receipt it was of this note which caused him to hasten a measure on which he had already determined; and he accordingly ordered his horses to be saddled, and a suitable train prepared, and set forth on his ride before the cocks had crowed their matin song. The occurrences which befell him afterward, and especially the discovery of Wyvil's horse by John Sherlock, close, as it was represented, to the place where the fugitive was first missed, and within a few yards of the fishing-house, scarce left a doubt on his mind of the secret agency of Alice in the young cavalier's escape. It is, of course, unnecessary to say, that to Chaloner this agency—however much inconvenience it might produce to himself, or peril to the fair young girl—did not appear in the light of an offence against any laws, either human or divine; and it is scarcely to be doubted, that had he himself been situated as she was, despite his official duties, he would have acted as she did, and facilitated the evasion of a fugitive whom he certainly regarded as unfortunate, and perhaps mistaken, rather than criminal or guilty.

Entertaining these opinions, therefore, the thing in the world which he least wished at this moment was that by any casualty he should be forced to discover the hiding-place of Wyvil. Averse, in the first place, to cruelty or blood-shedding under all circumstances, convinced that in the present crisis leniency was the true and politic course for the restoration of tranquillity and peace, and confident, moreover, that within a short space of time he could bring about a material change in the views of the government, he dreaded to have this case of Wyvil so brought before his eyes that he should have no alternative but to arrest him, when his fate, and not his fate alone, but that of all who had assisted him, would be decided on the instant.

At the same time, he was too rigid in his views of duty and of right, to connive secretly at any act which he would not avow in public—all personal consequences he would have discarded instantly, as utterly unworthy his consideration; and had he with his own hands taken Wyvil in the open country, or found him in the hands of troopers who had so arrested him, he would have very probably discharged him at his own peril, if satisfied that he entertained no views against the peace of England. To do this, however, if he should be detected under the roof of Selby, would be of no avail to save the old man and his lovely daughter from forfeiture of all their worldly goods, and from a long imprisonment, ending perhaps in death upon the scaffold. He felt that, with the information laid before him, he had no course left but to investigate the case completely, and if it should prove needful, to order a fresh search! And hating, as he did, to contemplate the possibility of the young man's being brought to judgment by his means, and dreading, as he did for a thousand reasons, the consequences to his friends and kindred at the Hall, who shall be moved by wonder if Henry Chaloner, despite all natural advantages of equanimity and fortitude—all supplemental aids of discipline, philosophy, religion—was ill at ease, and anxious and unhappy?

An hour or more had passed since he despatched the groom to the Hall, an errand which should not, as he conceived, at the most have occupied one half that time; and after looking out of the window anxiously two or three times within five times as many minutes, he ordered his horses to be again got ready, and determined to ride down the road, feeling assured that he should meet his messenger returning before he could reach the gates. He had just given these instructions when the sounds of a slight bustle reached his ears from the rooms below, and immediately after some words spoken in a low silvery voice, which fell upon his soul like the memory of some familiar tune heard in the happy days of boyhood, and unforgotten through all the sins, and strifes, and miseries of manhood, even to remote old age. It was but a few words—or to speak more correctly, the tones and accents of a few words, which were themselves inaudible—that reached him, and these too dulled and deadened by the distance, and by the obstacles through which they were transmitted: yet at the first faint note he started to his feet, listening intently, and apparently recognising the speaker, in a moment took up his hat and sword, and hastened down into the kitchen, whence the sounds proceeded. The moment he opened the door from the small turnpike staircase, with the full morning sunshine pouring in through the open casement on her beautiful features and graceful figure, Alice Selby stood before him, conversing in tones full of soft considerate kindness with the old afflicted woman and the young widow, who were listening to all she said with an expression not of love only or respect, but of the deepest and most reverential gratitude. Chaloner's servants, their morning meal concluded, had long since gone out to attend the horses, and there was no one in the room except the members of the family, and an old gray-headed serving man, in a plain livery of green and gold, with a stone jug, holding perhaps two quarts, slung in a leathern belt across one shoulder, and a large wicker basket by his side, who was wiping his forehead, as if somewhat tired with his load, although there was a cheerful smile upon his weather-beaten features, showing that he grudged not the easy labor.

Alice was speaking at the moment when her cousin paused at the open door; but as it was placed in a dark angle of the room, and as her eyes were turned in a direction somewhat different, she did not see him, but went on in the same low musical accents, which had so pleasantly affected him: "So when I missed you, Marian," she said, "from our little congregation at the Hall on Sunday, I was afraid there was something amiss with Dame Rainsford or poor Martin, and I should have come over yesterday to see you all, but I was somewhat occupied in the forenoon within doors; and, to say truly, I forgot all about it after dinner, and went out to walk in the park, and fell asleep, I believe, in the fish-house; and was frightened a good deal afterward—which was certainly very foolish in me, Maria—by some parliament soldiers, who rode by smoking and laughing, and making a loud rude disturbance. But when I saw this morning that neither of my little pets, Bella, nor my god-daughter Alice, were at school, I was quite sorry, and ashamed of my neglect. So I put on my cloak and hood, and made old Jeremy bring down a bottle of the choice Canary, which Doctor Trowbridge thought so good for your mother's ailment, and a few cates and simples from my own laboratory for poor Martin."

"Oh, you are kind! God bless you, Mistress Alice! and he will, I doubt not; but there is nothing much amiss; my mother, it's true, was ailing somewhat on the Sunday morning, and that was the reason of my not coming up to chapel; but she was quite well yesterday again, as well that is, as she can hope to be, and in good spirits, God be thanked! and there is no harm done this morning, though the soldiers were very rude and brutal, and used Martin so that he got one of his bad fits, and is only better of it now, and has just dropped asleep!"

"Soldiers!" said Alice, turning very pale; "what soldiers? are they here now? Quick, good Marian!" and as she spoke, she pulled the hood farther over her features, and looked wildly around.

"None, my fair cousin," answered Henry, before any of the others had time to reply, advancing into the room with his head uncovered. "None at all, Alice, unless you count me one; but if you do, I do n't believe you'll judge me very formidable."

"Oh, Cousin Henry, is it you?" she answered with a gay smile; "you startled me at first a little, for I did not dream of meeting you here. No, I do n't think you very formidable, although you are a soldier; but that is more than we can say for all of your good parliament troopers, since some of them are rude, not to say brutal."

"Of which I had a very clear proof here but now," Chaloner answered; "and in truth, if you will pardon me, I do think you were best confine your walks within the limits of your father's grounds just now; these Ironsides, flushed with their victory at Worcester, are scouring the roads all round, and, I fear much, abusing shamefully their power, and the trust reposed in them. I will see these things righted ere long, if I am to hold the district as commander; but for a few days, Alice, take my advice, and let your park walls be the limit of your wanderings."

"Indeed I will, Cousin Henry," she replied; "indeed I will take your advice, and thank you for it. They came and searched our house last night, for some one whom they charged us with concealing; and one of them, an officer, a singularly ill, ungracious-looking youth, was positively rude to me."

"He will not so offend again, fair Mistress Alice," answered the young man; "for if, as I doubt not, your friend was Cornet Despard, I have just sent him to headquarters in arrest for most unsoldierly and brutal conduct here this morning; and I will take care he is duly punished. But come," he added, "it seems to me your visit of charity and kindness is concluded. I was about to ride down to the Hall even now, to wait on your father, who signified to me by letter a wish that I would see him touching this business you have mentioned. Suffer me to send on my horses, and on foot escort you homeward."

"No, thank you, cousin," answered Alice, with a smile; "I am playing Lady Bountiful this morning, and have to pay two visits more to two of my old pensioners in the village. Since you have driven these rude discourteous warriors home, like a fair and gallant knight, an errant damsel may hold herself safe for this time. But, jesting apart, Henry, I *must* go a little half mile farther; and Jeremy has the key of the small postern gate beside the heronry wood, and I shall go in by that entrance. So go your ways, good cousin, and commune with my father, and then come join me in the park. You 'll tarry dinner with us, surely! Nay, I 'll have no denial; and, now I think of it, my father means, I fancy, to detain you over night. Fare you well for the present; fare you well, dame. Here be the simples, Marian, and give your mother a good cup of the

Canary straightway; poor soul, she needs some comfort. Fare you well, Bella; one kiss, my little Alice." And among the blessings of all, and the fervent thanks of the old matron, in whose opinion Alice was an absolute angel, too beautiful and good for aught below, she vanished from the room, leaving it, as Henry Chaloner thought, lower, and darker, and more gloomy than it had ever seemed to him before; and after a little while he too, having paid his reckoning, mounted his horse and rode away slowly toward the hall-gates, before reaching which he met his servant coming up at full gallop, the bearer of a verbal message from Master Selby, praying that "Major-General Chaloner would visit his poor house with all convenient speed!

CHAPTER VIII.

It was at about the same hour of the same day at which the rustic party were interrupted by the arrival of the Ironsides at the Stag's Head, that the squire of Woolverton—the morning meal being finished, and all the household busied about their wonted avocations—gave orders to the steward that he should not on any account be disturbed for a couple of hours, and, locking the library-door with jealous care behind him, proceeded through the secret passage to the hiding-place of his concealed guest. It was, perhaps, fortunate that the habits of the old man, secluded, sedentary, and averse to much intercourse with man, were such as to prevent any speculation or surprise at such an order, it being his almost daily practice to shut himself up in the pursuit of some abstruse and difficult study, so that no one of the servants entertained the least suspicion on the subject. The greatest risk that Selby had discovered in the case was the providing food for the stranger without attracting notice; and this he was, in fact, only able to manage by robbing his own buttery nightly, after the people had retired to rest, much to the wonder and disquiet of the old housekeeper, who was continually missing corners of venison pasties, cold larded capons, remnants of neats' tongues, and whole loaves of bread; for the disappearance of which she could in no wise account, and concerning which she was perpetually worrying and fidgeting her fellow-servants to no end or purpose.

It was then with a basketful of cold provisions, two or three long-necked flasks of Bordeaux wine, a fresh supply of oil, a change of linen, and sundry volumes of the long-winded cumbersome romances of that day, that the old squire now sought his visiter. With a noiseless step, and a suppressed breathing, the good old man traversed the long and darksome corridors, now climbing steep and narrow stairways, now winding downward by deep gradual descents, turning short angles, and passing through trap-doors almost innumerable, until he reached the safe and distant crypt wherein he had left Wyvil to his slumbers on the preceding night. So deep had been those slumbers, and so completely had the young man been overwrought by the toil, the exertions, and the tremendous excitement of the previous days, that he lay buried still in profound and dreamless stupor; and it was well that Selby had brought a master-key, by means of which he gained admittance to the cell, since not by any signal that he dared make could he attract his guest's attention. Unlocking the door quietly, he entered, and setting down his load stepped lightly to the bedside. The brazen lamp was burning steadily upon the table, filling the whole of the small room with a smoky, yellow light, and pouring full upon the uncurtained features of the sleeper. His clothes, cast off in negligent disarray, were heaped upon the stools and table; his rich buff coat, all laced with tawney silk and looped with gold, hung on the back of the armed chair, moist and discolored by the waters of the moat, through which the wearer had swam on the previous evening; his cuirass of bright steel, inlaid with arabesques of gold, lay on the table, sending back the rays of the dull lamp in strong and dancing gleams of brighter lustre; his vest and trunk-hose of murray-colored velvet, his russet buskins with their long gilded spurs, and his embroidered slouched beaver with its black drooping plume, lay in confusion on the stone-paved floor; but the blue baldric of his rapier was twined round one of the posts of his pallet bed, so that the hilt was ready to his hand at a moment's notice; while, as a further precaution, he had thrust the point of his naked poniard into a crevice of the headboard, so that it could be griped with his left hand, as readily as the sword-hilt with his right, on the least emergency. Little, however, would either weapons have availed him now, had the intruder been an enemy; for he still slept so deeply that he might have been slain easily, without the possibility of making any adequate resistance

For a few moments Mark Selby would not arouse him from his state, as it appeared, of absolute insensibility, but stood gazing steadfastly upon the tranquil lineaments of the young sleeper. Those lineaments, which the old man had seen but imperfectly the night before, were certainly and eminently handsome. He had a profusion of soft, silky, light-brown hair, falling back from his brow in long straight masses, waved slightly on the temples, and curled as it would seem artificially at the extremity; his forehead was very high and prominent, but rather narrower at the temples than below, which detracted somewhat from the beauty of the feature; it was, however, singularly white and smooth, and perfectly unwrinkled, except that there was a deep indentation, as if of an habitual frown, at the inner point of the eyebrows, which were straight and well defined, of a color several degrees darker than his hair. His eyes, as could be seen even while he slept by the form and dimensions of the lids, were large and well opened, and fringed with long black lashes; his nose was thin, and somewhat sharply, though not highly, aquiline; his mouth, which by its firm compression and set downward curve, bespoke decision of character and absolute hardihood, had yet an expression of voluptuousness in the full prominent under lip, and in the fleshy curvature of the projecting chin; and the combination of the whole was, as has been already said, sufficient to constitute a face of decided and unusual attractiveness. The coloring was rich and manly; a complexion, which had been naturally very fair and florid, having been darkened by exposure to the weather into a ripe and mellow brown, which suited well the narrow dark mustache which he wore on the upper lip, and the small vandyke beard trimmed into the fashion of a fleur-de-lis, with two small upward curls and long point between; giving a soldier-like and manly air to a countenance which without it might have been termed effeminate, from the smallness and delicacy of all the separate features, rather than from any real want of energy or character in the expression.

It may as well be stated here, although Mark Selby saw them not at present, that his eyes were of a full dark blue, and that his mouth was filled by a set of teeth as regular and white and pearly as were ever set off by the coral lips of the loveliest woman. As the old man gazed on the comely features, he certainly thought that he had never seen a handsomer man, nor one with a more bland and beautiful expression; yet much of this last appearance was factitious merely, and depended on the present situation of the sleeper, who, completely overcome with toil, was sunk in the voluptuous and calm tranquillity of the deepest and most dreamless sleep. Had he been awake, however, while he would have admitted the beauty even perhaps more fully than at present, the squire would not have discovered by any means the same attraction in his aspect, nor drawn the same conclusions with regard to his character. He would then have perceived—as did all persons who thought upon the subject, until their judgment was overpowered by the fascinations of the young cavalier's demeanor—that there was an unpleasant look, a look of extreme audacious boldness, in the bright sparkling eye, aud moreover a wavering, changeful, vacillating glance, indicative of a fickleness if not feebleness of purpose, and remarkably at variance with the resolved and even obstinate expression of the mouth, and he would moreover have detected something hollow and almost mocking in the style of the smooth dulcet smile which was continually playing about the half-open lips, and revealing the pearly teeth within. None of these drawbacks to the appearance of Wyvil were at this time perceptible, nor were they indeed ever discovered in their true light by Selby; for he was now so strongly prepossessed by the features of the sleeper, wrapt as they were in soft and placid languor, that he retained the first favorable impression afterward, and, becoming very soon habituated to the man, thought no more of his appearance. While he looked on, however, the character of his guest's repose was altered; a shadow flitted over the fair tranquil lineaments—a dark, frowning shadow—and anon the sweat broke out upon his brow in large and beaded bubbles; he writhed his limbs to and fro with a convulsive motion, and grinded his set teeth with a fierce energy.

Short inarticulate sounds came struggling from his lips, and at last the listener heard him mutter: "Over! it is all over!" and again, after another violent struggle, flinging his right hand abroad violently, and clutching the bed-clothes with a stern savage gripe, "I have thee by the throat, dog! damned dog! Plead not—plead not to me for mercy! thou didst stab Musgrave in cold blood, when he had yielded him a prisoner! Ha, ha! plead not to me!" He fumbled with his left hand impotently in the bed, as if he were grappling for a weapon, and then, still maintaining the death gripe, as he thought, with his right, "How the dog struggles!" he continued. "Plague on 't, I 've lost my dagger. Here, Edgar—Edgar Beaven—run me thy rapier through this hound, or blow his brains out, while I hold him! Ha! ha!" he added furiously, his whole face kindled with a wild fiery glare; "ha! down with thee to hell! and there boast of his murder! Ha! ha! ha! ha-ha!" and he burst into a fit of convulsive savage laughter, which gradually died away, and left him again all relaxed and dreamless.

"Poor youth! alack, poor youth!" murmured the poor old man; "how fearfully the dread strife and the death-grapple darken his fresh unhardened spirit. God pardon him the sin of blood-shedding, since surely he did strike for the right cause! Lo! he frowns now again, and the cold sweat wells out at every pore."

"Charge! charge!" muttered the sleeper, interrupting the tenor of his meditations. "Charge once more. Kill! kill! kill! no quarter to the rebel dogs! the damned blood-drinking roundheads!"

"Ay! he is in the very agony of the hot heady fight. I will awake him;" and suiting, as he spoke, the action to the word, he laid his hand lightly on the arm of the sleeper. It was like the work of magic; for scarcely did the old man's finger touch the wrist of Wyvil before he started up, unsheathing his rapier with one hand, and snatching the poniard with the other, and stood erect upon the floor, with eye, hand, and foot, on the alert, in posture of defence. It was scarcely a second since he was struggling in the visions of his tortured sleep upon the bloody banks of the Team, and now he was in the full possession of his senses, cool, self-collected—armed in mind and body, prepared for any fortune.

A quiet smile crossed the fine face of the old squire, and fading away instantly, left a grave and even sad expression in its place, as he addressed the youthful cavalier.

"Nay, nay, it is no foe; nor have you any need of weapons—"

"Ha! my kind host," the other interrupted him, lowering the point of his sword as he spoke. "I crave your pardon; I saw not that it was you."

"You slept in truth heavily," replied Selby; "and your slumbers were so disturbed and restless, that I had the less hesitation in arousing you. Besides, I have much to say to you. In the first place, I have brought you food, and wine, and raiment, and all appliances to make your toilet; some books, moreover, and oil for your lamp. Here is a little charcoal likewise, and there should be a brazier somewhere. Ay, here it is in the corner; best make yourself a fire forthwith, and dry your dripping garments. But first I must require you to plight me your sacred oath of honor, never by any means to publish or divulge to any living creature the secret of your hiding-place."

"I were ungrateful else, and base indeed," replied Wyvil; and laying his hand on his heart, he continued: "Most solemnly I plight my sacred honor, never by word or deed, by sign or hint or writing, to reveal aught that you shall show to me in furtherance of my escape and safety; and should I ever, or by any chance, forget this pledge hereafter, so may God forget me even at my utmost need!"

"No more," said Selby, taking him by the hand; "no more; nor had I asked even this, but that it is enjoined on me to do so. Never must these things be revealed to any, save the head of the house and his next heir, but in the case of extreme peril, and then under the sanction of an oath. This, then, sufficeth. Now tell me, sir, what hopes you have of aid from without?"

"None, presently," answered the youth. "If I could but reach France, I might do well; for on the outbreak of the war, and since at many times, I have remitted thither much jewelry and gold. But how to reach the coast, or when there to get shipping, in truth I know not."

"And have you no friends anywhere, whom you might trust, nor any faithful agent! We may conceal you here, it is true, for a time; but every hour, nay, minute, will increase the hazard. Suspicion is awake already, and, I might say, peril is around us."

"No friends; no friends, at least, who could assist me; but there is one, a secret agent of the king's partisans, though deemed a spy in the pay of Cromwell, known as the pedlar Bertram; if I could make him know my case, if any man could do it, he would effect—"

"I know the man," interrupted Selby; "I know the man, but only as a travelling trader. I know him, and it may be can discover him ere many days; but are you sure he may be trusted?"

"No man in these times can be *sure* of any one!" Wyvil answered, after a moment's thought; "but I dare trust myself with him. He has been often tried and trusted, and so far has proved always faithful."

"I will proceed straightway to have him sought out. As far as may be we will secure his faith, not paying him a crown till you are safe on shipboard."

"That will not avail anything. Bartram, as he is called—for that is not his name, in sooth—takes no reward from cavaliers."

"That speaks well for his trust, at least. I'll see to it. Now, mark me; I do not doubt but that search will be made again to-morrow, or to-day; nor do I very much doubt but that, if one I know conducts the search, this chamber will be readily discovered. So many of the old houses have similar contrivances, which have by chance, or treachery, or acute wit of the searchers, been discovered, that they have got the trick of them; and this, though not altogether easy, is by no means to be considered as impregnable. It hath, however, further secrets. First, let me tell you there is no lack of fresh air here, although there be no windows; for everywhere throughout the thickness of the walls there have been framed long winding spiracles, else were it unsafe to burn charcoal. Now, Captain Wyvil, mark every word I say, for it may be your life depends on your clear memory. There is a strange contrivance here; a long metallic tube, framed like a trumpet, but with ten times the power—one whisper at the farther end fills all this chamber with a reverberating din, that would awake the soundest sleeper though he were drugged with opium. By this tube notice shall be given you ere any search commences. An hour, at the least, must elapse, ere any one except myself or Alice could reach this central hold; but notwithstanding, when you shall hear that sound, make no delay, for be assured there will be desperate peril. If, when they search this spot, they shall find any signs of recent occupation, be sure that you are lost; with you it rests to keep all things so ordered, that they shall be in place as though not touched for months. Pile all the furniture together; leave not a scrap of food, nor a drop of wine, to tell tales, in any drinking-glass—heap the books on the highest shelf; and, lo! here is a bag of dust and rubbish and old feathers; shake this out freely over all, tie the wine-flasks and lamps, and aught else that might create surmise, to the leaden weight and hook which lie by the trap-door I showed you, and sink them in the water; do this as speedily as may be, and then fly! And, now I think of it, keep no fire any more in the brazier, when you have dried your raiment; so, I doubt not, we may frustrate their expectations that would work us evil."

"But how, or whither must I fly? I see no means at all, nor any—"

"We will waste no time, Captain Wyvil," answered Selby, "but you will follow me, so please you;" and with these words he unlocked both doors, which had remained unopened the preceding night; and entering that nearest to the stairs, by which lay the descent to the well and trap, was followed closely by the young cavalier, whose attention had been firmly riveted on every syllable the old man uttered.

The greater part of an hour had elapsed before they returned; and when they did so, it was by the other passage, so that it was apparent that Marmaduke had now been made acquainted with all the different modes of egress from his friendly prison-house. They were both somewhat pale, and the lamps which they bore burned very blue and dim, and all their clothes were soiled in many places, and besmirched with much green mould; the old man was, moreover, so much exhausted, that he sat down for a while in the arm-chair, panting and seemingly quite overwrought by the fatigue, and the bad atmosphere he had imbibed in traversing the gloomy vaults and corridors of that dark labyrinth.

After a few moments' rest, however, he filled himself a beaker of the generous wine of Bordeaux, and pushing the flask across the board to Wyvil, motioned him to fill up, and emptied his glass at a single draught.

"Well now," he said, "remember, I beseech you, the clew in the right hand passage is the number three! to the right throughout—every third turning to the right!—those to the left, and all the others, are but false turnings and deceptions. In the left hand it is five. Now, if the alarm be by day, neither of these are very safe ; both opening as they do in the clear country. By night it matters not much which you take, but be careful that that there be no one watching ere you issue out. If, then, the alarm be by day, you were best try the other, and tarry there until you hear the signal. Now, then, give me your hand ; farewell. I may not now wait longer, lest I be missed. Alice or I will visit you this evening. And now, young man, consider—I would have you—and weigh well the vast trust I repose in *you*, a very stranger ; all for pure charity, and my own sense of duty ! My own and daughter's life ! my own and daughter's honor ! No more, sir, one word is enough ! No answer, I beseech you ; and, above all, no protestation ! Deeds, my good friend—deeds done hereafter will outstrip a whole ton of words at the present. God bless you, and farewell !" and saying this, he left him quite abruptly, and locking the door after him, hurried away with all speed to his own private study.

Well was it that he did make haste ; for he had not been there ten minutes, and had but just replaced the volumes which concealed the spring upon the bookshelves, adjusted his disordered dress, and seated himself, pen in hand, at his desk, when a quick footstep without followed immediately the slamming of a distant door ; and was succeeded by a tap on the panel, and the voice of a domestic announcing the arrival of a messenger bearing a letter with despatch from Major-General Henry Chaloner.

Rising instantly, with his pen still in his fingers wet with the ink into which he had the presence of mind to dip it for the purpose, Selby unlocked the door, and received the note, with an explanation that the bearer had been detained an hour or better, no servant having ventured to disturb him until the time should arrive which he himself had specified.

" It is well," answered he, when he had read the hasty scroll ; " then will I not delay him any longer. Bid him say to his master, Launcelot, that Master Selby greets him, and will rejoice to see him at his own good convenience !" The man bowed, and withdrew ; and the old man seated himself again quietly, and after a moment's thought—"Ha!" he said—"ha! now comes the trial!" and without any further meditation, or any sign of care, he took up the Eumenides of Æschylus, turned to the difficult and obscure chorus at the 876th line, and read, and methodized, and made notes as he went on, some in the margin of the volume itself, and some in a large brass-bound vellum-covered book, labeled, "Ephemeris Classica Variorum," as tranquilly as though he had nothing of more immediate or pressing urgency upon his mind than the emendation of a corrupt reading, or the restoration of the true text. It was not affectation—it was not even the result of an effort—he yielded to the force of ancient habit, and in five minutes after the man had left him was completely wrapped up in his subject, mindful of archæology alone, and utterly forgetful of all sublunary matters, and so remained, until he was again aroused to consideration of earthly things by the announcement of his cousin Chaloner. Of a truth was it said, that we are fearfully and wonderfully made!

CHAPTER IX.

For two hours at the least did Henry Chaloner remain closely engaged in deep and painful conversation with his ancient relative, who, understanding well his difficult and delicate position, appreciated fully his considerate kindness. Henry did not affect for a moment to conceal from him his opinion that the young cavalier was secreted somewhere on the premises of Woolverton, nor did he pretend to disapprove the motives which had led to such concealment however much he might regret the consequences which he considered likely to arise therefrom. He showed the proclamation to Mark Selby, and did not hesitate to confess his own dislike to the duty imposed upon him, and his sincere wish that the young fugitive might escape, until such times as the government should be induced to remit somewhat of what he termed their cruel and unchristian rigor.

"At the same time," he said, "I have but the choice of two alternatives—to resign my commission and the command of this district, or to perform with strict accuracy all the duties thereby laid upon me. To resign at present," he continued, "I do not think advisable, not as regards myself—for that, of course, I should not at all consider—but as regards the welfare of the country; for should I do so, some other would be at once appointed, who would, it is most likely, be harsher and more rigorous than I, and much harm might well come of it. Now, Cousin Selby, I am not, as you know, a man of many words or large professions, wherefore I shall go straight to the point. I believe the young man to be here, and, in fact, I am *forced* so to believe by these documents;" and he laid the papers he had received the night before on the desk as he spoke. "I hope sincerely I may be mistaken, or, if not mistaken, that I may be unable to discover where you have hidden him; for it is very sure that it will go very hardly with you if he shall be discovered here. I will do all in my power, should such be the case, as I am sure I need not promise you, to smooth the matter, and hope I may be able through Cromwell to provide your safety; but, I speak plainly, cousin, with all this evidence before me, I must order a search. I must send for a detachment of the soldiers to Low Barnsley, which is their nearest station, and I *must*, and pray believe me that I *will*, exert every faculty I may possess to capture the young man. I ask you no questions, nor wish to hear any answers, and I will not allow yourself or Mistress Alice to be at all interrogated. For the rest, I must do my duty; and you will not, I am sure, think hardly of me for so doing. I shall send off a messenger forthwith to Keating, with orders to bring hither two troops of the Ironsides to-morrow at day-break; till then I will remain with you myself, if you will give me quarters, and you will not, I fancy, find me a difficult or troublesome inquisitor!"

"Oh, you are quite right, cousin, you are quite right in one thing," answered Selby, laughing good-humoredly; "you are quite right in one thing, though very wrong indeed in another. You must search the premises, that is quite clear; I knew that from the very first—and, indeed, I rather desire it than otherwise—for I suppose when it is done and over, I shall be left in peace; and until it is done by some one in authority, I shall have no rest at all, but shall be worried day and night by these redcoated gentry; and you know, Henry, I 'm not very fond of worthies of your cloth. You must search the house, and the more strictly the better; for then you will be satisfied yourself, and will be able to satisfy others. So far you are quite right! but very wrong indeed, I do assure you, when you imagine that you shall find any one hidden here! For you will not, Henry—you will not, I can tell you, however carefully you may search soever, and however much you may suspect it! Of course, I shall rejoice to have you stay with me, and so will Alice. She hath gone forth this morning to the village, to carry some medicaments, I fancy, and some dainties to the poor old souls down there; but she 'll be home to dinner; and after you have searched to-morrow, if you will ride out with her, and see Gilbert Falconer's long-winged Norroway hawks fly at a heronshaw, you 'll please the girl, and the honest knave too—in good faith you will; but for me, I care not for such toys!"

"Well, well," said Chaloner, "I trust it may be as you say; for if I do not find anybody, it will, of course, be all over, whether there be anybody here or no! But, I beseech you, do not depend too much upon the secrecy of your devices. I have seen many of your old houses, and know the general plan of their concealments. From this very room, I dare say, if it were well examined, some avenue might be discovered; but as you say so, I dare say I shall find no one, and I am sure I hope so. Now, if you will permit me, I will write a brief order to Colonel Keating, to march hither a squadron or two of horse to-morrow at daybreak. One of my fellows can ride over with it now, and I will tell the others not to mount guard exactly, but to keep a peaceful watch on all that is going on to-night. Your people it will be needful to interrogate to-morrow."

"You will get nothing, Henry, out of them, I promise you. Meanwhile do just as you will, till one of the clock, when we dine in the hall below. If your own horses be tired, send one of mine, good Henry."

"My horses are quite fresh," answered Chaloner, as he removed toward the writing-table; "and now I will write to Colonel Keating without delay, and walk out, when I have despatched a fellow with it, to join Alice in the park. I met her at the Stag's Head as I came, and wished then to escort her homeward; but she was going farther, and bade me join her in the park, when I had finished talking with you, down by the heronry wood."

It did not occupy the young soldier many moments to finish the official note, and shaking his cousin affectionately by the hand, whom he both respected and loved, as being the nearest relative he had on earth—his mother having died within a year of his birth, and his father not having long survived her—he put on his hat, and sauntered slowly through the long suite of rooms; now pausing to admire some rare painting or antique statue, now gazing out of the windows, across the courtyard and the moat, over the sunny park, which he could see stretching away for a mile and a half in length till it was bounded by the heronry wood, and the deep narrow river—a rich and beautiful perspective. He was, indeed, now in a very different mood from that in which he paced the parlor floor of the Stag's Head; for the unconcerned manner of the squire, and his reiterated assertion that no person would be found concealed in the Hall, had produced, and very naturally too—for he well knew the strict probity and truth of the old man—a strong impression on his mind; and though he had observed that Master Selby did not positively deny the concealment, or assert that there was no one hidden, he was considerably tempted to believe that such was the case. Indeed, the very fact of his finding Alice so far abroad, and seemingly so unconscious, had at the moment somewhat shaken his opinions; and now, when he recurred in his thoughts to her calm smile and fearless, unembarrassed air, he could not believe her privy to any scheme of peril.

As he reached the oaken staircase, and passed slowly round the gallery on which it opened, he caught through the tall Gothic window another view of the grounds in the opposite direction; a view of much greater extent, including nearly three miles of open lawns, with belts of timber-trees, and deep withdrawing dells between them; these lying broad and fair in the mellow noontide lustre, those full of cool blue shadows, with here and there a rippling reach of the stream flashing among the thickets — all terminated far off to the westward by the park wall, and the gigantic range of elms which screened it from the road. It was put a passing glance that he threw over the lovely landscape; for he had marked it oftentimes before, and was familiar with its beauties; but even in that transient glance, his eye was arrested by two moving figures far off in the distance, which, distant as they were, he recognised for Alice and her old attendant.

The sight quickened his movements, and he ran down the broad easy steps, calling to his men as he descended; so that one of them met him from a side door as he reached the little hall at the stair-foot. He was not engaged half a minute in giving instructions, in his own clear and precise method, to the servant, but passed onward immediately through the paved court and formal garden to the gate-house, intending to join Alice within a few minutes at the farthest. But very variable, indeed, and uncertain are the intents and resolutions of mankind, and very liable to interruption even when they appear the least so — and thus it proved in this instance: for, in the first place, an old woman, the wife of the porter, who had known him from his childhood upward, came tottering out from the lodge, and detained him a short time by a series of silly and disjointed, but kindly meant interrogations, which it was not in the heart of Chaloner to treat with neglect or coldness; and then, when he had got rid of this annoyance, and issued into the road through the park, whom should he see trotting up the avenue but stout John Sherlock, on Wyvil's coal-black charger. In a moment he remembered how he had directed the good yeoman to wait and speak with him, and how, forgetting all about what he had wished to say, he had ridden off afterward, leaving him asleep under the oak-tree. Again, therefore, he was obliged to pause in common courtesy; but he contrived to learn from honest John all that he had to tell concerning the horse, the place he had found him, and his intention of consulting Master Selby as to the wisest method of disposing of him, without the loss of much more than a quarter of an hour; and then at length, having expressed his approbation of the worthy farmer's conduct, he set forth in good earnest to join his beautiful cousin.

'How tiresome," said he within himself, as he proceeded on his way—"how tiresome that I should lose so much time; she will be well nigh home ere this, and I shall get no opportunity of talking with her after all;" but at the same time he stepped out at the top of his speed, and had soon passed over two thirds at least of the distance between the house and the spot where, from the windows, he had seen Alice half an hour before. When he had come thus far, without discovering any signs of her he sought, or hearing any sound of her voice, although he stopped and listened once or twice, he began to grow weary lest he should have taken a wrong path and missed her; for it seemed to him that she ought to have been at least so far on her way homeward, if no farther.

The spot on which he stood as he thought thus was in the bottom of a gently-sloping dell, planted with tall old beeches, quite free from any underwood, and carpeted, wherever the shadow of the thick foliage had not overpowered its growth, by soft and mossy greenwood. At this point the path, which he had followed hitherto, separated into two branches—one leading straight on to the postern of which Alice had spoken, and the other winding away to the left hand toward the fishing-houses. Both of these paths, as he well knew, crossed the river on narrow rustic bridges at a few paces distance only, and wound through thickets and plantations so tortuously that it was not possible to see a person till you were quite close up with them. While deliberating which of the branches he had now better follow, a sound reached his ears which sent the blood rushing through all his veins like torrents of hot lava—a long, shrill, piercing shriek—another! and another! in the well-known tones of the sweet girl of whom he was in search. The cries proceeded evidently from the direction of the postern, and uttering a shout in answer, he dashed forward through the trees with speed scarcely inferior to that of a hunted stag. A few bounds carried him across the little hollow, and up the acclivity beyond it; and before him lay the stream wheeling on, dark and deep, but very narrow—not above twenty feet at the utmost—between steep banks, spanned by the single log which formed the foot-bridge. On the farther side was a stony ridge covered with stunted evergreens, and over that another small ravine feathered with underwood and tufts of furze and broom, into which the path divided abruptly. Hence, as it seemed to him, the voice proceeded; and with another shout, which to his great surprise was answered faintly from behind him, he ran across the rugged arch, climbed the steep rocky brow, and plunged into the dell half frantic with excitement.

Scarcely, however, had he made ten steps beyond the summit, before a sight met his eyes which would, if anything, have forced him from his self-control. In the very bottom of the glen, prostrate upon the ground, with a tall ragged ruffian furiously and unmercifully belaboring him about the head with what resembled greatly the truncheon of a broken pike, lay the old servant Jeremy; and a little farther off, just where the ground rose on the other side, in the violent gripe of two savage-looking men, who by their dresses were evidently disbanded desperate wanderers from the royal army, as pale as death, and trembling in every limb, stood Alice Selby.

One of the wretches, who held her tightly grasped by one delicate wrist, had thrust the muzzle of a huge horse-pistol, cocked, as the ready eye of Chaloner observed in an instant, within a hand's breath of her temples; and was, with loud and beastly imprecations, threatening her with instant death if she spoke or resisted; the other had already torn a jewelled pendant from one of her ears, and that so brutally, that a drop or two of blood had fallen on her shoulder; and, just as Chaloner came into sight, attracted by a glittering brooch which secured her kerchief, he thrust his sacrilegious hand into the sanctuary of her bosom, and by one violent effort dragged away both the brooch and kerchief, rending her robe itself, and leaving all her snowy bust exposed to their foul glances. So greedily were they occupied in their unholy calling, that the villains had not observed the repeated shouts of Chaloner, and consequently he came on them quite unawares; he was indeed upon the first almost before he was aware of it himself, and rushing at a tremendous pace down the steep slope, drawing his rapier as he came, he kicked the brute who was in the act of stooping over his groaning victim, head-over-heels into the broken gully among the stones and brushwood, and dashed on, without pausing to see what became of him, to succor the terrified girl, who, seeing aid so near, again sent forth one of those wild, ear-piercing screams, which she had been deterred from uttering, since the first moment of her peril, by menaces of instant death. Her shriek, and the noise of their comrade's fall, were the first intimations the other robbers had that they were interrupted! He with the pistol, diverting his aim instantly from Alice, levelled the weapon with cool deliberation at the young soldier's head, and pulled the trigger, when he was scarce six feet from its muzzle. Happily for him, however, and yet more so for her whom he alone preserved from robbery, and perhaps worse outrage, it had been greatly overloaded, and recoiled so heavily that it threw up the hand which fired it, for it had been correctly aimed; and, as it was, the ball pierced the crown of Henry's hat, actually grazing his hair in its passage. Before the ruffian had time to note the effect of his discharge, the point of Chaloner's sword was glittering between his shoulder blades, while the guard knocked against his breast-bone, so forcibly was the thrust driven home; and with a fearful execration he dropped to the ground, the blood gushing from his mouth, and from the wide wound in his bosom, like water forced out of a pump.

So rapidly did all this pass, that the wounded man was actually prostrate before his comrade had unsheathed his broad-sword; and when he did so, he was still so confused and startled, that parrying easily an ill-directed lunge, Henry was able to catch Alice round the waist, and rush back through the underwood, avoiding the place where the first ruffian was now struggling out of the ravine toward the river. He had hoped to be able to cross over, when he doubted not that he should have little trouble in defending the narrow bridge, by which one only could pass at a time, until help should arrive; and he was confident that help was not far distant, from the shout which had so promptly responded to his own; but he was disappointed, for he had barely mounted the ascent, and reached the river bank, when both the robbers were upon him sword in hand. To attempt to traverse the bridge, leaving his back exposed, would have been insanity. Setting down his precious charge, and bidding her run for her life, while he kept the pass, he again shouted at the pitch of his voice, and as he did so, was engaged instantly in hand-to-hand encounter with two swordsmen.

Few men of that day were at all equal to Henry Chaloner in the management and mastery of his weapon, and he derived from his cool and collected disposition an advantage hardly, if at all, inferior to his skill in the fence. Had one only of the ruffians now opposed to him been able to assault him at a time, the affair would have been decided in ten seconds; but even a master of defence has his hands full enough, when attacked hotly by two tolerable fencers, and such at least might be considered the bravoes, who now pushed at him with fierce, savage oaths, encouraged by the hope of booty, and burning to avenge their comrade, and half maddened by despair and want. Even at this disadvantage, the brave young officer would, it is probable, have proved still superior, had he fought with his wonted coolness; but now his eye wandered too often from the flickering points of the brandished rapiers in pursuit of his cousin; and when he saw her, after staggering a few steps toward the bridge, sink down upon the grass in a dead faint, he was so much diverted from what he was about, that he received a thrust in the left breast that would have finished his career upon the spot, but that it glanced off from a button of his coat, inflicting a sharp wound as it grazed him, and running quite through his left arm. The effusion of blood was very great, although the sword-blade by good fortune had missed the artery, and the robbers at once saw their advantage.

"Fight steady, Joe," cried one, "for by the—" and he swore an oath too blasphemously fearful to be written down—"he 'll bleed away by inches, and we can finish him at our leisure."

And accordingly they both assumed the defensive, menacing him it is true at times, both with edge and point, and at times pressing him back toward the river, but keeping off, and waiting the time when loss of blood should render him a weak and easy victim. Now he exerted every nerve, and practised every feint and foin to tempt them from their guard, and even succeeded in drawing blood from each by turns, though slightly. And now he perceived the advantage which they had gained, and which they seemed so resolute to keep; and as he felt his strength ebbing out drop by drop, and a chill sickening faintness gathering at his breast, and no help drawing nigh, and she he would have died to save lying there senseless and inanimate, a ready spoil to those worse than brutes as soon as he should fall, a sensation nearly akin to the cold dull agony of despair fell on his soul; yet still he fought undauntedly, and still they dare not close with him, though every moment he felt more and more that he could strive only a little, a very little longer. Then, to augment the wretchedness, if anything could indeed augment it, of his feelings, even at that moment of unutterable torture, as if in mockery of his situation, the clear, loud, merry sound of the dinner-bell came clanging through the sunny air from the neighboring Hall—telling of joy and merriment, and succor near at hand, yet really as far from him as though it had been fifty leagues aloof. He felt it, felt it bitterly and keenly; and though he almost staggered from exhaustion, knowing that all depended on himself, he lunged with fierce impetuous thrusts, raising once more as loud a shout as his quivering lips could utter.

By Heaven! the shout was answered—close at hand rang the cry—a loud stentorian whoop from the beech covert, and the thundering tramp of a horse at full gallop.

"In with you, Joe, in with you, man," muttered the ruffian, who had spoken before; "thrust at him, both at once;" and they did so, again and again; and at the third pass again wounded him. Still he kept up his guard, and feebly answered the approaching clamor.

And now, bareheaded, in fierce haste, lashing the fiery Arab to yet more fiery speed, Sherlock drove up the hill beyond the river. The men looked doubtfully at one another; yet still, although dispirited, pressed on!

"Damn it, don't give it up now!" the man, who had not spoken hitherto, now cried with terrible malignity. "Finish this fool at once! the other has no arms, and before he can dismount, and cross the bridge, we can get off, and bear her with us!"

"Revenge!" the other answered, with a yet fiercer rush on Chaloner, than any he had ventured yet to make; but the assurance of prompt aid had reinvigorated the ebbing strength of Henry; and he not only parried his thrust completely, but lunged in his turn, and gave his assailant a sharp wound in the shoulder. The ruffians had, moreover, counted without their host; for Sherlock never once thought of dismounting, nor drew the rein at all, nor checked the thundering gallop of Wyvil's black Arabian. No! not he! He flung his hat, with which he had been thrashing the charger's sides in lack of a better goad, high up into the air, and setting himself firm in the saddle, charged with a wild, shrill cry full at the perilous leap. Bravely the gallant brute drove at it, with his expanded nostrils red as fire, and his wide eyeballs glancing with a keen spark of vicious lightning—bravely he drove at it, with the speed, as it seemed, of a whirlwind, the solid greensward literally shaking beneath his furious gallop. Not a second did he pause, no, not the twinkling of an eye! on the sheer verge. The treacherous turf, at the extreme brink, yielded, broke in, under his forefeet, but it was all too late; a moment he was seen sweeping through the air, and then alighted with a stern dint on the rocky ridge, amid a cloud of dust and fire, ground from the flinty surface by his heels! "Hurrah!" screamed the excited yeoman. "Hurrah! surrender ye black thieves, or ye are but dead men!" and, as he spoke, reining his horse up by the side of Henry, he plucked one of the empty pistols from his holster, and levelled it. "Down with your arms," but the sight was all sufficient. Seeing that Sherlock had no sword, and judging from his dress that he was a mere countryman, they had persisted even after his bold leap; but when they saw the motion of his hand toward the holster, they took at once to their heels, one even throwing away his sword, and dashed into the scattered bushes, flying in mortal terror.

The farmer's blood was up, and though unarmed, he would have still pursued; but Henry called him to desist, and lend his aid to Mistress Alice. Water was soon procured from the stream, and after two or three deep sighs, and a long fluttering struggle, she returned to her senses, and with them to a full appreciation of her peril, and of her cousin's gallantry in her behalf. In a few moments a bandage was applied to the young soldier's wounded arm; and Sherlock undertaking to carry the poor old servant, who still remained insensible from the terrible beating he had undergone—home on the black horse by the postern; and to send people to look after the slain bravo—the young pair crossed the bridge and hurried homeward, both silent and affected beyond the power of speech; one by the intensity of his excited feelings acting on a debilitated system, the other by the conflicting influences of joy, and gratitude, and terror.

CHAPTER X.

LONG before they reached the hall, however, they were met by several domestics who had come forth to seek them; or who, seeing the abruptness with which Sherlock had wheeled his horse out of the carriage-road, and galloped across the park, had suspected some peril to their young mistress, and rushed out, although too late, to her assistance. Manifold were the exclamations of wonder, pity, and dismay, that fell from their lips, as they beheld the testimonies of her danger in the rent sleeve and bloody dress of her bold protector, and heard in a few words what had passed; but indignation prevailed in their minds, and anger over all other sentiments. Two or three who were armed—for a park-keeper with his musquetoon was one of the number, and a falconer with hawking-pole and wood-knife, started immediately in pursuit of the insolent ruffians who had dared to insult their beloved lady within the very precincts of her own grounds; others ran to the park-gate to meet the worthy farmer and lend their aid to the old major-domo Jeremy; and many others hurried back to the house to collect weapons of all sorts, and scour the country round, and all the neighboring woodlands, determined at all hazards to seize and punish the marauders.

Meanwhile old Master Selby, having been made aware by the bustle and running to and fro that something more than common was in progress, had come down from his library, and learning there, not without some exaggeration, what had taken place, rushed out, bareheaded as he was, in more than mortal terror. Words can not paint the deeper and more powerful emotions of the human mind; at best they can but feebly image to our senses the external signs of the strange workings constantly in process within that finest of volcanoes—the secret heart of man. A deep flush shot across the high and pallid forehead of the father, and the big drops gushed out like summer rain from those eyes long unused to weep at any earthly sorrow, as he clasped to his bosom, full of thoughts far too deep for speech, his innocent and lovely child; while she with like emotion clung to his close embrace, and wept in silence within the sheltering circle of the frail arms which trembled as they pressed her.

"Blessed be God!" he faltered forth at length. "My child! my own, own child!" and with the words kissing her pale fair brow, he surrendered her to the care of her maidens, and turned to grasp, with scarce inferior energy of love and gratitude, the hand of her defender. "And thou," he said, "Henry, thou, too! thou, that hast ever been my affectionate kinsman and true friend, be now, henceforth for ever, be my son!" and he drew him to his aged breast, and held him for a moment there, like himself speechless from the very force and depths of his feelings.

But scenes like this must, from their very nature, have speedy terminations; and, although in that instance all the spectators fully and freely sympathized with the emotions of the actors; though there was no broad glare of idiot curiosity, no sneer of apathetic dull brutality, to jar and jangle on the nerves attuned to so high a pitch, it was—as always is the case with spirits of a sensitive and elevated order—with a sense of something nearly akin to shame, that on recovering from their ecstacy, they withdrew from the gaze—too near, though it was friendly—of the small group which stood in mute attention around them.

It was some time before any of the three were again visible. Henry was borne off to a chamber which from his childhood upward had been set apart to his use, and designated by his name; and there his hurts were looked to with a solicitude that could not be surpassed, and with a degree of skill, which, although often found in those days possessed by persons not professional, would now be looked for only in a regular surgeon of high practice. Alice retired with her women to the seclusion of her own apartments, and it was not a little while before she could control her agitated feelings enough to reflect with any degree of calmness on the dangers she had that day undergone, much less to bring down her mind to other matters, equally at least, if not more, pressing.

The noontide meal passed that day, for the first time at Woolverton in many, many years, unhonored by the presence of any member of the family; and those who were collected round the ample board, the higher servants namely of the household, instead of displaying by an increase of levity, or any show of boisterous merriment, their freedom from restraint, imposed by the presence of superiors—as would assuredly be the case now-a-days—were graver and more silent than their wont, and even downcast, if not sad, in the expression of their homely features. The afternoon passed dully; the arrival of the servants, headed by Sherlock, bearing on their shoulders the still senseless body of the old butler, tended in no degree to produce any alteration in their feelings for the merrier. So severe were the injuries, and so critical the state of the faithful servitor, that—his case evidently requiring skill far beyond that of the housekeeper, famed though she was through all the parishes about for the rare virtue of her simples—an express was sent off to Long Darringford, a little country town some five miles distant, for Doctor Trowbridge, who on his coming gave an opinion, guarded indeed and far from positive, that he would painfully and tediously recover. Having administered a soothing potion to his fair patient, whose first entrance into this world of pains and sorrows he had witnessed, and having honored with his approbation the strings and bandages wherewith his rival—as he always called her—worthy mother Trueman, had accommodated Henry's arm, and which he refused to remove or alter, he backed his short-legged round-barrelled cob, and trotted soberly off between his well-stuffed saddlebags, to the benefit of some poor sufferer at ten or twelve miles' distance.

Soon after his departure Alice sent down a message to her father, praying that he would visit her forthwith; and on his coming she dismissed her women, and they remained for more than two hours alone in close and anxious conversation. At the end of this period, having apparently recovered quite from the trepidation and embarrassment which had been the natural consequences of the morning's terror, and showing only by an unusual paleness of her pure delicate complexion that anything uncommon had befallen her, she descended leaning on her father's arms to the library, where she lay down upon the cushioned ottoman which fitted the embrasure of the deep window, and soon fell into a calm and gentle slumber, the old man watching over her with almost painful tenderness. Meanwhile the sun set calmly in the west, and his last rays ceased to gild the sere tops of the lofty forest-trees which sheltered the old mansion, and the hoarse cawing of the homeward rooks was heard no longer; but in Mark Selby's library no lamp was lighted that night, nor did he pore over his favorites of bygone ages, immersed as he was for a little while in a more anxious study, as he hung over his fair child, sole idol of his widowed heart, still sleeping in so tranquil and immoveable a stupor, so ashy white withal, and so supernaturally calm in the expression of her face, that but for the faint fluttering pulsation of her sweet bosom, it might have well been taken for that long trance whose bed is the cold grave, whose waking is eternity. Suddenly, some few moments after the last echo of the last chime of the stable clock-house, as it struck eight o'clock, had died into utter silence, she sat up, wide awake in an instant, and perfectly collected, as the quiet tones of her tuneful voice proved beyond doubt.

"Father," she said, for it had now become quite dark; "are you there, father?"

"Surely," replied the old man, "I am beside your head, and have not moved thence, darling, since you first seemed to sleep. How fare you, dearest, now?"

"Quite well," she answered cheerfully; "oh, quite well, father. My long sleep has refreshed me, and I am now as strong and well as ever. I have not, I trust, slept overlong; the hour has not passed, has it? Oh, father dear, you should have roused me sooner."

"Nay, nay! be not alarmed," replied her father; "be not

alarmed without cause, Alice. The clock has but this moment stricken eight, and Launcelot hath not yet announced supper. I will now call for lights, and then go down to the hall. I shall forbid that any of the household enter in hither, lest they disturb your slumbers. Compose yourself again for a while, and then you may fulfil your purpose."

"Well, if it must be so; yet, father, I do feel no small repugnance to visit the young gentleman alone, so far removed, too, from all earthly witnesses."

"It *must* be so, my Alice—it must be so, however," answered he. "Already once to-day was I well nigh found absent, when so to be found would have been utter ruin. Moreover, dearest child, the force of circumstances is vast; and that which would in one case be judged, and rightly judged, unmaidenly and forward, becomes in another the most natural thing in the world. He were a villain, too, such as nor earth has ever held, nor heaven looked down upon, if he could ever dream of wronging you."

"Oh, no! no, father," replied Alice, a deep blush mantling all her lovely features; "I never even thought of that—I only feared that I might seem to him, as you have said, unmaidenly and over-bold."

"Ever strive *you* to act rightly, child," the old man answered, "as with your upright soul and pure heart you will, I fear not, always, and never heed what this man or that woman think or say of it. If they be pure-minded and noble, why then they will judge candidly and nobly; if other, then it matters not how they regard it."

"Well, father," she replied, "I will go visit him anon; tell me, I pray you, where you have hid the basket?"

"It is within the passage, Alice," he replied, "and a light burning. Tarry awhile, and listen on your return before you come in hither, lest Chaloner should quit his chamber and seek to find you here. Farewell, dear child, and linger not over-long." Once more, as he ceased speaking, he folded her to his breast, whispered a gentle blessing, and, without waiting any further answer than the kiss which melted on his lips, left her alone in the dim twilight chamber.

For some time afterward she did not move at all from the couch on which she had been leaning, but continued buried in deep and painful meditations, reluctant to set forth upon her self-elected duty, to which—now that the first excitement and novelty of the adventure had passed away—she felt herself unfitted by something of timidity and bashfulness, which she had never experienced at any time before so heavily oppressive. At last, manning herself, as it were, with a sudden courage, she started to her feet hastily, not, perhaps, daring to trust her own thoughts any longer, lest they should quite overpower her firmness; and opening the concealed door, not without some embarrassment, hurried into the vaulted passage, closing the entrance carefully behind her. It did not occupy her many minutes to thread, with her light step and ready knowledge of the way, the intricacies of that gloomy hiding-place, and she was at the very door of the secret chamber before she had fairly collected her thoughts for the half-dreaded, half-desired interview. One little moment she paused at the door, her cheek suffused with a deep crimson flush, and her heart throbbing with so convulsive violence, that she felt quite exhausted and at the point of fainting. She rallied however instantly, and tapping the panel very gently, "Open," she uttered, in her soft low-toned voice—"open to me, Captain Wyvil; it is I only, Alice Selby."

The instant she spoke, a hurried step sounded within, the bolts were withdrawn, the door was thrown open, and the young soldier led his bright hostess to a seat, pouring forth all the while such protestations of eternal gratitude, couched in words so feelingly yet simply eloquent, and those words uttered too in tones so rich, so full of manly melody, that no created ear of woman but must have given them heed.

"Oh, how—how may I ever prove," he said; "how speak in living language, the tittle of what I feel, dear lady? Words may not tell—the human heart itself may barely comprehend its own deep feelings; for do I not owe life, and more than life, to your calm, gentle courage—to your sweet sympathy with the good cause—to your brave, generous, self-oblivion?"

"Do not, I pray you, Captain Wyvil," she replied, her presence of mind having come back to her at once, when the first step was taken; "do not, I pray you, put me to the blush by praises that savor more, I fear, of courtly *politesse*, than of hard-featured, honest truth. I should imagine you but spoke in mockery, did not your courtesy forbid construction so ungentle; for surely I did nothing that any other lady would have doubted to do in like circumstances for any of the gallant soldiers who have so faithfully done battle for King Charles."

"Most natural it is that you should deem so, lady, seeing that the pure and noble-hearted ever, till sad experience has taught them the reverse, believe the souls of others to be all truth, and honor, and high generosity; and find in everything about them, so strong does their undoubting fancy work, a clear reflected portrait of their own inborn worth. But trust me, lady, when thou didst step forth boldly to succor the distressed and flying stranger, ten would have fled in selfish terror, leaving him to the mercy of his bitterest foeman. Where thou didst take no thought of self at all in sympathy for one thou didst not even know, save as a fellow-being, ten would have taken no thought else. Nay, more; of the few noble spirits who would have aided, had the time been given for calm deliberate action, half would have doubted till the occasion had gone by—half pitied merely, or marvelled till too late; or, had they even resolved to act at all, would have so acted, with hurry, fear, and trepidation, that all had been discovered and rendered useless. Oh! no, dear lady, no! it may not be denied that I owe life itself to your kind sympathy, to your energy, decision, and courage! Nor, now that I have seen my fair deliverer, would I for untold worlds be free from that sweet obligation; henceforth, for ever, I am yours—your bondsman, your sworn soldier, and your slave!"

"Well, be it as you will, sir," answered Alice, with a calm smile. "It can not but be most agreeable to me to know myself in any wise the savior of a human life; and if you so esteem it, I can not be so churlish as to refuse your thanks. Meanwhile, as it seems necessary that you should be a prisoner for some days yet in this dark den, I have brought you some trifles whereby to make your time pass the less gloomily—some wax-lights, books, and wine; and I must tell you now, ere I forget it, that fresh search will be made for you betimes to-morrow. My father has instructed you how to avoid your enemies, and you shall not want timely notice; but one thing has occurred to me, which I believe my father had forgotten. You must not bar the door within, and the key must be left without; forget not this, I do beseech you, else will all our endeavors be lost labor. And now," she added, taking up her basket, the contents of which she had deposited upon the table during the conversation; "now I will bid you farewell; I fear I may be missed, an if I tarry longer."

"Oh, go not yet—go not yet, lovely Mistress Alice," exclaimed the young man passionately, rising up from his chair, as if to detain her; "you do not know, you can not dream, how wearisome, how terrible a thing it is for one used from his boyhood up to the free liberal air, to the broad face of the sun-lighted heavens, to the green loveliness of earth, to be pent here, taking no note of time, without so much as a stray mouse to bear him company, day after day, night after night, in solitude and sadness. Oh, go not yet, I do beseech you! linger a little while, to make this gloomy cell radiant by your bright presence. You know not, oh! you know not, nor can fancy, how I have watched, and prayed, and panted for this interview—how I have dreamed all night, and pondered all day, on the sweet half-seen features of you, my guardian angel. How I have fancied for the words in which I would embody my deep gratitude, my deathless fealty; and now that the long-wished moment has arrived, my tongue clings faltering to my jaws, my spirit finds no voice to give its feelings utterance. Oh! go not, lady, I beseech you; who is there that should miss you, as you say, saving your excellent father?"

"My cousin, sir, who is now with us as our guest; my cousin, Henry Chaloner."

"What!" exclaimed Wyvil, hastily; "what! Chaloner, the rebel major-general, whose leading of the horse at Marston contributed so fatally to the success of Cromwell—who fought by Fairfax's side at Pasely, and was the first to cross the Team at Worcester? Can it be such a one who shares the hospitality of Woolverton?"

"Even so, Captain Wyvil," answered Alice, not altogether pleased by his manner. "Even so; Henry Chaloner, my father's honored cousin, and the defender of his daughter's honor!"

"Oh, now I have offended you," cried Marmaduke—"offended you, I fear, past hope of pleasing any more. And yet I spoke but thoughtlessly, and from a passing moment's irritation—the pardonable irritation of a defeated soldier against his more successful rival; but had I known, dear lady, had I at all suspected how high this rebel soldier stands in your fair esteem, then rather had I died than breathed a thought against him."

"Nay, now you misinterpret me," she answered quietly, but blushing deeply as she spoke; "since Henry Chaloner was naught to me before this day, except my father's friend and my good kinsman; and if I did esteem his nobleness of mind, his singleness of purpose, his perfect truth and dauntless courage, yet more did I regret the strange hallucination which had induced him to link qualities so fair and good unto a cause so black, so impious, and unholy! But Henry Chaloner has this day bound my soul with obligations which must endure for ever;" and simply, but with deep feeling, she told him the events of the forenoon, her peril from the ruffian cavaliers, and her bold rescue by the Puritan leader.

High colored Wyvil's cheek, keen flashed his eye, as she proceeded; and when she told how they had torn the earrings from her lacerated ears, and placed the muzzle of the pistol to her brow, he started to his feet, and half unsheathed his rapier, muttering through his close set teeth, "Villains, accursed villains!" but when she spoke of Henry's daring onset, of his encounter, single-handed, against the two marauders—of his wound, and her fainting fit, and of John Sherlock's late arrival on the field; he bit his lip till the color faded from it quite, and while his face grew pale as death—

"Happy man! happy!" he exclaimed, "and, indeed, thrice happy! Oh, that it had been mine so to do in your cause; and doing so to have died there and then. For then, although the jewel, the all-inestimable jewel of your love had been surrendered to this Chaloner, regret had still been mine, and the sweet meed of kind and sorrowful remembrance. But wo is me! Fortune was never yet the friend of Wyvil."

Again the deep red flush shot over the fair brow of Alice, and she frowned slightly, and her voice was very cold, and almost stern, as she replied—"Nay, Captain Wyvil, now you are overbold, to speak to me of love! Toys such as these, sir, suit not so brief acquaintance as that which rests between us; nor should I like them better, even if we were better known. When next you need a visitant, my father shall wait on you."

"No, no!" cried Marmaduke, impetuously springing forward, and throwing himself at her feet, so as to grasp the hem of her garment. "No, no! you must not quit me so. Oh, not in anger thus—not in contempt, sweet lady! Pardon me, pardon, I beseech you; for I am quick of speech, and have ever been but too prone to speak the promptings of a heart, too warm perhaps and ardent, but neither obstinate, believe me, nor wilful in offending; pardon me, and revoke that cruel sentence, and say that you will visit me again, and cheer the hapless prisoner's solitude with some brief gleam of bliss!"

"Rise, sir; rise, I beseech you. I do believe you think me indeed a country-girl, and a most silly one too, that you rave thus and mouth it. Rise," she continued, smiling, she scarce knew why, at the evident sincerity of his emotion, "and we will part good friends."

Then without further words he rose and led her to the door, and bowed respectfully upon her hand, and raising it a little, just touched it with his lips as she departed, uttering in a half-choked voice that passionate, sad sound, "Farewell!" Alice raised not her eyes to his face—for her life she could not have done so! but trembled violently in every limb of her fair body, as, in accordance with the fashion of the day, he kissed her unresisting hand. She knew not why it was she trembled; she knew not why it was she could not meet the glance of his clear, brilliant eye—she was unconscious of all cause for shame, for fear, for any strong emotion—yet was she moved, and mightily! But when, just as she closed the door, she cast a furtive glance between her half-closed lids toward the cavalier, she saw him standing in an attitude of deep dejection, with his arms hanging idly by his side, and his fine head with its long silky love-locks drooping despondently upon his breast. She marked, and marvelled at this singular display of feeling; and with a fluttering heart, full of a hundred wild and whirling fantasies, she hastened back, locking the door behind her, and reached the quiet library all agitated and quite breathless, and resumed her seat on the sofa, ere any one had discovered or even suspected her absence.

It was not, however, destined that she should pass even the few remaining hours of that eventful day without some further agitation; for she had not been many minutes in the library before her cousin entered, having his left arm in a silken sling, and looking somewhat pale from loss of blood, although he walked quite firmly, with his fine form erect and graceful as its wont. A servant came in with him, bearing a lighted lamp with several burners, which having placed upon the table, he at once withdrew; but while he was yet in the room, Alice had sprung up from the sofa, and darting forward, seized Henry by the unwounded right hand, exclaiming, as she did so—

"Oh, I am so rejoiced—so more than glad and happy to see you thus again, dear, gallant Henry! for I had feared that you were very badly hurt; and had anything befallen you, I never could have pardoned myself at all, for it was owing altogether to my silly weakness, in fainting the very moment when I ought to have been most collected. It was indeed most weak and childish, but in truth I was sadly frightened; and are you not so much hurt, Henry?"

"Oh, no!" he answered, gazing with an enthusiastic eye upon her beautiful pale face; "oh, no! not hurt at all. It is a mere scratch, which would not have disabled me in the least, had it not bled so copiously that it made me too something faint, which is far weaker in a soldier you know, Alice, and more shameful, than in a pretty lady; who is entitled, if she please, to faint at least three times a day in mere caprice and wantonness. But you are not, I know, one of these gew-gaw puppets of the court, who die away at a warmer ray than common of our mild English sun, and shiver at the least breath of the fresh breezy air; you are not one of these, but my own sweet and gentle cousin, whom I hope one day"—dropping his voice to a lower and more tender tone—"to call by a yet dearer title. *May* I hope, Alice?"

For a single moment, so suddenly did the surprise come on her, every drop of blood in her veins appeared to rush at once into her face; but in an instant it was gone, and she was pale as death, even to her lips, and so icy-cold and shivering, that her teeth almost chattered.

"Alas!" cried Chaloner, quite alarmed at the effect of his words; "alas! I have been all too rash and hasty. I should have recollected, dearest one, how your nerves have been shaken by this morning's terror. Forget it, Alice, forget it altogether, or think of it no more until a fitting season;" and as he spoke, he supported her to the sofa whence she had risen on his entrance, and knelt beside her, holding her hands in his, and striving to soothe her by every soft and delicate attention, entreating her to rest, and make no answer for the present to his ill-timed address. But after she had lain a moment or two on the soft cushions, she sat upright, and collecting herself with an effort, spoke very firmly—

"No, no!" she said, "I must speak now; I must answer fully, for, Henry, your words have pained me very deeply."

"You can not—no, you can not be offended," Chaloner interrupted her; but before he could finish his sentence, she in her turn broke in—

"Oh, not offended, but pained, grieved, saddened; yes!

made me sick at heart; sick at heart for you, Henry, and sorry, ay, almost doubtful of myself. But, Henry, Henry," she continued, increasing in vehemence as she proceeded—"as God is now my witness, and shall hereafter be my judge, I never dreamed of this; oh! never, never! and now that it has broken on me all at once—oh! it is very sad and terrible; for I will not attempt those frail and commonplace, and, as I think, insulting modes of consolation, which worldly girls may offer to court-lovers; and though I never dreamed you loved me other than as your cousin, your good little Alice, to whom you have at all times been so kind and gentle—now that I do know it, I also know what disappointed love must be to such a heart as yours—a heart which, if it love at all, must love devotedly, and with its all of energy and fire. I feel what it must be to tell you that you must not even hope; and feeling so, judge, Henry, judge how I must suffer, when I must by my words blight, for a time at least, the promised happiness of one who—besides that I love him most dearly as a true friend, a valued, proved, kind kinsman—has this day saved my life, and more, my honor, at fearful peril of his own! What must I suffer, Henry, knowing that I must give him evil for his good, and kill his hopes who has given life to me?"

"Oh, Alice—Alice," answered Chaloner, "think not of that one moment! Do not, do not, I pray you, fancy for one moment that your poor kinsman is so mean, so truly poor of spirit, as to build any claim on what the humblest varlet in your household would have done gladly without guerdon, and thought it, when done, but as his own good fortune. The little service I did you this forenoon had nothing in the world to do with what I said to you but now, save that it set me thinking, made me consider how wretched I should have been had I not been in time to save you, and by filling my whole heart full of warm thoughts, all unchained and run-riot, led me to speak in words what I have long since felt in silence. For the rest, I am in your hand; do with me as you think the best, the happiest for both."

"That I must do, although it rend our hearts within us for

the moment, and leave them sore, it may be, and tender to the touch of passion, for many a day hereafter. But I must not, dear Henry, I must not do myself, do thee so foul wrong, as to let any doubt of what I feel, or any hope remain beyond this moment. The truth is, Henry, I can not be your wife — it is impossible — I *can not!* Giving you all regard, all friendship, all esteem, I can not give you love. Honoring your high qualities of soul, your perfect truth, your noble upright candor, the whiteness of your spirit, your fearlessness, your honor, your renown — admiring your bright intellect, your deep unworldly wisdom — loving your gentleness, your kindness, your soft, pitiful, good heart — yet, Henry, yet I can not love you — love you as *you* should, *must* be loved by her who calls you husband — as *I must* love the man to whom I give, not my hand only, but my whole heart and mind and soul here and for ever. I am a wayward girl, dear cousin; the spoiled, wild orphan of my dear widowed father; and it may be from him — my tutor, and almost my nurse — that I have caught strange fantasies, become a muser from my childhood, and a day-shunner, a lover of wild haunts and wilder legends, a creature of romance and poesy and fancy. Gifted, I fear me, with a dower which tends not to the growth of real and substantial bliss, I can not love unless my fancy have been won, and my heart through that fancy. I grieve for you, dear cousin, I grieve for you with my whole strength, and likewise for myself, for, why I know not, there is a something here within that whispers me with solemn augury the pain which I now give another shall be mine own hereafter — the bitter, hard, cold anguish of unrequited love. I shall know nothing more of happiness until I see you happy."

"At least, dear Alice," Chaloner answered, "at least you shall see me calm. You have dealt by me nobly; and never, never will I forget your goodness. To say I am not grieved and sorrowful at your decision, were to say what is false; but, Heaven be praised, I have a hope, a Comforter on high — a hope that will not let me be cast down by any mortal anguish — a Comforter, whose consolations are most nigh when they are needed most, and never are breathed vainly on the heart. And now, before we part — for this has been an agitating day for both of us, and with the morrow perchance will come new troubles — let me say to you, that you shall never lack a friend, a counsellor, a guard, and a defender, while life is warm in this poor bosom. Never fear, Alice, never fear to call on me for aid, advice, or friendship. Fear not that by so doing you will awaken vain hopes, or call forth old presumptions; for, now I understand your sentiments, I would not for the wealth of Eldorado disturb their even tenor, or move you any more to so sad thoughts as these. Promise me this; will you not, Cousin Alice?"

"Indeed I will, indeed I will, dear Henry," she replied, her beautiful blue eyes swimming with tearful tenderness. "There is no one upon earth on whom I would call half so willingly, with half so true a trust. And now," she added, stretching out her fair hand to him, "good night, and blessings be about your head, and peace for ever."

He caught the proffered hand, and held it for a moment, wistfully gazing in her face; then, as if by a sudden and irresistible impulse, snatched her to his bosom, and strained her there the while he pressed a long cold kiss upon her snowy forehead. "Pardon," he said, as he released her; "pardon; it is the last—the last. Oh! Heaven!" and in a burst of feelings most unaccustomed to that self-restrained and philosophic spirit, he rushed from the apartment, and was seen no more that evening by any inmate of the Hall.

CHAPTER XI.

At a very early hour on the following morning, before the household had assembled to their first meal, the trumpets of a squadron were heard in the park; and very shortly afterward the clatter of hoofs, mixed with the sharper clash of their accoutrements, ringing and clashing with the speed at which they rode, came nearer yet and nearer on the soft morning air, and only ceased at length when four or five troops of the Ironsides halted before the gate of the courtyard. Scarcely, however, had they halted, before Chaloner came out alone to meet them, and having held brief conference with Colonel Keating, their commander, and seen above a hundred of the men dismounted and drawn up round the house, each within gunshot of the other, he led the officers through the parterre into the house itself, the other troopers remaining in the court till further orders. This time the visit of the soldiery was orderly and civilly conducted; for Keating, who had come out at their head in person, was himself a gentleman of old and honorable family, and had borne arms in Germany and the low countries with good repute, before the civil war broke out in England; and he had, in compliance with a hint from Chaloner, selected the more polished of his subalterns for this day's expedition. Just as they were admitted to the Hall, the breakfast-bell rang out, and all the household was assembled, the Ironsides receiving a request that they would partake of the hospitalities of Woolverton before proceeding to their duties. Alice had not as yet descended from her bower, though all the rest were seated, when Henry Chaloner with several officers in full costume, with their long broadswords clanking in their iron scabbards, and their spurs jingling on the oaken floor, joined in the domestic group; but in a few minutes she too entered, looking a little paler than her wont, and very simply dressed, a few stray ringlets of her rich sunny hair escaping from a plain lace cap which covered her whole head, and her form somewhat shrouded in a loose morning-robe of grave sad-colored satin—but still so lovely, that even the rude officers of the parliamentarian army were moved by the grace and quiet dignity of her appearance, and rose at once to greet her. But little conversation passed during the ensuing meal, and even that little was constrained and uneasy in its nature, and very vague and general in its topics; so that it was perhaps a relief to all parties when the company arose from the table, and Chaloner announced to Selby his intention of proceeding with the search forthwith.

"The quicker things of this nature are brought to a close the better, so we will waste no time in empty compliment, but go on straightway to the point. Now, Colonel Keating, order in, if you please, one troop dismounted with their carbines; the rest may form an outer cordon in the park, without the ring of sentinels. Now, Cousin Selby," he continued, "will it please you to designate a chamber where all the household may be held in ward until our search is ended. Yourself and Mistress Alice will give us, I doubt not, your company in the book-room above."

"As you will, cousin," answered Selby; "but, as I told you yesterday, you are giving yourselves much needless trouble; for surely you will find no man here, but we who are even now assembled. As for the rest, there can no better spot be chosen than this same dining-hall; you see it has but two doors, and you can place a sentinel at each, inside or out, as you think best. My daughter and myself will, as you have suggested, wait your convenience in my study."

"Be it so," Chaloner replied. "Now, Colonel Keating, if you will take my counsel, you will detail a small guard with a lancepesade in the courtyard without, and post a cornet or lieutenant at either of these doorways, letting none have egress or entrance. You will then take your men and search the whole house thoroughly; taking especial care to do no damage, and replacing whatever furniture or hangings you may be forced to move from their position; looking especially for sliding panels, false chimney-backs, moveable pictures, and the like, which *may* give access, and do often in such old tenements as this, to hidden galleries and chambers wrought in the thickness of the wall. Be diligent, I pray you, and leave no means untried to find what you suspect to be the case. Should you want any aid or counsel, I will await you in Master Selby's library; should you discover aught, pray summon me. Here are the keys of all the chambers, which my good friend has voluntarily given up to me. You will post a small party at every corridor and landing-place, that the concealed malignants, if there be any here—which I doubt much—may not dodge to and fro, and so escape you. I deem it best you should commence here in this parlor, and now we will be no check on your movements."

As he ceased speaking, he offered his hand to Alice, and led her, with the old man following them, to the small, cheerful chamber, wherein so many of the events which it has been our lot to trace occurred; and there the trio, seated around the fire, conversed on ordinary topics as calmly and contentedly as though no search, involving life and death, was going on within the walls—as though two of the three who sat there, seemingly so happy, had not their hearts pierced to the very core by strong and passionate emotions. Such is proverbially, however, the course of all things human! such the deceitful and false semblance of the world! where hardly aught is real, saving the sin and sorrow that lurk beneath the specious glitter—the foil and tinsel—of that thin gorgeous tissue which men think fit to term society! Two hours perhaps passed thus, or something more, when Keating with two subalterns came in—a dozen privates halting at the door—saying that, after a most strict and tedious search, no place had been discovered wherein a mouse even could find concealment.

"This chamber searched, then, all our work is ended," Chaloner answered; "but now my task commences. Now, my good cousin, may I request you to remove the panel which hides the secret passage. Let your men fetch some torches, if they have got none with them, and look well to their weapons, Colonel Keating, and to the priming of their carbines. So you will not disclose it? Well, it was only to spare time I asked you! Here, lancepesade, jump on those steps, and take out all the volumes which fill that third compartment, the third there from the window. I saw you open it once, Master Selby, many long years ago, when you thought no one marked you. There, that is it; now tarry;" and stepping up to the identical place where the nail-heads and screws which worked the springs within were all made clearly visible by the removal of the books, he began to tamper with them, and after some considerable time succeeded, so that the portion of the wall revolved, and the mouth of the low passage was disclosed to the greedy gaze of the fierce Ironsides.

"Now we will soon see what is hidden! Give me a torch, and light a dozen more. Leave three men at the entrance, Colonel Keating; you and the others follow!" and with these words Chaloner drew his rapier, and entered the dim vault, the soldiers rushing after him with brandished swords and blazing flambeaux, rejoicing, as it seemed, already in the contemplation of some valuable capture. Far stretched those long and devious corridors, through many a nook and labyrinthine angle, up steep long flights of stairs, down long and gradual descents, with many a false turn leading their steps astray, and ending in dead walls, or guiding them back to the spot whence they came, far from the light of day, full of garnered dust, cobwebs, and filth of ages—the atmosphere so dense with foul and noxious vapors that the lights waned, and some went out, and all burned blue and ghastly. Yet still with stanch indomitable perseverance the soldiers struggled onward. Guards had been posted here and there at all the points of intersection, so that, when at last they reached the chamber, having been upward of an hour in traversing a distance which Alice, knowing the real clew, would have accomplished easily within ten minutes, there were but four privates left with Henry and the officers.

"Ha! we have reached the citadel at length," said Chaloner; "and, lo! the key on the outside, suspended to the staple; I doubt we have but lost our time and labor."

He unlocked the door, as he spoke, and entered the little cell, which had the night before been Wyvil's hiding-place, but now it was all vacant and deserted—no food or raiment, no light, or other token of any human visitant, was to be found in its narrow precincts—the bed, the board, the stools, the shelves against the wall, and the few articles that were piled on them, were covered with the thick white dust, as it appeared, of ages ; feathers, and bits of flock, and clots of matted cobwebs, were scattered over all the floor and walls ; and in the brazier were a pile of cold white ashes, which, as the disappointed soldiers swore, had not been lit these ten years. The other doors stood open, and for form's sake alone, for all were now convinced that no one was concealed at all within the building; those passages were likewise searched, but this was speedily accomplished ; and when they found that the first staircase ended abruptly in the wall, which has been heretofore described, aud that the doors at the end of the others were locked and bolted in the inside, with all their bars and chains so matted over with the network of five hundred spiders, that they had evidently not been removed for many months at least, then they gave up the search as useless, and making their way back to the library, with far more ease than they had come, in the first instance, after a few apologies to Master Selby, and an assurance that his house should be no further troubled, the Ironsides departed. Then, after a little while, Chaloner, resisting all Mark's efforts to detain him, took his leave also, convinced, as fully as the rest, that his kinsman did indeed know nothing of the young cavalier, and that his fears on his behalf had all been overstrained and needless.

Within two hours, the same cell which had been so strictly searched, and found so sordid and neglected, was neatly swept and garnished—the board was spread with a clean damask cloth, two bright wax-lights were burning in tall candlesticks of silver, a cheerful fire of wood was crackling in the brazier, and by the board sat Wyvil, with his long hair all curled and arranged carefully, and his rich dress in accurate order, sipping a glass of rich and fragrant Bordeaux wine, and reading, so to deceive the time, a huge romance of Calprenade or Scudery; while on the table at his elbow stood several plates and trenchers, with the remains of a fat roasted capon, and the long flask from which he ever and anon replenished his Venetian beaker, so little had the search availed to find the real secrets of that old rambling manor.

CHAPTER XII.

For many days after the second search of the Ironsides, the family at Woolverton pursued, as it would seem, untroubled, the wonted round of their calm quiet daily avocations. No visiter disturbed the even tenor of their way, no stranger came within their gates. The good old man, whose age, and the well-known seclusion of his habits, should have exempted him, in the opinion even of his few Puritan neighbors, from any such suspicion as would have justified a search, returned, apparently scarce conscious of their violent interruption, to his old bookworm customs; and read, and pondered, and dreamed days away; and wrote huge volumes on abstruse and crabbed points of classical lore—volumes, which it would glad the heart of many a regius professor now to discover, but which were never destined to see the light of any broader sun than that which stole in through the shadowed casements of their perhaps too unambitious author's study. Never, except at meal-times, or when some message of slight moment summoned a servant to his library, was he seen even by his own household, saving that once or twice, when the clear radiance of some brighter morning than was common at that season, invited her forth to inhale the fresh breezy air of autumn, Alice persuaded him to don his sad-colored riding cloak and broad-leafed beaver, and lend her the support—mere nominal support, indeed, and worse than useless, had any need occurred to make it requisite—of his frail arm. Then for an hour or two at a time, he might have been seen loitering by the side of his fair daughter beneath the shade of his old elm-trees, or sitting on a bench of stone under the southern wall, to solace himself with the faint beams of the September sun; while she, not far aloof, tended in her parterres some bright late-flowering survivor of the summer, and stripped away its withered leaves, or fitted it by her neat-handed preparations to meet the coming winter.

At times, too, though less often than before her perilous adventure in the park, she went her rounds among the village poor, dispensing comforts, and working that sweet gratitude which ever greets calm and unostentatious charity, through every cottage, how poor and sad soever it might be, of which she crossed the threshold; but now, instead of the old superannuated servant who had been used to follow her steps, as he had done her mother's many a year before on all her merciful errands, the treasures of her laboratory were carried by an athletic, broad-shouldered young fellow, whose broadsword girded on his thigh, with the small buckler swinging from his left shoulder, would have proved a far more efficient guard against marauders than the oak staff and feeble hand of poor old Jeremy. Two or three times, indeed, she took wing, as it were, for a longer flight; and then the country-people looked on with an admiring eye, a smile on every lip, and a blessing on every tongue, as she swept through the soft green lanes on her dapple-gray palfrey, with two grooms galloping behind her, and a whole host of dogs—Talbot the mighty bloodhound, and Cynthia the soft silky setter, and Romp and Rupert, thorough-bred Blenheims both, and half a dozen others, sporting about her pony's feet, as she rode forth to visit, at rare intervals, the ladies of some neighboring family—the Foleys, or the Fairfaxes, which last, although strict Presbyterians, had ever been close friends, while she was yet alive, of her lost mother. Still these were but exceptions, for it was very seldom, comparatively speaking, that Alice left at all the precincts of the park; and even within these, it began to be noticed by the old servants—licensed gossips of the household—that she was less often visible than of yore, and that a far greater portion of her time was passed in the seclusion of her father's study — strange choice for a young, lively girl! — for, heretofore, she had been very lively, and even mirthful; but now it could not fail to be observed that she was greatly changed — that her young lip was seldom visited by smiles — that a subdued and conscious expression pervaded her bright eyes and sunny lineaments—an expression, not of grief at all, nor of thought altogether, but of deep, pensive feeling. It might be of hope tremulous and deferred; it might be of that half-real, half-ideal melancholy, which is not all unusual to spirits of an imaginative and poetic temperament; or it might be perhaps the dawning of deeper thoughts, and warmer passions, that cast, like coming events, their dim prescient shadow over the tablets of her virgin mind, reflected thence on eye, and brow, and lip, and every speaking feature.

Much of her time was, indeed, passed now within the library, so far at least as the domestics had the means of knowing; but she and her old father alone knew where and how it was consumed. For his years, and disinclination to taking any active exercise, had speedily induced Mark Selby to delegate to his sweet daughter the task of daily visiting their concealed guest, nor did he in truth again seek the crypt after the Ironsides had searched it. From that time forth, then, it became the task of Alice to see him each succeeding day, ministering to his wants, soothing his sorrows, cherishing his high hopes of brighter fortunes in the future, and forming, as it were, the sole connecting link between the bright external world and the dull prison-house of the proscribed and hapless cavalier. For several days at first it needed a strong effort ere she could task herself to the performance of a duty, which, if she did not feel it altogether irksome, to say the least, was both embarrassing and painful; but gradually, as the restraint of a recent and irregular acquaintance faded away and was forgotten—and this occurred the sooner, that on no subsequent occasion did Marmaduke discover any of that affected and half-flippant gallantry which had almost offended her in their first interview—and as she learned to look upon it as a thing of course, she began slowly, and as it were half reluctantly, to take a lively interest in her imprisoned guest, looking forward when she must seek his cell with a sort of excitement, and regarding the young man himself—as women ever regard anything, whether it be the tame bird, or the pet spaniel, or beloved infant, to the safety of which their care is essential—with an uncertain, half-affectionate solicitude; which, while she could not altogether affect even in the depths of her own secret heart to misunderstand or deny it, she could neither discard from her bosom, nor confess to her inquiring conscience.

It became, moreover, so very soon unquestionably evident that Wyvil looked upon those brief hours, stolen as it were from solitude, as constituting his whole day, all the rest being one dull, dreary blank; and so respectful and considerate was the tone of his admiration, so delicately gentle his attention, so proudly humble the earnestness with which he supplicated her to bestow upon him, in mere charity, as many of her leisure moments as she could spare from more pleasurable occupations, that it was not in woman's nature but to feel gratified and pleased by evidences of his esteem and gratitude, so natural and unforced in their development. There could not have been in fact devised, had it been the aim of any social Macchiavelli to frame wily schemes for that purpose, any more dangerous artifice for ensnaring the affections of a young, ardent, and romantic girl, than this entire abandonment of her whole time, her thoughts, her fancy, to the discretion, as it were, of a brave, dashing, captivating gallant; and that, too, under circumstances beyond all others calculated to work on the imagination, to rouse the dormant sensibilities, and, through the blended influences of pity and protection, to reach the heart of woman. It would, perhaps, at first sight seem a paradoxical remark, and one susceptible of easy refutation, to say that all men, and yet more, all women, are readier to attach themselves to those whom they have aided, than to persons who have claims upon their love or gratitude from benefits conferred, or onerous obligations; but we are certain that the more fully this shall be considered, the more it will be found that it is true and natural. Why this should be, it is not for us to investigate at present; but throughout the whole range of human nature, the same strange contradiction, as it seems, will be found prevalent. The children of her agony and sorrow are dearer, dearer a thousand-fold, to the young nursing wife, than the mother who brought her forth in suffering, and watched her infancy with tearful eagerness of hope, and cherished her fair youth with tender and solicitous affection. In this, perchance, may lie the germ of all the matter; from this instinctive natural devotion of woman to those who are dependent, and whom they love, as it would seem, the more from the very helplessness of that dependence, perchance may spring that tendency in all our race to love, we will not say our benefactors less, but those whom they have benefited more. Be this, however, as it may, the fact will be found to be as we have stated it; and for one girl who gives her whole heart up to one whose claims to her regard are based on gratitude for services performed, nine yield their love to men whom they have heard maligned, and so defended—whom they have succored in distress, or what is the same thing, whom they imagine they have succored.

And so at last did it fall out with Alice Selby. Predisposed, from the share she had already taken in his fortunes, from the very perils she had incurred, and from the uncertainty of his final destinies, to feel an interest in the young cavalier whom she had saved from death; when she found him afterward intrusted wholly to her care, depending on her discretion for his life, on her attentive ministering for his subsistence day by day, on her society for his sole intercouse with the fair world, that interest was naturally increased tenfold! And then his eloquence, his bravery, his gratitude expressed in words of living fire—his noble person and high intellectual features—all the advantages which nature gave him, and sedulous accomplishment had carried forward to their utmost limit—all these things, cast as it were before her feet, witnessed by her alone, called forth as it appeared for her sole use, profusely lavished for her pleasure, had, as they needs must have, their due and full effect. It must not be supposed, however, that Alice was won easily, or that she was indeed won at all; for not a word of love had ever passed between the pair, nor is it in the least probable that so much as a thought of it had as yet crossed her innocent mind; since it may be deemed certain that if anything of the kind had once suggested itself, her jealous bashfulness would have at once taken the alarm, and by rendering her aware of danger, would simultaneously have rendered that danger quite innocuous. It is true that she thought Wyvil, as indeed he was, the most accomplished and high-toned gentleman she had ever yet encountered: she admitted to herself that he was the most agreeable; that his conversation, enriched as it was with anecdote, sparkling with brilliant humor, pervaded by a rich vein of feeling, strong and poetical, and tinged not slightly with romance, was the most captivating to the senses of any she had ever listened. Then, too, his feelings were conveyed to her ear through the medium of perhaps the most perfect voice that ever breathed its fascination into a woman's soul; it was rich, deep, well-timed, yet soft as summer music, and it had, too, that peculiar spell of music which caused its every tone to haunt the hearer's brain, like a remembered tune heard suddenly after long years of absence — and there is certainly no fascination so vast as that embodied in a sweet, powerful, cultivated voice. She saw that he was handsome likewise; but that, as is ever the case with women of that class and station in the world whose love is in the least worth having, had scarce availed him anything with Alice, unless he had been gifted eminently, as in good truth he was, with all the noble treasures of intellectual manhood. And from all these things it resulted, by a most natural consequence, that — although she had never yet thought of the man at all, except as feeling that in some degree his presence and society, which in the beginning she had so much dreaded, had even now become a pleasure, and pitying his endangered fortunes — the beautiful young woman was half in love already, and quite prepared to wake at once into the consciousness of passion, when any casual word or trifling accident should break her day-dream of security.

So stood affairs at Woolverton, when a full fortnight after the visit of the Ironsides, on a still gleamy afternoon, when all the world was dressed out in its brightest guise of beauty, and everything on earth, in heaven, was peaceful and at rest, sweet Marian Rainsford was seen traversing the park, her slight and delicate figure shrouded in a loose cloak of dark blue woollen, and her soft brown hair covered by a deep gipsy hat of home-made straw; and asking at the gate for Mistress Alice, was instantly admitted to her presence, and that without creating any wonder or surmise, for her blind aged stepmother and the poor idiot were special favorites of the young lady; and rarely did she pass a second day without either seeing them or hearing of their welfare.

"Well, Marian," exclaimed Alice, "well; how fares your mother, and how poor helpless Martin? I should have been down one day this week to visit you, but that I have been so engaged at home, that I have really lacked leisure."

"They are as well, my dear young lady, as they can ever be this side the grave," replied the fair young widow; "but it is not on their account that I have come to seek you. I know, too, that you have been close engaged at home, and I believe I know *how* likewise; or, if I do not know, I at least have a shrewd guess at it. Nay, lady, answer me not, I pray you; but listen to my errand, for I have much to tell you, and you must act as you deem best when you have heard all I have got to say. The pedlar, Bartram, of whom you have bought, I think, wares at sundry times, is at the Stag's Head since last night, and on his part I come to you."

"To me, from Master Bartram! but wherefore, wherefore, my good Marian?" asked Alice, blushing deeply as she spoke, and endeavoring to avoid, she scarce knew why, the quiet, melancholy eye of her young visiter.

"Oh! you may trust me, dearest lady; surely you can not doubt that you may trust me! for have not I too suffered in the same cause; and does not that one bond of suffering link me more closely to my fellows in that sorrow, than any ties that earth has now to hold me? I would give everything but life, myself, to buy his safety for this young gallant gentleman—and life itself how joyfully! were there not those yet living to whom that life is needful. But think not that I wish to pry into your secret, if you have one; I only speak to let you see my mind, and understand my motives. And now, this is mine errand. Bartram is at the Stag's Head now, or will be there anon, and bade me say to you, he has obeyed your father's bidding, and all is well-nigh ready. But he must see you, lady, either at our poor house, or in the little park beyond the river, after it is quite dark this very evening—he dare not come up to the Hall upon this business."

"Oh, now I understand you," answered Alice; "I understand you now quite well. But tell me, Marian, has Bartram explained nothing to you of all this?"

"Not a word, Mistress Alice, though he said he did not doubt I should understand; and that very likely you would trust me with the whole."

"But I will not," said Alice—"I will *not*, Marian;" then seeing instantly that an expression, not of vexation or offended pride, but of regret and disappointment, was written legibly on the young widow's speaking features, she added with a smile, "not that I have the least doubt of your faith and truth, or the least fear of your prudence, but that such confidences are very dangerous to those who are intrusted; and I would not involve, without the plea of strong necessity, another in the risk which I run myself willingly. If need be, however, Marian, be quite sure I *will* trust you. But now, how to arrange this meeting will be, I fear me, not so easy. Who knows of Bartram's presence hereabout?"

"No one at all," Marian replied, "except myself so far, for he tapped at my casement long past midnight, and bade me let him in quite silently. And I did so at once, for I guessed partly what he was about. And after he had charged me with this message, he sat beside the kitchen fire till it was nearly daylight, and then letting himself out of the back door, locked it after him, and flung the key into my window. He has gone now, I well believe, to Farmer Sherlock's; but he will be back before nightfall, and I have left the lattice open in the two-story parlor to the rear, that he may climb the park wall, by the elm-trees, and thence mount into the house unseen. Then I will carry him your answer, and he will meet you where you will.

"In the park, then," said Alice — "in the park, under the large oak-tree, beyond the third foot-bridge; there I will wait for him from seven of the clock."

"I know not," answered Marian; "I know not. I do not think the park so over-safe. They say stone walls have ears, and on my word I think green leaves have ears and eyes, too, now-a-days; for as I came across the little park, just by the very tree you mention, there is, if you forget not, a small steep hollow place, an old sandpit or quarry, quite overgrown with weeds and bushes; just as I passed the brink of it, I heard a kind of scraping sound, as if some person were dragging himself on his breast along the ground, and then a rustle as if of branches parted by a strong careful hand; so I looked round quite naturally, not as if I had heard anything, and made believe to call a little dog, but I saw quite distinctly two full dark eyes gleaming out from among the tangled thorns and briers. I took no notice then, however, for I perceived at once that I could not discover any more of the features, but passed on a few paces farther, and then turned round again and chirruped for the dog, though I had no dog with me; that time I got rather a fairer view, and saw the whole of the man's face — for a man it was — although he did not think I saw him! A grim and truculent countenance as I ever beheld, with a close crop of foxy hair, and the most evil aspect in the eye you can imagine. I am sure, too, that I have seen the face before, though where or when I can not bring to mind. It seems to me, though, that it was not long since; and I can not but think it was connected with some painful scene or other. I have been tasking myself ever since to try and recollect, but I can not do so were it to save my life. Of this, however, I am assured, that he lay there in wait for somebody or other. I think the better way would be, dear Mistress Alice, that I should leave you now, and come back somewhat suddenly when it is growing dark; then you may take a servant or two armed with you, and they can wait in the kitchen while I lead you up stairs, as if to see the children or Martin, who, to say truth, is somewhat ailing."

"I see," said Alice, after a moment's thought — "I see, and think as you do. This is unpleasant news, however, concerning the spy in the park, if spy he be; but might he not have been a poacher, lying in wait for the deer, think you, Marian?"

"I think not, lady," she replied. "There was, I know not what, that made me think of homicide or treason in his eye. He had not the dare-devil look of a deer-stealer. It was a hypocritical, bad, downcast visage, as ever man wore on his shoulders."

"Well, 'tis too late to look to this to-day, to-morrow he shall be seen after. In the meantime do as you have suggested, Marian; come for me about six o'clock, and Charles and Launcelot shall go with us. You will return by the road, will you not?"

"That would be unwise, lady; and if he be a spy, might lead him to suspect something, and so to change his ground. Besides, it is quite clear that I have nothing to apprehend; he had me in his power before, had he thought fit to harm me. No, I will go back as I came; and see, I brought my empty basket for an excuse, and I will get it filled with simples by Dame Trueman, and go my way, my errand being done."

"But stay, but stay a moment," Alice cried, "and tell me what ails Martin?"

"Oh, in good sooth, not much; but he is altered greatly since that bad officer entreated him so rudely, and since the soldiers killed his mastiff; and he sleeps not so much in the daytime, nor is so quiet, but has become a rambler of late, which he never was before, wandering off into the woodlands for whole days, starting so soon as the sun rises, and sometimes not returning until the moon is up; and, though he brings back poppies and late field-flowers, and sometimes blackberries and hips and haws, I think it is not after these he roams abroad, for I fancy that the expression of his eye is changed too, and that not for the better. He wears a cunning and suspicious glance at times, and seems for ever as he were seeking to track some one to a hiding-place; but yet it may be nothing but my fancy. We tried at first, when he took up this habit, to confine him; but then he had such awful fits and paroxysms, that we were forced to let him go his own way, trusting his welfare unto Him 'who tempereth the wind to the shorn lamb.' I hope, however, that I am in the wrong about his change of temper; I hope it is my fancy."

"Mere fancy, Marian, be sure of it," answered Alice, rising; "and now farewell, and recollect to call for me;" and as she spoke she led her out to the stair-head, where the servants might hear what she said, and shaking her warmly by the hand—"well, good-by," she continued; "pray get those things you want from Trueman as you go, and don't forget to come for me should Martin have another seizure. I will go with you at a moment's notice;" and then they parted, Alice to seek her father's study and there request his counsel, and Marian to hurry home, with fearless port but trembling heart, along the path which she believed waylaid by lurking ruffians.

CHAPTER XIII.

It was not altogether without some trepidation, if not positive alarm, that Marian Rainsford hurried homeward; for, in spite of her strong natural sense, and her conviction that no evil was intended toward herself by the man she had seen in the park, it was still a position quite sufficiently alarming to be at the mercy of an unknown individual, whose motives, to judge from his demeanor, could scarcely be compatible with uprightness or honor. That portion of the park, too, was very solitary; and indeed was but rarely visited, except by the forester on his appointed rounds, as had been proved by the boldness of the late attack on Alice Selby—a boldness well-nigh justified by that gilder of all human actions—ultimate success. The youthful widow was, however, of a temperament which, naturally calm and self-restrained, had been yet further schooled by hard and sad experience; she had thought on many subjects, and rarely indeed acted now on impulse; the same cool foresight, therefore, which had made her determined to return homeward by the same path which she had taken in going out, the better to deceive the lurking spy—who, if he were indeed a spy, must be presumed acquainted with her person and her dwelling-place—taught her, that to avoid the danger she must avoid showing fear of it; so with a quiet, easy air, and with a step slower, if anything, than common—though, it must be admitted, that her heart thrilled painfully, and that her ear marked every trivial sound—she neared the brink of the old sandpit. Nothing occurred, however, to disturb her self-possession; nor did she see or hear aught which could be held to betoken the presence of a living being, if it were not a thin blue wreath of vapor, which curled up lazily out of the tangled brushwood that fringed the verge and all the steep sides of the little quarry, and which, when she had seen it from a distance, her eye, unpractised to such accidents—as a painter might have termed the effect—had confounded with the evening mists already floating up all gray and ghastly around the damp and marshy woodland. As she passed by, however, she instantly detected its true character, and yet she misinterpreted its meaning; for as she could not catch—although she listened with her every sense on the alert—the slightest sound of conversation, she came to the conclusion that those who had lighted the fire for their own purposes had ere now left the spot, the rather that a robin perched in full sight upon a leafless bough was warbling his simple tune within ten paces of the place whence the blue smoke was rising into the evening air, and that two large and lazy hares were pasturing quite fearlessly beside the pathway. This error, for error it was, had well-nigh led her into very serious peril; for she was on the point of going forward to examine the ground, when suddenly, she scarce knew why, a sense of terror fell upon her, and she moved onward at her wonted pace till she had passed the nearest clump of trees, and then she fairly took to her heels, and never ceased from running until she reached home, breathless, but uninjured. Lucky it was, indeed, for her that she did not leave the beaten track—lucky that she did not even pause, for the song of the bird, and the lazy tameness of the hares, indicated not that there were no human beings near at hand, for such was not the case, but only that they had made no movement recently—it being characteristic of such animals to entertain no fears, even of the great tyrant man, so long as he sits or stands motionless and silent. Lucky it was, indeed—if that may be called lucky which was the result of forethought more than of any accident or chance—since at that very moment, sheltered from view by the precipitous banks of sandy gravel, and the thick bushes overhanging them, three strong and ruffian-looking men were seated round the fire which sent up the thin smoke that had caught Marian's notice.

It was a singular and exceedingly well-chosen spot for an ambuscade or post of espial, for you might pass within ten feet of its brink without imagining that there was anything more than a small shallow basin full of brushwood; while, in reality, it was a deep and abrupt pit, with sheer-cut sides of nearly twenty feet, whence at some distant period the sandstone had been quarried for purposes of rural architecture. It was indeed quite small, not above fifteen yards in length by half that width, and so luxuriantly had the broom and evergreen furze shot forth from the brink of its banks, that they almost entirely overcanopied it. The ground in this quarter of the park was broken into abrupt rounded hillocks, and this pit had been sunk in one of these, close to the crest of the knoll; so that when it had attained its utmost depth, an irregular and narrow cart-track had been cut through the slope into the nearest hollow; this track, however, having been long disused and half choked by the earth and stones which had rolled from above, and overrun completely with every species of tangled underwood, was quite forgotten, and would doubtless have been quite obliterated too, but that a little thread of running water, the offspring of a tiny well-head which had been opened as the stony strata were cut through, found its way down the narrow gorge to join the neighboring rivulet. So insignificant, indeed, was the whole surface occupied, and so completely was it sheltered, that there were not perhaps five people in the country who knew of its existence, although it lay, as has been stated, within ten paces of a regular footpath. Some two or three of the old servants, had they been questioned, would probably have recollected that they had seen or heard of it, and the game-keeper knew the gully well, for it was a favorite haunt of woodcock when all the marshy woods were frozen hard, though it is scarcely probable that he had ever followed the streamlet upward to its source. No fitter den could, therefore, have been chosen by any person, whose object it might be to join seclusion with the ability of keeping watch over the dwellers of the Hall; since its steep banks concealed it from all observation, and sheltered it from every wind of heaven; while its pure spring afforded an unfailing antidote to thirst, and heavy must have been the storm which should beat down upon its inmates between the tangled branches of the thicket overhead.

In this sequestered nook, around a fire which evidently was but just kindled, of dried leaves and such broken branches as would give forth but little smoke, three men were seated, silently superintending the preparation of their evening meal, for which there lay ample provision on the dry mossy greensward, in the shape of a hare already stripped of his furry coat and trussed for cooking, and a brace of superb cock-pheasants, when they were interrupted by the crackling sound of a dry branch, several of which they had disposed for that very purpose across the path, so that it would have been no easy matter for any one to have avoided treading on them, even had he been desirous of so doing. As no such thought had entered Marian's mind, she trod on one or two quite unsuspiciously, and the sharp crackle with which they yielded to her light springy tread, reached ears, as we have seen, keenly awake to every passing token. One of the party rose immediately, making a sign of caution to the others, and scaling the bank easily by the aid of steps cut into its hard strata, and stakes set firmly in the looser portions, brought his eye just above the surface; and speedily discovering who was the passer-by, and seeing that she walked straight on quite fearlessly, descended again to his comrades, and resumed his seat, saying, in answer to their inquiring glances—

"Nay; it was but the young wench of the inn, who passed an hour ago, or better, when I was on the watch."

"It was but right," answered one of the others, with an appalling oath; "to strip off her duds if she has nothing more about her, and give her a walk home *in cuerpo,* as the Spaniard has it, this fine fresh afternoon."

"No, no; that would not do at all," returned the first speaker, a sullen, dogged, puritanical-looking youth, dressed in a strong new doublet of buff leather, such as was worn by the Ironsides when off duty, and a slouched gray felt hat; "I do profess, that you would ruin the best scheme that ever wit hatched by your rash rakehelly marauding. I almost do regret I have consorted with you; I do, as my soul hopes to see salvation."

"As your soul hopes to see hell-fire!" replied the other man, a tall, rawboned and tawdrily-dressed soldier, with huge mustaches and a peaked beard upon his chin; the very caricature in fact, of a debauched and roistering cavalier, as was the other of a fanatical independent—"to see hell-fire, you should say rather—for as the courses you run here lead not that way, the road is very different, I trow, from what the preachers tell us. But if you are so sorry you have joined with us, what keeps you here with us? Too much of honor is it for a d—d scurry roundhead to be admitted to go shares with gentlemen who have fought for the king. Why do you consort with us, Master Despard? I trow we never sought your company."

"Because he can not help it," said the third man, who had not spoken before—"because he can not help it, Beverly. Why do you ask such silly questions; seeing you know as well as he does, that since he was broken and dismissed the Ironsides, he has no help for it, but to take toll as we do?"

"Then I should rather ask," retorted Beverly, "why we, two cavaliers of honor, allow this canting psalm-singer to hang upon our skirts, and carry it so high as if he were our leader?"

"That can I tell you," said Despard, for it was no other than the tyrannical and brutal cornet, who had been cashiered and disgraced at Henry Chaloner's instance; "that can I tell you very shortly. Because five words of mine, just five! of mine would send you to the gallows at Low Barnsby Moor; first, as proclaimed malignants, second, as common pads and michers, and third, as the assaulters of sweet Mistress Alice Selby; five words of mine would do this piece of very notable justice. I do not know, 'fore Heaven, why I don't speak them."

"Then will I make sure that you don't," replied the taller ruffian, starting to his feet, and laying his hand where the hilt of his sword should have been, but where there only swung an empty scabbard. Despard, however, did not quit his seat, nor indeed move at all, though his dark, jealous eye watched every movement of his man with eager scrutiny; but when he saw him clutch the useless scabbard, he uttered a low, sneering laugh.

"Pity," he said, "'tis pity thou didst throw away a weapon thou seemest so prompt to handle, and all in empty terror for an unloaded pistol, when, had you but possessed half a man's courage, you might have pinked that straight-laced idiot Chaloner, and clodded the knave-farmer into the deepest hole of the river, and turned the girl to your own uses afterward. Tush man, you cavaliers and kingsmen, for all your braggart ruffling, are fit but to rob hen-roosts, and frighten country cullions. Tush! I say, tush! Hugh Beverly, we are not here to wrangle or to fight, but to be well revenged upon our enemies, and to amend our fortunes, as thou knowest!"

"Curse Chaloner, and you too!" answered the other gruffly, resuming his seat, however, as he spoke; "for had *he* not thrust himself into that which concerned him nothing, we had won gold enough to carry us to merry France long since: and then must *you* come in with your confounded schemes and plots. Hung! by the Lord! if we were hung at all it should be for what we are planning now, to yield up an old kingsman, and a comrade too, to the filthy roundhead butchers. But if we do 'scape hanging for't, we shall not 'scape the stings of our conscience. For my part I do not like it half!"

"But recollect," put in the other cavalier, "recollect, Beverly, how he set you in the bilboes and swore that you should taste of the strapado."

"And if he did, if he did, Paul, I can not say but I deserved it," the tall man interrupted him, "but plague upon the bilboes! If Captain Wyvil could see us as we are, he would right freely share his last crown with us; and not to save his own life ten times over would he betray our hiding-place or yield us to the hangman."

"Well, Beverly," returned the other, "If you think thus of it, you were best bridge, and seek your fortune elsewhere, Master Despard, and I will do the job without you. But as it must be done, whether you will or no, it seems to me you were best share the deed, and go thirds in the guerdon. Think, man, a hundred crowns to each of us, and a free pardon!"

"Damn the crowns!" Beverly replied, "I would not do it

for ten thousand, if I could only get myself quietly away to France."

"But that thou canst not do, friend," said Despard, who thought it full time to strike in, now that his comrade's virtue was yielding fast to the temptation; "but that thou canst not do, were it to save thy soul from sure perdition. Here thou art, many miles from sea, with all the roads patrolled on every side, and not a tester in your pouch! Thou hast no choice but to join with us or to perish. Besides, it may not go so hard with this malignant Wyvil, after all. For of a verity I owe him no grudge; and, for me, he might go safe wherever he listed, were it not for the price upon his head, and for the certainty of proving Chaloner guilty of treacherous connivance, and bringing down his cool, proud insolence of bearing, to infamy and ruin, for all he lords it now so fairly! Come, pluck up heart, man, thou must needs on with us."

"I fear you say true, and I must," Beverly answered; "but I would not, by all the fiends in hell! I would not, could I at all do otherwise! Pass me the bottle, Paul, pass me the bottle;" and grasping, with the words, a huge black leathern flagon, half-filled with spirits, he gulped down his qualms of conscience in a deep draught of the liquid fire; and, dropping it again, folded his arms upon his breast, and frowning, fixed his eyes doggedly on the ground, as one resolved to act against the dictates of his better reason. For a minute or two no further words were interchanged, but Despard screwed his features into a hideously acute grimace, and winked at the ruffian who had been called Paul, pointing, as he did so, with his thumb over his shoulder to the lesser villain, Beverly, and then a grim smile kindled both their visages, as they exulted over the last vanquished glimpse of their companion's nobler nature. After a little pause, however, Paul addressed the Puritan in a subdued voice, not necessarily to attract attention from the other.

"But are you sure," he said, "are you so very sure after all, that Wyvil is concealed up here at the manor? I can not see, for my part, how he can well be there, after such a thorough searching, nor if he be there, how you can know it."

"I tell you, man, he *must* be here; did we not chase him down to the very bridge in full sight of our party, and when we turned the corner, lo! he was vanished away; and was not his horse found close beside the river, where he had tied him in the woodland; and did not our first squadron see this girl at the fish-house, who had departed thence when we came hither, and is not this good proof?"

"It may be good suspicion, but hardly proof, I think. It were the devil's own hash, to be foiled in this matter, after we have been loitering hereabout so long."

"I tell you we will not be foiled; keep thou but sharp watch; for while I lay watching the forester under the old park wall, I heard that pedlar knave, that Bertram—I never miss a voice I have heard once before! chatting with the quean Marian, of the inn. I could not catch all that they said; but I am sure I heard the pedlar send her to fix some time and place where he might speak with Mistress Alice, doubtless to scheme this Marmaduke's escape; and I doubt not it was to that end she visited the Hall. As soon as it grows dark, we will part company; you, Paul, shall watch the lane and the park-gates, Beverly here shall hang about the fish-house, while I will take my old post by the wall."

"But are you certain," Paul again inquired, "that when we have found out the time, we shall be able to entrap him? are you assured you have discovered all the outlets of that same hiding-place of which the soldiers told you?"

"I tell you, yes; fool, yes!" returned the other; "there be but two, and I have found them both; one in a drain that opens out beneath the park wall, eastward of the gates, into the old green lane—the other has its mouth in the stream's bank, not much bigger than a foxearth. I had not found it, had I not well known from the troopers the true direction of each passage?"

"But after all is done," said Beverly, who had been listening all the time, although they knew it not, "we shall be in the dark as much as ever. We can not possibly learn by which of the two gates they mean to let him out, and we are not sufficiently strong-handed to beset both."

"Oh, for that I have taken thought," said Despard; "we will force them to take which we choose. That in the river bank will be the easier of the two whereat to seize him. And I will so arrange it, that there shall be a troop of horse posted before the entrance of the drain that night. I have some old friends yet among the soldiers, and it is but the sending a false letter."

"Ay! that will do—that will do bravely! and we can seize him meanwhile, and carry him at once to headquarters," cried Paul exultingly, rubbing his hands as he spoke. "But come," he added in a moment afterward, "come, let us roast the hare, and get our supper; the fire has burned bright, and it will cook him quickly. We must put out the embers, too, before the keeper takes his round, and it is getting dark already. It was a wonder the wench saw not the smoke as she passed by. Art sure she did not, Despard?"

"Trust me for that; she never lifted once her eyelids from the ground," the Puritan replied, "else had I twisted her head round, before she could have called for succor, had there been any near."

And then, without more words, they all three set to work in earnest about the cookery of the game; and in less than half an hour—just as the night was closing in, and objects were but indistinctly visible at a few paces distance—they had not only prepared, but discussed their supper, flung a few handfuls of sand upon the embers, and gathering up their weapons, gone off in different directions into the growing darkness.

CHAPTER XIV.

Meantime, all unsuspicious of any plots against her, Alice awaited the return of her humble friend; and scarcely was it dark before, according to their preconcerted scheme, Marian came up quite breathless from the lodge, and sent a message in, praying that Mistress Alice would of her kindness walk down to the Stag's Head, since Martin had been taken, as they feared, death sick. Old Mark looked up from his book quickly, as the word was delivered; for she was sitting with him at the time, engaged about some graceful feminine handiwork, and began saying something about the lateness of the hour, and the darkness; but he perceived, as he looked up, a meaning in his daughter's eye, which checked him as he did so, and he made no further opposition, when she said calmly—

"Oh, father, I must go; I shall not be away above an hour or so at the utmost. I will take Launcelot and Charles, with weapons and a lantern, so there can not be any danger."

"As you will, Alice," the old man replied; "but I must say I think it foolish, seeing that to go in the morning would probably do every whit as well. The men, however, must carry firearms, if you will go. See to it, Peter," he continued; "see that they carry pistolets beside their broadswords." Then, as the servant left the room to execute his bidding—"what is there in the wind now, Alice?" he said anxiously, "for I am certain there is something; I can read that in your eye and heightened color."

"Oh, read your Æschylus, dear father," said she smiling, as if to reassure him; "instead of wasting your acumen upon my silly cheek. You shall know all when I return, and all good news, I fancy." And she stooped over him, as she spoke, and parted the long snowy hair from his broad brow, and kissed him tenderly before she left the room.

Nothing occurred of any moment on their way, except that

Marian told her how Martin had in truth come home from wandering in the park far more distempered than he had been since the outrage; that he had raved so furiously about the soldier, that he had terrified them all, and had then fallen into the worst fit she had ever witnessed. Bartram had not arrived when she left home, but she feared not he would be there before them. And so, indeed, he was. For, when they reached the Stag's Head, after desiring the two men to make themselves comfortable by the kitchen hearth, over a pot of spiced ale which stood simmering in the chimney corner, all mantled over with a rich creamy froth; and sending off the girls on the pretext of putting the blind woman quietly to bed, Marian lit a hand-lamp, and led the fair young lady by the same winding staircase, into the same neat chamber wherein Chaloner had breakfasted on the eventful morning which sealed his earthly fate. Here she set down the light upon the table, and opening a small door into an inner chamber, looking to the back of the house, and quite overshadowed by the tall elm-trees of the park, which grew within ten or twelve feet of the latticed window—"Bartram," she said in a low whisper, "are you there Master Bartram?"

"Ay," was the answer, in a yet lower tone; "ay, but be very cautious, I fear we may be watched. Is Mistress Alice with you? I need not ask though, I hear her gentle tread; come in, then, come in both of you now quickly; leave the light there, oh! leave the light, it would betray us outright; and hark you, Marian, reach me that old steel cross-bow, and the bolts that hang above the chimney; it is as well to be prepared for the worst always."

Alice immediately entered, and went up to the pedlar, whose sturdy and athletic form she could discover indistinctly near the window, saying, in a sweet guarded tone, "Well, Master Bartram, I have come to hear what you can have to say to me; something of greater moment than the last modes, or the price of French taffeta, I hope."

"Yes, indeed; yes, indeed, lady," he replied; "but, I beseech you, come and sit here by me, that I may speak quite low to you. I do not like the shadow of those trees; a man might lie upon the coping of the wall, within six feet of us, and we no thought the wiser."

"Then why not shut the casement? or, better yet, go to the her chamber?" said Alice; doing, however, quietly as he directed her.

"Because," said Bartram, still gazing out into the darkness, "this is the only safe room in the house; in all the rest the servants would overhear us; and as for the casement, four of the panes are broken, the worse luck on it; it slipped from my hand as I entered, and fell back against the tenter-hook in the house-side. So if I were to shut it, it would but hinder us from seeing what's afoot without doors, while it would be no safeguard in the least to us within. Ay, that's it, Marian," he continued, as he reached the cross-bow from her hand, and instantly applied himself to bend it, and fit the quarrel, or steel-headed bolt, to the stiff cat-gut string. "Now keep your watch there in the parlor, but do not shut the door, lest Mistress Alice be afraid, nor move the lamp at all—it is well placed now, since it casts no glimmer hitherward. Now, lady, listen; listen with all your ears, that you may perfectly remember, and *that*, if possible, without obliging me to answer any question. We have but little time to talk; and if I be not more mistaken than I am very often, I saw the shadow of a man dogging me in the park; and if it were so, he was not half so far as he should have been when I climbed in here at this window."

"Do not fear," answered Alice, "that I shall clearly comprehend, and perfectly remember what you tell me; go on at once, I pray you, for the sooner I reach home the safer it will be for all of us."

"Well, then," he said, still speaking very low, and pausing every now and then to listen for a moment, and keeping his eyes fixed upon the summit of the park wall, which was nearly on the level of the window—"well, then, all is prepared for the young cavalier's escape. A sharp, fast-sailing lugger, is lying off the Welsh coast; relays of horses are already posted in spots where none will think of looking for them; I will accompany him to the seashore myself, and see him safe aboard. Ha! what was that? did you not hear a sound?"

"It was a bird," Alice replied; "only the cry of a little bird, and hark! that is the flutter of his wings as he takes flight; go on, good Bartram!"

But he did not go on, but sat there with his head bent forward, his rapid roving eye glancing continually over every object, and his ear drinking every sound, however small or trivial. But there arose no further noise, although he listened for ten minutes at the least, moving not nor speaking. Then, with a doubtful and dissatisfied shake of the head—"It was indeed a bird," he said; "a missel thrush, awakened from its roost by sudden fear; that much is clear enough to all who know the habits of the bird; but what should have compelled him to take wing so wildly, it would require a wiser head than mine to fathom."

"How can you think so deeply on such a trifle?" said Alice, wondering greatly at the pedlar's manner. "What can it signify what roused him? a fox, perhaps, passing among the shrubs below, or a night-owl, it might be, or perhaps a snake."

"As for trifles, lady," the pedlar replied very gravely; "I trust in heaven that you may never learn, as I have, to take the closest note of all such seeming trifles—taught so to do by the hard, bitter teacher of the best earthly wisdom—painful and sad experience. I have been hunted day and night by savage bloodhounds, and men more savage yet, and have 'scaped only by my knowledge of such trifles. Lady, God has not given one small instinct to one of the smallest of his creatures, but has its clear and proper meaning—but speaks to him who comprehends, with voice as plain and audible, and far more true, than any human accents. There is not a bark or whine of the hill-fox, not a yell of the wild-cat, a shriek of the night-wandering owl, not a note of the meanest warbler, nay! not a croak of the garrulous frog, but I have learned to mark them, and draw deep warning from them each and all! But it was none of those things which you named that startled that poor throstle. A fox would not have roused the bird at all, for it roosts high, and knows as well as we do that foxes climb no trees—night-owls prey ever in the open meadows, and strike their victims on the ground, never among thick woods or even in high bushes; then, as for snakes, the cold nights this week past have driven the snakes all into their snug holes under ground for winter quarters. No, if that thrush did not wake up scared by a dream—for birds dream also! Mistress Alice, although I do n't suppose you will believe me—it was a man that forced it to take wing, and yet I heard no footstep, nor any rustling of the branches."

"It was a dream, then, I dare say," said Alice, not a little surprised and rather restless at his long discussion; "for surely had there been a man, we must have heard him; go on, I pray you, with our more urgent business."

"Well, as I said then, all is ready, and I have picked a stout and bold companion to see us clear at starting. Now, lady, mark me well; the third night hence there will be no moon, none at all; and, as I think, the weather will be cloudy. We shall need all the hours of darkness, for if the day dawn on our road we are but lost men all. At eight o'clock, then, to the moment, we must start. Now tell me clearly, you, where are the mouths of the two outward passages? This you must speak out fearlessly, for we *must* know it, or we shall never meet, but wander, it may be, all the night long in the park at cross purposes."

"One opens in the lane, sixty-four paces due east from the lodge; a large arched drain comes out through the park wall, just opposite a tall old ash-tree; you can not miss the spot. The other—my father told me this, that I might tell it to a trusty friend in case of urgent need—communicates with a low natural cave, not much larger than a foxearth or rabbit-burrow; the mouth is in the steep, red gravelly bank of the rivulet, an arrow-shot above the first of the three bridges; it is within a foot or less of the water's brink, and in high floods is sometimes quite submerged; there is a clump of very thick dark hollies on the bank's edge, and one of the same trees, a variegated one, about midway the steep declivity exactly over it."

"Hush!" whispered the pedlar; "hush!" laying his hand on her arm in the excitement of the moment; "heard you not that?" as a slight grating sound, like that which a person might make creeping along the top of a rough-hewn stone wall, became quite audible; and, as he spoke, he rose carefully to his feet, holding the cross-bow ready in his hand for instant service. The very next moment the noise was repeated, and was followed closely by a loud rustling of the branches of the elm, which could be indistinctly seen to shake against the dull horizon, though there was not a breath of air abroad to stir them. As quick as thought the cross-bow rose to Bartram's shoulder, a hoarse clang broke the silence, and then the whirring of the heavy missile! the boughs were more violently agitated yet, as if some heavy body was breaking its way through them, and in a moment the marked and peculiar sound of a soft heavy mass falling upon the ground succeeded, with something that resembled a faint groan.

"Good God!" cried Alice, clasping her hands in all the agony of mortal terror—"good God! you have killed some one; oh, how could you be so rash, so unthinking?"

"I hope I have," Bartram replied, speaking in a louder voice than he had ventured to adopt before, and not without some real dignity. "I hope I have slain some one, for that one must have been either a night-robber or a spy; and which he was soever, death is his fitting meed. But I believe I have not: for I shot quite at random, and I fancy the bolt broke his arm; at least he was alive as he dropped through the branches, and seemed to catch at them as if to break his fall."

"He may be wounded, then," exclaimed Alice. "Oh, heavens! wounded, and bleeding his life-blood away upon the cold damp ground, without a helping hand to soothe his tortures. Let me call Charles and Launcelot, to go and search for him with torches!" and, as she spoke, she darted toward the door; but Bartram caught her firmly but respectfully, and held her fast by the arm.

"Unhand me sir;" she said, with not a little indignation in

her tones, though they were still instinctively suppressed; "unhand me, for I will go forth."

"Not for your life! dear lady—for all our lives—I say!" responded Bartram. "Yours—Wyvil's—mine—but that is little worth, and ready at a moment's call!—and your good father's!" and seeing that she was struck by his words, he released her and continued—"Now hear me, Mistress Alice, but twenty words more, and then return straightway to the Hall, taking your servants with you. As soon as you shall have departed, I will go look for the man I shot at—I will, by all that I hold sacred! Now this is all that still is left to say. I understand the spots you have described distinctly. Of these the first will be the best, if it be possible to use it; therefore, let him try that the first; but, as it opens on the road, something may well occur to make it perilous. Therefore let him look for this token. If he find not a glove within the drain, at some five yards from the arched mouth, directly in the centre of the dry channel—for it is dry, I well remember—let him go back at once, and he will find us at the other. He must be at the drain mouth shortly after seven, that he may have full time to get back to the other entrance if he find not the symbol. But, for no cause whatever, let him go forth until he hear me whistle thrice; he knows my call, I trow. Now, do you understand distinctly? Let him be at the drain by seven, and if he find the glove, lie *perdu* there until he hear the signal; if not, back with the speed of light to the cave by the river."

"Yes, yes; I understand distinctly," she replied; "but—"

"Oh, no buts, no buts, dear lady," cried the pedlar; "we have no time for buts! You have the whole plan now before you, and if you manage rightly, then his escape is certain; if not, then on their heads be the blame who mar it in the acting. Now, Marian, light her down stairs; take your men hastily, I do beseech you, Mistress Alice, and get you homeward with all speed, this is no place for such as you at such an hour. God's blessing on your head, and be of a good heart, for all shall yet go well. And trust me I will go forth instantly, and see what has befallen yonder; though I am well assured his life is safe, and his wounds, if he indeed be wounded, quite superficial. It is as well so, too; for he heard nothing of our conversation, nothing at least that could do good or evil."

He led her to the door as he said this, and while Marian conducted her down to the kitchen, and saw her set forth for the Hall under the keeping of her sturdy yeomen, he lifted from the table, where they had lain during his interview with Alice, two brace of large long-barrelled pistolets, and a broad-bladed wood-knife; the latter of which he thrust into his belt at first, whereas he opened the pans of the others, and felt that the powder was both dry and loose, and the flints firm fixed, before he consigned them to the girdle. This done, he mounted on the window-sill, caught a large flexible branch of the elm-tree in both his hands, and swung himself, with far more agility than could be looked for in a man of his years and thickset frame, to the top of the park-wall, alighting on it firmly, and balancing himself a moment before he stooped; and grasping the projecting coping with a strong hold, lowered himself to arms' length, and then dropped safely to the earth within the park of Woolverton. There he searched diligently and for a long time, if he might discover any trace of the man he had shot at; but there was no one there, alive or dead; nor was there any sign that anything had fallen from above, except that one small bush was beaten to the earth, and some of its thin shoots battered and broken as if by some heavy body.

CHAPTER XV.

It was already very late when Alice entered the park-gates, for the walk and her interview with Bartram had occupied much more time than they had imagined, and supper was already ended; but so well had the whole scheme been arranged, that her unusual absence excited in this instance neither suspicion nor surprise. Desiring that some light refreshments with wine and water should be carried up into the library, she ran up thither instantly, thinking, it is true, very little about such matters, and eager only to disbosom herself to her father as soon as possible of her important tidings. This was soon done; and so much pleasure did the old man exhibit at the intelligence, that, though she spoke not of it, his very evident joy seemed selfish and unkind to Alice; who, though she knew not why, felt a sad sinking at the heart, a melancholy and foreboding gloom upon her spirits, so often as she thought of Marmaduke's departure. After brief conversation on the subject, for neither felt inclined to talk at length, Alice, fatigued by the exertions and excitement of the day, retired without visiting her captive guest, her father having seen him in his crypt during her absence.

Long she lay tossing, sleepless and restless, on her innocent couch; distracted with strange fancies; doubts, and suspicions, and perplexities, succeeding one the other, like billows on an agitated sea. Now, for the first time it would seem, a dim, indefinite perception of the state of her affections began to steal across her mind. At first it assumed the form of a simple anxiety—a longing fond desire to know if he, whom she had so long tended with so affectionate care, would feel the same despondency and sorrow at quitting his poor place of refuge, which she endured already at the mere thought of his departure; then, as she asked herself, "Why should he? why should he grieve at being rescued from a dull, dreary prison-house, and let loose again to active life, to liberty, and daylight? nay, rather why should he not rejoice with an extreme triumph and exultation?" it naturally began to suggest itself to her that her own sorrow and despondency was something more than ordinary; and, though she strove hard to convince herself that it was a mere natural regard for one with whom she had passed latterly many delightful hours, a common and unselfish interest in a fine noble-minded man, who was no more to her than any other late acquaintance, all the heart's sophistry availed her nothing; but she was forced to entertain the question, "Did she then love? Could it be possible, that all unasked, uncourted, she had surrendered her soul's deep affection to this young gallant? whether it could be that a secret instinct, undreamed of at the time, and unsuspected, of love for Wyvil, had led her to meet Chaloner's addresses with so unqualified and final a rejection? No! she discarded the idea by a strong impulse of alarmed and jealous modesty! It would have been, she thought, the height of overbold, unmaidenly effrontery, to love, herself unloved; it was impossible! it was not so! And then she closed her eyes, and breathed a short pure prayer, and turning on her other side, bade such vain imaginations avaunt! and resolved positively, as she thought, to entertain the like no more. But such thoughts are insidious and most subtle guests; and once admitted into the sanctuary of the human mind, can scarcely be yielded thence, but will creep forward—onward, and forward still—till they have reached the very shrine and altar of that wondrous temple, disguised perhaps and hidden under some specious mask, but still unchanged and vigorously active; and at the last shake off their counterfeited semblance, and kindle the whole place with the full blaze of confessed and over-mastering passion. And so, on this occasion, was it with Alice Selby; one question still suggesting others, so that she scarcely had resolved to think no more of such things, before she was asking herself—"And was it then so certain that she was unloved—was it so clear, that it was not a secret instinct that Marmaduke indeed did love her, which had called forth in her this mutual feeling?"

Then she began to think of the peculiar tones of his voice, as he had spoken to her; to recall to mind the deep and concentrated glance of his expressive eye, which she had caught so often dwelling on her features, when he believed it all unnoticed; to reflect how his whole demeanor had been gradually changed toward her, from commonplace, gay gallantry, to calm, though by no means cold observance. She called to mind how often she had seen him raise his head, and partly open his lips to speak after long intervals of thoughtful silence, and again check himself by a sudden effort, and relapse into meditation. She fancied, too, that he had become more deeply thoughtful than was common, or in accordance with his native disposition—that there was a vein of melancholy in the poetical, half-rambling strains of thought into which, now and then, his conversation would degenerate; and she was sure—the more sure, the more she thought upon it—that he had oftentimes of late endeavored, as it were, to probe her thoughts, to penetrate her inmost mind, and learn her real character, her style of principles, her temper, and such other matters, more carefully than a mere passing guest would have been likely to do concerning the acquaintance of a day. Thus her imagination still advanced, never one moment idle or at fault, till it had overleaped all obstacles, and had persuaded her, before she sank into a perturbed slumber, and that she was loved by Wyvil, and almost led her to confess that she loved him in turn.

The following morning she awoke all pale, and worn out, as it seemed, with mental excitation; but after breakfast she passed an hour or two in "chewing the cud of sweet and bitter fancy" in the delicious flower-garden, and returned thence refreshed, indeed, by the pure autumn air, and the fresh scent of the rich, upturned mould, but only confirmed the more fully in the almost intuitive conviction which had come over her in the course of the past night. All that day long, however, she went not near the cell; excusing herself on some trivial plea, and prevailing, not without some small difficulty, on her father to relieve her of the charitable duty. It seemed, moreover, as if anxiety and care were now to be the lot of all the family of selby; for, on his return from Wyvil's hiding-place, an eye considerably less acute than that of Alice could have discovered that something of far more than common moment had disturbed the serenity of old Mark's calm and steady equanimity. He settled himself down, indeed, to his books as usual; but it was very evident that his mind was no longer in the task, for he would look up and fix his eyes steadfastly on the vacant air, and gaze for many minutes, and then shake his thin gray locks doubtfully, and heave a long-drawn sigh; and then apply himself as it were reluctantly to the old commentaries once again, and read or write earnestly and eagerly for a few minutes, till gradually his powers of abstraction would prove unequal to the struggle against the powerful thoughts within, and he would raise his eyes once more to rest them upon the lovely features of his fair pallid child, and seem as if he were about to speak; but finding himself unequal to the task, would clear his throat with a deep husky cough, and brush away a tear from his gray lashes. Thus passed the day gloomily, cheerlessly, although the sky was bright, and clear, and sunny; and the air balmy, although fresh and bracing. Thus passed the day, with nothing worthy of note to mark its fleeting hours, except that the head-forester, who had been sent out with all his men, charged to search all the brakes and dingles of the park, but more especially the old sand-quarry, returned at nightfall, and reported that there certainly were no strangers now within the precincts of the park; although, as certainly, there had been poachers there a day or two before at farthest; for in the old stone-pit he had found the white embers of a wood fire, the skin of a dead hare, the feathers of several pheasants, and, last but not least, a bunch of admirably-manufactured gins and springes, proving, beyond all question, the quality and occupation of its late visiters.

Night came, and passed away; and on the following morning, when Alice would again have eschewed visiting the young man, her father so decidedly, and, as she thought, with so much meaning in his tone, refused to take her place, and prayed her with an air so earnest—reminding her that she would have this duty, which seemed so irksome, to perform but one day longer — to go at once, without more foolish and unkind delay, that she could not decline it; but found herself obliged, though most reluctantly, to visit Marmaduke with her accustomed burden. It would have been, perhaps, difficult for Alice to have explained why she felt that reluctance; for she of late had certainly looked forward to the hour for those stolen interviews with interest, and not unpleasurable agitation; and most assuredly, had Wyvil been at that moment a visiter at large in her father's hospitable mansion, she would not have shunned meeting him, or even wished to eschew his company. Most probably it was a secret, and not unnatural, sense of modesty, now that she had become apprised of her own feelings, which hindered her from seeking, as it might appear, an interview with one she loved, but whose attachment toward herself, if that he was indeed attached, was unavowed, and buried in the depths of his own heart. She felt, too, it is more than likely, that most unreal, but at the same time most natural dread, that he, concerning whom her thoughts had been so much engaged during the last two days, must have arrived during the same period at the same conclusion with herself — must have penetrated her secret sympathies, and become the lord, as it were, and judge of all her hidden sentiments. So that, she fancied, it would appear to him as if she had come thither — had sought him out, in short — only to seek a solution of her own doubts and fears; to give him an opportunity of telling his passion, and of learning that it was returned by equal, perhaps earlier, passion of her own! The very thought made her cheeks burn with painful blushes; made her limbs tremble, and her tongne falter; so that it would, in truth, have been impossible for any man of common penetration not to perceive that Alice, as she entered on that morning the hiding-place of Wyvil, was under the influence of some strong mental agitation. So certain is it that in women of the better order, the existence of deep passion is far more frequently discovered to those from whom they wish the most to hide it, through the very means they have adopted to conceal it, than by direct and open revelation. Besides this, it is very rare that a man, himself loving or inclined to love a woman, can long remain in real ignorance of her sentiments toward himself, unless in those flagitious cases, where direct means are taken by the designing and coquettish to keep him in suspense and darkness. When, therefore, Alice entered the small chamber, though she had done so fifty times at least before without exhibiting the smallest signs of confusion, it was with such an air of conscious bashfulness, that Marmaduke at once perceived the alteration in her manner.

It would be now of no avail to trace the progress of his sentiments, to note how first the seeds of future passion were sown within his bosom; for to no one who, with a fancy disengaged and a heart free, has been thrown accidentally into the constant and familiar society of a young and very lovely woman, can it be a matter of wonder that Wyvil, shut up as he was in absolute seclusion from all the world except one sweet and beautiful girl, pre-eminently gifted with all the charms that most adorn her sex and captivate the other, should have become enamored; especially when to the strong attractions of beauty, wit, and gentleness, are superadded the strong plea of gratitude. From the first moment of their meeting, marked as it was on her part by so much of high though gentle spirit—by so much generosity, and readiness of mind, and courage, a deep sense of admiration had possessed him; and daily, more and more, that admiration, blended with warmer gratitude, and fostered by the constant observation of her sweet womanly character, her gentleness, and easy grace, and artless frankness, had grown up into strong and burning love. Some hint of this Wyvil had casually and indistinctly, perhaps half-unintentionally, dropped to her father; and instantly perceiving the change which followed his words in the expression of the aged man, and coupling with that grave sad shadow the absence of Alice from his cell during two whole days, he had been torturing himself wlth every kind of vague and jealous fancy, till he had worked himself into such a fever of hope, and rivalry, and anxious passion, that he felt almost ready to sacrifice and surrender everything so he could only be resolved what was the nature of her feelings. And now when she came in with a faltering step, a cheek suffused with momentary crimson, and in a moment after pallid as monumental marble, a downcast eye that suffered not one radiant glance to flash through the long lashes, and a perceptible air of timidity and agitation in her whole bearing and demeanor, he started hurriedly from his seat, and rushed to meet her, with his whole spirit beaming from his every feature.

"Oh," cried he, in a passionate and broken voice, "why—oh, why, have you deserted me? You do not—oh, no! you can not think how wretched I have been; how miserably sad and anxious. Have I offended you in anytning? Oh, surely, surely not; for rather would I die a thousand deaths, than that one thought of mine should wound you. Or can it be that you are wearied—wearied, as well you may be, of wasting your bright hours with a poor prisoner in his cheerless cell? Yet, dear, dearest lady, could you but know how exquisite the pleasure is which you confer even by your briefest visit, so it be lighted by your kind smile, one gentle glance of those compassionate eyes, you would not grudge a little weariness, you who are so soft-hearted, so charitable to the feelings of all others, so careless of your own the while! and that, too, when so short a time remains before your task will have an end for ever. Yet, perchance, even this—this end which I can not so much as contemplate without a thrill of horror, is unto you a source of pleasure, of congratulation! You do not speak—you do not answer me!" he went on, without even giving her the time to answer if she would, impetuously, and carried away by the torrent of his passions—"You *will* not answer me! I doubt not that you *are* glad I leave you." As he spoke thus, Alice, who had stood paralyzed, and almost frightened at the rapidity and vehemence with which he poured forth this quick flood of words, raised her long lashes slowly, and looked full in his face, with her large soft blue eyes dilated with surprise, not all unmixed with apprehension.

"I do not understand you," she said simply, after a little

pause; "I do not at all understand you, Captain Wyvil. Of course, I am glad that you are about to be set free from prison, which you find naturally so very dull and dismal — of course, I am glad that you have a certain prospect of escape from your blood-thirsty enemies. I have continually been in terror since you have lain here hidden, lest they should find you out. Of course I am glad, Captain Wyvil."

"I thought so! yes, by heaven, I thought so!" exclaimed he; "glad to be rid of the poor, helpless, ruined, runaway cavalier, who has been for so long a time a burden on your hospitality, a clog upon your gayer pleasures. By God! I do believe it is a joy to you to think that you shall never look upon me any more, that you stand there so calm, and quiet, and unmoved. Why, you had shown more of emotion at the departure from your house of a mere servant — ay, I do well believe, even of a dog!"

"For a dog," answered poor Alice, quite dismayed at his strange vehemence, "would not turn and rend the hand that had been kind to him!" and with the words she burst into a flood of weeping so passionate and so convulsive, that if she had before appeared unmoved and self-possessed, such charge could now the least of all attach to her.

"You weep," he cried; "you weep. O heavens! can it be that you feel any care, any regard — "

"Unkind," she answered; "oh, ungenerous and unkind! Have I not risked *my* life, and what is dearer fifty-fold, my beloved father's! to conceal, and shelter, and protect you? Have I not gone forth in the night, provoking misconstruction at the least, if not insult and actual outrage, to plan your safe escape? Have not I come to visit you and cheer your solitude at all hours of the day, and almost all of night — that some might call me forward and unmaidenly — that now you should affront me with such questions? Out on it! is this generous or noble?"

"But all this," he replied, "you would have done as much for any other. It was an impulse, a kind, and noble, and heroic impulse! but still an impulse only, that induced you at the first to offer me an asylum from my enemies. You would have offered it to Astley, or Prince Rupert, nay, to the profligate Wilmot, as you did offer it to me."

"Ay," Alice answered him indignantly; "ay, or to any nameless fugitive who had fought for his king, and whose life was in instant peril; ay, by my word, to any Puritan even, whom I had seen with the avenger panting at his heels, and the sword thirsty for his life-blood. To any man, however poor, or mean, or humble, I would have given shelter in the like case until the peril were overpast. But if you think I would have risked my good report to aid one whom I did not believe worthy—if you imagine I would have given my poor company to one so far above me as Prince Rupert, much more to one so base as fame speaks my Lord Wilmot—you neither honor the character of a true woman, nor comprehend the heart of Alice Selby!"

"You would not!" he exclaimed, a strong and joyful light illuminating all his face, and his voice sinking to its tenderest and lowest tones—"you would not, Alice, and you have not avoided me from any feeling of distaste; and you will not forget me so soon as I have left your doors; and you will suffer me to write, and tell you of my future fortunes?"

"It would be strange, indeed," she answered, "if I could forget one very speedily whom I have known so familiarly and well. If I were capable of doing so, my regard or remembrance were little worth the having."

"But shall I have them, Alice—but shall I have them?" he cried eagerly; "for by my soul, if I have not, I care not for my life a maravedi! I care not whether I escape at all! I would to God you never had stepped forth to save me! that I had never looked upon your face, for it will haunt me to my grave, imprinted on my heart's inmost core in living fire! Shall I then have them, Alice, and will you let me write to you?"

"Most surely I shall not forget you; most surely I shall often think of you, shall be glad to hear of your welfare. My father doubtless will rejoice that you should write him of your whereabouts and your well-being ; for me, it were not maidenly to receive letters from a stranger."

"A stranger!" he broke forth again, half angrily, half sadly; "a stranger! and is it I—I who have for days, nay weeks, but lived to watch each glance of your soft eyes, but fed upon your smiles—is it I whom you call a stranger? Oh, cold! how cold and haughty!"

"Oh, say not cold! oh, say not haughty! Captain Wyvil," she answered eagerly, while the blood rushed in torrents to her pale cheek; "for indeed, indeed, I am neither; but, tell me, what else but a stranger could the world term you?"

"The world!" he said, "the world!" with a contemptuous sneer curling his upper lip, and a thick frown gathering on his brow; "the base, uncharitable, fickle, cold, hard world! And is it—can it be Alice Selby, that bends to the brute clamor of the knaves and fools, whom all trucklers and cowards, fawners upon the great and grinders of the poor, have styled—as if in mockery—THE WORLD? Can it be, that she shapes her conduct to meet the whimsies of the beggarly mob, or regards any way the censure of that blast of frowzy and unsavory breaths that bruit the world's opinion?"

"It can be," she replied; "it is! and I am sorry that you should think otherwise. I think I have shown already that in a good cause, where humanity or honor point our way, while the world's opinion might be deemed likely to lead elsewhere, I think I have shown to which I yield obedience. But, where the general voice is confirmed by the small still voice within, the voice that speaks the loudest in dead silence! or in all cases, where to obey is to conflict with no superior mandate, to bar no higher duty—be quite sure Alice Selby *does* regard the censure, *does* shape her course to the opinion, of what men style the world—to make up which, there go not all the knaves and the fools only, but all the great and good, the virtuous, the high-minded and the noble, of this and bygone generations! Be sure that Alice Selby does bend to this great voice; and be sure, Captain Wyvil, oh! be sure, that she who does not, is neither a high-minded lady, nor yet a pure-hearted woman!

But to pass this, what would you have me style you—what would you style yourself, if not a stranger?"

"Your lover!" he replied impetuously, throwing himself at her feet, and clasping her small trembling hand, which she strove feebly to withdraw and impotently—"your true, devoted, honorable lover! You must have seen, you must have known, oh, Alice, Alice! you can not have been ignorant thus long how deeply, passionately, *madly*, I adore you. You can not but have seen, have known all this; and knowing it, you can not have permitted me to rush unchecked and hopeful into the agony, the anguish, the despair of loving you, adoring you in vain!" and with the words, as she had let her head fall almost on her bosom, while her hand rested passively in his, and he might see the big tears stealing silently down her pale cheeks, he rose and stood respectfully beside her; and after gazing for a moment earnestly on her emotion—"I hope," he added, "I trust, Alice, I have not now mistaken you; these are not tears of grief, or of vexation, Alice?"

For a second's space or more she stood in breathless silence, then with an effort as it were she raised her head a little, and strove to look him in the face; but she could not effect it, and let fall her eyes again sobbing and panting as though her heart would break.

"Oh, Alice! lovely Alice!" he whispered tenderly, "answer me, I beseech you; or if you may not answer, press but my hand, give me some slight token;" and then he paused, and no sign was given that she heard or would regard his fond entreaties. "It is but right, and fitting your own dignity," he said, something more coolly than before, but still affectionately, for there was something in her manner that told him she was not insensible to his affection, "that you should give me now an answer. For do not fancy for a moment—I am certain that you do not fancy for a moment, Alice—that I am one who would entrap a maiden into engagements unknown to her parents. Not for worlds—not to win thee, even thee, Alice, would I do aught, require aught that could provoke the sternest father's censure; that could call forth a blush, a sigh, a sorrow, a regret, from her whom I would make my wife, when long years should have flown, and the deceptive meteor of strong passion faded from the horizon of the mind. I am a gentleman, as Master Selby knows, of honorable birth, of station, once of fortune! not, though I say it, all unknown to fame; and, though deprived of my estates by this disastrous civil strife, not so impoverished or needy, but with a bold heart and my good sword to boot, I can maintain my lady as a Wyvil's lady and a Selby's daughter should be maintained—in honor. Now, therefore, Alice, since I have laid my whole heart open to you, since you can not but say that I have dealt with you in frankness and sincerity, surely you will be frank with me and open. If you can love me as I hope—O heaven! how fervently! as I sometimes have almost thought you could—let me speak of it to your good father; if not, at least relieve me from the agony of this suspense, and let me go my way a wretched and heart-broken being, to seek my death as the best boon that God can grant me, at the pike's point or the cannon's mouth. Will you not—will you not say, then, that you love me?"

While he was still in the act of speaking, the little hand which he had held so long imprisoned in his own, returned the pressure of his fingers, but that so slightly and with so timid and so fluttering a touch, that it was scarcely perceptible; still it was felt, it gave him hope, that he continued to the end, observing that she listened to his every word with deep attention; and that her tears, although they still flowed, gushed not now with that convulsive violence which had almost alarmed him at the first, but trickled from her long dark lashes in a calm, unpainful current. And now, as his voice ceased, she raised her eyes to his, full of a sweet and dove-like tenderness that stilled his every apprehension in a moment, and a bright radiant smile glanced through her falling tears, like a first April sunbeam shimmering through the raindrops of a morning shower. Words were perhaps scarce needed, for the calm light of that pure artless face, fraught with a quiet happiness, spoke more than volumes; yet, feeling that it was her duty to speak out—

"Oh, Captain Wyvil!" she said, in a voice which, though low and musical, was now quite firm and trembled not at all; "Oh, Captain Wyvil, now you have made me very happy!"

"Alice—my own, own Alice!" he exclaimed, clasping her by a sudden impulse in his arms, while her fair head, with all its rich profusion of brown curls, dropped on his shoulder like a lily overcharged with dew-drops; "will you indeed, indeed, be mine for ever?"

"For ever! Marmaduke," she faltered forth in tones scarce audible; "for ever and for ever!" Their eyes met as she spoke the words, full of true chaste affection; and as he drew her fondly to his bosom, their lips met likewise in the first love kiss; while from behind, a deep, sonorous voice, firmer than often issues from the organs of the aged, breathed forth, "Amen! amen! my children—my blessing be upon you both; and may God's blessing, without which mine is nothing, be with you both for ever!"

It was Mark Selby, who, alarmed somewhat by the protracted absence of his daughter, had come to seek her, and actually had stood in the full sight of both—although they were so much absorbed in the strong ecstacy of passion, that they had neither ears nor eyes for aught besides themselves—during the last ten minutes. Marmaduke started at the voice, and turned round with a hurried gesture; but the expression of his features was tranquil, open, and quite fearless.

"I pray you, think not," he began; but ere he could say any more, the old man interrupted him—

"I have no need to think, Captain Wyvil, for I have heard every word you have spoken these ten minutes past. I did not mean to listen, you may be quite sure; but I had heard so much before I could attract your notice, that I believed it best to let this dear child answer you, before my presence could any way affect or influence her choice. I thank you for your noble, manly candor; and I can give you no more proof of my belief in your high qualities, than in surrendering to you this peerless jewel—this my heart's latest idol." And he embraced the lovely girl with a long, agonizing ecstacy of fondness, while the big tears rushed forth like summer rain from his old lids, and mingled with the calmer drops that dewed the cheeks of Alice. "God grant that you prove worthy of her, and bless you both, and keep you here and hereafter, with his boundless mercy!"

CHAPTER XVI.

Three days had passed since Bartram's interview with Alice, and the third sun had set, and night was falling fast over the lovely scenery of Woolverton, when three strong men well armed with quarter-staves and broadswords, but without any firearms, came cautiously out of one of the dense coppices that lined the old park wall, and stealing with light steps and watchful eyes across the open lawn, ensconced themselves in a thick brake of holly bushes which grew on the brink of the stream, not very far from the bridge which Chaloner had so manfully defended, and the scene of Sherlock's bold equestrian exploit. A few minutes after they had hidden themselves, the gate-house clock struck seven; and while its chimes were still ringing through the woodlands, the distant flourish of a cavalry trumpet came floating on the night-wind, and the faint sounds of a squadron on the march.

About half an hour later, in the green winding lane that led from the Stag's Head past the lodges into the Worcester turnpike, some hundred yards below the park-gates, a troop of the Ironsides were drawn up, the men sitting motionless on their strong horses, with their drawn broadswords in their hands; while their captain and two subalterns, having dismounted from their chargers, stood a few paces in advance conversing eagerly, though in low, guarded tones, keeping strict watch as it would seem even while they talked most earnestly.

"I do believe, for my part," whispered one, "that it is a

mere cheat and trapan. For what, I do beseech you, should we watch here, where any one could see us at fifty paces' distance, or farther if he had occasion to fear anything?"

"I do somewhat mistrust the same," replied another; "yet sure I am that letter was in Despard's hand, and he was ever a stanch bloodhound on the track of any cavalier. Besides, we have our orders; and at the worst it is but a night's ride, and a cold halt here for an hour or so. Move hence I will not until the clock strike nine. Hush! was not that a sound by the ditch side there?"

At the same moment when he spoke, a vidette, who was thrown forward some eight or ten yards in advance, brought up his carbine to the port, and challenged loudly; but no reply was made, nor was the least noise heard again, though the whole party listened with ears sharpened by the most anxious expectation.

Just as these things were going on without the park, matters were drawing rapidly toward a crisis within the walls; for, as it grew more dark, two other men, one a tall, stout, athletic countryman, the other a short, thickset figure, somewhat apparently advanced in years, but active still and vigorous, came out from a plantation nearer the Stag's Head inn than the coppice whence the three former had emerged; and coming up to the stream, which was quite shallow in that place, rippling swiftly over a gravel bed, couched themselves in the long grass exactly opposite the mouth of a low cave, which lay in a right line under the holly brake wherein the others were ensconced, at some ten paces' distance. The three men who had come first to the ground surveyed the others quietly as they came up, and remarked to one another, with a grim air of satisfaction, that they had no arms except staves, and perhaps pistols, which they would not, even if they had them, dare to use for fear of attracting observation. But neither they nor the new-comers saw that a sixth man was soon after added to the number, who came out crouching from the coppice at the very spot whence the first three had issued, with strange and uncouth gestures, stooping at times quite to the ground, and crawling on his hands and knees, seeking as it appeared for some track on the dewy grass, which he examined carefully with his hands, and seemed at times even to snuff at, like a hound trailing a doubtful scent. By these means, and by slow degrees, he followed exactly on the steps of Despard and his comrades—for it was they who lay hid in the hollies—till he was now within six feet of their very lair; but in so total silence had he crawled up from behind, and with so much sagacity, as it appeared, of caution, that they had neither heard him nor suspected his approach; then raising his head somewhat, he cast a wild glance round him, and again seemed to snuff the air; and then, as if contented, sank quietly down into the covert, which grew thick and shadowy on the river's margin.

At the same silent hour, in the deepest part of the heronry wood, hard by a narrow path winding among the swampy brakes, upon the firmer ground, which led from a narrow postern in the park wall to the same green lane which has so many times been mentioned, entering it a mile or more westward of the Stag's Head, stood a young man appareled as a forester, holding two noble chargers; one a blood-bay with coal-black mane and tail, the other a dark iron-gray, both of them evidently thorough-bred, and that of the best strain of blood, but very plainly harnessed with hunting-saddles somewhat old and used, rude leathern bridles, and coarsely-fashioned holsters—yet they were exquisitely groomed and in superb condition, their skins as smooth and soft as velvet, and so bright that they actually glittered even in the few faint starbeams that stole through the floating clouds which clothed the moonless skies. A short but heavy musketoon leaned against the bole of a huge ash-tree close beside him, with a large noble bloodhound lying upon the ground near to it.

Meantime, within the Hall all had been carefully prepared for Marmaduke's escape; a tearful and most passionate farewell had passed between the cavalier and his affianced bride; between whom it had been arranged, that so soon as they should be certainly advised of his arrival on the safe coast of France, every exertion should be made to procure his free pardon—a thing by no means to be despaired of when he should once be out of reach of capture! and failing that, and no change for the better occurring in the state of politics at home, that Alice, under her father's escort, should follow him to France, and there become his wife, under a milder rule and in a happier realm than poor distracted England. This settled, when they had torn themselves for the last time asunder, old Selby led his guest through all the devious passages, and let him out at the gate which communicated with the arched drain, promising to wait there for an hour unless he should return before that period had elapsed. He had not long to wait, however, as it happened, for within twenty minutes Wyvil returned in haste and breathless, and told his anxious friend, how finding that the token he expected was not in its place, he had crept cautiously to the drain-mouth, and thence discovered a party of the Ironsides posted as if upon watch, with carbines ready and drawn broadswords—that he had been challenged by a vidette, but had got off, as he believed, unseen and unsuspected. This explanation passed while they were hastening, after the gate had been sufficiently secured behind them, toward the other outlet; and when they reached it, once more affectionately pressing the young soldier to his bosom, the noble-minded old man bade him go once more, taking God's blessing with him, and waited long and anxiously, holding the door in hand before he ventured again to make it fast; but no more was he disturbed that night, and when two hours had passed, he rejoined Alice, to soothe her with the comfortable tidings that doubtless her young lover had escaped so far securely on his way seaward.

The clock had not struck eight when Wyvil reached the mouth of the low cavern; and though, as he peered stealthily out of its narrow opening into the misty darkness, he could discover no sign of any persons on the watch, he was yet mindful of the pedlar's message, and took good care to show no part of his person, not so much as the tips of his mustaches, beyond the entrance. He did not lie there very long, however, before a keen shrill whistle rose from the tall fern on the farther margin of the rivulet, and was again and again repeated, with an interval of perhaps twenty seconds between each signal. No person indeed showed himself, yet Marmaduke, who had on many a former occasion held intercourse with Bartram, knew the sharp call so well that he did not hesitate a moment to extricate himself from the sandy burrow and descend into the channel of the stream. At the very instant, however, in which he left the cavern, several heavy stones and a quantity of loose earth came rolling down the bank from above, and before they had reached the bottom of the declivity three stout men, by whose feet they had been spurned from the summit, leaped down upon him, calling aloud, and bidding him surrender "in the name of God and the commonwealth of England." Marmaduke had in fact scarcely got sure foothold when the enemy was on him; yet he turned sharply round to face them, drawing his rapier when he did so; while, even in that anxious moment, he had presence of mind to take notice that Sherlock and the pedlar had sprung out of their covert at this unexpected onslaught, and were rushing down to his assistance with all speed. Too late, however, was he in his movement; for ere his sword was well out of the scabbard, and long before he could shift it to parry or to strike, a sweeping blow of a huge two-handed quarter-staff was dealt him on the right side of the head, which felled him instantly into the channel of the stream. Very lucky was it for him that he had turned completely round before the blow took effect; for as he dropped the first man sprung upon him, kneeling upon his breast as he lay face upward in the shallow water, and grappling his throat with both hands; so that, stunned as he was by the blow, and helpless to arise, he must have necessarily been suffocated, had he fallen on his face, before the struggle ended.

Meanwhile the other ruffians, seeing that Marmaduke was for the moment quite unable to resist, rushed upon Bartram and the gallant farmer, pressing them so hard with their long two-edged rapiers, against which the others had nothing but their oaken staves, that it was quite impossible for them to offer any aid to the young cavalier; and now they had more than enough to do to defend themselves, and must have been slain speedily or have surrendered, had not a new auxiliary rushed suddenly, and that, most unexpectedly, upon the scene. A long-protracted and most fearful howl gave the first note of his approach, as the person who had lain hidden in the brake immediately behind the ruffians darted with strange fantastic bounds and frantic gestures down the steep river bank, and seizing Despard—for he it was who knelt so cowardly on the young soldier's chest—tore him away from his hold as if he had been a mere child, and shaking him for a moment at arms' length, with another howl, fiercer and shriller, and more fiendish in its tones than any yell that ever issued from the lips of man—even of the untameable and savage Indian!—hurled him to the earth, and leaping like a tiger on his prey, grasped with his fingers, strangely and fearfully contorted, the windpipe of his tortured victim; compressing it with all his might, and dashing his head up and down upon the ragged flints till the blood gushed from it in torrents, gibbering all the while, and uttering a low chuckling laugh of triumph, that, when connected with the savage fury of his onset, was perhaps even more revolting than the long beast-like howl which had preceded it.

All this passed in a moment—in far less time than it has taken to describe it; for as soon as he was released from the weight of Despard—the temporary faintness produced by the stunning blow having immediately yielded to the effects of the cold water, which had completely overflowed his face and temples—Wyvil sprang to his feet, brandishing the sword which he had never let go for a moment, and hurried to the aid of his companions, whom he saw overmatched in the unequal combat; but eagerly as he leaped forward, he was yet all too late! for when they heard that wild and devilish outcry, and saw a fourth man rushing from the brake, which they had believed to be tenanted by themselves alone, and dealing such extraordinary retribution on their comrade, the superstitious terrors—the only terrors to which they were accessible—of the desperadoes were aroused.

"It is the fiend!" cried one; "fly! fly! in God's name!" and with the word, leaving their late opponents unquestioned masters of the field, and wondering only that they were not pursued, the ruffians broke away, and rushing through the scattered bushes, sought the wild woods, and actually ran miles before they paused even for a moment, in mute and breathless consternation.

But not for that did the death-struggle cease between the disgraced roundhead soldier and his uncouth antagonist. Strong as he was, and desperately as he struggled for his life, striking violent, though impotent blows with the dagger which he had contrived to draw, and striving by the most fearful muscular efforts to dislodge his inveterate antagonist; yet all his efforts were in vain, for his persecutor clung to his throat with an iron grasp, and wrenched his head completely round, still muttering and gibbering, and laughing with a fierce, fiendish glee, and making horrible grimaces — grinding his strong white teeth till the foam flew from his lips, like froth churned from the tushes of the hunted boar, and falling on the face of the dying Puritan, was blent into a frightful lather, all clotted with the gore that flowed from his deep wounds.

And now the smothered imprecations — the broken sobs and gasps of the throttled roundhead — were changed into the dread death-rattle; his eyeballs rolled up meaningless; his lips were painfully convulsed, and white as ashes, while all the rest of his countenance was purple almost to blackness with the blood forced into all his pores by that strong gripe; the dagger fell from his relaxed and nerveless fingers; a sharp, quick shudder shot through his whole frame, and then all was still. The powerful limbs, collapsed and flaccid — the staring eyes, half starting from their sockets, glared with a dull, white film — the chest, that heaved of late with energy so terrible, inert and motionless; aud all the fiery passions, the inordinate lust of gold, the hot insatiable ambition, the recklessness of human life, the strong fixed purpose, the undaunted courage which but now fluttered in that living, throbbing heart — all quenched, and darkened, and at rest for ever!

Ere Wyvil and his trusty friends could reach the scene of the protracted struggle — for, although he was himself quite ignorant of the persons both of his assailant and his rescuers, Bartram and Sherlock suspected the identity of both, *knew* that of one from the first utterance of the awful outcry that harbingered his coming — all was completely over; and as they came up, Martin Rainsford — for it was the poor idiot, whose instinctive hate for Despard had worked out Marmaduke's deliverance — uprose from the dead body, and actually danced on the cold, senseless clay, in the wild exultation of his mad revenge.

"Ha! ha!" he cried aloud articulately, and in a clear high voice — "Ha! ha! rogue roundhead, wilt kill more faithful guardians of the weak? wilt beat poor Martin? wilt do more evil now? wilt shed more blood? Not thou, I warrant me — not thou! Ha, ha! ha, ha!" and then the spirit of appalling vengeance which, it would seem, had gifted him with a new and strange instinct, to hunt out and destroy the slayer of his favorite mastiff, deserted him at once, and he fell down as helpless and nerveless as the body of his victim, upon the blood-stained sod beside it, in a dread epilectic paroxysm.

"Now, before heaven!" exclaimed the pedlar, who, as he looked upon that awful spectacle, bold as he was, and fearless, and well accustomed to look unmoved on bloodshed, felt his cheek pale and his hair bristle; "now, before heaven! although we owe our safety to it, this thing is very terrible! The idiot boy hath slain him, and is, I do believe, sped by some chance blow likewise!"

"Now, God forbid it be so!" cried John Sherlock, kneeling down as he spoke beside the boy; "for if it were so, it would kill the old dame outright, and bring sweet Marian to the grave ere many months had flown. But no!" he said, "but no! he is not dead, nor even wounded; he hath but fallen into a fit, such as he ever takes after uncommon and unusual excitement."

"Who is he, then?" asked Wyvil; "who is he? do you know him? and who is this that he has slain?"

"We have no time to talk of such things, Captain Wyvil," answered the pedlar, hastily; "we must fly straightway. Meantime we must leave you, John Sherlock, to settle all the rest. I fear me much this dead man, and those runaways, will call forth fresh suspicion against good Master Selby."

"Not it! not it!" cried Sherlock; "those cowardly dogs who ran, were but chance fellows of that dead ruffian yonder. I know them well, they are the same thieves who set on Mistress Alice, disbanded desperadoes of the royal army, escaped, I trow, from the defeat at Worcester, and forced to rob and pillage by sheer want. How they fell in with this knave Despard, I know not, and marvel at it too; but we may rest quite certain, that they will not tell aught of what has passed this night—in truth they dare not, for they will fly the Puritans as the hare flies the grayhound; and for their lives, they dare not tell a cavalier how they would have betrayed and captured one of their own party—no! no! no fear of them, and as for this dead dog, I will tie such a stone about his neck as shall find its way with him to the bottom of the deep black pool underneath the waterfall below there. It will rain hard too before daylight, and that will wash away all traces of the scuffle. I will get Martin home anon; and frame some story how I found him in a fit out in the fields—that will account too for the blood upon his garments, and if he say aught of it, as he is not very like, poor fellow! seeing he does not speak thrice between Lent and Christmas, no one will notice it at all. Now, God give you speed, Master Bartram; but tarry not here I beseech you, else shall we but lose our pains. Safe journey to you, captain; I think you will 'scape scot free, after all's done. But I say, Bartram, not a word to Frank Norman of this job—not a word for your life!"

"No, no," replied the pedlar; "it is a bad business as it is, and I'll not make it worse, depend on it. Come, Captain Wyvil, John's in the right of it, we must make hay while the sun shines;" and with these words, he started at a long swinging pace that brought them within a few minutes to the postern gate which had been left ajar on purpose, so that they passed unhindered into the herony woods, closing the door which was fastened by a spring lock carefully behind them. A few steps farther brought them to the spot where Norman held the horse; and mounting instantly, scarce interchanging five words with the forester, they rode away as quickly as the nature of the ground would permit, until they reached the lane. There Bartram set spurs to his bold bay horse, and put him resolutely at the strong, quickset hedge, which separated it from the cultivated fields, clearing it with a gallant leap. Marmaduke followed not a horse's length behind; and thence they drove at a hard gallop athwart the open country, sweeping in their career across wide brooks and over stiff enclosures, unchecked and fearless—for they dared not trust themselves on the high-roads, which were patrolled by parties from the neighboring garrisons—until they reached a lonely hovel at the verge of a vast tract of forest-land, with the Welsh mountains rising dark beyond it against the cloudy sky. There a small clownish boy was stationed with a relay of fresh horses, equal in strength, and blood, and spirit, to those which had so nobly borne them hitherward; and mounting upon these without a moment's pause, they again dashed into a wild wood road, already twenty miles at least from the park walls of Woolverton, and farther yet from the headquarters of the Ironsides. Long before midnight, as Sherlock predicted, it began to rain; and in less than an hour from the commencement of the storm, it waxed into as wild a gale as ever ushered in the winter equinox, with heavy rain and sleet, and raving gusts of wind, and ever and anon a crashing peal of thunder, yet they paused not, nor slacked their long hard gallop, for liberty and life were on their speed, and they were not the men to lose them by any lack of hardihood or daring.

CHAPTER XVII.

Above six months had passed after the flight of Wyvil, yet had no tidings of his safety arrived to cheer the gentle heart of Alice; for it was autumn still, when he effected his escape from Woolverton; and now winter was over, and the earlier months of spring-time; and the young days of June were scattering their sweets over the smiling earth. But it was on a different scene from any yet described, and in a distant country, that the sun, verging fast toward the west, was pouring his soft light, when the events occurred wherewith we purpose to resume our narrative.

It was a wild and broken country, covered in many parts with heavy wood and tangled thickets, full of ravines, and intersected by a number of small streams and rivulets, and altogether as unlike the environs of a great city as can well be imagined; yet it was in the very heart of France, scarcely ten leagues from the metropolis, lying between Corbeil upon the Seine, and the small town of Villeneuve, yet nearer to the gates of Paris. Among the defiles, then it was, which intersected at that day the forest land that covered so much of that part of France, and at an advanced hour of the evening, that a small band of horsemen were advancing slowly and with much caution, as if they had been almost in the face of an enemy. They were not above ten in number, and consisted, as might be seen at a glance, of two gentlemen with their train of armed attendants; yet there was something in the style of their accoutrements and harness which showed that they were either actually engaged in some military service, or at least were prepared for some unusual danger; for although those were times wherein no gentlemen went forth unarmed, or without soldier-like retainers, still it was quite unusual for either men or masters to wear defensive armor, unless in actual warfare. The leaders of the party, who rode some two or three horses' lengths in front of their followers, were both young men, and eminently handsome; but as different as it is possible to conceive in the style of their beauty. He who rode to the right was clad in a complete suit of bright steel—an open helmet with a tall plume of ostrich feathers covered his head, and cast a darker shade over a face, the hues of which were naturally of the darkest that are ever seen in Europeans—his eyes were of a quick and lustrous black, full of enthusiastic life and rapid energy; his features manly and decided, yet at the same time delicately shaped and singularly handsome; a small coal-black mustache penciled his short-curved upper lip, and a profusion of black curls fell down beneath the rim of his bright morion, over the gorget and cuirass which armed his body. Taslets of steel were on his thighs, and his legs, from the knee downward, were protected by stout boots of polished leather, bedecked with the gilt spurs of knighthood; a long straight broadsword suspended from a scarf of white silk fringed with gold, and pistols of two feet in length, completed the accoutrements of the young chevalier. His comrade, though he was mounted on a noble charger, and though he wore both sword and pistols, was less elaborately harnessed; for in place of a helmet, he had a hat of black velvet with a band of white feathers running around it, a mode which was at that time in its first commencement, and deemed the very point device of military foppery. A coat of maroon-colored velvet, with cuirass above it, crossed by a white scarf like his friend's, breeches and gauntlets of white chamois leather, and polished riding-boots, were the nearest of anything he wore to military decoration. Something too of the same distinction, which would not but be noticed in the accoutrements of the leaders, was perceptible in those of the retainers; for while the four stout able-bodied men, who followed the last-mentioned rider, were evidently nothing more than the ordinary armed servants of the day, the others were unquestionably regular troops, and as such were equipped with the heaviest horse-armor of the day. It was not in their dress, however, nor in the style of their arms, that the principal difference between the party consisted; for while the soldier's hair and eyes and whole complexion were extraordinarily dark, his comrade was distinguished by all the attributes of English beauty, fair skin and rich brown locks, and—but it needs not to describe him further, for no one who had ever seen him, could have failed to discover in the gay cavalier of France, the person of the English Wyvil.

"Well, Captain Wyvil," said the dark-featured soldier, turning toward his companion, after a long pause in their conversation; "here are we now, within a scant league of Villeneuve St. George, and night fast drawing on, and not a sign can we discover, not a word can we learn from any one of this advance, so loudly bruited, of Monsieur de Lorraine. I begin shrewdly to suspect those intercepted letters were but a *ruse* of the princes to force Turenne to raise the leaguer of Etampes! I am in doubt how to proceed, for we have reconnoitred all the country hither, and the marechal's orders were distinct that we should not cross the Hyère; and here it is, just in the hollow way beyond that wooded hill. There, you can see its waters glittering in the sunshine three miles or so to the eastward, by the top of yon ash-tree."

"I scarce know how to counsel you, Bellechassaigne," replied the other, "not knowing how the country lies, nor what hamlets or farm-houses are scattered through this forest. It will not do, however, to fall back on the marechal, without some sure intelligence. If we can go so far onward, without incurring much risk of discovery, as to get a view from yon hill-top, I think we ought to do so; for thence we shall be enabled to overlook Villeneuve, and see, if nothing more, whether the troops of Lorraine have occupied that town in force."

"Forward, then, forward," cried the other gayly. "There is some peril in it, certainly; for if monsieur is in Villeneuve at all, be sure he has outposts on this side the river, the rather that the cross-road from Brie-conte-Robert and Grosbois intersects there with this by which we are advancing. But where the devil would the fun be in warfare, any more than in dull peace, if there were not a spice of danger in it? So forward, I say, forward!"

"Let it be quickly, then," said Marmaduke; "for, as you said but now, it is fast waxing late, and, if we are to have some fighting, we may as well have light to do it by; and if not, then it behooves us to look out for a snug place to bivouac, before it grows too dark to choose one."

"Forward, then; trot!" cried Bellechassaigne, raising his voice, so that its tones could reach the ears of the men behind, striking his charger at the same time with the spear. "And, now I think of it," he added, "it were as well to be upon our guard. Unsling your carbines, look to your matches, and be ready!"

As the last order issued from his lips, they had reached the bottom of the small sandy hollow—the road bordered on either hand by a thick growth of coppice, here and there a tall tree interspersed, and winding up a large ascent in front of them to the summit of the woody hill, whence they expected to overlook the level country toward the junction of the Seine and Marne, in which direction it was reported that the Prince of Lorraine was advancing. The command was obeyed promptly, and with their musketoons thrown forward, and eye, ear, heart, on the alert, the troopers trotted rapidly up the rough stony hill. And now they were within a hundred yards of the summit, and a few seconds more would have placed them on the verge, in full view of whatever there might be beyond its woody screen, when suddenly a faint, long note, as of a trumpet keenly winded, but far distant, came down the summer wind. The quick ear of Bellechassaigne caught it upon the instant.

"Halt!" he cried; "halt! we are upon them, Wyvil."

"Let us two then dismount," returned the Englishman, leaping to the ground as he spoke; "we may creep on under the covert of those fir-trees, and reconnoitre them with ease. Here," he continued, turning to his servants; "here, Adam, hold my charger, and see you stir not without orders. Best doff your helmet, Bellechassaigne, its glitter would betray us if a stray sunbeam should flash upon it."

The gay young Frenchman smiled and vaulted lightly from his charger, unclasped the chin-strap of his morion, and passed it to the nearest of his troopers; then drawing out his pistols from the holsters, he waved his hand to Wyvil, and they advanced together with stealthy steps till they had reached the brow of the hill, when they crept into the covert to the right hand of the road, where a thick tuft of stunted fir-trees afforded a sure hiding-place, and were lost to the eyes of their followers. Scarce had they made three steps into the shadow, before a vast and glorious landscape was spread out like a map before them; a wide rich champagne, covered with the tall crops of waving grain and fertile pastures, checkered with woods and orchards, and dotted with a thousand hamlets—the broad bright courses of the Seine and Marne rolling in silver labyrinths among the verdure, and the blue domes and Gothic spires of the metropolis just seen through the thin haze which curtained the horizon. Nearer, and in the foregroud as it were of this grand picture, lay the small town of Villeneuve, beyond the river Hyère, which wound—now seen, now lost among the glades of the thick wood that clothed the northern slope of the height whereon they stood—down to the margin of the stream, and the broad yellow road by which they had advanced receded in long clear perspective downward to the stone bridge and the barriers of the town.

It must not be supposed, however, that the two partisans had any leisure to survey the scene, or even to consider whether the landscape in itself was beautiful or not, so absolutely were their senses occupied in reconnoitring its military points, and judging of its occupation by the enemy. Nor was it very difficult to form a judgment on this point; for at the first glance they might see a hostile standard hoisted upon the bridge, and a small guard of horse in foreign uniforms on duty at the gate; while in three different spots of the more distant champagne, they could distinguish clearly three large and powerful divisions, evidently each in communication with the others, marching as fast as possible on Villeneuve.

"Now," exclaimed Bellechassaigne; "now we may go our ways as hard as we can gallop, and tell Turenne what we have seen, for here are the advanced guard of the Lorrainer's horse on the Hyère already, and certainly the rearmost of those three infantry divisions will be within the town before to-morrow noon. The marechal must march right rapidly if he means to fight monsieur before he can cross the Seine. So let us get to horse, good friend, and make the best of our way back to Corbeil; we will halt for an hour or two at the little village where we breakfasted, and we can join the marechal before daybreak."

"Hold! hold a moment," returned Wyvil; "one moment, Bellechassaigne. Look down into the valley yonder—there in that hollow by the holly bushes—just where the other road comes in, the cross-road from Grosbois, about which you were speaking. Is it not the same?"

"Yes, yes! but what of that?" asked the young officer. "Ha! by my soul!" he added, as he turned his eyes to the spot indicated by his comrade, "they are in ambush there—two—four—six; now, by St. Dennis, there are a score of troopers in the thicket. What, in the devil's name, can they be waiting for?"

Just as he spoke, however, his question was answered by the appearance of a mounted servant or *avant courier*, dressed in a livery of dark blue cloth, splendidly laced with gold, who wheeled into the main causeway, and turning his horse toward the hill whereon the partisans were standing, came that way very rapidly without perceiving the soldiers who were lying in the thicket. A moment or two afterward one of the heavy coaches of the day, drawn by six horses, with postilions dressed in the same handsome livery as the courier, came lumbering round the corner of the wood, two stout armed servants following; one of whom led a charger, equipped with demipique and holsters, and the rich housings of a general officer of the king's party. Scarcely had the last servant come fully into sight, before the quick flash of a carbine streamed out of the dark evergreens; and before the sound of the report was borne to the ears of the young soldiers, the courier, horse and man, fell headlong to the ground, rolling over and over among the clouds of dust which surged up from the sandy road, and for a moment cut off all view of the scene of action. The rattle of a volley, however, which instantly succeeded, showed that the cowardly murder which they had seen committed was but the prelude to worse outrage. As quick as lightning, Marmaduke, when he saw the flash, and almost before he could perceive its result, turned round and rushed toward the horses, waving as he did so to his men to come forward; and they, catching his signal on the instant, came up so promptly that he was in his saddle before Bellechassaigne overtook him, though he had followed him in hot anxiety, fearing some deed of rashness on his part, the moment he observed his movements.

"Are you mad, Wyvil?" he exclaimed; "are you mad? that you think of charging twenty armed troopers with a handful such as ours; and that, too, when the twenty will be supported within ten minutes by a hundred; and, above all, for a matter that concerns us nothing? By heavens! man, we shall be cut to pieces or made prisoners in five minutes; and, what is worse than that, Turenne will get no tidings of the advance of these Lorrainers. Tête Dieu! it's well he sent me with you, as a curb on your impetuous valor."

"By the Lord! but it does concern us, Bellechassaigne," answered Wyvil hastily; "did you not see the housings of the charger? There is a general officer of the king's there; and I doubt nothing it is Sir Henry Oswold, whom Monsieur de Turenne and our good Duke of York are hourly expecting from Sedan, by Chalons and Coutomiers. I will die with my men or rescue him. Bear you the tidings to Turenne. Forward, men; gallop!" and, with the word, he dashed his spurs into his horse's side, shook off Bellechassaigne's grasp which was upon his rein, and followed by his servants, dashed over the brow of the hill, and thundered down its other slope at a pace which made itself audible to the ears of his comrade, for a moment at least after he had lost sight of him. The trooper shook his head, and muttered a few words very bitterly; but he too mounted, as his horse was led up by his soldiers, and rode, though with much caution and a slow pace, to the brow beyond which Wyvil had just disappeared. But that impetuous and daring youth was plunged already into the midst of action, before his cooler-headed, though no less brave companion, had gained a fair view of his precipitate, fool-hardy onset.

The spot at which the conflict had taken place between the servants and the ambushed force of the Lorrainers, was a small hollow way that made a deep indenture in the side of the long sloping hill, about one fourth of the way between the summit and the town; and was so situated, that although it was completely overlooked by any person standing on the brow, it could not be perceived at all by one at the base of the ascent; so that, as Marmaduke saw at a glance, there was no fear of any reinforcement coming up from the bridge, unless it should be called for by some fugitive from the scene of action, and that in this case many minutes must elapse before it could arrive upon the ground. All this he had considered before he passed the brow of the hill with his men, so that he was completely free, his plan being matured already, to take note of everything — the most minute that was occurring — which might tend to the defeat or success of his intended exploit. The smoke and dust which had obscured the scene, as he had looked upon it last, had drifted quite away, so that nothing was now hidden from him which it was in the least important for him to know or understand. He could see, therefore, that the firing had not apparently excited any surprise or interest in the guard at the gates; from which he judged that the whole matter had been carefully devised beforehand, and the attack made in numbers so overwhelming as must, in the opinion of the plotters, insure success beyond the possibility of question. And it had been so far successful; for midway the steep descent, between the summit and the hollow way, lay the horse of the courier, where it had fallen by the first shot, quite dead and motionless; while the man, having extricated himself from the carcase, which had fallen on him, sat by the road-side with his head leaning on his hand, grievously wounded. Of the two other servants, one was stretched beside the chariot-wheel motionless and lifeless, with the sword which he had just drawn grasped firmly in his cold right hand—his fellow leaning against the vehicle, and striving fruitlessly to stanch the blood which was welling from his side in torrents; two of the horses which had drawn the carriage had fallen, with their postillions, at the volley, and the rest, their traces having been cut at the first charge of the Lorrainers, were in the hands of the rude victors. Resistance, therefore, was completely at an end; for just as Wyvil cast his eyes upon the scene, he saw a tall and noble-looking man, who had sprung sword in hand from the carriage, and done some execution in the ranks of his opponents, mastered, disarmed, and bound by some of the ruffians; while others were engaged in ransacking the carriage, cutting loose the trunks which were fixed to it, and even tearing out the curtains of rich silk which bedecked its windows. The sight, however, which most inflamed the fiery blood of Wyvil, was a tall, elegant-looking girl, whom, by the splendor of her dress, he could discover, even at that distance, to be a personage of consequence and rank, struggling madly in the grasp of two or three of the licentious soldiers, who seemed disposed to treat her with indignity and insult.

"Now, my men," he exclaimed, as he drew his sword from the scabbard, "out with your carbines, and when I bid you halt, pour in your fire—every one pick his man, and see you throw not a shot away—then draw, and charge upon the gallop;" and with the word he dashed down the steep hill at the top of his horse's speed.

Down they came; down! all abreast, each with his carbine cocked, and pressed against his side. "Halt!" and the well-trained chargers stood motionless as marble statues, and the quick firelocks poured forth their streams of glancing fire, Wyvil accompanying the volley with a pistol-shot; and four of the marauders, who, taken somewhat by surprise, were mounting in hot haste, and mustering to meet the onset, fell, either killed outright, or wounded mortally; their startled horses plunging ungovernably through the field, and terribly increasing the confusion, as they yerked to and fro with their armed heels, snorting with rage and terror.

"Charge!" shouted Marmaduke, standing up in his stirrups, and hurling the long-barrelled pistol which he had just discharged full into the face of a subaltern officer, who was in the act of lunging at him with his rapier. "Charge! and strike home! down with the villains!" The ponderous weapon hurtled through the air, and full between the eyes, under the peak of his steel morion, smote the Lorrainer! For an instant he reeled blindly in his stirrups, then pitched headforemost to the earth, and lay there stunned, and to all appearance lifeless, while Wyvil's bay horse, forced by the keen spur of the rider, bounded across his prostrate body. One sweep from left to right of his long broadsword, and one of the stout men who held the lady staggered back with a deep gash in his brow, the blood streaming into his eyes, and leaving him blind for the moment and quite senseless. His men were close behind him, and for a little while it seemed that the bold exploit was successful; so greatly had the suddenness and vigor of the onset paralyzed and subdued the courage of the fierce marauders. But when they saw the small force of the party that had charged and half defeated them already, they rallied, and stood to their arms stubbornly; the fellows who had been engaged in rifling the baggage leaping down from the roof of the carriage sword in hand, and the troopers who were yet mounted bearing down in a body on their rash assailants. A pistol-shot at this critical time, while Marmaduke was cheering on his men to a fresh charge, took effect in his charger's breast, that he stumbled, sank on his knees, and despite all the efforts of the cavalier rolled over on his breast; at the same instant a heavy sword fell like a thunderbolt upon his hat, and cut through to the hair, but turning flatwise in the hand of him who wielded it, the blade inflicted no wound, though it had nearly beaten him to the earth. But all undaunted he sprang to his feet again, and repaid the blow by a straight thrust that staggered his antagonist, although his buff-coat saved him from a wound. Still it was evidently hopeless; and, though he fought on desperately, striking down trooper after trooper, and though his servants backed him as if they emulated his example, they were so thoroughly hemmed in, and overdone by odds, and all of them now wounded, that it was too apparent even to the young soldier that he had but a choice between death and surrender — when suddenly a clear, high voice, heard above all the din, like the blast of a silver trumpet, struck his ear with a note of joyous tidings.

" France! France! St. Dennis! Bellechassaigne for France!" and with that far-famed battle-cry the daring partisan drove into the melée, sheathed in impenetrable steel, his horse curveting and bounding, so that each downright blow fell with redoubled force, three of his men-at-arms cutting their way by dint of mighty prowess after him.

" Stand to it — stand to it, my men," he shouted, so that the enemy might hear him. " Stand to it, Wyvil, cheerily — help is at hand ; strike out, Seguin is close behind with thirteen hundred horse."

Already daunted by the fresh charge, the Lorrainers, the moment that they heard his words, betook themselves to flight, throwing away their arms, and leaving dead and wounded to the kind mercy of the victors. While, to augment their terror and confusion, Bellechassaigne ordered his men, who had been forced to charge with their carbines loaded for fear of injuring their friends in the melèe, to give their fire and pursue.

" Meantime," he called to Wyvil, " get these good people to horse straightway ; the lady must ride, too, for we shall be pursued ere we can right the carriage. I go to drive these dogs into the river, and terrify them so far as I can ;" and without further parley he drove his spurs into his war-horse, and in a minute was in advance of all his men, hewing down, riding over, and unmercifully trampling under foot the scattered and disorganized marauders.

Wyvil, who had been hurt in several places before the timely succor had arrived, and who was beginning to feel faint from the loss of blood, gazed round him with a slightly vacant air, as though he scarcely comprehended what was said to him ; but at that moment the aged officer whose rescue he had achieved so gallantly, came forward to address him, saying,

"Your friend is quite right, sir; we have no time for anything, not even for the thanks which you have won so nobly, for doubtless they will sally from the town forthwith. But, good God!" he continued, seeing the young man stagger and turning pale, "I fear you are hurt seriously!"

"No, no! not seriously," Marmaduke answered instantly; "but I am bleeding fast, and I must get these cuts bound up before I can sit on horseback—and so I fear must these poor fellows, who all of them are more or less hurt."

"Oh, if that be the worst, we will soon set all that in order. Here, Isabella," and he turned toward his daughter as he spoke, who stood all terrified and trembling in the midst of the carnage, scarce conscious if she were indeed preserved from outrage—"here, Isabella, see if you can not stanch the wounds of this young gentleman, who has so gallantly incurred them for your sake. Take my scarf, girl," he added, unbuckling his baldric of white taffeta, "and bind his left arm tightly—that is the worst cut, I suspect. Meanwhile, these worthy fellows must look to one another, while I essay to catch these frightened horses, and to prepare a pillion whereon you may ride until we can procure some suitable conveyance."

"We shall do well enough your honor," replied the man whom Wyvil had called Adam, and who was hurrying up, having a handkerchief bound tight about his temples, to assist his master; "we none of us be hurt so badly, but what we could ride fifty miles if it were needed."

"Well said, my hearty fellow," returned the officer in English, for hitherto the whole conversation had been carried on in the French language; "we are all English here I fancy, so we had just as well talk in our mother-tongue as in their cursed jargon, which is not fit for anything but their court-apes and popinjays. Come hither quick, the lady will attend your master better by half than you can. Catch yon gray charger by the rein that plunges there so wildly—he is the best of the lot, and belonged to that officer your master felled so neatly; and as that bay horse which he rode will carry him no more, he must be mounted as best may be for the moment. Cleverly done! soh! soh! now pick that pistol up and take its fellow from the dead horse's holster—they are old friends, I warrant them. So, now he is equipped and mounted. Now, what's thy name, good fellow?"

"Adam, Sir Henry—Adam Brandon," the man answered; "and I know your worship too, Sir Henry. I was not far from you at Edgehill; and I saw you—"

"Well, never mind that now," exclaimed the officer, "but lift up that poor fellow that lies there bleeding by the wheel," pointing to the servant who had been standing up, though sadly wounded, when Marmaduke arrived upon the field.

"Is he dead, Adam?"

"Ay is he, poor lad," answered the servitor, letting the body down; "ay is he, dead as a door-nail!"

"Poor fellow!" cried the other in a thick husky voice, while a tear twinkled in his eye; "poor Lauriston, to fall in such a paltry brawl, after so often—well, well, we 've no time for wailing; so Anthony, I'm glad to see thee safe," as the third postillion, who had escaped all but some trifling bruises, extricated himself from the fallen horses; "thou art the only one left whole, of six as faithful fellows—"

"No, no, Sir Henry," the lad interrupted; "old Mathew yonder," and he pointed to the courier, who was now limping down the hill, "has got off free I believe."

"Catch him a horse then, boy, and do as much for yourself; we must be stirring presently."

While he had been thus issuing his orders, attending to and talking of a dozen different matters, the veteran had arranged a sort of temporary pillion, by means of a cushion from the carriage, attached to the cartle and crupper of his demipique by two or three stout silken cords which had festooned the curtains of the vehicle; and now giving the bridle of his own led horse to Brandon, who was already holding the charger which he had accoutred with Marmaduke's own war-saddle and housings, he strode up to the spot where his fair child, kneeling among the dead and dying, by the side of her young preserver, was binding up his wounds with all the tenderness of a sweet gentlewoman, and almost all the skill of an accomplished surgeon.

That was a singular and striking picture—the evening sun pouring a flood of gorgeous light over the bright green foliage of the woodlands, and the yellow sand of the road, which was contrasted fearfully by the broad streaks and puddles of dark gore—the bodies of the men and horses who had fallen, all grim and gashed and gory, some dead already and fast growing cold, some struggling fruitlessly and groaning in their great agony, hopeless of any succor from the travellers whom they had but now so brutally assaulted—and in the midst of this wild, ghastly medley, the noble figure and superb attire of the young cavalier, as he sat on a little knoll by the wayside with that soft, lovely creature, so sedulously ministering to his need, for she was soft, indeed, and lovely. It was not only that the whole contour of her tall, finely-moulded person was exquisitely beautiful, combining all the slender, graceful symmetry of girlhood with voluptuous roundness of feminine maturity—it was not only that every feature of her speaking face was perfect in its classic outlines, that all the coloring was rich and delicate in its harmonious blending, but that there was an air of inborn nobleness and worth—an outflashing of intellect and soul from the full, spiritual eye—a music breathing from every dimple of the mouth—a character and mind that could not, by the most casual observer, be confounded with aught sensual or common or ignoble, pervading every varying expression of her lineaments, every small movement of her easy figure.

Yet, beautiful as Isabella Oswald was, her beauty was by no means of an English style—her hair, which was of an extraordinary length and volume, was perfectly jet black and glossy as the raven's wings, without one shade of gold or auburn mingled with their dark tints, and with the slightest tendency to wave or curl that can be fancied; and there was something oriental in the mode in which she wore it, a broad and massive braid plaited in many strands, sweeping down over either cheek and looped behind the small and beautifully-formed ears, that suited admirably with the expression of her features, and the rich sunny coloring—for she was a decided and even dark brunette—with a clear olive skin, through which the mantling blood showed like the ripe blush on the sunny side of a soft peach—black eyes, that flashed at times as if they had been fraught with liquid fire, and at times melted into that lovely languor that is so seldom seen except in climes far to the southward of her native land—and a mouth exquisitely arched, and tinged with the most burning crimson. It was on such a face, and such a form, that Marmaduke, faint from the loss of blood, and dizzy from the fierce excitement of the struggle in which he had been so severely handled, was gazing through his half-shut lids, scarce conscious of what had happened; when, all the arrangements made for their departure, Sir Henry drew near the couple.

"How fare you, sir—how fare you now?" he asked, in his hale, hearty tones.

"Well, I trust—well by this! or by the Lord that lives! we shall be taken yet."

While he was in the act of speaking, the stunning roar of a heavy cannon came crashing down the wind from the direction of the town, and instantly the clang of bells and the deep roll of drums, was blent with the alarum of the shrill bugles, calling the garrison to arms.

"There is no time to lose—no time! To horse, at once! to horse, and away speedily!" and catching his child by the arm, he swung her to the crupper of his war-horse, and sprang himself into the saddle with the agility of a young cavalier; while Marmaduke rose to his feet, somewhat unsteadily indeed, and rallying his disordered senses by a considerable effort, contrived by the assistance of his servants to mount his gray, which had been furnished with the equipments of his fallen charger. Once in the saddle he seemed to gain fresh vigor, and looking with a lively and quick air about him, he made some brief inquiries concerning what had passed during his faintness, and issued his commands with promptitude and spirit. His servants, who had already bound up each other's hurts as well as time and their scant means permitted, together with the courier and postillion—who alone, of Sir Henry's train, had escaped scatheless—were all on horse and ready, their fire-arms reloaded by Wyvil's order, to start upon their hasty route; and the word was just given to advance, when the hard clang of his furious gallop announced the partisan; and, closely followed by his men-at-arms, Bellechassaigne dashed up to the fugitives, all blood from plume to stirrup.

"Get on," he cried, even before he reached them; "get on, with no more tarrying. Put the hill-top between us and the town, and we shall do well yet; which, by the light of heaven, is more than I expected or even hoped for!"

At his words, fancying some urgent peril close at hand, the little party struck instantly into a hard trot, which rapidly increasing to a gallop, soon carried them beyond the summit of the slope, and far into the vale beyond it, before Bellechassaigne could so far overtake them as to make himself distinctly understood. But as they reached the bottom of the hollow, he shouted "Halt!" in his sonorous tones, so clearly that all instantly obeyed the order; and, as they did so, he came up laughing heartily, and in the highest spirits.

"Here is no need," he said, to blow your horses, or to pound that fair lady to a jelly, by riding thus over these hills like madmen. These coward dogs have made report that all Turenne's light horse are coming down on them; and as I chased them so far, that I cut down my last man on the *pont levis* as they raised it, and did not fall back till they began firing their ordnance, they have some reason to believe so. Trust me they will not send a party out, even to reconnoitre, for an hour to come; and as their march lies not in this direction, for they design to cross the Seine above Charenton, we have but to keep moving steadily, and my life on it we shall hear nothing more of them. So, gently, Wyvil, gently, my good friend! and as for you, my pretty lady, we will find a horse-litter or a coach of some kind, wherein you may journey softer than on that great Bucephalus, ere we have ridden half an hour."

And, reassured by his blunt speech, they rode deliberately on their way, but without losing time; and just as it was growing dark, they reached the hamlet where they had halted in the morning without the slightest interruption.

CHAPTER XVIII.

It was a small and scattered group of houses only, along the margin of a swift stream which turned the wheel of a little watermill, in the midst of which our party drew their horses up, just as the glorious summer moon began to show her silver orb above the tree-tops on the hill, although the richer hues of sunset were still alive among the cloudlets along the western verge of the horizon; yet small although it was and humble, it still afforded a neat comfortable inn, and more, a village-surgeon of skill sufficient to replace the rude extemporaneous dressings which had been applied to the hurts of the sufferers, by bandages and ligatures in order, and of sufficient confidence in his own skill to assure all his patients that within two or three days at the farthest they would be fit as ever for any martial exercise.

Meanwhile, Bellechassaigne, who had come off entirely unwounded, was all alert, and actively seeing the horses fed and properly rubbed down, and looking to the preparation of a vehicle, wherein the lady might accomplish the remainder of her journey more pleasantly than she could do on horseback. The last was not arranged without some difficulty; and, when arranged, the two-wheeled cariole, springless and rough, and built of coarse unpainted timber, presented a wide contrast to the luxurious well-appointed carriage in which she had set out from Coulomiers that morning. Nevertheless, by piling it with soldiers' cloaks, and other fleecy textures procured from the inn, it was at last made tolerably comfortable; and, when two strong fleet horses had been harnessed to it tandem fashion, to be driven from the saddle by Sir Henry's own postillion, it promised to unite the qualities of speed and safety in a higher degree than could have been expected from its appearance. These preparations finished, the partisan was summoned by a rosy-cheeked peasant maiden, to partake of the evening meal; and hastening into the single stone-floored apartment, which was at once parlor and kitchen to the rustic inn, he found the board spread with a clean, though somewhat coarse cloth, on which were laid four covers, a huge piece of fresh beef boiled almost to rags, a salad, and a loaf of black rye-bread; a pewter salt-cellar, a bowl of excellent butter, two or three flasks of ordinary wine, and several tall drinking-glasses, completing the apparatus of the humble meal, which found however no fastidious sharers in that moment of haste and half-apprehended danger.

But few words had been spoken, as may be well conceived, during the hot ride hitherward; but now there was a thousand questions to be asked and answered, that soon led to a quick and animated conversation, and—so true it is, that one short hour in circumstances of excitement and romantic situation, will produce greater intimacy than years of ordinary life—ere half an hour had passed, they were all talking unrestrainedly, as if they had been acquaintances of half a lifetime's standing.

"Well, be that as it may," exclaimed Sir Henry after the board was cleared and supper ended, in reply to some remarks of the young men deprecating any praises or expressions of high gratitude; "I can assure you that you have done me no small service, inasmuch as I happen to be aware of what you know probably nothing—that Monsieur de Lorraine, had I been so unlucky as to fall into his hands, would in all probability, though contrary to all the rules of honorable warfare, have held me as a hostage for the safety of some traitor lord or other, with whom his eminence of Mazarin has in contemplation to deal somewhat harshly. So that, had you not acted as you did, with generosity and skill and courage such as I have but seldom seen, the best I could have looked for would have been close imprisonment, and the worst, six paces and a file of musketoons, or it might be the block and headsman. And so, sir, as I have told your friend before," he continued, addressing Bellechassaigne, who had just risen from his seat at the table, "it is to you that I owe my life, and peradventure my child's honor."

"Now, by my faith," returned Bellechassaigne, laughing bluntly, "you are most grievously mistaken. For all that you owe me, is for striving strenuously to divert this hot-headed countryman of yours from riding down to help you; but it seems that he knew you were expected by his grace of York, and fancied, when he saw the housings on your charger, that it was you indeed whom the Lorrainers were attacking; or what, I believe, is the truth, he had some secret instinct that so beautiful a lady was in question as mademoiselle here; which, I entreat you to believe, Sir Henry, had I known likewise, I would have been beside him in his first onset. But, as it is, I do assure you, that you have nothing for which to be grateful to me; unless it be for doing all that with me lay to induce this fair youth, who sets so simply blushing to the roots of his hair, to ride off toward Corbeil, and leave you to your fate."

"If this be your modesty alone, fair sir," interrupted Isabella, "you carry it indeed to a great length, that you would lead us to believe base things of you, whom we have seen perform such feats of gallantry and daring. When Monsieur de Bellechassaigne wishes to be believed, in slandering himself, it must be before those who have not seen him in the field of honor, or profited by his undaunted valor!" She spoke with a slight degree of excitement in her tones, and her eyes sparkled as she did so with generous enthusiastic admiration; and at the same time a rich flush, when it flashed on her mind that she was speaking thus unguardedly to one almost a stranger, rushed like a torrent over her clear transparent brow.

"Upon my honor! upon the honor of a French gentleman and soldier," answered the partisan in an earnest tone, laying his hand upon his heart as he spoke, "dear lady, you do me at the same time too little and too much justice. Too little, when you doubt the truth of what I have just said; too much, when you ascribe the glory of this exploit in the least point to me. I do assure you, that I not only did my utmost to dissuade Wyvil from assisting you, but absolutely refused to join with him. It was his own deed altogether, and you will be disposed to laud it even more than you do at present, when I tell you, that in charging down that hill to your assistance he incurred many a danger of which you know nothing. Had he failed in his object, and had our party been cut off and taken, the day that had seen his release would have seen likewise his military execution for disobedience of orders. That is as certain as that the moon is shining now into your window—"

"How so? How so?" Sir Henry interrupted him. "Who is he, and what orders did he disobey? You called him, I think, but a while ago, my countryman; is not he, then, a Frenchman? Explain, I pray you. You, I know very well, Sieur Bellechassaigne; by reputation only though, for we have never, I think, met before this day; but who is your companion, to whom, by your account, we owe so much? I fancied him an officer in your horse regiment, and knowing you, believed him your subordinate."

"I am indeed your countryman, Sir Henry," returned the cavalier; "Marmaduke Wyvil, late captain in Sir Philip Musgrave's horse at Worcester field, now bearing the same rank in the most Christian monarch's service, but with a staff appointment under his royal highness, our duke of York!"

"By heaven!" exclaimed the old man, springing to his feet, and grasping the young officer's hand warmly; "by heaven! sir, right glad I am to hear it. I honor you, sir, for your loyalty. We must have fought together on the same side ere this, I fancy; that is, if you bore arms before the murder of the royal martyr. I thank you for your ready help; I thank you for your valor! Why, girl—why, Isabella; why sit you there so shy and silent? do not you hear? He is your countryman—one of the northern Wyvils; an officer of our good king; and, now I think of it, you were one of the fifty gallant spirits who held to the king to the last—ay, after the last too! Where is your tongue, girl, and your hand for your preserver?"

It would perhaps have puzzled Isabella Oswald, quick as she was of intellect, and bright at repartee, and used to the great world, had she been called on to explain why she could speak to Bellechassaigne, and thank *him* for his gallant aid, with eloquent tongue, and frank, unembarrassed manner, looking him in the face the while with bright, unblenching eye; and why, when she would have performed the same easy duty toward her own countryman, she should have been embarrassed and confused, and scarcely able to express herself in words at all. She did indeed rise from her seat, and all the rich color had vanished from her cheek, and her whole frame shook visibly as he raised her white fingers and pressed them to his lips; and as she faltered forth a few words of acknowledgment, she almost stammered in the effort; and then, as raising her deep liquid eyes she met the clear bright glance of Wyvil, seeming to read her very soul, she blushed—brow, cheeks, and neck and bosom—the deepest and most burning crimson; turned pale again as death upon the instant; staggered, and would have fallen, had not the young man started to his feet and caught her in his arms, when she was relieved, as it seemed, from fainting only by bursting into a violent and half-convulsive fit of tears and sobbing. Her father hastening up, Wyvil consigned her to his arms, saying as he did so—

"It is no wonder! the perils and excitement of the day have been too much for her. We will retire, and leave the servant-girl to aid you. I doubt not but a little rest will restore her."

"I trust it will be speedily," said Bellechassaigne, with an anxious brow, "for it is time even now that we should depart. We were detached to reconnoitre Monsieur de Lorraine's march, and I know that our report is looked for even now; besides, it is too probable that the enemy will send out their videttes to scour the country, and if so, you are far too near their quarters to be safe."

"Oh, I shall soon be better," answered the fair girl, mastering her confusion as she spoke. "It was a sudden faintness only that came over me. Fetch me, I pray you, Rosalie," and she turned to the serving-maid, "an ewer of fresh water; and by the time our horses are prepared, trust me, I will be ready."

"A noble girl," exclaimed Bellechassaigne, as the door of the kitchen closed behind them; "a noble girl, and well suited to be a soldier's bride. But, in the fiend's name, Wyvil, what did you to the girl to scare her wits away?"

"Faith, nothing I, Bellechassaigne," Marmaduke answered; "not for my life can I conceive what so much overcame her."

"Then, most assuredly," replied the Frenchman, "you are one of two things—either the least observant, or the most modest of mankind. By heaven! if I had such a fortune, I should not be so long in apprehending it, nor, despardieux! in profiting by it likewise. A pretty fellow you, to be so able a proficient in the art of warfare, to have defended indefensible positions, and carried keeps impregnable, and not to see that you have sapped, almost without an effort, the first defences of a fair lady's heart. Make you but two or three assaults in quick succession, and my life on it, when you call a parley, she will beat her charade straightway, and offer you a carte blanche in the bargain."

"Tush, tush!" said Wyvil, with a smile, that denoted how much the jest of his comrade had gratified his self-complacency, "the thing's impossible, Bellechassaigne; why, she has hardly heard me speak, scarce even knows my name."

"I crave your pardon, beau sire," the soldier answered mockingly; "I knew not heretofore that it was with men's names fair ladies fell in love; but you are doubtless a greater adept in these things than I. But, jesting apart, Wyvil, she is a most rare beauty—that deep, wild, languid eye—that superb hair—that figure so magnificently rounded. By my soul! I can scarce believe that she is one of your cold, half-animated countrywomen—this creature of ethereality and fire; she seems to me some passionate romantic madrilena, or houri of old Mahomet's Elysium—well worth the turning Mussulman to win, even beyond the grave. Are you not overhead in love with her already? you too, who have but to thrust out your hand and grasp her — "

" Nonsense," repeated Wyvil; " nonsense, Bellechassaigne. Our English ladies are not so easy, I assure you, to throw themselves into the arms of the first gentleman that does them a slight service."

" Slight service, by my soul! if you call it slight service to charge a score and a half of well armed-troopers, with four ordinary retainers, I should like to know what you call heavy! Slight service, by the lord! If I had done my duty, and ridden back to Corbeil, as I ought, with my intelligence, I trow you would have found the consequences anything but slight, let the service be what it might. As for the rest, I dare say she is a trifle prudish; most of your pretty islanders are so. But, what then? it were a poor game at which we should win ever, without check or hinderance. Now look you, if you mean not to push your conquest, just say so, and I'll fly my hawk at this fair quarry."

" Oh, fly it when you will, Bellechassaigne; I have no thought, I do assure you, of adventuring, though she is as you say very beautiful; and for that matter, if I had, would it avail me anything I fancy, so far at least as aught has yet occurred to aid me. But we had better make our men bring out our horses; we shall have sharp work yet to join the army before daybreak. I doubt not the fair Isabella has rallied her composure before this;" and almost as he spoke the words a servant followed them out from the inn toward the stable-yard, whither they had turned at the suggestion, and told them that the lady and Sir Harry were quite prepared to set forth on the route, so soon as all should be made ready.

" Sound them to horse!" Bellechassaigne cried. " To horse, to horse! it is nine by the night already; and we have leagues to ride ere daybreak."

The bugle instantly sent forth its long, clear summons, waking a thousand echoes through the still evening; and with its first note the ready soldiery came forth, leading their chargers orderly, and mounted and fell in; while Wyvil and Bellechassaigne aided the lady to ascend her rude conveyance, and then sprang to their saddles.

"Pardon me, gentle lady," said the Frenchman, bowing as he spoke till his tall plume was almost blended with the tresses of his charger's mane; "pardon me, that I use so rude a word as *must;* but we must travel fast to-night, as fast in fact, as our steeds will carry us. Sir Henry will accompany your carriage with his *chasseur*, while Captain Wyvil with his servants will scour the road in front, and clear all obstacles away; and I, with my four troopers, as the best armed, will follow you in the rear and cover you. Only remember this, and now I speak to you, good comrade mine, should you hear any noise or tumult in the rear, ride on as best you may, and bear our tidings to the maréchal; any attempt to aid me would destroy not only yourself alone, but the whole army—the whole *cause* indeed of the king! and so God speed ye, and set on!"

The eyes of Marmaduke turned half-reluctantly at the fair face of Isabella Oswald, lighted up as it was by the bright lustre of the summer moon, and caught a sidelong glance from hers, which were, however, instantly averted; and for a moment he appeared to hesitate, but before any one could comment on his seeming indecision, he too bowed low, and turning his horse's head down the road, led the way, followed by his servants at a swift, regular, hard gallop. All night they rode at a sharp, steady pace, pausing twice only to breathe their horses by some lone well-head or clear streamlet, hearing from time to time the rumbling sound of the rude calash which bore the lady, far behind them, but never halting so long as to suffer it to overtake them. They met no opposition on the route—in fact, no human being, whether friend or foe, crossed their path as they hurried onward—and, save a stray wolf from the neighboring forest of Senârs, no living creature, until, just as the moon was setting, a sentinel by the wayside levelled his arquebus, and called on them to stand and give the countersign.

"Turenne, Turenne!" cried Wyvil, and, dashing on, scarce

stopping to return the deep salute of the fautassin, entered the streets of Corbeil, and halted in the market-place, amid the earliest crowing of the awakened cocks.

Wild thoughts had flitted through the brain of Wyvil during that hurried ride ; wild, whirling, passionate fancies ! Hard would it be indeed to shadow forth the thick tumultuous images, which rushed in like an entering tide, and filled his whole mind for a space, and were in turn displaced by a fresh sweep of conflicting feelings, for it assuredly would have been beyond his power, himself to account for or explain them. The past, the present, and the future — gratitude, honor, love — sudden and almost overwhelming passion — ambition, avarice, and above all, the lust of power — were all at once fiercely striving in his bosom. The words of Bellechassaigne had, like the puissant spells of a magician, called forth a host of demons, that would not now be laid to rest by any effort of the mind which they tormented. A passionate admirer of all female loveliness, Wyvil had been much struck, at first sight, by the extreme beauty of Isabella Oswald ; and there was something in the romantic nature of the accident which had brought them acquainted ; in the close contact into which they had been thrown while she dressed the wound incurred for her sake ; in the mixture of sudden familiarity with conscious bashfulness ; that added much to the effect of her charms on the fancy of Marmaduke Wyvil — for it was, indeed, but his fancy that had been touched, and that very slightly, when, by the chance words of the partisan, a far more dangerous and subtle element of his disposition was started into action. Wyvil's besetting weakness — for in him, though it often led to good, oftener perhaps than to evil, it was a crying weakness — was vanity. The vanity of being first in all things ; vanity, not ambition ! though casual observers would designate it — though he himself would fain have palliated it to himself — have dignified it by the title of that far higher and more potent passion. It is true that it led often to the same results in Wyvil to which ambition would have led a man of sterner nature. But he had nothing of the Cato in his mood ; he never would have chosen the *esse, quam videri bonus;* his leading object, his first aim, was ever to shine prominent, to be the present wonder filling the mouths of men, to be *held* brave, or elegant, or fortunate, even though he himself knew the falsehood of the world's opinion.

This was, indeed, the one great flaw in Wyvil's character; and though it was associated with many a high and noble quality—though he had that fine sense of innate honor, that he would have spurned indignantly from his soul the mere suggestion of aught base or sordid—though he was brave, even to headlong rashness—though his heart was kind, and good, and full of noble impulses and holy aspirations—though his head was in other respects strong, clear, and capable of judgment—yet this one failing went far, like an alloy of copper with fine gold, to corrupt and debase, and render nugatory those admirable sterling qualities of which he was undoubtedly the master. And now, although he certainly loved Alice Selby with all the strength and truth of which his wild and somewhat vacillating character was capable—although he would have scorned and loathed himself, if he could at that time have even momentarily contemplated the desertion of her to whom he owed so much—although he would have spat upon the man who would have counselled him to do her any wrong—although, above all, he cared not even in his fancy, beyond the moment's passing admiration, for Isabella Oswald—Bellechassaigne's words had wrought upon that solitary weakness, and kindled it into quick action. A bright triumphant vision of winning that high beauty, for whom, as fame had bruited it abroad, already half the gallants of Paris were vainly sighing—of being signalized through the gay court of France as the conqueror of that impregnable and cruel heart—of being the possessor of the most brilliant bride in all that land of beauty—of riding as it were unchallenged, unresisted, and at a *coup de main*, into the stronghold of that cold and haughty maid's affections—flashed, vivid and impetuous as the lightning, across the mirror of his fancy.

True, it was instantly driven out, discarded, by a strong impulse of the better nature which was yet strong within him; true, it was with a sense of shame and self-reproach, that he became conscious on the instant that his heart had swerved for a second's space from its fealty to sweet Alice Selby; true, it was some time ere the finer feeling lost its power, ere memory, the memory of the calm, pure affections, of that fair gentle girl, of her heroic self-devotion, of her deep fervent feminine love, faded from his mind; but no less true, it *did* fade. It did fade, and the more dazzling charms of the superb court beauty, replaced the image of the country-maiden. Again indignant conscience rallied its forces, but it was only by a stronger effort than before, only by summoning his sense of gratitude, his sense of honor, to its aid, that his heart once again was won back to its allegiance. And so, throughout that long and hasty ride, his mind could be likened only to a confused and whirling battlefield, where the fierce hosts of the tumultuous and fiery passions were mustering fast and thick to the attack of principle and virtue; and when repulsed time after time, banding anew their scattered legions, and summoning, at each fresh charge, fresh and more foul allies to aid in their fell onslaught. Such conflicts are, alas! but of too frequent and familiar occurrence, to create anything of wonder, or even of much interest, in the mind of every-day observers; but it is from them only, that the keen judge of human nature derives his intimate acquaintance with the individual heart of man, with the general heart of the world; it is from a deep and continued study of them only, that we can learn the sage's hardest and last lesson: "the knowledge of ourselves."

The minds of all, the best of us no less than the worst, are subject to these rude assaults, these violent temptations; the minds of all, even the best, at times succumb to the assault; the minds of all, even the worst, at times resist their tempters. But it must be observed, that in the species of resistance there is a broad distinction; there is a steady, resolute, and organized resistance, the consequence of the exertion of thoughts influenced by principle; a resistance which, when it has repulsed the first attack of its insidious foes, though possibly it may carelessly relax from its first vigor, and so be liable to surprise, is nothing weakened in itself, but can at any moment rally and drive back its assailants, which, from their very nature, are more disorganized and scattered at every subsequent repulse, until they in the end become entirely weak, and frustrated, and powerless for evil. There is, again, a quick and fiery, though unstable and irresolute resistance, the child of a mind acting ever upon the impulse; which, though it may beat back the first onslaught of evil passions, nevertheless retains a recollection of the strife, receives as it were, an impression from the shock; and, when again attacked in the same weakened point of its position, though it again comes off victorious, is still so much enfeebled by its own irregular and impulsive opposition, that each succeeding victory but renders it the less unable to resist, but fires the daring of its enemy, until its whole defences sapped, the heart of its lines carried, it yields at last ignobly, and surrenders, as it were at discretion, to foes who, foiled often, have gathered strength and purpose, less from their innate qualities, than from the defects of the system that pretended to confront them. Such, during all that night, had been the state of Wyvil's mind, harassed and agitated by a continual occurrence of thoughts and half-formed wishes, which, while he felt them to be evil, and exerted himself from time to time to beat them back and banish them, he yet lacked the steady energy of will to repress utterly, and crush, as it were, in the bud.

The consequence of this with him, as it must naturally be in every case, was that the mind became habituated by constant repetition, to suggestions from which at first it shrunk abhorrent; and that, although he would not have admitted it, he became half familiarized with the idea of forsaking Alice Selby, even before he had in reality at all contemplated doing so. He was in some sort then bewildered still and confused of mind, when he halted his party, a little while before daybreak, in the market-place, ignorant what to do, or whither to direct his course, until Bellechassaigne should come up, for he had never been in Corbeil before, except to pass through it at a trot on his outward march the previous morning. He had not been there, however, many minutes, before he found himself surrounded by a dozen or more privates and non-commissioned officers belonging to a troop of royal horse, which had been quartered there some time, in order to command the passage of the Seine, and insure the advance or retreat of the king's army. From these he had already learned that good accommodations could be obtained at an inn in the *Rue Royale*, known as the *Lion d'Or*, when the rude vehicle came up creaking and groaning over the rugged pavement, escorted by the daring partisan and his bold troopers; so that as soon as they came into sight, he merely waved his hand to them to follow, and led the way to the great gates of the inn-yard, where he was standing when they overtook him, thundering with his dagger's hilt upon the oaken portals, though seemingly with no effect, except to wake a thousand echoes through the deserted streets, and to excite the furious baying of one or two gaunt half-starved mastiffs, which were chained within the courtyard. On the arrival of Bellechassaigne, however, all this was speedily corrected, for at his order, the bugler of his party set up so loud and long a call of his shrill instrument, that half a dozen casements were speedily thrown open in as many different houses, and sundry male and female heads, clad in strange night-gear, suddenly protruded to learn the cause of the disturbance. A moment afterward, a shuffling step was heard within the gates, and after reconnoitering the company for half a minute through the *grille*, despite the oaths and objurgations of the angry soldier, the slipshod hostler unbarred the leaves, yawning and rubbing his half-open eyes, and ushered them into the bass-court of what had been at some time, before it was degraded into a house of public entertainment, the mansion of some rich proprietor. Here they were met by the portly landlord, profuse, though scarce awake, of promises of entertainment and apologies for their detention; and here, having assured their fair charge that she was in absolute security, Corbeil being in possession of a strong royal garrison, the young men took their leave, amid the unfeigned thanks and warm acknowledgments, no less of Sir Henry than of the lady.

"Rest sure, Sir Henry Oswald," were the last words of Bellechassaigne, "that you will advance yourself nothing by moving any farther on this route, even when the day breaks. The army, I am certain, is on the route already hitherward; and as the tidings which I carry will only expedite their progress, you may depend on seeing the maréchal *here* before the day is six hours older. If then you will be ruled by my poor counsel, you will remain here till the post comes up, and obtain such repose as the fatigues and apprehensions of this fair lady must render indispensable."

"I will, sir," cried Sir Henry, "I will, and that right willingly. And now I will not bid you tarry, as knowing that the first duty of a soldier is the prompt execution of his orders; and trust me, you shall lose nothing with Monsieur Turenne for your service; and now farewell for a short space, seeing we shall soon meet again." And then, their parting salutation made on both sides, the cavaliers rode off as hard as they could gallop, Bellechassaigne calling out to Wyvil with a light laugh—

"Despardieux! but I am not half so certain as the good English chevalier, that our service shall seem so good to the maréchal as he deems it. Seeing that it was his aim to surprise the duke of Lorraine, it may well be, that he will scarce thank us for beating up his quarters, and telling him, as plain as we could speak, that all the army, which I'll be sworn he fancied at Etampes, was on this side of the Seine. I should not be surprised, for my part, if we were both ordered into arrest directly; and, if it take that turn, our lives will depend on the good or bad generalship of the Lorrainers!"

"I see not that, however," answered the Englishman, spurring his horse sharply as he spoke, to keep up with his volatile companion; "what the devil has the duke's generalship to do with it?"

"You are less apprehensive than your wont, then," replied the partisan. "See you here—you know well that Condé has been building, these two weeks, a bridge of boats a little above Charenton, whereby Henry of Lorraine may pass the Seine and join the army of the princes. Now, seeing that the duke heard of our onslaught last night before sunset, and must be sure from that of Turenne's movement to cut him off from Paris, if he has acted with the smallest judgment, he is before this time at Charenton: and before we have crossed the river, here at Corbeil to the eastward, will have made good his passage to the westward, and broken up his bridge and joined the princes at his leisure. That, as you know, will utterly foil all our plans for the campaign; will leave us in the face of a superior force; will probably completely ruin the king's cause; and, what concerns us most of all, will be the consequence of our misconduct, and will afford a very pretty pretext for treating each of us to a file of musqueteers and a volley at twelve paces. So now you begin, I suppose, to apprehend how far it concerns us whether the duke of Lorraine be a good general or a bad one!"

"You take it coolly enough, notwithstanding," exclaimed Wyvil, not altogether liking his companion's mode of putting the case.

"Of course I do," answered the other, laughing; "why should I not, pray? You would think it very odd, if I were *not* cool in contemplating the result of a volley from five or six hundred Spaniards, or Lorrainers; and I have yet to learn that a score or two of Spanish bullets do less harm than a dozen French ones. Tush! man, our business is to die when we are wanted, and what odds does it make whether it comes by a platoon in battle, or by a file in execution? There is this in it, notwithstanding, that the faster we ride the less the chance of being shot by Frenchmen, and the more by the Lorrainers. So if you, as you seem to do, prefer these last so much, you were best spur that gray brute somewhat sharply. Don't let him tumble on his head, though," he continued, as the horse, urged beyond his speed, made a bad stumble on the rutty road—"well saved! well saved! You English do ride well, that must be granted—and lo! here is the Seine and the bridge, and there comes the sun above the tree-tops. Hark! hark! by heaven! there go the trumpets; and see—see there, how the dust surges up beyond the hill—we shall soon leave the worst of it!" and galloping violently on, they soon encountered the advanced horse of the royal army, and in less than an hour were busily employed in threading their way through the dense columns of the centre, now in full march upon Corbeil, in search of their renowned commander.

CHAPTER XIX.

A COMFORTABLE chamber, supplied profusely with all the luxuries and appliances which an *auberge* of that day, and in that country, could be expected to supply, the chief of which was a convenient and well-curtained bed, soon brought forgetfulness of her terrors and fatigues to Isabella Oswold; yet, ere she sunk into absolute sleep, she could not but think much and deeply on the occurrences of the past day—of the great perils she had seen—of the enthusiastic, daring valor of her young countryman, exerted, almost in despite of hope, for her protection. Nor is it strange she should have thought of it deeply; for at all times, and in all countries, there is perhaps no quality of man which strikes at first so strongly the imagination of the weaker sex, as gallant and fiery courage. At that day, too, when the sword was the surest—almost indeed the *only* instrument whereby to clear the path of honor; when the spirit of chivalry was yet alive and burning in every noble breast of man or woman, a high and perilous emprize was sure to win the admiration and regard of all for the successful gallant. To this, in Isabella's case, was added a romantic sense of gratitude—a feeling that this bold deed had been wrought for her sake alone, and that, as the existing cause of a chivalric exploit, she, too, must be a sharer in the glories of the actor.

It must not be forgotten, either, that Wyvil, both in form and feature, might be esteemed a model of masculine and vigorous beauty; that his attire was rich and splendid, and bore sure witness to the exquisite taste of the wearer; that his air and demeanor were unusually high and noble — easy, at the same time, and dignified — graceful and polished as the bearing of the most courtly Frenchman, yet tinctured with a strain of frankness, and largely fraught with a sort of proud humility that she had never observed in any of her lighter and more volative adorers. What wonder, then, that she should ponder long and thoughtfully before she sank to rest, and that the thought of her defender should have been blended, after her eyes were closed in slumber, with the disturbed and whirling visions which, rising naturally from the occurrence of the past day, floated a wild phantasmagoria through her brain.

Isabella Oswald was not, indeed a girl of ordinary qualities, or every-day character; but, born with the perilous dower of uncommon genius, coupled, as it almost invariably is, with a quick, sensitive temperament, with powerful affections and strong passions, she had, unfortunately for herself, been educated so — if that can be called education, which in no respect ever aimed at correcting the defects of nature — as to exaggerate rather than diminish the extravagances of her native character. Her mother, a Spanish lady of great wealth and the highest rank, whom Sir Henry had married at the time when an alliance with the infanta had been contemplated by the unhappy prince who had since expiated his faults and follies on the scaffold, died in her daughter's early childhood; and from that period, the young Isabella had scarce a guide beyond her own wild inclinations. Her father, who in his youth had been one of the chosen councillors and courtiers of the First Charles, with a prescience of events which it had been well for his hapless master to possess, leaned only to the moderate councils of Hyde and Falleland, and those wiser spirits, whose prudence, had it been listened to by the misguided monarch, would have spared England years of bloodshed; and soon foreseeing that the neglect of these would lead to fatal consequences, had remitted the whole fortune of his lost bride, and not that only, but the price of all such portions of his own patrimony as he could alienate, to France, where he concluded a safe asylum would at any time be open to the servants of the crown. It so fell out, however, that long before he contemplated any instant peril, he was qualified by circumstances to judge of the wisdom of the measures; for, whereas he had looked forward to exile, as to the consequence of adhering to the fortunes of his royal master in opposition to the rebellious and fanatical will of the people, he was doomed to experience, first, coldness and neglect, then persecution—from which he was but too happy to escape by flight—at the hands of that very king whom he was ready to support through right and wrong with undiscriminating loyalty. Restless and active in both mind and body, he had scarce entered France before he plunged deeply into the intrigues which were harassing the vitals of that kingdom; and adopting the court party, from the natural bias of his mind, had risen speedily to eminence; had distinguished himself greatly, both in the council and in the field; had been advanced to a high station in the army, and occupied a situation as prominent as could be held by any foreigner in the great nation. This, and the circumstances, no less than the character of the man, his want of domestic ties or attractions, his fury and headlong appetite for all and every kind of wild excitement, his constant absence from home, in the field or at the court, contributed to deprive his child of the advantages of any solid supervision or home-government; living as it were alone, and mistress, when she was yet but a child, of her father's grand hotel in the fauxbourgs, with carriages and horses and attendants at her command, and the old governante who nominally ruled her, in truth the most obsequious of her servants—it was not wonderful that Isabella Oswald should have grown up a wild, untamed, high-spirited girl, with no guide for her actions but her own eager impulses and active sensibilities, with little powers of self-government, and still less mental discipline; but it was somewhat to be admired that she did not become a more wilful and capricious beauty, reckless and violent and headstrong, the slave of her own passions, and the tormenter of all who should be thrown into the sphere of her attractions. From this her natural genius, and a certain resolute strength of mind, which she inherited from her mother, had happily preserved her.

An eager, passionate ambition, which was, perhaps, not the least striking feature of her mind, coupled to an insatiable thirst of knowledge, had saved her from frivolity; and, while she would not hear the least dictation in matters that related to demeanor, to all the masters from whom she could derive instruction she yielded an implicit and unquestioning obedience, that in itself assured advancement and success. Thus, at an early age she had not only mastered all the accomplishments which were esteemed in that day requisite to ladies, but many which were rare even among men, except those who were destined to the learned professions. An enthusiastic and complete musician, a dancer second to none in that land which then, as now, was the great theatre and school of that gay science; she was, moreover, a linguist of no mean capacity, speaking and writing the French, and Spanish, and Italian tongues, as fluently as her own native English. Nor was this all; for she had dipped somewhat deeply into the wells of ancient lore, so that she was far better qualified than most men of that day to converse with the great and learned on high and interesting topics.

This course of reading, it is true, had strengthened the powers of a mind naturally strong—had filled the storehouses of her brain with manifold and valuable knowledge—had perfected her taste, matured her judgment, and developed all her natural gifts in an unusual degree. But in effecting this, it had produced other and far less favorable consequences; if it had strengthened the powers of her mind, it had also in no less degree strengthened her confidence in them; if it had perfected her tastes, it had increased her desire of consulting them alone; if it had amplified her judgment, so it had led her to respect no opinions that tallied not with her own sense of what was right and proper. It had, in short, contributed to foster in no small degree the independence of a spirit already perhaps too independent; so that even in her fifteenth year, Isabella Oswald, with more than all a woman's talents and accomplishments, possessed a degree of energy and decision that was sure to make her a singular and distinguished, though it was highly questionable whether it was like to make her a happy or contented woman. It seemed, indeed, that there was something not far removed from a direct destiny—if such a thing could be—in the events which had formed the character of the young beauty; for just at that critical age when she was budding into womanhood, and when from her increasing years she was becoming a companion to her father—who, had he fallen into more domestic habits, as he was indeed gradually doing, would not have failed to notice, or noticing to counteract, the undue tendency of her young mind to form decided judgments, to act upon the impulse of the moment, to consult its own opinions only, and to do many things which could not be deemed other than unfemininely and unduly independent; just at that critical period, the war broke out in England between the king and his parliament; and true to his chivalric sense of loyalty, Sir Henry overlooked the many wrongs done to him by the man, in sympathy with the misfortunes of the sovereign; left his asylum, took up arms for the crown, and trusting his child to the doubtful guardianship of an old marquise of the *vielle noblesse* — who, to complete the mischief, was something of an *esprit fort* herself — fought to the very last, even to Astley's fatal overthrow at Stow-on-the-Wold, with a determined valor that, had the cause for which he bled succeeded, would have placed him among the first men of the nation.

As it was, he who had been at the first banished by the king, was now proscribed by the parliament; and once again escaping to his old asylum, found the daughter whom he had left a bright, precocious child, grown up into a dazzling woman, captivating all around her by her rare gifts and striking qualities; but formed completely and matured in character, already almost beyond the possibility of changing, whether for good or evil.

Such had been the early history, and such were the habits, of the beautiful girl for whom Wyvil had, unhappily for all parties, performed the brilliant and successful exploit, which had at once so powerfully wrought upon a fancy, the natural tendency of which was strongly sensible to anything romantic or poetical, that it had paved the way for warmer and more passionate sentiments, should any circumstance occur in future to call them into action. That she was deeply interested in the handsome young cavalier, who had so daringly encountered peril in her cause, can not be doubted; and as she fell asleep on that eventful morning, it is quite certain that the last tangible thought of her mind was upon Marmaduke. Quite overcome by exertion and fatigue and terror, she slept long and soundly; and although many a strange and startling noise rose from the street below her window, and that too before she had been long asleep — though squadron after squadron of the king's cavalry passed at a rapid trot, clanging and clattering with their iron harness over the rough stone pavements — though the loud shouts of the people, awed into loyalty by their imposing numbers, greeted the royal troops with stunning acclamations, and were responded to by kettledrum and trumpet — though a field battery of ponderous guns, with their caissons and tumbrils, groaned, creaked, and lumbered through the street; she did not stir from her heavy sleep until the sun was already high in heaven, and all the vanguard of the army had well nigh reached the village where she had supped on the preceding evening.

Just as she awoke, however, and had so far collected her ideas as to be aware where she was, a prolonged flourish from a distant band of music called her attention; and conjecturing at once that the sound must announce the army of Turenne, she dressed herself in haste, and hurried to the window, just as a column of arquebusiers, marching extremely fast, shoulder to shoulder, in the closest order, began to fill the street from side to side. In a few minutes these had passed, and were succeeded by six fine Scotch and Irish regiments, under the royal standard of King Charles of England, clad in the uniform, and officered by cavaliers of their own country — Monsieur de

Navailles, whom Isabella well knew, followed with a detachment of the French horseguards, whose trumpets she had heard from a distance ; and then, surrounded each by his proper staff, and many a mounted officer besides, the Marechals Turenne and D'Hocquincourt rode by, in deep and earnest conversation. But it was not to these great men, nor to the gallants who swept by, glittering in gorgeous arms and fluttering with scarfs and favors — though many of them were acquaintances, nay, friends and suitors — that the eyes of the fair Isabella were directed ; though with an earnest and inquiring glance she ran her eyes over the splendid concourse, as if in search of something which she found not. After the leaders of the army had passed out of sight, there was a little break, as it were, or interval in the line of march ; and then a squadron of well-mounted cavaliers, led by a tall and noble-looking man, whom she recognised as the earl of Bristol, came up at a hand-gallop, as if endeavoring to make up the ground which they had lost. While these were yet beneath her windows, the drums and fifes of another Irish regiment, playing one of their wild, heart-stirring melodies, swept cheerily down the wind ; and, almost keeping up with the gallop of the English horse, the splendid files of the duke of York's own regiment came dashing through the dust, trailing their pikes, at the long swinging trot peculiar to the natives of green Erin. What was there in the sight of that wild regiment, that so excited the bright girl who gazed upon them ? Her color came and went, her heart beat almost audibly, her small hands trembled so that they scarcely could support her, as she leaned far out the casement to survey them. They did afford, indeed, a gay and spirit-stirring sight, those loyal islanders ! The lithe and stalwart limbs, bearing them, free as the deer on their own pathless mountains, at a pace no less different from the trained march of the more drilled mercenary, than is the gallop of the desert steed from the procession-amble of my lady's palfrey — the merry hawklike glance of their blue laughing eyes — the hair that floated in loose tresses on the wind — the reckless jest, the soul-fraught merriment which rang in every tone, which breathed from every feature — the wild, clear shout of *faugh a ballah*, which every now and then rose shrilly from the heads of the column, as they pressed on the track of the cavalry — combining to make up and picture the very opposite in all respects of the stiff, rigid martialists of that age of stern and iron discipline. It was not this, however, that stirred the heart of Isabella, with a strange sense, she knew not what, of mingled hope and apprehension. She had not failed to note, in the few words that Bellechassaigne let fall, that there was some reason for dreading evil consequences from the slight breach of orders — slight in her opinion, and venial, if not praiseworthy — of which both had been guilty in attacking the Lorrainers; and having heard from Marmaduke's own lips, than he held an appointment on the staff of the English duke, her whole soul was in terrible suspense to see if he was in his place beside his princely master.

The last rank of the royal Irish passed; and immediately behind them, mounted upon a Polish carriage-horse, dun-colored, with a long white mane and tail, a young man, richly dressed in a suit of dark-brown velvet, cut in the fashion which has derived its modern name from the great Flemish painter, with russet leather buskins and a superb cravat of Valenciennes lace, cantered lightly on. He wore no armor, not even weapons, except an ordinary rapier hanging from an embroidered scarf; but in his hand he held a leading staff, or truncheon, and round his neck he bore a glittering chain with the effigy of St. George, and on the left breast of his mantle, the diamond star of the Garter. He was above the middle height, graceful and slender in his person; and he rode easily and well, with a firm seat and a delicate light hand — but although very young at that time, the darkness of his complexion, his heavy eyebrows, and the hard, deeply-cut hues of his rigid and inflexible lineaments, caused him to appear many years advanced beyond his real age; an impression which was in no degree diminished by the harsh periwig of coarse black hair, which he wore under his low-crowned feathered hat, falling quite down upon his shoulders. Yet, though he was decidedly ill-favored and harsh-featured, no person at that time could have failed to see that he was a man of consequence, and character to match his dignity—there was a quickness in his clear, dark eye, that spoke intelligence, and spirit, and high-daring; there was a firm and resolute curve in the muscles of the close-set mouth, that promised an unblenching steadiness of purpose. Such was the duke of York, as he was in the days of adversity, the steady and right counsellor of his more vacillating brother. Such was the duke of York, when he fought side by side with Turenne—such, when he gave the promise, afterward well-fulfilled by skill, and conduct, and unquestioned valor, displayed as lord high admiral against De Ruyter and the Dutch: ere power and priestcraft had debased his every quality of mind—until the conqueror of Opdam sank into the weak driveller and coward of the Boyne.

A pace or two behind the duke, but still so near that they could easily converse with him, were three or four English gentlemen, among whom Isabella recognised the earl of Berkely and Colonel Worden, his gentlemen of the bed-chamber; but there was not one in his suite whose post or air in anywise resembled the gallant Wyvil: two or three grooms and equerries followed, one leading the duke's battle-horse, and the others bearing, dispersed among their number, the various pieces of his armor. The fair girl's heart sank as they vanished from her sight, and were succeeded by the rear-guard of the army, composed of the regiments of Picardy, Richelieu, Uxelles, Carignan, Burgundy, and a strong detachment of the French guard, closing the long line of the march. Heart-sick and faint, she drooped into a seat, and letting fall her head upon the window-sill, buried it in her hands in sad and anxious meditation, until, after a long and silent pause, the groaning crash of heavy wagons again excited her attention. It was the baggage of the host of artillery carts, and huge wains, piled up with chests of arms and clothing, and mules laden with tents, and foragers, and sutlers, and abandoned women, and all the base and worthless rabble that ever follow in the train of camps and armies. A dozen light pieces of artillery, and a small body of musketeers, accompanied, or rather brought up, the rear of this disorderly multitude, and she began to reassure herself in the idea, that now indeed *all* had passed by, and that to the country—as was in fact quite true—had proceeded the main body of the troops. As soon as this idea took hold of her mind, her sanguine, fearless temperament, caused her at once to assume it for a truth, and having, scarcely a minute before, been quite depressed by the imagination that her deliverers were suffering disgrace and perhaps danger, she now amused her mind with many a gay, visonary dream how they might have been promoted for their gallantry, and sent on with the foremost, filling the perilous post of honor.

Already satisfied, and for the moment happy, she had turned to the mirror which graced the antique toilette-table, and was arranging her magnificent tresses, humming a gay provençal ballad as she did so, when she was once more summoned from her employment to the window by the trampling of horses. She turned, it is true, to look at what was passing, but it was with a listless air of unconcern, that was as different as possible from the excited, restless agitation with which she had watched every separate company as it swept onward, before she hit upon the thought which now possessed her. A single glance, however, sufficed to change her air of unconcern for one of the deepest and most agonizing interest. Every drop of blood rushed back from her cheeks, and left her pale as ashes; she clasped her hands, and wrung them bitterly, and one faint shriek burst from her lips, and even reached the ears of those whose situation caused it. The horsemen whose march had attracted her, were a small party, fully armed, and led by an officer, who rode at a foot's pace, with his sword drawn, at their head; six troopers, three and three, came after him, all with their carbines ready, the butts resting on their thighs, and their matches lighted; two more with drawn swords followed, and between them—his horse's reins linked to the bits of their chargers, and the sheath of his rapier empty—Marmaduke Wyvil! Six troopers more succeeded, like the first, with their matchlocks in their hands; and then, guarded like Wyvil by two soldiers, but with a gay and scornful smile on his dark features, the brave Bellechassaigne! A dozen dragoons more, and another sabaltern, completed the sad escort. The face of Marmaduke was perfectly composed and calm, though somewhat paler than its wont; until the shriek of Isabella falling upon his ear, he raised his eyes and met the wild and careworn glance, and noted the strange paleness that had supplanted her rich warm complexion—then a quick burning flush covered his face with crimson, as answering her passionate look of inquiry with a deep-meaning glance, and a bright, half-triumphant smile, he doffed his plumed hat and bowed low, laying his hand upon his heart as he did so. Bellechassaigne caught likewise the faint accents of the lady's cry, and he, too, smiled and bowed; but there was nothing but high daring, mixed with a touch of scorn in the expression of his face; and as he bowed he raised his voice, and called aloud:

"Fear not, dear lady—fear not at all for us; this is a matter of mere form—believe me, we are in no danger!" She heard, it is true, what he said, and waved her hands mechanically in reply, but her mind scarcely comprehended the sense of the words; and even if it had done so, the grave voluntary shake of the head with which the officer, who had them in charge, received the speech, would have entirely counteracted their effect. She watched them for a moment or two, and observed that they took not the route of the army, but turned off toward the castle, which she had seen on the right-hand as she drove into the town that morning; and then, as they passed round the corner of the street, rushed out into the antechamber, calling, in tones that were almost a shriek, upon her father.

CHAPTER XX.

It was about two hours after sunrise, when the last files of the royal army extricated themselves from the streets of Corbeil; and although some difficulty and delay occurred in consequence of the narrowness of the bridge and ways through which the army had been forced to defile, yet so ably was the advance conducted, that no breaks were made in the line of march, but the communication between the van and rear was maintained uninterrupted. As the troops cleared the suburbs, their order was changed in regular succession, the fronts of the several columns being increased to the full width of the broad highway, and their depth in the same degree diminished; the cavalry of the advanced guard was held well in hand, and the open woodlands on either side of the causeway occupied by strong bodies of light troops, sweeping the country a league's breadth, and keeping somewhat in advance of the main army.

It was a beautiful gay sight—the long files winding rapidly along, now seen, now lost among the leafy screens of the dense forest—the many-colored pennons of the cavalry glittering through the tree-tops, and their bright armor flashing out in many a line of dazzling lustre. Rapidly they advanced throughout the whole of that fine summer's morning, so that just as the sun had reached the meridian, the heads of the advanced column, mounting above Villeneuve St. George, came into sight of the enemy, posted in force upon the elevated ground between that town and Charenton, with a small battery of heavy guns planted on the steep knoll commanding the streets of the town, and enfilading the bridge across the Hyère, which lay at its base; at the same moment the two marshals, each with his staff, galloped across the summit to reconnoitre the position of Lorraine. It took but little, for a general of Turenne's unequalled skill, to form his plan and act upon it. One brief glance showed him that to attempt the passage of the river, which was unfordable, and only to be traversed by a long, narrow bridge of stone, commanded by the cannon on the hill, and defended by a strong *tête de pont*, would be a mere loss of valuable time, and only to be effected by a vast sacrifice of life; while it would have left it in the power of the duke, by leaving a small part of his infantry, to defend the town and dispute the bridge, until such time as he could fall back with all his horse, composing the main force of his army, to Charenton, and then crossing his bridge of boats, effect his junction with the princes. This, in effect, would have frustrated all his views; and it is certain, that for the time, the royal army was in a situation full of difficulty if not danger, from which it was extricated only by the splendid genius of its commander. Turenne, knowing the country well, and being aware that at the distance of some three or four miles toward Brie the Hyère was fordable in many places, determined instantly to march along its banks to the eastward, and passing it as soon as possible, to turn the enemy's position in the direction of Grosbois, and force him to a general action. In order to do this, it was, however, necessary to alter the whole order of his march; his cavalry, which had up to this time composed the van, being now wanted in the rear; which it would be in the power of the duke to attack, while countermarching, by throwing his light troops across the Hyère.

This change was rapidly and splendidly effected. The forest of Senârs, which covered a great portion of the country between Villeneuve and Corbeil, broke off entirely midway the slope, which has so many times been mentioned, and left the foot of the declivity and all the banks of the little river quite open and free from incumbrance to the left hand; although toward the right, the woodlands stretched in an uninterrupted range quite down to the angle, formed two or three miles off by the junction of the Hyère with the broad Seine. A narrow road, the same by which Sir Henry and his daughter were travelling when attacked on the preceding day, came into the highway at a little hollow some hundred yards above the meadows, into which it descended shortly, skirting along the edge of the great forest; and by this narrow defile it was now necessary for the whole host to pass.

The cavalry, under D'Hocquincourt, was moved down by the main causeway to the meadows, and there deploying, formed front toward the bridge in a transverse line from the Hyère to the edge of the forest, facing northwesterly; and half a battery of field-pieces were planted on the road, so as to sweep the bridge in case of any sally. This done, the infantry filed, corps by corps, through the narrow lane, until they had all gained the level ground to the eastward of the cavalry; and then they fell into solid columns, filling the whole space from the edge of the road by which the guns were moving, down by the margin of the stream. Until the whole of this intricate manœuvre was accomplished, Turenne sat quietly upon his horse, with all his staff about him, watching the enemy's position with jealous scrutiny, and sending now and then an officer to expedite the movements of the various regiments. Once only did he quit his station after the royal regiment of Irish had passed him, cheering as they did so, when he rode down a little way from the hillock which he had occupied to meet the duke of York, whom he requested to halt for the present, and remain near his person; nor had this happened long before the last of the infantry had formed on the low grounds, and all the cannon were in full march by the road immediately above them; when Turenne—having despatched one aid-de-camp to D'Hocquincourt, with orders to draw off the cavalry, and form them in the rear, and sent another to the van to set the troops in motion—cantered down from his stand, and wheeled into the lane, by which he could communicate at his ease with any portion of the column. Just as he turned the corner from the causeway, the quick eye of the great commander fell on the broken carriage of Sir Henry Oswald; which, all stripped and dismantled, had been dragged into the low brushwood on the roadside by the pioneers of the vanguard. About it lay the bodies of seven or eight horses, their housings and rich harness plundered; and not less than a score of human corpses, entirely naked, as they had been left by those human harpies, the foragers of their own party, and showing by the terrific wounds which seamed their ghastly limbs, the prowess of their daring conquerors. Turenne pointed toward the hideous pile, as he rode by with his leading staff, and turned to the duke —

"This proves," he said, "the perfect truth of Bellechassaigne's relation; and, by my word! although in contradiction of all military order, as gallant an onslaught as ever was made yet by four men upon forty. Tête Dieu! each man of the assailants, not to exclude Bellechassaigne's troopers, must have killed three men with his own hand!"

"And this, I trust," replied the duke, "will prove a good defence to them, especially now that their indiscretion has had no evil consequences."

"No, no! your highness," answered the general, laughing; "that last were a poor reason. They must not get off quite so lightly. Had that been possible, I would not have refused so slight a matter to your gracious intercession. Consider, this was a very grave offence — directly contrary to orders — and actually imperilling the whole army, the whole cause of the king. Besides, our cavaliers, all independent as they are, and serving with their own men for loyalty and honor, with neither pay nor profit, are ever insubordinate, and readier to consult their own rash fancies than to obey commands, especially of such as suit not their headlong and absurd caprices. No, no! this was too flagrant, and we want an example."

"Surely — oh, surely," the duke interposed again, with an expression of strong interest displayed in his harsh features, and his voice actually quivering from the agitation of his mind, "you do not think of a military execution? Two such fine gallant youths; it were too horrible!"

"Not I," replied Turenne, quite quietly; "not I, indeed! Good officers are not so plenty on his majesty's side now-a-days, that I can afford to shoot them. As for Bellechassaigne, too, we can not spare him possibly; he is the life and soul of the whole army — half the most desperate things that are done he does himself, and all the rest by proxy, driving all our young fellows half mad with rivalry and hot ambition. No, no! we can't spare Bellechassaigne; and as to this young English fellow, by the Lord! I believe he is the madder of the two. Fancy a charge, in a velvet hat and coat, with four unarmed retainers, upon two score or better of well-appointed troopers. I half believe I *should* have shot Bellechassaigne, if he had obeyed his orders and left him to his fate, as he should have done. What does your highness know of this young devil with the unpronounceable name? Has he ever been such a dare-devil?"

"I have heard say," answered the duke, "that in the long civil war, though he was then very young, scarcely indeed more than a boy, he was the shrewdest and most daring of all Goring's officers; and in this last unfortunate affair, he was undoubtedly among the best of all my brother's partisan commanders. In fact, it is to him that his majesty is indebted for his own personal escape from his rebels. It is said, moreover, and I fear *truly*, that if the king had followed Wyvil's counsel, and charged with all his horse, while Cromwell's men were in confusion—for they were beaten back, and all their cannon taken by a sally from the town—the fatal fight at Worcester might well have had a different conclusion."

"Ha! he is something more, then, than a mere swordsman," said Turenne. "I wonder what induced him to make this escapade? He could scarce hope for success, I should think, and the risk far surpassed the object to be attained, unless indeed he had been smitten by the *beaux yeux* of this fair Oswald, who they tell me has turned the heads of half our gallants."

"Oh no, it can not, I am sure, be that; for I am certain he had never seen her till that day. It is but a little more than five months since he came to Paris, having with difficulty made his escape from England. Since that time he has been constantly about my person; and from the 21st of April, has been upon my staff with the army. In the meantime, Sir Henry Oswald has been, as you know, in the Low Countries, on business of his eminence, and this young lady with him; so that I feel quite sure that they have never met till yesterday. If I am right in my opinion, it is but an ambitious craving for distinction, joined to a spirit naturally bold and ardent, that has led him into this deed of rashness. Besides this, maréchal, there was a story how he effected his escape by the aid of a beautiful young girl, to whom he is said to be troth-plighted."

"Well," answered Turenne, "since no harm is done, we can hold them under arrest until this battle has been fought with Monsieur of Lorraine; it will be something of a punishment to these men, such as I know Bellechassaigne, and such as you describe the other, to hinder them from the honor of this field. After that we can call them to a court-martial, and sentence them to be reprimanded. By my faith! the next time Bellechassaigne gives me any trouble, I'll sentence him to serve in the army and not to draw his sword for a whole campaign. But come, your royal highness, the vanguard must be nearing the fords of the Hyère; we were best gallop on, and see what goes on there. If monsieur is on the alert, and has sent some of his horse to dispute our passage, we may have something to do yet." And with these words he put spurs to his horse, and with the duke of York and his staff, rode forward as fast as he could for the obstruction offered by the guns and tumbrils of the artillery, until he passed beyond them all, when he galloped forward at full speed, and reached the leading regiments of infantry just as they reached the first ford.

The little river at this point spread out to several times its ordinary width, rippling rapidly over a gravelly bed in several channels, with narrow islands of meadow-land intervening; above this, for about a quarter of a mile, the stream flowed between deep banks in a strong and sluggish volume; and then another ford, somewhat deeper and narrower than the former, but still passable for horse, occurred where the sandy road wound down from the hill and crossed the bed of the Hyère. The third and best ford was still a quarter of a mile higher, and there the river was easy to be passed by five hundred men in front at a time. On the farther side the meadows were quite open, so that Turenne could overlook them for more than a mile in distance; and not a brake or thicket was in sight that could conceal a dozen skirmishers.

Halting upon a little knoll beside the upper of the three fords, the general sent off his aids-de-camp in all directions, to hasten the march of the infantry to the spot where he stood, to direct the artillery to come down from the hill, and pass by the lower ford of the three, and to bring up the cavalry with all speed to the deepest passage. All this was brilliantly and successfully conducted, and before sunset several regiments of infantry had crossed over, and had been formed in line of battle, facing almost due west, and having the high road from Brie-conte-Robert to Grosbois—from which last place they might be something more than three miles distant—on their right hand, and the river which they had forded on their left. About the same time the guns were got across, though not without much labor and some difficulty, and placed in a second line behind the advanced infantry, which had been pushed forward so as to cover all the three fords from the army of Lorraine, in case it should advance to meet them. At this time, just as the cavalry—which, when it was evident that no attack would be made on the rear, had gained the road on the hill side, and so outstripped the centre and rear of that—were beginning to defile toward the low grounds on the river, the general, who had taken no refreshment since the army had left Balacour before sunrise, ordered a halt, that the men might cook and get their suppers—it being his intention to make no longer pause than was necessary, but to march directly on Villeneuve. Fires were lighted now in all directions, and nothing could be fancied or described more wildly picturesque and striking than the scene that was presented on both sides of the river, in the soft, rich light of the summer sunset; the splendid uniforms and glittering armor of the confused and busy groups that bustled round the camp-fires, or sat in lounging attitudes on the soft green sward—the long line of stately chargers picketed in advance of the dismounted cavalry—the number of bright standards, and many-colored pennons, pitched in the ground at the head of every regiment and squadron—the mounted officers careering to and fro amid the whirling crowds—the frequent stacks of arms, flashing and twinkling in the sunbeams ; and, over all, the broad blue shadows silently creeping, as some great cloud swept across the sky, before the soft west wind, and intercepted the now level rays of the setting sun! Close to the margin of the river, hard by the upper ford, a group of three tall ash-trees—the only trees, indeed, which were to be seen in the meadows—overhung a small limpid basin, from which a tiny rill of crystal water stole away through the long thick grass, to join the broader stream.

Under these trees a Persian carpet had been spread on the ground, and a large piece of scarlet cloth stretched over the shafts of three or four long pikes extended from tree to tree, forming a sort of rude extemporaneous pavilion, under the shade of which the Maréchal Turenne with several of his principal officers, and among these the duke of York and two or three of his personal attendants, sat jesting and conversing merrily; while round a blazing heap of fagots at a short distance four or five servants were at work unloading a stout sumpter mule, and making preparations for the evening meal of their masters. Two or three hampers had been unpacked already, and their contents, in the shape of sundry cups and platters, and other implements of silver, were displayed on the carpet, about which the officers were sitting; while in the basin of the spring a dozen or more of the long-necked flasks, which from time to time almost immemorial have been consecrated to the rich sparkling wines of Champagne, were in process of cooling for the banquet.

While this was going on, and many a lively quib and repartee were passing round that merry circle, the quick glance of the maréchal detected a slight bustle in the lines of the cavalry that were the highest on the hill-side—a dozen or two of the troopers getting in haste to their chargers, and falling into order as if they expected an attack. The next minute, a single man came into view galloping very fast down the forest-road, and instantly some five or six more followed him at the same hurried pace. On reaching the little squad of mounted men, who had ridden out to receive them, they halted for a few seconds, and then, an orderly accompanying them, came down without relaxing their speed toward the general's station.

"Whom have we here, in such hot haste?" cried Turenne, gazing anxiously at the approaching riders; "messengers from the rear? It can not be that the Condè has followed us in force. No, no! impossible! Nor can Lorraine, I think, have marched on Charenton. Who is it, gentlemen?—who is it? I thought I had known every officer of the army, and yet I can not make him out at this distance. It is an old man, too!" And while he was yet speaking, before indeed any one of his train had time to answer, a tall, fine-looking veteran, with a stern, aquiline countenance, a profusion of long, silvery hair, and a pair of thick, white mustaches, came up at the gallop; and checking his horse slightly, alighted at a few paces only from the ash-trees. He was clad in a rich suit of half-armor, with a buff coat magnificently laced with gold worn over the cuirass; a high-crowned, broad-leafed hat, with a black feather, covered his head, his morion being carried by one of his servants, and his long basket-hilted rapier hung from a broad scarf of blue silk; his air was highly proud and military, but neither his port nor his complexion—which must have been, before it was embrowned by wind and moonshine, unusually fair and florid—at all resembled that of a Frenchman. All seemed to recognise him as soon as he dismounted, for all rose up to greet him; and Turenne himself, accompanied by the English duke, advanced some two or three steps, the first exclaiming—

"Ha! I am charmed to see you, good Sir Henry; such men as you are ever well met with, upon the eve of battle. We heard, too, that we were in some danger of having lost you altogether yesterday."

"To which, indeed, you owe the fact of my being here—advantage I will not call it, notwithstanding that you are pleased to be so complimentary. I was indeed desirous of seeing you even earlier in the day, but I had difficulty in getting men and horses in Corbeil. I had gone out across the river in the direction of Montl'hery, where I expected to meet with my servants, before you entered, and I did not return until it was past noon. There, having learned that the two gallant gentlemen, to whose good service I owe my life and my daughter's honor, are in disgrace, under arrest, and in some danger, I have made all the haste I could accomplish to overtake your excellency, and beseech your pardon for them; which I sincerely trust you will not think too much to grant me, seeing that I have fought some years for the same cause with you, and done, as you have been good enough to say, some service to the king, our master."

"Sir Henry Oswald," Turenne replied, very gravely, "you are too old, and far too good an officer, not to be well aware what detriment arises *ever* to our armies from the determination—for I can use no other term to express what I mean—of our young gallants to act on their own impulses and responsibilities, instead of obeying orders. In this case, the positive instructions, given by myself to these gentlemen, were to discover themselves, *on no account whatever*, to the enemy—my object being a surprise! Their conduct in disobeying such instructions, to say the least, was utterly unpardonable. I scruple not to say, that had Monsieur de Lorraine acted with one half his accustomed foresight, all we should ever have seen of his army would have been the last files of his rear-guard crossing the bridge at Charenton; if we had even got up thither in time to witness that. As it is even now, to-morrow's noon will show whether I can prevent his junction with the princes. Had Monsieur de Bellechassaigne obeyed orders, and returned to me undiscovered, we should have fallen on him unawares, and beaten him ere this, God willing! You must perceive, Sir Henry, that in this matter martial law must take its course. Had it been possible for me to gratify you, it would have given me the highest pleasure. If in aught else I can oblige you, it shall be done forthwith."

"Monsieur de Turenne," answered Sir Henry haughtily, "I hardly thought to have been refused at all in a thing of so slight moment. Not when you promised me of your own accord, upon the breaches of Hesdin, to grant me any possible request, did I expect that I should have occasion to remind you of your words; as it is, maréchal, I recall that promise to your recollection, and claim this as my first — my last request.

"But, sir," Turenne made answer, with cold inflexible politeness, "your request is *not* possible. Had it been in *my* power to grant it, you would have no need to prefer it. For, in that case, I should have been too proud to oblige his grace of York, to whom, within the hour, I have been reluctantly compelled to make the same denial. One thing I can assure you, and I do so with much pleasure, as your strong interest in their behalf is natural, that neither their honor nor their lives will be perilled; further than this I can not speak, nor should you ask me. And now to change the subject, which can not be agreeable to either of us, we are about to sup, or dine; if you have not done so already, will you not join our party? I know not well what we can offer you, but I doubt not that Merlache yonder will make us tolerable cheer; and I am sure we have got some right good wine. Come, come, old fellow-soldier, lay by that brow of gloom, and sit down with us."

"I must request your excellency," answered the veteran, with a deep and formal bow, "to excuse me, seeing —"

"But if his excellency do so," said the duke of York, taking a step in advance, and cutting him short in the middle of his sentence, "I can not. So, Sir Henry Oswald, you will be seated; I command, on your allegiance to his majesty, my brother. What, man," he added with a gay smile, which pleasingly illumined his dark features; "what, man, would you have the maréchal grant you a boon, which he has, not one hour ago, refused to the blood royal? Tush! you forget your manners; but a word in your ear — our good friends will be cared for; and so sit down, and prove yourself, as the dons have it, *buar camarado*."

To this, of course, there could be no reply. The veteran, half-satisfied, yet half-reluctant, joined the gay circle. Supper was served, and the bright wine went round, and flashing repartees, and keen wit, and light laughter, became the order of the evening; until at length after the sun had set, and darkness spread over the festive host, and torches had been lighted for more than an hour, the general rose from the carpet, which served his company for seats and board alike, and gave the word for the drums of the infantry to beat to arms, and the trumpets to sound, "Boot and Saddle!"

CHAPTER XXI.

THROUGHOUT the livelong night, the meadows and the banks of the Hyère were lighted by the ruddy blaze of many a flitting torch, borne by the fast succeeding regiments, and the yet broader glare of many a beacon, kindled along the line of march, to indicate the route to the rear of the army. Midnight was passed already before the last of the royal host had extricated themselves from the ford, and formed themselves in line of battle across the meadows on the farther side. This feat having, by vast exertion on the part of the officers, been accomplished, the trumpets sounded the advance, and they marched on, all through the hours of darkness, at the best pace the obscurity of the night, which was much overclouded, and the obstacles they encountered—in the shape of marshy ground, and of many small rivulets, and brooks, which made down to the river, from the hills beyond—permitted. At length the day broke, clear and promising, and the great sun came forth, just as the army had passed partially through, but principally to the left of the village of Grosbois, a little better than a league from Villeneuve St. George, where the duke of Lorraine was supposed to be still posted. As soon as it was quite light, so that objects could be perceived at a sufficient distance, Turenne began to press the advance, urging the men to march as fast as possible; and throwing forward advanced parties of light infantry and horse to reconnoitre, keeping the higher grounds himself with the duke of York and his staff, to the right of the line. It had not been long day, however, before a party of the cavalry, who had been pushed forward, were seen returning at a smart trot along the high road from the direction of Villeneuve; and, when they drew so near as to render the recognition of particular persons possible, Monsieur de Beaujeu, a friend of the cardinal's, who had been employed by him in negotiations, which had been going on uninterruptedly with the duke of Lorraine, and Monsieur d'Agecourt, captain of the duke's guards, were discovered to be of the number. A few minutes sufficed to disclose that Monsieur of Lorraine was well disposed to treat; the purpose of his envoy being to request Turenne to delay his advance for the present, and to acquaint the duke of York that the king of England was in the camp of Lorraine, whither he had come on the preceding evening, with the hopes of effecting an accommodation. After a short pause of reflection, the maréchal requested the duke to ride back with the envoy, who was empowered to plight the duke of Lorraine's honor, that he should be safe to come and go, inasmuch as his brother was desirous of conversing with him on the subject.

The prince immediately consented; and being charged with Turenne's ultimate conditions, which were comprised in three brief articles—"that the duke of Lorraine should immediately destroy the bridge of boats at Charenton, subject to the instructions of Monsieur de Varenne, who went for that purpose with the duke of York; that he should engage to quit the boundaries of France within the space of fifteen days; and that he should pledge his honor to give no further aid to the princes"—rode off, with a few personal attendants only, to the duke's quarters.

In the meantime, however, seriously doubting the good faith of the duke, and fancying that his object was only to gain time, Turenne continued to advance as fast as he was able, taking advantage of every favorable position, and keeping himself in readiness to act at a moment's notice on the offensive.

Meantime, the duke of York made his way to the position

above Villeneuve, extending from that town on the right flank to the road from Grosbois to Paris on the left, which Monsieur of Lorraine was fortifying with all the skill of an able general, added to all the personal activity of a shrewd soldier. As the young English prince rode up the gentle slope, at the southern base of which the town was situated, he was struck very forcibly by the strength of the position, and formed a high opinion of the ability by which it had been made tenable, as it certainly seemed to be, against a superior force. All the night had been spent in unintermitted labor at the construction of five strong earthen works, in which the main part of the infantry had been placed, one powerful battalion having its post as a division of reserve behind the principal redoubt in the centre of the line. Behind the foot, which did not amount to above three thousand men, the cavalry, five thousand strong, were drawn up in two lines of battle; and above these, upon a height near the junction of the rivers, his cannon overlooked the whole from a small barbette battery, at which the duke himself was laboring like a common pioneer, pickaxe in hand, when his noble visiter approached him. But Monsieur de Lorraine, before receiving him, sent one of his equerries to conduct him to the quarters of his brother, who was at that time in the town hall of Villeneuve.

Charles, who was seriously desirous of accommodating matters between the court and the duke, expressed his apprehensions that the latter would never consent to them. "I tell you, James," he said, "he has so strongly promised the princes, that he can not, od's fish! he can not now turn back."

"Then must the sword decide it, for certainly the maréchal will not relax one tittle," answered his brother; and as he did so, the duke of Lorraine entered the apartment, and having received the message of Turenne, continued for some time to joke and trifle in his accustomed strain of half-sneering badinage with the princes. It was not long, however, before the duke of York was convinced by his manner that much of his raillery was forced, and at variance with his real sentiments. With regard to the destruction of the bridge, he readily assented, and despatched several of his officers with Monsieur de Varenne, to order his engineers to cease from the construction for the present; but as to the rest, he protested vehemently that nothing ever should induce him to affix his signature to conditions so dishonorable. Then, finding that the duke would give him no hope that any others would be accepted by Turenne, he begged the king to send Lord Jermyn back with the duke as a mediator, saying, in a manner half complimentary and half sarcastic, that he feared much his royal highness would be led, by his chivalric and martial disposition, to cast his vote on the side of war rather than of peace. To this Charles willingly assented; and after a few more compliments the duke of York returned to the royal army, and Monsieur de Lorraine hastened away to complete his arrangements for receiving the attack of Turenne.

It did not take the duke and Lord Jermyn many minutes to reach the advanced parties of the maréchal, which were already almost within cannon-shot of the Lorrainers; while the whole meadows were filled with the bright lines of the compact and orderly foot regiments, pushing on very fast with an unbroken front, their standards fluttering gayly in the light summer wind, and the steel heads of their pikes, and the long barrels of their polished muskets, flashing back the early rays of the morning sunshine. The field-pieces, with their caissons and tumbrils, which had been drawn along the high road on the right flank, were moving down toward the centre of the front; and interspersed among the dense files of the fantassins, the squadrons of the gayly-equipped cavalry were pressing forward, or wheeling round from the rear so as to gain the flanks, with hundreds of brilliantly-colored pennons flaunting above their clear steel morions, and gorgeous scarfs and cassocks partially covering their polished armor. It was a splendid spectacle, indeed, to unpractised eyes; but those who now looked on it, had been too long accustomed to all the pomp and pageantry of warfare, to contemplate it in any other light than as a combination of scientific movements—a living game of chess, played at by one who, in those days, and for full many an after-year, had no superior in his knowledge of that terrific art. Galloping on as fast as they were able, and constantly inquiring where they should find the maréchal, the envoys made their way among the regiments, several of which, as the duke passed, cheered him with the wild homage of their Irish acclamations. They soon reached a spot where, surrounded by his staff, the noble general was standing on the ground, with his charger held by a groom beside him, while his attendants were engaged in putting on his armor.

" Well, you have come back in good season," he said merrily, " Monsieur le Duc — and as I judge in vain, since the Lorrainers hold the height in force, and we might see just now the cannoneers at work loading the guns in the battery yonder. Your men are in the rear," he added, pointing with the leading-staff, which he still held ; " but not far off. You were best ride to them at once, and arm yourself, for we shall be engaged I fancy before half an hour. But who is this you have brought with you ?"

" My Lord Jermyn ; who seeks, on the part of monsieur, to bring your excellency," answered the duke, " to accept some more moderate conditions."

" It is impossible — utterly !" Turenne interrupted him very quickly ; and though Lord Jermyn employed every argument that he could think of to persuade the maréchal, all was in vain ; and after an ineffectual attempt to prevail on the duke of York to return with him, he galloped back as hard as his horse could carry him to the works of the Lorrainers.

Meanwhile Turenne had finished arming, and riding forward to the centre of his advance, was making all his dispositions for the attack, when, to the surprise of all parties, the king of England himself came down to prefer the same request, which he asked as a personal favor to himself ; but finding that Turenne was still inflexible, he begged him once more to send the same terms to the duke. Monsieur de Gadagne was then despatched with the conditions fairly written out, and with instructions to have them signed upon the spot, in default of which the signal would be given instantly to commence firing.

No halt was made, however, and now the cannon were unlimbered, having been placed in battery against the enemy's works upon a little rising ground; and the different corps which had been ordered to storm the redoubts took up their position, while a strong force of tirailleurs were seen wheeling round the right, with a view to occupy the great woods which covered the left flank of the duke's army. Everything seemed to denote the approach of a great action; and the hearts of all men were filled with that strange and awful feeling, which is not fear, nor yet impatience, but an inexplicable blending of the two, which all have at some time experienced before the step is taken that throws them into imminent peril.

It was at this critical moment—just as the duke of York had armed himself from head to foot in a complete suit of beautifully-finished Spanish steel, and was in the act of mounting a strong charger, which was held ready for him by a dismounted trooper—that several figures came into sight on the meadows in the rear, riding very fast from the fords of the Hyère. There was something so peculiar in the appearance of one of these figures, even when seen at a very great distance, that the attention of the prince was attracted to it instantly; so much so, that after gazing fixedly for a minute or two, he called to an orderly to give him the perspective glass, which was slung in a leathern case across his shoulders. He had scarce received this, and looked through it for a moment, before he closed it with an exclamation of extreme surprise, at seeing that the person was no other than a female, splendidly mounted, and habited in the richest costume of the day. He paused a moment, and raised his hand to his forehead thoughtfully, then turning his horse's head toward the new-comers, rode swiftly a few yards in that direction; but again, as the thought struck him that he was riding away from the enemy, and that, too, at the very time when they might be expected to open their fire, he drew in his bridle, and, casting one more look to the group in question, wheeled his horse round, and took his way to rejoin Turenne in the centre of the front line. At this moment he could see the maréchal, who was sitting on his charger within point-blank range of the cannon on the hill, and scarcely out of musket-shot of the foot in the principal redoubt, raise himself slightly in his stirrups and wave his truncheon, pointing toward the works.

The regiments of Picardy and Carignan, which were the nearest to the maréchal, taking the signal as soon as it was given, advanced at a quick, steady *pas-de-charge*, toward the great redoubt, with their pikes levelled, and expecting every instant to receive the volley of the duke's fautassins; but as they moved, the regiment of York, or royal Irish, who were a little to the left of the centre, jealous of the French troops, and fearful that any others should be under fire before themselves, set up the wild and thrilling cheer of their country, and dashed forward, brandishing their arms, at a pace that would have precipitated them before many minutes into the hostile lines.

Perceiving this, the duke set spurs to his war-horse, and drove across the open ground at the top of his speed, taking three or four small ditches in his stride, until he overtook his regiment, which was perhaps two, or at most, three hundred yards from the breast-works. The pace at which they had rushed forward was so great, that they were quite unable to sustain it for the whole distance; and the consequence was, that some of the men outstripping the rest, the line was much shaken and disordered, and, had it continued its impetuous and uneven progress, must very soon have fallen into entire disarray.

In some respects, however, this was fortunate; for the subaltern officers, who, in the first instance, had been infected with the same rashness which had overset the discipline of their men, had found time for reflection, and had perceived the fatal consequences of the headlong rush by which they were now hurried on themselves, powerless to control their soldiery. The men themselves, moreover, were many of them breathless and overdone; so that when the duke overtook them, and wheeled his horse round their right, pulling him up in the face of their lines, midway between them and the enemy, and raising his leading-staff high in the air, called to them in a voice full of determination and authority to "halt," they did so on the instant. Ashamed of their own mad precipitation, the officers toiled strenuously to reform the shaken ranks; and in less time than it has taken to describe it, the lines presented an unbroken, regular front, ready to march in steady order against the fortified posts of the Lorrainers.

The duke addressed them in a few words of high and somewhat harsh remonstrance; and then perceiving that the French columns, which had been entirely outstripped by the headlong rush of the Irish, had in the interval come up and formed an even line, drawing his sword from the sheath dismounted, giving his horse and leading-staff to Colonel Worden, his equerry. "Now, gentlemen," he said, "we will advance together; so, in God's name, for Ireland and France—forward—ma——"

But the word died upon his tongue before the order was pronounced; for as he raised his voice to give it audibly, his eye fell upon a broad white ensign, which was displayed from the barbette-battery on the hill, and on the forms of several mounted officers galloping down to the redoubts, as if in obedience to some new and sudden order. Within the space of a few seconds, before he had time to consider well the meaning of the movement, a small white flag was hoisted on each of the redoubts, and the next minute the French regiments to his left halted; so that now, doubting nothing but that the duke of Lorraine had consented to the maréchal's condition, he gave the word to his men to halt and stand firm; and immediately remounted his charger, and resumed his truncheon. He had scarce settled himself, however, firmly in his saddle, before an orderly rode up, and informed him that an accommodation had been made, and that the maréchal required his presence, begging him to leave orders with the lieutenant-colonel of the Irish, to hold them steady to their arms, as there might well be treachery; but not to stir a pace without fresh orders.

The duke gave the directions necessary, and without loss of time returned to join the maréchal; but long before he reached him, he saw the female figure, whom he had noticed at a distance, gallop up to the assembled officers, amid the undisguised astonishment and noisy exclamations of the soldiery, and springing from the saddle, throw herself on the ground before the general's charger, clasping her hands about his booted leg, and seeming to address him with wild vehemence. It may be readily supposed that a sight so strange as this prompted the young prince to hurry even faster than before to the spot where it was enacting; but it was not mere curiosity which urged him to make haste, for, from the moment of her first appearance, he had suspected who the lady was that dared to brave, not only the dread terrors of a battle-field, but the world's censure, which must follow proceedings so unfeminine and rash.

Rapidly as he spurred, however, he could not come up to the presence of Turenne in time to witness all that passed; for, in the first place, several servants, in liveries which he well knew, followed their mistress at full speed to the spot, covering the group beyond from his gaze; and, in the second, all the staff had simultaneously leaped from their horses, and gathered round the lady and the general. For some short space it seemed to the duke that the press was so dense around the latter as to prevent him from dismounting, for his plumed hat and noble head were clearly visible above the crowd, though bending down toward the suppliant at his feet. Presently these, however, disappeared, and it was evident from the motions of the group, beginning to diverge, that he had alighted and was conversing with the lady.

In virtue of his rank and illustrious birth, as soon as he had come up and given his horse to one of the equerries, way was made for the duke of York; and in a moment he perceived that his suspicions had been too correct, and that it was indeed Isabella Oswald, who had actually ridden through a great part of the night, and made her way—exposed to rude surmise at least, if not to actual contumely—through the disorderly and vicious followers of the camp, to prefer, as it seemed, some personal request to the maréchal upon the very field of battle.

The first words that fell on the duke's ears were from the lips of that lovely girl; and although under circumstances so unusual, and at a time so fearful to the nature of a delicate woman, her voice faltered not the least, nor were her accents tremulous or hurried; but every tone, though low and femininely soft, was clear, and evenly pitched, and thrilling as a silver trumpet.

"I have your word, then, Maréchal Turenne—a word which never yet was questioned, much less broken—pledged for their liberty and honor."

"You have, indeed—you have, indeed, dear lady," answered the general, in tones that manifested his strong sympathy. "They are free from this moment; and had I deemed it possible that you, the daughter of my old friend and comrade, could possibly have been exposed to this, by all my hopes of heaven! I would have cast down rank and power, and life, and all, save honor, as I cast down that gilded bauble"—and with the words he tossed away his marshal's baton—"rather than so much as arrest them! For God's sake now, dear lady, let there be no more said about it, but presently withdraw; peace is concluded here—and I will send you with a trumpet, and a befitting train, into Villeneuve St. George, until such time as I can have Sir Henry summoned from the woods yonder, where he commands our tirailleurs, to take charge of you. I pray, no words, young lady. You know not, can not dream, what risks you have run last night, or what will be said of this hereafter."

"I come of a bold race, maréchal," she answered with a scornful motion of her head, tossing away the ringlets which had fallen over her high brow and flashing features; "nor am I the first daughter of it that has looked on a foughten field, if annals tell the truth, that I should shrink from doing right for the risk of a little peril!"

"There are some risks, lady," the general made reply, with an impressive and grave air, "which none, however rash, should incur ever! some perils which the bravest should avoid! Honor is not a thing to risk, nor repute to peril; and—"

"Honor! repute!" she interrupted him, her clear voice

ringing supernaturally shrill, and her eyes blazing with indignant anger; "my honor! who dare question it? My repute has never been risked; or if it have, I know how to defend the one, how to avenge the other! But you mean kindly, and, I am certain, honorably, maréchal," she continued, her momentary anger vanishing, as she perceived and appreciated the general's motives; "and with thanks for your kindness, I will submit to your dictation."

"Indeed I do, dear lady," Turenne made answer; "and so far from impugning your repute, or questioning your honor, there is no gentleman in France who would so gladly draw his sword to right you; nor did I mean to say that you had risked them, though I must say you have acted rashly, and given some scope to ill tongues, which everywhere abound! but, by my honor, were I Sir Henry Oswald, I should know how to deal with the knaves that led you hither!"

"It was Sir Henry's own fault," answered she, somewhat more meekly than before, "if fault there be, that I am here at all. He promised, when he left Corbeil, that he would send me tidings when he saw you; and here you tell me that he knew last night these gentlemen were in no peril, yet hath he sent me no word of it; and all the town was ringing with rumor that they should die this evening. Believe me, sir — believe me," she went on, speaking with much feeling and some vehemence, "I felt and knew that much might be said against my coming hither; but I knew likewise that, with six trusty followers, there could no real risk befall my father's daughter, even from the basest of the king's army! and I felt, more than all the rest, that it would comport ill indeed with my honor, that two brave gentlemen should fall disgraced upon the scaffold for rescuing that honor, and I not move a step to aid them. These, noble Turenne, only these were my motives! The gentlemen we speak of I never saw till two days since! never may see again! and scarce should recognise if I did see them!" She broke off suddenly; and overpowered quite with the revulsion of her feelings, burst into a paroxysm of violent and convulsive weeping.

Greatly distressed by this occurrence, at a time, too, when he was deeply occupied with other matters, and when his presence was indeed momentarily called for, the maréchal looked anxiously about him for a moment ere he spoke; then, "Monsieur de Clairvilliers," he cried, turning to an old officer of very high rank, "you are, I think, a dear friend of this young lady's father; and those gray hairs, blanched in the service of two kings of France, may well defy all scandal. Will you not, with our good duke of York here, taking a trumpet with you, and a fit escort, lead this young lady to Villeneuve, and see her suited with apartments and proper female tendance? Meanwhile, I will despatch a message to the duke of Lorraine; and our good friend Laloge here will spur his Barbary horse, from his pure love of the fair sex, until he find Sir Henry Oswald, and conduct him to his fair daughter." The gay young officer bowed low, and darted away like a swallow over the level meads in the direction of the great woods to the right; while Turenne, taking Isabella's hand in his own, kissed it respectfully and said—"And now farewell, dear lady; all will go well, trust me! And now I must beseech you to excuse me, for I have pressing calls upon my time; and his majesty must not have reason to complain that, besides pardoning his officers for disobeying orders, all for the bright eyes of a lovely lady, I, his commander in the field, neglect myself his service; even although the cause should be so worthy a true chevalier's devotion!"

His tone of badinage did much to reassure her, and she soon wiped her tears away, and was assisted to her horse by the young prince himself; but though she wept no more, she was extremely grave and unwilling to converse, replying in monosyllables to such remarks as were addressed to her, until she was installed in safety in handsome lodgings without the gates of Villeneuve; when, thanking the duke and the other gentlemen who had accompanied her, she expressed a wish to be left alone, and retired to her chamber, there to reflect upon the strange events of the past days.

CHAPTER XXII.

THERE stood in those times a small, ancient castle, a part of which was believed to be the work of the Romans, on the outskirts of Corbeil, although within the walls, of which, indeed, it formed an important angle, jutting out into the bosom of the broad Seine, and partially commanding the bridge, which, crossing the river, formed in this place the grand communication between the Orleannois and the Isle de France. It was old even at that time, and has long ago fallen into decay so total that there are now no vestiges to be seen, even of its foundations; but although small, it was then by no means deficient in strength, and, having been repaired quite recently, and mounted with a few heavy cannon, it had been garrisoned for some time past by a small detachment of artillerymen and a squadron of light-horse; the town being occupied by a whole regiment, and sometimes even a stronger force of infantry.

From these circumstances, and from its isolated position, it had been often used as a sort of state-prison, whether for officers of the king's party, accused of any serious breach of military discipline, or for such prisoners-of-war as were not admitted to a parole of honor, or as were liable to charges of high treason; and to its walls Wyvil and Bellechassaigne had been conducted on the morning of the advance against Villeneuve. It was in a suite of apartments, if one moderately large room, with two light closets containing each a truckle-bed, can be called a suite, at the top of the principal tower, which was perhaps something better than a hundred feet in height, that the two friends were confined. Their quarters, had they not been designated by the term prison, a term capable of rendering even a palace hateful, though neither large nor sumptuously furnished, would have been by no means unpleasant; for, owing to their elevation above the paved court-yard, and the height of the outward walls, the windows were not barred; and, from the situation of the building, projecting far out into the current of the river, they commanded an extensive view over the richly-cultivated, although somewhat flat expanse of the Orleannois, and over two bright reaches of the broad, winding Seine. Yet, notwithstanding this advantage, and although they were attended by their own servants, served with an excellent table, and permitted the use of books and papers, the time lagged wearily with the impatient and high-spirited prisoners; for both these men, however different in other points of view, were of that class, who, like Scottish Douglas of remoter times, ever preferred the green fields and the azure vaults of heaven, to the soft Persian carpets and gold-fretted roofs of those luxurious days; who had rather hear the lark sing than the mouse squeak, as the old borderer had it; and to whom life itself, though coupled to every charm of power and luxury and wealth, if it had not also been enlivened by change and peril and excitement, would have been wearisome and odious.

The first long day wore over, and that perhaps more lightly than could have been expected, for there was something of an adventure even in their situation; something to excite thought and create surmise; something uncertain, and even trifling, in the doubt of what should follow after; that strung their minds to a high key, and rendered them in some sort heedless of the present. But when the second day succeeded, and no signs, as they had anticipated, showed themselves, either of a court-martial, or of a summary execution, their minds began to wax uneasy, and their spirits dull, and their souls heavy. Soon after breakfast Bellechassaigne began to pace the floor with quick, irregular strides, pausing occasionally to look out of the window over the wide sunlighted landscape; and turning suddenly away with a brief, bitter curse, to traverse and retraverse the narrow limits of the chamber; and so, with little intermission, he continued during the whole day, answering shortly and impatiently to the chance words of his companion; and hurrying round and round the walls, as if to seek an exit, with the impatient gestures of the caged hyena.

Meanwhile, the English exile, no less disturbed and ill at ease than the young Frenchman, displayed the disorder of his mind in a way as different as possible from his companion. He had sat down at a small table by the window, to while away the time with the wild conceit and strange fancies of the Gargantua of Rabelais; but, though for the first half hour he had turned a few pages, and smiled a few times, and once even laughed aloud, he soon lapsed into the depths of his own mind, and sat there quite immoveable, and seemingly unconscious of all external things; with his brow bent into a gloomy frown, pondering the past, the present, and the future; turning no leaf, reading no line of the licentious, witty author, until afternoon had long stricken, and the servant had come in and out, and arranged the board with wine and meat and all the preparations of the mid-day meal, without his raising so much as an eye from the book which he scarce knew to be before him—his wilder fellow-prisoner slapped him on the shoulder, and burst into a loud, rallying laugh.

"Despardieux! we are good companions, and rare fellows, too, to call ourselves tried soldiers—particularly you, who have been shut up, as you told me, for weeks together, without fresh air or daylight—to take on thus absurdly for a few days' confinement in good quarters! for that, I trow, will be the worst of it."

"Ay, that is it!" answered Wyvil, a little wildly, as if he did not altogether catch the sense of Bellechassaigne's words; "that is just it; that is what I was thinking of."

"Well, wake up then, man; and see here is dinner ready; they mean to fatten us, I trow, if they do not intend to kill us!"

And thus, for a short space, they both shook off the presence of their cares, and ate, and drank, and chatted, ay, and jested, as cheerfully as though they had been both at large; but when the meal was finished, after a little effort to sustain a laborious conversation, their spirits flagged again, and both returned to their occupations; the partisan, of restless and excited motion—the exile, of deep, painful meditation.

Meanwhile night fell, and candles were lighted in the prison chamber, and, at Bellechassaigne's bidding, a stoup of wine and glasses were set upon the board; and for a space the two companions talked cheerfully enough about their future prospects, and the events of the campaigns; the partisan expressing his surprise that they had heard no sounds of cannonading, which, had a battle taken place at Villeneuve, they could not have failed to do, and drawing from the fact strong cause for apprehension that the duke of Lorraine might have fallen back on Charenton upon the first alarm, and actually crossed the bridge of boats before Turenne had overtaken him.

While they were eagerly and anxiously discussing this, their attention was attracted by the sounds of some arrival, which created a considerable bustle in the courtyard below. The creaking of the *port levis*, as it was lowered, the drawing of the hoarse bolts, and the screaming of the rusty hinges, was succeeded by the clatter of horses' hoofs upon the bridge, and the jingling of spurs upon the pavement, as trooper after trooper leaped from his saddle; torches were seen flashing to and fro, and lusty voices heard calling for the governor. Amid the tumult the prisoners soon detected, as with every sense on the alert, they listened to the din without, the words repeated many times—"News from the host—a message from Turenne!" and Bellechassaigne had just turned round to his companion, exclaiming, "Now, then, we shall soon learn our fate!" when a quick step came up the staircase, and along the corridor; and instantly the door of their prison was thrown open, and the head warden entered with a smile on his countenance.

"I bring you pleasant tidings," he said, "noble gentlemen; you are discharged from my custody. Here are despatches from the army;" and he laid two documents, addressed to the prisoners, upon the table. "The orders for your release," he added, "have been received in due form by the maréchal himself, and you can set forth on the instant, if it please you. Monsieur de Flamarin, with a party of light-horse, awaits you at the gates."

"Lead on, then—lead on!" exclaimed Wyvil; "for by the Lord! I do not love to breathe the air of a jail a moment after

I may quit it. Your orders are the same as mine, I fancy, Bellechassaigne."

"A simple mandate," answered the partisan, "to report myself at the headquarters of my regiment as soon as may be!"

"Precisely," replied Wyvil; "so now to horse! to horse! where shall we find our horses and our varlets, monsieur warden?"

"They have been cared for, gentlemen," answered the man very civilly; "you will find them below, I think, by this time. Monsieur de Flamarin bade us send for them instantly, when he arrived, and one of my men ran down with his orderly to the Golden Lion, where they were sent yesterday."

No time of course was wasted, and before many minutes the friends were in the saddle, and away toward Villeneuve, which they soon learned from their friendly escort, had been evacuated on that morning by Lorraine, and occupied by the royal army. Much had De Flamarin to tell them of the operations of the army, of the repeated intercessions in their behalf by the young English duke, and by Sir Henry Oswald; and last, not least, of the arrival on the field of battle, just as the signal was on the point of being given, of a young lady, who had ridden all night through to win their pardon of the maréchal. He had not himself seen her, he declared, nor did he know who she was, but all the camp, he said, was ringing with the praises of her strange loveliness, the exquisite taste and fashion of her dress, her superb horsemanship, and above all, her high and dauntless spirit, in traversing the midnight roads, swarming with the licentious followers of the host; in riding up to the very muzzles of the enemy's cannon, even then about to open, and in defying, as it was said she did, the great Turenne, when at the head of the king's forces. Both the companions, of course, instantly suspected who was the lady that had interposed to save them; and sundry were the questions which both put to De Flamarin; but all that they could learn was, that she was tall and of an extreme loveliness, and that it was reported she had ventured so much for the love of the English cavalier.

"I told you so," exclaimed Bellechassaigne, with a gay, ringing laugh—"did I not tell you so, the night before last, Wyvil? It all comes of your luck, man, in charging home with a velvet coat on, instead of a greasy elk-skin cassock and a steel-harness. I knew no female heart in France could resist that passmented pourpoint, and the feathered hat! By Heaven! I'll charge in my shirt the very next chance I get, but I'll outdo you!"

But Wyvil answered nothing to his friend's raillery, seeming to be absorbed in deep and serious meditation; and it was observed, and commented upon by both his comrades, that he was unduly grave, and almost sad, during the whole of their ride to headquarters. De Flamarin, however, replied instantly—

"No, you won't, not a bit of it, Bellechassaigne. I heard the maréchal himself tell his highness of York, that he should sentence you to serve the whole campaign in the front of your regiment with your sword in the scabbard, and you know he's a man to keep his word!"

"I know he is, De Flamarin," said Bellechassaigne, still laughing; "and you know, too, that I am not exactly one to forfeit mine; so, trust me, if he sentence me to that, I will serve in a shirt over my uniform instead of a cuirass; and, if my sword be nailed fast to my scabbard, why I must have three inches added to the length of my dagger, and trust to that and my pistols in the melée."

De Flamarin was not slow to reply, and though Wyvil continued silent and abstracted all the time, the march through the dark woods was still enlivened with loud merriment, and now and then a song, until they reached the outposts of the army, which had been pushed nearly a league in advance of the bridge over the Hyère, on the road toward Corbeil, to guard against the possibility of any movement on the part of Condè, who, it was apprehended, might cross the Seine, and attack the rear of the king's army. The first intelligence they had of the existence of such a picquet—it had in fact been posted after De Flamarin had left Villeneuve, in consequence of the appearance of the prince's vanguard on the other side the river, which had come up in less than an hour after the duke had abandoned his position and begun to retreat—was the glare of a watch-fire, lighted by the road-side on the crest of the hill so often mentioned, and the loud hum of many voices. No sentinel, it seemed, had been thrown out by the officer of the picquet, and very little of precaution taken to guard against surprise; from which, however, the nature of the ground in some degree protected them. What was, however, even more blameworthy, so loud and jocund was their revelry, that it entirely drowned the noise which the other party made in approaching, until they had come so near that they might see the whole of the picquet, which consisted of cavaliers of Lord Bristol's English horse, and two or three officers of the French guard, all of them, even to the privates, gentlemen of blood and honorable lineage. To this it was attributable, that no distinction was made of rank or dignity as they sat revelling round the fire, while many a flask went round, and the old forest rang with their bacchanalian glee.

Bellechassaigne, ever full of broad wit and wild humor, entreated De Flamarin to halt his party, and steal up quietly, and so surprise the revellers; and he assenting, as they crept up among the bushes between the feasters and their arms, which they had stacked at a little distance in the rear, the following words met their ears, loudly chanted by a mellow though untaught voice, and were followed by a jovial chorus of applause, that might have been heard far and wide in the silent midnight.

Trowl, trowl the brown bowl—
Merrily trowl it, ho!
For the nut-brown ale shall never fail,
However the seasons go.

Drink, drink! he who'll slink,
When circling goblets flow,
That knave, I swear, will never dare,
Like a man, to meet the foe.

Then steep, steep your souls deep
In the wassail-cup to-night;
For the next day-spring shall surely bring
The dry and sober fight.

CHORUS.

Trowl, trowl the brown bowl—
    Merrily trowl it, ho!
For the nut-brown ale shall never fail,
    However the seasons go.

Wine, wine! comrades mine,
    In wine the pledge must be,
When drink the brave "to a soldier's grave,
    Or a soldier's victory!"

Hence, hence with all offence,
    Though foes of old were we
Our future life shall know no strife,
    But who shall foremost be!

Then up! up! with each cup,
    From whatever land are ye—
Whether knights of the lance, from merry France,
    Or old England's archers free.

CHORUS.

Wine, wine! comrades mine,
    In wine the pledge must be,
When drink the brave "to a soldier's grave
    Or a soldier's victory!"

So loud and long was the burst of acclamation that followed this characteristic melody, and so completely were all hearts taken up with it, that Bellechassaigne and De Flamarin saw their opportunity, and springing forward, so as to cut the party off from their firearms, shouted to them "to surrender on the instant, or they were all dead men!" bidding their own men, at the same time, "level their carbines and take aim;" but, although taken by surprise, beset and surrounded, not one of the picquet dreamed of yielding.

"Draw your swords, boys," cried the singer, springing to his feet, and unsheathing with one motion, his poniard and his rapier; "draw, and fall on! there be but a score of them." And he was bounding forward to the charge, when a loud shout of laughter, and the cry, "Friends! Turenne! Turenne!"

arrested them, and all was for a few minutes loud and wild confusion, but when this ceased—

"You keep good watch," exclaimed De Flamarin; "and lucky is it for ye that we were not the rounds; as it is, ye are mulcted in a flask of wine, which we will discuss presently, and then to horse again; but if you will take my advice, you will detach some two or three videttes, for I esteem it very like that some of the generals will go the circuit of the posts between this time and morning!"

"You're in the right of it there," answered the captain of the party; "so Mainwaring and Digby take up your carbines, and be off and post yourselves a hundred yards apart, down the hill side—I will relieve you in an hour—here is the wine—but will you not sit down and join us—"

"No, no, we must away, else worse will come of it," Bellechassaigne made reply; "so here's to your good health, fair comrades—and a light watch to ye—and may ye 'scape the provost marshal as well as we have done—Wyvil and I—for by my life, I hoped for nothing better than to be shot to-morrow morning!"

"Well, if you had been," answered De Flamarin, laughing, "that were a better fate than the soothsayer foretold me at the siege of Etampes."

"Why, what was that, De Flamarin?" asked one of the English cavaliers.

"Oh! that I should die with a rope about my neck," he replied, laughing.

"By St. George! but that's pleasant," exclaimed one.

"Yes, and probable, too," answered Bellechassaigne, "when he has the privilege of decapitation in right of his nobility."

"A mighty pretty privilege that, on my honor," replied an Irish trooper of the regiment of Clare; that's a prerogative now, I'm not over anxious to be earning—but praise be to the saints for that same! they can't make me out to be noble, any way"—and in the shout of laughter which chorussed this naïve observation, the others mounted and rode away, and without any more adventures, made their way safely to headquarters.

Several days elapsed after this, without the occurrence of any event of importance; Wyvil and Bellechassaigne having rejoined the corps to which they were attached, and quietly resumed their duties, no notice being taken whatever of their conduct, either by the maréchal in person, or by their own immediate superiors. The count, meanwhile was at St. Denis—the citizens of the metropolis, divided among themselves, and pretty equally balanced between the causes of the cardinal and princes, holding themselves in a sort of disaffected mutuality, with their gates closed, and refusing ingress to either party; and it was soon understood by the gentlemen whom her decided and impetuous activity had preserved from the disgrace of a court-martial, that Isabella Oswald was in attendance there on the queen-mother, Anne of Austria. Thus, for some days, no intercourse could possibly take place between the English cavalier and the lady, in behalf of whom his heart was hourly declining from its allegiance to another. This fact, however—as often is the case in the commencement at least of attachments, before the first romance of incipient passion had been dissipated by too familiar intercourse—tended, as it would seem, only to fix the wavering mind of the young soldier more steadily upon the wild, high-spirited, and head-strong beauty, whose every charm was seen through the misty veil which absence casts upon remembrance, exaggerating, like the haze of the spectral Brocken, in proportion as it renders indistinct, the outlines of whatever it enshrines in its poetical and visionary fold. Day after day, the more he shunned his comrades, wrapping his soul in deep abstraction, and giving every minute he could spare from his military duties to wild and whirling fantasies. It must not be imagined yet, that no thought of the fair and gentle being to whom he had now begun to meditate so foul disloyalty, was intruded on his waking dreams; for it was to no lack of kind or honorable impulses, but to want of steadiness, of direct, persevering energy, of overruling principle, that the defection of the young man was attributable. In the early moments of his new fascination, the sweet, calm face of Alice would constantly recur to his mind, and as often as it did so, the pure and maidenly loveliness of her character, its thoughtfulness, its absolute neglect of self, its charity toward the faults of others, and above all, its feminine devotedness of love toward himself, smote deeply on his repentant spirit. But alas for human nature! too true it is, that when we have once admitted evil thoughts to be our counsellors; when we have once listened to the voice of the charmer, who, alas! ever charms too wisely; unless we banish the dark spirit instantly, by one strong effort, so that he never shall return at all—the pleadings of the consience wear weaker still at every iteration, till they are drowned wholly by the trumpet-tongue of passion—the whispers of the false one, whom we have suffered to become the second time a visitant, recur more frequently, gain strength at each recurrence, until he has become the lord and tyrant of our bosoms. And so it was with Wyvil, he was from his birth upward, pre-eminently subject to that "one touch of nature," which, as the great poet of the human heart has written,

"Makes the whole world kin—
That all with one consent praise new-born gauds,
Though they are made and moulded of things past;
And give to dust, that is a little gilt,
More laud than gilt o'erdusted."

To this he owed it, in the first place, that he became so readily, although so worthily, enamored of Alice Selby—to this he owed it, too, that when she was afar, and a fresh "Cynthia of the minute" was brought upon the stage, his "present eye" was prompt upon the instant "to praise the present object." Moreover, so unsteady was the right principle within him, so little had he of the stern, obstinate determination to do well, let what *may* come of it, that, though his good impulses at first leaped out unbidden to do battle for the absent, he yet repelled the tempter with so little energy in the first onset, and suffered him so soon to make another and another charge, that almost ere he knew it, the lodgment was effected and the old garrison expelled—now in its turn to attack, but as a faint and ineffectual antagonist, the citadel which had so treacherously yielded. It had by this time, therefore, come to pass, that although thoughts of Alice Selby would still at times sweep back to his false heart, they were now thrust aside by a mental effort, as most unwelcome and intrusive visiters; for the voice of remonstrance, never too welcome to humanity, when it has been once hushed, though it may rouse itself again and again, is listened to each time with less attention—greater reluctance—till the object itself, which gives rise to the self-reproval, becomes by association itself hateful and repulsive. Through all these processes, then, had the mind of Wyvil passed, since the day on which he had so accidentally assisted Isabella Oswald. From having his soul full of remembrance, and of such affection for Alice Selby as he was capable of feeling—with now and then a strange and passing thought of Isabella intruding itself, and repulsed faintly—he had come to ponder all day long on the charms and perfections of the latter, on the chances of winning so bright and beautiful a prize, and on the means of recommending himself the more effectually to her favor; while, if the half-reproachful face of Alice was summoned for a moment by his guilty conscience, to look into his very eyes, it was dismissed at once by the most rigorous and resolute exertion of volition. Yet even, when this was the case, it could not have been said of him truly, that he had resolved to aim at gaining Isabella's love, or to act with base treachery to Alice. This fact was simply this; that he was too indolent, too irresolute of mind, to determine anything; that he left himself voluntarily, like a boat cast on the billows, oarless and rudderless, to float which way soever the stormy winds of passion or the capricious tides of fortune should waft him devious on the sea of life.

He had thus far become a traitor, that he had willingly permitted treason to grow into the continual and licensed subject of his meditations. And who is he of mortals, that having once admitted the evil one to be the guide of his steps, the prompter of his secret thoughts, can say to him, "thus far shalt thou direct my footsteps, thus far shalt thou advise my soul—thus far—thus only?" Several days elapsed, and the troops of

Turenne halted inactive at Villeneuve, but this pause of seeming indecision was destined to be of short duration; for the great leader, having learned that beyond doubt the duke of Lorraine had retired beyond the frontiers, determined to resume the offensive, and act against the prince of Condè, the only enemy now in the field against him, with vigorous decision. Accordingly, he broke up his encampment on the twenty-first day of June, and marching northeasterly, by slow degrees, to Ligny, he there crossed the Marne, and, turning westward thence, arrived on the second of July, and encamped at La Chevrette, a little village, about a league distant from St. Denis, on the east side of the Seine; the prince of Condè, who had vainly quitted Etampes in the hope of effecting a junction with Lorraine, being posted a little higher up the river, on the opposite side, at St. Cloud. Both armies were prepared in earnest for a general action, for on the very day of his arrival, Turenne began to bridge the Seine in several places, which is here very wide, and interspersed with islands, and Condè hastened to oppose him. Continued skirmishes and constant cannonading now took place, and every opportunity that could be fancied, was afforded for deeds of desperate and daring partisanship; and what would seem most strange in these days, but was then deemed nothing unusual or remarkable, the residence of the court being so near the scene of action, parties of gay non-combatants were constantly made up to ride or drive down to the eminences overlooking the scene of strife, so that scarcely an hour of the day passed without some gorgeous cavalcade, with gilded carriages and bright liveries, and even ladies of high rank among the number, being seen literally in the line of fire, while it was scarcely a less singular feature of the times, that in the middle of a war of rebellion and civil discord, all extreme points of courtesy were insisted upon with the minutest etiquette, so that in fact there was little danger to the fair and gay amateurs, except from a chance shot or spent ball, which would now and then come ricocheting through the dust, and set them all a scampering. It will be readily imagined, that with a field like this before them, such men as Bellechassaigne and

Wyvil were constantly devising some new deed of daring; vying with one another in every sort of hazardous and wild excitement, and setting all the young spirits of both armies in a flame with martial rivalry. Day by day, night by night, sometimes together, but oftener apart, they were for ever in the saddle—now cutting off a convoy, now capturing a picquet, now making a general officer in his own quarters prisoner and carrying him off by surprise, till every eye was fixed upon them in astonishment and admiration.

Several times, while engaged in scouring the country in search of some adventure, Marmaduke had encountered Isabella, riding upon her fiery English horse, to the envy and surprise of the Parisian dames, escorted by her father, and surrounded ever by the noblest and most fashionable idlers of the court; but though no opportunity was given for more than a passing glance and hasty salutation—for Wyvil was at all times upon duty—still so deep was the blush that still accompanied the lady's greeting, so marked and speaking was the glance that seemed to linger on her features, that he could scarcely doubt but that he had awakened something of interest already in her bosom; that he was stirred to aim at winning some higher token of regard, by wilder and more desperate exploits. Meantime Turenne, whose working parties had been much annoyed by the interruption of the enemy, posted the two foot regiments of Laferté on an island in the river, somewhat more elevated than the opposite shore, to the point of which the bridge was in process of construction, and by this able movement prevented the light troops of Condè from harassing his workers, hand to hand, as they had done in the first instance. So great was the advantage which the royalists gained by this disposition, that, on the following morning, the princes seemed disposed to make a general attack, several heavy corps of foot having been seen at an early hour moving with horse and cannon toward the point in question. It was as beautiful a morning as could be imagined; the country all arrayed in the richest green of summer, the fields enamelled with ten thousand wild flowers, that perfumed every breath of the soft, mild, west wind; the great sun laughing out of the azure skies, and filling the earth and air with warmth and lustre. The scene, too, was of the most delightful—the meadow banks of the blue Seine, with sloping eminences, wood-crowned, and decked with hanging vineyards on either hand; and all the rich and cultivated champagne, with hundreds of white villages, and here and there the grand and massive towers of palaces and abbeys, lying stretched out, broad, bright, and beautiful, to the far distance; while to the left-hand of the gorgeous landscape, loomed up the dark magnificence of the metropolis, with all its piles of antique masonry. What wonder, then, that all the gay court insects were abroad, to gaze upon the pageantry and pomp of the approaching conflict. In a small meadow, near the bridge, sat Turenne on his charger, surrounded by his staff, calmly observing the advancement of his works, and the movements of the approaching enemy. Before him, to the left-hand, lay the island occupied by the infantry of Laferté, with their bright armor and tall standards; behind him, on a little eminence, commanding the river and part of the opposite banks, was a long line of cannon, with the artillerymen and cannoneers busily pointing them upon the heads of the enemy's advance; and in the low fields to his right, many small bands of horse were wheeling to and fro, distinguished from each other by many-colored scarfs and fluttering pennons, and the cassocks of their partisan commanders. The mass of the royal army was, for the most part, concealed by the low range of hills on which the cannon were disposed, although the heads of their pikes, glittering in the sunshine, and the tops of their ensigns shining above the trees and hedges, showed that they were in force and close at hand, should they be needed; while, to complete the picture, scarcely a pistol shot behind the cannon of the royalists, three of the king's carriages were stationed, with their bright train of liveried attendants and magnificently-appareled courtiers, among whom were pre-eminent the distinguished forms of Sir Henry Oswald and his unrivalled daughter.

Two or three shots had been fired from the royal cannon, which, though they had done no real damage, had already checked the advance of the prince's columns; for these had not been supported by artillery, so that it began to appear doubtful whether anything of consequence would take place that day; and the fair amateurs were even beginning to display some such feelings as would be now called forth by the non-appearance on the stage of some popular tragedian, whose announcement had called them forth, when suddenly a small party of perhaps two hundred fantassins, rushed down from the main body with such rapidity, as set at naught the fire of the artillery, which opened on them furiously as they came, and took up a position behind the brow of a little sloping hill, which sheltered them entirely from cannon shot. It evidently was impossible to drive them from that post by any missiles then in use, for although bomb-shells had been introduced in the attack of towns, the management of mortars was so little understood, that hardly any aim could be taken; and this was the more to be regretted, that they kept up so terrible a fire on the regiments which held the island, not being above a hundred yards from the river bank, that the men might be seen falling by scores at every volley from their unseen assailants, and that the working-parties ran in, unable to sustain the constant and well-aimed discharge. Meanwhile, a dozen squadrons of dragoons moved down, and drew themselves up in line of battle, a little way in the rear of the fantassins, while several regiments of foot came winding down a hollow way to the left, as if with the intent to cross over to the island under the cover of their ambushed tirailleurs.

The brow of Turenne grew dark as night; and, in a moment a cavalier went at full gallop from his side to the artillerymen, who instantly commenced a furious cannonade upon the horse in the rear, which were exposed to their fire, and within half an hour forced them to fall back to a mile's distance; although they did so most reluctantly, making two or three different attempts to rally at successive intervals, and losing nearly a third of their number, before they gave up the point. Still the foot-soldiers continued undisturbed behind the hill, and poured their balls in an incessant stream of quick glancing fire into the dense ranks of Laferté, which had no means of returning the discharge by which they were so cruel sufferers. For this there seemed no remedy; and now the maréchal was on the point of sending an order to the relics of those regiments to abandon the island, until such time as he could erect breast-works during the night to cover them, when on a sudden, one of the troops, which have been mentioned as wheeling to and fro in the meadows on the right, like birds of prey seeking to swoop, came up at a light canter to the general's station. This little handful, for in truth it was no more, consisted but of fifty men besides their leader; but they were mounted, one and all, on fine gray horses, with headpieces and corslets of clear, polished steel; and were distinguished from all other parties of the kind, as well by the exquisite finish of their whole equipment, as by their parti-colored plumes and scarfs, which, like the pennons that waved over them, were singularly blended of bright blue and yellow, with fringes and embroidery of silver. The officer who led them was a tall, slender youth, with a profusion of light curls falling down from beneath his helmet, and a buff coat superbly laced with silver, instead of a cuirass, crossed by a silken baldric of the same colors as those borne by his retainers.

The cloud passed partially away from the brow of the maréchal as he observed the movement of this party, and he even told the orderly whom he was just despatching to the regiments of Laferté, to await further orders, observing, with a half smile, to the duke of York, who stood beside him —

"Now, then, I fancy we shall have some strange proposition from yon dare-devil, though what it can be is beyond my guess, to dislodge those accursed fantassins who are playing havoc with our men yonder! By heaven! if he succeeds, it shall go hard with me but I will have amends made to him where best he'll value it. Let us hear what he has got to say, duke;" and as he spoke he moved his horse a little way from his staff, to meet the partisan; while a loud murmur of applause, not unlike that which often greets a favorite actor, rose from the concourse of spectators, who seemed to anticipate some high gratification from one so much renowned already for his extravagant and dashing valor.

Halting his band at some short distance, the young man rode up to the maréchal, and humbly asked permission to swim across the river with his men, and bring away the marksmen who were so much annoying the infantry upon the island.

"Bring them away, Captain Wyvil!" exclaimed Turenne; "I am sure I shall be much obliged to you if you will; but, for my life, I can not see how you will set about it."

"There is a large bark there, your excellency," answered Marmaduke, pointing to a little cove on the opposite side, where a vessel of some five-and-twenty tons was moored to a rude dock; "my head upon it that we bring them if you will but permit the guns to cover us as we return."

"Well, sir," replied the maréchal, "I give you my permission; the guns shall open as soon as you turn back toward the shore; see to that, will you, Dunmont," he added, looking to a young subaltern of his staff, who rode away to the cannoneers immediately.

Wyvil bowed low and looked much gratified, as he received the answer of Turenne; and, instantly having rejoined his men, addressed a few words to them, which they received with a loud cheer, and put their horses at once to a hand-gallop; while all the cortége on the hill began to move down nearer to the river, in the anticipation of some animated spectacle. Nor were they disappointed; for just as his band began to gallop, Wyvil dashed to their head, and seizing his pennon from the hand of the bearer, led them at a tremendous pace across the meadow to a spot where the bank shelved gradually to the river, showing a hard and gravelly soil. It scarcely seemed a moment before he reached the brink, and giving his good horse the spur, was in deep water, his troopers setting up another loud cheer as he rose from the stream, which had at first almost ingulfed him, and following without a second's hesitation. The river was both broad and deep; and though not swift, the current swept along in dark and turbid eddies, and it required the utmost strength and skill in horse and rider to stem its powerful tide. Yet not one charger failed—not one trooper faltered!

The regiments upon the island, now seeing the intention of the movement, set up the cry of France, known for so many ages—their cry upon the battle plain, or at the festive board, in the extremity of peril, or in their height of rapture—"Vive le roi! vive le roi!" and the heart-stirring, deep hurrah, of the few English cavaliers, responded to the mighty acclamation with bold and dauntless greeting. Luckily for the little troop, the very elevation of the ground which sheltered the fantassins of the enemy, prevented them from aiming at the daring swimmers; and when the cavalry of Condè, who, being on the upper ground, saw what was concealed by the sloping banks from the skirmishers, once more attempted to move down, the royal cannon again belched forth, through flame and volumed smoke-wreaths, their hail of iron bullets, and scattered them in wild confusion.

Heavily the white clouds swept down, and curtained for a moment the bright Seine, and shut off the scene of action from the anxious eyes that gazed on it. They cleared away, and, lo! Wyvil had landed safely, had formed his men upon the hostile bank, and was in the act of charging, with battle-cry and trumpet-note, the surprised and dismayed fantassins. Furious and loud now waxed the cheering from the island, while from that little troop the clash of blades, on morion and corslet, and pistol-shots glancing among the melée, made meet accompaniment to that fierce, stormy chorus. But the affair was ended in a moment. Taken entirely by surprise, cut down, and trumpled under foot—their leader killed, and their position forced—the skirmishers threw down their weapons and surrendered. Five minutes more saw them embarked in the sloop under a fitting guard, the mooring ropes cut, and the vessel drifting with sail and oar toward the other bank; while, without losing horse or man, the gallant partisan swam back, among the redoubled plaudits of his party, uninjured and in triumph.

As he returned, the marèchal rode down himself to meet and

thank him, at the head of his whole staff; and, having done so, ordered a dozen field-pieces to be passed over with a company of engineers, who should intrench the island, in the same bark which had brought over the fantassins. But yet another and a higher gratification awaited the ambitious partisan; for, as he wheeled his men back to their quarters, he met the royal cavalcade returning to St. Denis. Many a high encomium was passed upon his conduct by tongues not wont to commend lightly; many a glance and smile were flashed on him from eyes and lips that rarely glanced or melted but for the mighty and renowned; but one soft sigh was faltered forth, which went more deeply to his soul than all the eulogies of chiefs and princes—one hurried, speaking beam, was shot from an eye half-averted, that thrilled his heart more hurriedly than all the fascinations of all those gay court beauties. The cavalcade swept onward; but as they passed, there fell at Wyvil's feet a lady's kerchief of pale lilac, with a broad gold border. From out ten thousand, the eye of Marmaduke would have discovered it, and sworn to its transcendent owner. Thenceforth he wore that kerchief knotted upon his arm—that owner enthroned nighest his seat of life! From that time forth, whatever he had been before, Wyvil was false to Alice!

CHAPTER XXIII.

Months had elapsed since Marmaduke effected his escape, and everything at Woolverton, except the thoughts of Alice Selby, had fallen back into their customary old routine. Winter, with its keen frosts and driving snow-storms, diversified by long, slow, sloppy thaws, and dark gray fogs, had come and gone; and spring had clothed the woods with fresh green foliage, and called the wild flowers into life, and waked the wild birds into song; and summer had succeeded, with its mature and glaring flush of noonday beauty: yet no news arrived of Marmaduke, his whereabout, or his well-doing; nor had the pedlar Bertram been seen or heard of in the neighborhood since the tempestuous night whereon he accompanied the cavalier in his flight toward the seashore. One thing had occurred only that could be supposed to have any reference to the subject which, it may be believed, was ever uppermost in the disturbed and anxious mind of Alice. A few days after Christmas, a strolling mercer had left a little parcel at the lodge, addressed to Mistress Alice Selby, Woolverton Hall, near Worcester, accompanied by a mere verbal message, "That it contained the goods which had been paid for in the autumn."

This, when it was opened—not without many a surmise as to its contents, for no one could remember that anything had been ordered, much less paid for in advance—was found to enclose a dozen pair of French kid gloves, superbly fringed with silver, and embroidered with rare skill, according to the fashion of the day. No note, however, accompanied the gift, for such it evidently was, nor was there any clew by which so much as to guess the giver; but on a close examination, Alice discovered that, contrary to what was usual, every glove bore the same device—a bird folding its wings as if just alighted under the shelter of a tuft of lilies, with this refrain, or poesy, as it was vulgarly denominated—

"Sauf a l'abri
De fleur de lis!"

It flashed upon her mind, therefore, instantly, that this must be intended as an intimation that her lover had made good his escape, and was now in security under the protection of France, as indicated by the chosen emblem of its ruling race. There could, indeed, be but little doubt that this was the case; and while the vigilant and jealous system of espionage, continually exercised in everything regarding intercourse with France, under the present government, was taken into consideration, the delicacy and skill by which this morsel of intelligence was transmitted, in such a manner that it should not awaken the most remote suspicion, could hardly be enough admired. For a short time the heart of Alice was relieved of care, and she lived, as it might be said, from day to day in the hope and confidence that she should ere long have the pleasure of receiving full and sufficient information of him whom she almost regarded as her husband. But when month after month lagged on, and no news came, although she learned at times that other persons throughout England received tidings from their royalist friends in the neighboring kingdom, a cold and heavy feeling of despondency, mingled with apprehension, settled down, a fixed and grievous weight on her young spirits. She could not—though she strove against the thought, which still, as often as she repressed it, rose spectre-like before her—she could not but believe that she was deserted—that she had never been loved, as she loved herself, with the whole, deep, interminable fondness of a sincere and single heart; and that now, in the first brief absence—the first small separation, which, even with the most fanciful and fickle liking, is wont rather to add than to deduct something of deeper interest and romance—she was already overlooked, forgotten, and betrayed. Brighter days would, indeed, at times break in, and with that beautiful and holy trustfulness which forms so exquisite a feature in the pure love of woman, she would frame many an excuse, and fancy many a reason, for her lover's silence; and at times would reproach herself for doubting, even momentarily, the faith and honor of him she so devotedly adored. Yet still, month after month, the adverse feeling grew more palpably and strongly on her reason; until at length it was so firmly rooted, that she would almost have been more surprised to hear that he was faithful, than that he had already broken his plighted faith and violated his allegiance.

Well was it then for Alice Selby, that though her whole soft nature was imbued with even more than all a woman's tenderness, and delicate and retiring trustfulness, there was yet in her untried soul a deep spring of resolved and patient firmness, a never-failing source of self-sustaining, humble, pure religion.

It was well for her that she had learned, even in the young days of her all-joyous, unmixed happiness, to raise her thoughts and hopes above these transitory scenes, and fix her heart on those fair mansions, where sorrow never comes, nor sin, nor suffering. It was well for her! for by that patient firmness, and in that high religious hope, that longing after something happier far, and holier and more exalted than can be looked for here, she was enabled to endure her trials, nor to endure them only, but to smile even when her pangs were keenest—and to be herself happy in the performance of her duties, and in diffusing happiness around her. There were not, it is true, so many, nor so radiant smiles on her bright face. There was not such a mirthful and continual sunshine as had been wont to beam from all her sparkling features. There was not such a bounding and elastic joy, as used to manifest itself in every motion of her light fairy frame. She fed her birds as fondly, tended her flowers as sedulously as of old; but there was something in her every act and movement, as if her feelings, those even which were the most pleasurable, had lost a part of their intensity—as if for her the earth had lost its glory. One pleasure, one alone, not only seemed to have remained unblighted, amid the desolation of the rest, but to have gained a fresh zest and vigor—the pleasure of administering to the wants, and comforting the sorrows of the poor, the aged, and the sick. Always, even from childhood upward, the eyes of many a sad, bed-ridden sufferer had brightened at the gentle sound of her light footsteps! Always the needy and the woful had been accustomed to look, not in vain, for the aid of her bounteous hand, the comfort of her low, soft voice! Always, for miles around her quiet and unostentatious home, the prayers of the grateful peasantry had been wont to call down blessings on her out-comings and in-goings. But now, more frequently than ever, her footsteps might be traced among the sad and sordid haunts of rustic want and wo—more frequently might she have been found sitting by the bedside of the fevered cottagers, assuaging by her kind promises the parting agonies of some sad, dying mother, of fatherless and helpless babes, or soothing the impatient griefs of wayward orphans! There was a deeper pathos in the tones of her most musical voice, as she read out, beside the death-bed of some penitent sinner! A sadder, yet a holier meaning in her smile, as she wiped off the tear-drops from the cheek of some forsaken maid, and pointed, as her surest consolation, to the comforts of the day-spring from on high!

It was not that she entertained so vain a thought as that these things should be imputed unto her for righteousness above. It was not that she nursed a hope so ruinous or so delusive, as that, by this mere exercise of actual duties, she could bribe Heaven to favor her weak wishes! Oh, no! she was too well taught in the truths of that which is indeed the Book of Life; she knew too well the imperfection of all human virtue, the inutility of aught save faith, and humbleness of heart, and deep contrition, to fall even for a moment into so wild an error. No! it was rather, that as she came herself to learn the fickleness of every human fortune, the fallacy of every human hope, her bosom yearned the more toward those who sorrowed, and there was none to comfort them. Her father, buried although he was in his beloved classics, with almost all his mind abstracted and engrossed on bookish meditations, was not so perfectly inapprehensive, as to notice nothing of what was passing in his sweet child's mind; nor yet so ignorant of the world's wisdom, as to deny the justice of her solicitudes and fears; but though he saw and understood the whole, and sympathized with all her sorrows, and trembled for her fate, there could not perhaps have been chosen a less fitting, or a less apt consoler, than Mark Selby. Himself originally a man of deep and overflowing passions, yet at the same time even from his youth a secluded scholar, having set all his happiness upon a single cast, and in the death of his beloved wife having lost that all by a single blow; despite his wisdom, his philosophy, his Christian fortitude, he had been able to discover no better remedy for his incessant grief, than to shut himself up apart from all his friends, among the very scenes that most recalled it to his spirit—than to brood over it in solitude and silence, till it had come to be the sole companion of his life, unfitting him for all exertion, and setting as it were a great gulf between him and the ordinary cares and pleasures of mankind.

It is true, that at times, under the sudden stimulus of some exciting circumstance, he could be roused from his stupor, and even spurred to energetic action and quiet thought; but with the emergency, the brief spirit to which it had given birth passed away likewise, and left him as before, the listless and unworthy student. This present grief was not, however, in any sort one of those which could operate to arouse him, lacking as it did any of that suddenness which seemed alone to stir him; caused as it was, rather by the cumulative evidence of many slight and almost imperceptible circumstances, than by any one striking or important incident. Then, though the old man would sometimes wonder that no tidings should arrive from Wyvil, and sometimes in his secret soul doubt the sincerity of his affection for his child, he would relapse almost immediately into forgetfulness, and hardly seem to recollect that the events had taken place at all, which had exerted such strong influences on the peace of his domestic circle. Sometimes, indeed, he would observe the unwonted silence, not to say solemnity, of his sweet daughter's manner. Sometimes he would gaze at her wistfully, as she sat by his side engaged in some graceful feminine occupation, with downcast eyes, and an unusual air of placid calmness shadowing her expressive features; and as the sorrowful conviction would steal upon him that the same fatal blight had smitten that young heart which had converted his own prime to ruined desolation, a tear would steal to his withered cheek, and he would shake his thin white locks in hopeless resignation. Yet he dreamed not of altering his mode of life—of interrupting his secluded habits—of seeking for a change of associations by a change of scene, in her case more than he had done in his own. It may be, that he knew not the efficacy of so slight causes to "raze from the brain a rooted sorrow;" or, if he knew it, he had lost the energy to practise it. So he left her to brood over her sorrows, even as he had done himself; and if the result did not prove the same, it was that the girl's mind was framed of sterner stuff than the philosopher's, and the girl's love derived from a far deeper source of wisdom than the schools of the stoic or the stagyrite.

Months had elapsed, and it was now the very height of summer; the birds, which had filled all the woods with joyful song a few weeks earlier in the season, were now all hushed and voiceless: but, as if to compensate for this, the air was vocal with the hum of myriads of bright insects, and perfumed by the odors of unnumbered flowers. It was a glorious morning in the first week of August: the heavy dew which had fallen nightly for some weeks, indicating, by its presence, the very loveliest of summer weather, was hardly yet exhaled from herb and flower, when, tempted by the fresh coolness of the time, Alice was wandering among her parterres, now one rich blush of many-colored roses, when she was disturbed from her pleasant task by the light sound of an approaching footstep. Looking up quickly from the bush which she was trimming, she recognised at once the form and features of Marian Rainsford, the gentle widow of the village-inn, and advancing a step or two to meet her—

"Ah! Marian," she exclaimed, "I am glad to see you; but I hope nothing is amiss at the Stag's-Head to bring you abroad so early. How is your mother these two days?"

"Better, I thank your kindness, Mistress Alice," replied the fair, pale widow, in answer to Alice's last words, "I think she is something better, though it is true there is very little change in her since our poor Martin was taken from us. She felt it as a sad shock, and never has been able to look on it as I do, in the light of a most merciful and blessed release—for surely he had nothing to enjoy but the mere sense of existence, and, as you know, dear lady, after that terrible night when the young cavalier escaped, he never was himself at all, but relapsed ever from one wild fit into another. Oh! lady, I am certain there was some dark mystery befell that night, of which nor you, nor I, know anything at all; and if I ask Frank Norman, or honest

Master Sherlock, they only shake their heads and make no answer. But I am wasting time, and forgetting that I came for. I much fear there is something wrong, though I can not tell what—last night a pedlar-man put up at the Stag's-Head, whom I once saw a year or two ago with Master Bartram, and all the evening long he seemed uneasy, and desirous to speak with me apart; but, knowing nothing of the man, I kept aloof from him, and I am sorry for it now, for this morning early a dragoon from London stopped there, to take breakfast and refresh his horse, on his way, as he let fall, with despatches for Major-General Henry from the Lord-General Cromwell; and when the pedlar saw him coming down the lane, in the uniform of the Ironsides, he was quite awe-stricken, and besought me to let him out by the little door in the end of the house, and would have left his pack behind if I had not reminded him of it. Well, Mistress Alice, just as I let him out, he told me that he had come down hither to warn you; for that Bartram had been caught at last, and that he bade him come down hither. And he said something more about a letter, but I could not distinctly understand, for he spoke very hurriedly and low; but I made out this much, that there was danger to your house somehow impending; and that his purpose was to warn you. But then he pointed toward the front door by which the soldier was just entering, and said it was too late, and fled as quickly as he could up the road, and I saw nothing of him more. But when the trooper had gone on his way, which he did very soon and seemingly in much haste likewise, I came up hither to tell you all that I know; but grieved I am, to say that it is all too little."

"I know not, Marian, I know not," answered Alice thoughtfully, "nor can I even guess what it should mean. Sorry I am to learn that Master Bartram has been taken, but I can not imagine what evil should arise to us from his arrest; but this man, my good Marian, this pedlar, do you know his name? did Bartram ever say that you might trust him? nay, do you even know who Bartram is himself?"

"No, lady," replied Marian, "no, I never heard this fellow's name; nor ever saw him except once, as I have told you; and what is more, so far from Master Bartram telling me to put trust in him—I have no certainty that he himself yielded him any confidence. I have seen Bartram oftentimes consort with men of all conditions, and all politics; and when he came in with a stranger, none of us ever seemed to know him, unless he spoke the first. I can not recollect now, were it for my life, how he behaved that night this man was in his company. I think, however, that they seemed friends; or I should else have thought more deeply of the matter and so remembered it."

"He might, however, well be a trapan or wily spy of Cromwell," said Alice, after a moment's musing; "I have heard tell of such things; was it not the young Cholmondeley of Chonandeley Royals, who was arrested after he had been concealed quite safely for half a year or more, all through discoveries made by a spy pretending to be a confidential agent? I should not wonder if this were something of the kind. I am almost glad that I did not see him. But, Marian, you have not told me what you know of Bartram."

"No, Mistress Alice," replied Marian, her whole face covered by a deep crimson blush, "I have not told you; and I must not, though I know very well. He is not what he seems, however, but a gentleman of birth and breeding. You may be just as certain of his faith as if you knew him, as I have done for years."

"Well, Marian, "Alice answered, "I do not see that there is anything to do, or even to consider of, thus far, if there be evil coming, we have no means of judging what it is, much less of averting it at present. All that is left to us is to be patient. If ill there be, sure am I we shall not wait long before we hear of it; and to hear nothing will be to learn that nothing is amiss. One thing, I would urge on you, Marian, should this man by-and-by return, beware of letting him discover that you at all comprehend—but ha! what have we here?" she said, interrupting herself, as the clattering sound of several horses' feet made itself heard upon the gravel-road. "Upon my word, it is our cousin Chaloner; he has not been here for these many weeks; and he looks grave, I think, even at this distance. Nay, Marian, now I fear that you are right, and that some danger is abroad."

"That do not I, Mistress Alice," answered Marian; "General Henry is not the man to bring ill tidings to his friends; unless he brought withal their remedy."

"Well, we shall soon see. Come, Marian, I will go meet him, as he passes by the wicket;" and with the words, she turned into a long alley bordered by shrubbery and flowers, across the end of which Chaloner was obliged to pass, in order to reach the gates of the hall. But, as if he had anticipated her intention, and was desirous of frustrating it, he put spurs to his horse the moment he saw her turn; and passed the head of the walk at a rapid trot, bowing very low, but wearing no smile on his handsome features, before she had accomplished half the distance.

"There! see you not that, see you not that, Marian? Be sure that he bears some ill news, which he would break to my father ere he reveal it to me. I will return to the hall; and, riding at that pace, he will be there long ere I reach it. So farewell, farewell for the present, and pray believe me that I thank you much for your kind services. Should anything occur, wherein you can assist me, depend on it, I will send for you."

"I pray you do so, lady," answered the gentle widow, "for we owe you a very heavy debt of gratitude, and I would fain do something, if it were possible, to prove to you that we are not insensible to your great goodness—not for a moment dreaming of repaying you: for that I could not, nor would wish to do, if I could; but that it is sweet to serve those we love, however humbly. But I will not detain you, Mistress Alice; for I can see, by your eye, that you are anxious. God bless and keep you, lady, and may all good go with you, as do the prayers of all the poor and sorrowful. Heaven only knows what would come of them should aught befall the house of Woolverton!"

The tears rose to the eyes of Alice, as the fair widow spoke; but she made no reply, for of a truth her heart was too full;

and not that only, but a presentiment of evil near at hand hung over her, depressing for the moment all her fine energies, and high elastic spirit, so that she dare not speak, lest she should lose her self-control entirely, and burst into a flood of weeping: waving a mute answer, she turned and walked rapidly, though with a faltering and uncertain pace, toward the hall, before the doors of which she found the horses of Henry Chaloner in waiting; and many of the servants of the household collected in a blustering, and as it seemed half-apprehensive group, talking in fast, low whispers, and seeming by that strange instinctive intuition which is so often possessed by servants, to have discovered that matters were not going well with their masters.

"Oh! Mistress Alice," exclaimed the old butler, Jeremy, coming up as fast as he could to meet her the moment she came into sight; "here is Major-General Henry Chaloner closeted with the master, this half hour, and they have asked for you thrice, Mistress Alice; the park-keeper has gone to seek you at the fish-house, and Abraham was sent into the garden."

"Never mind, never mind, good Jeremy," she answered quickly, as she hurried past him, fearful of being detained by the old man's garrulity; "I am here now, and Abraham, and John, the park-keeper, will not begrudge the trouble."

"Not they, not they, I warrant them"—but long before he had concluded his prolix assurances of the men's willingness to incur every trouble in her behalf, Alice had vanished up the staircase, and was already at the door of her father's study. There she paused for a moment to collect her agitated thoughts; for her heart beat fast and painfully, and her limbs almost refused to do their office, so certainly did she connect this unexpected visit of her cousin with the arrival of ill news, which, though she knew not why, she never for a moment doubted to be in some sort identified with Wyvil. She opened the door with a noiseless hand and entered, and as she saw the countenances of the pair, who sat with many papers scattered before them on the table, she was assured that her mind had been but too prophetic; for the fine face of Henry Chaloner, so passionless for the most part and calm, bore now strong tokens of vast care and perturbation, flushing at one time, and the next moment pale as ashes; his voice, too, was husky, choked, and indistinct; and his eyes swam with tears, which he brushed away every now and then with his gloved hand, as if he were ashamed to be seen weeping. The features of the old man, on the contrary, were much excited. The air of cold and careless abstraction which commonly possessed them, had given way to a high and spirited expression, and there was a quick and lively glance in his clear eye, a hectic color on his pale cheek, which Alice had not witnessed there for years. So quietly had she come in, that neither was aware of her presence; and her father went on speaking, unconscious that he was overheard.

"So, as it seems that no choice else is left to us, we were better set off on the instant."

"I fear so," answered Henry, gloomily—"indeed, I fear it must be so; for though this pass of the lord-general will secure you from all trouble or annoyance on the route, I can not but be apprehensive that should the parliament commissioners arrive, and find you still here, it might be construed into an act of contumelious malignancy."

"Well, if it must be so," replied the old man; "but it is hard, that one so old as I am—so old in honorable years and blameless studies—should be forced to fly from his country, like a thief or a murderer; and that for no harm done! But, it is not for myself, Henry! for I have but a little while—a few months, more or less—to wear away in this mortality; and what matters it where one, so useless and wornout as I, draw his last breath? It is not for myself that I feel, Henry—although I had hoped to see my last sun set over these peaceful trees, and to lie, when this vain world should be lost to me for ever, by her side in the long home of my fathers. But, Alice, Alice! oh, it will be difficult to leave her—as leave her I soon must—far from her native home, among mere hirelings, without a friend or guardian, and in a foreign land. Besides, she loves so dearly this old place, and all its memories, that it will break her heart to leave it!"

"No, father!" the sweet girl interposed, taking a forward step that brought her fully into view—"no, no! believe it not! There is not anything in the wide world that it would break my heart to leave, unless it were to leave you! Oh, no! I am quite ready to set forth at once, if it be needful—but whither must we go, and wherefore? tell me, I pray you, Cousin Henry."

"Grieved to the heart I am to tell you, Alice; but told it must be, pain us however much it may; so nerve yourself, dear cousin, for the worst, for this indeed is very sad and difficult to bear. It seems the pedlar Bartrand, or Colonel George Penruddock rather—for such is his real name and station—for whom the government has been long strictly watching, as an emissary of the exiled family, was taken six nights since, after a desperate resistance, at a small, obscure tavern in the borough; and when he came to be searched, there was found on his person, concealed within the hollow of a staff, a letter, among sundry treasonable papers, from Captain Wyvil to his friend and kinsman in the north, Vavasour; detailing accurately his escape from Worcester, his lying hid here in this house, and even going so far as to describe the very mode by which he was enabled to elude our search by diving through an opening in the wall of the well into a subterranean chamber. Your name and Master Selby's were mentioned at full length, so that there is not any room for denial or disproval, if you had been disposed to make such, which I am sure you are not. Unhappily, the papers, some of them having reference to an intended rising in the west, were deemed of such immediate interest, that, Cromwell being absent from town at Hampton Court, they were laid instantly before the council, and by them referred to the parliament, who proceeded without delay to take action on them. Had they been shown to the lord-general in the first instance, no evil should have come of it; for though he may esteem it necessary to punish heavily seditious plotters, or those who would disturb the constituted powers, he is the last man living to act vindictively, or to wage war on those who are now living peaceably in the land, whatever may be their opinions. A despatch was forwarded to me from him this very morning, by relays from the military stations; for he has often heard me speak of you, and knows our kindred, and how dearly I regard your welfare. Warrants, he tells me, have been issued for your and your father's apprehension—the penalty, you know, for the harboring and resetting proclaimed traitors is death, Alice — but that he has himself taken means to delay the messengers. He has sent his sign manual, by which you may pass everywhere throughout the realm, and sail from any port unquestioned; he urges upon me to prevail on you to set off instantly for France. He tells me in so many words, that had he learned these matters in due season, no peril should have come of them to you or any of your kindred; but if you be once taken, he can not, for state reasons which it is needless now to name, well interfere to save you. Further than this, all will go well. Sequestrated your estates must be; but Cromwell has given me his written promise that they shall be made over to me in perpetuity, and in my own power. I need not therefore say, that I shall hold them as your steward, remitting the rents to you wherever you may be, and looking to the welfare of your tenants and poor pensioners, as you would were you present. For the rest there is little doubt, or I might well say more — that the whole of this trouble will be reduced at least to a few months sojourn in France; for a free pardon will be granted to you easily after the first excitement of the business shall have died away, you living quietly in the meantime, as you will doubtless do, and taking no part in the angry politics of the day."

"Is that all, Cousin Henry?" replied Alice, feigning a pleasure which she was very far from feeling, and mastering her own feelings so as to induce her father to more self-control—"is that all that has made you and my father look so gravely? — a few months' absence only on the continent? I have longed ever to visit *la belle France;* and here, it seems, is a self-made opportunity; a little hurried, it is true, but the more haste the more excitement. You were best order the coach round at once, dear father. My girl will pack up a few things in half an hour. We will take Margaret along with us, and

Charles and Gregory on horseback, and two or three of the other men can ride on the road before us and lead relays! so we can drive to Bristol with our own horses; that will be the best way — will it not, cousin?"

"I think it will," he answered, smiling sadly. "You are quite a general, Alice, for that is just the plan I had myself laid down for you. There is a vessel too at Bristol, to sail in three days for Boulogne."

"I am glad of it, Henry," she replied — "I am glad; when we have anything to do not altogether pleasant, it is the happiest always where it can be done at once. Now, dearest father, will you not go and speak with Jeremy, and tell him simply that we are going to France for a little while, and that our Cousin Henry will remain in charge while we are absent, and bid him order out the coach, with two relays of led horses."

"God bless you, my beloved child! God bless you, and he will," replied the old man, as he rose sadly and slowly to quit the library — "and he will bless you. God's blessing follows ever such constancy and piety as this. We will dine early, and depart immediately. Chaloner, you will take your last meal with us —"

"And ride with you to Bristol, and see you safe on board; and then returning hither, take order here with all things, that you shall find them all, when you return, even as you left them."

"When we return! when, Henry?" cried Mark Selby, and his countenance fell as he cast his eyes around him, over his loved books, and the quiet study where he had passed so many years of his secluded, peaceable existence. "But go with me, good Henry. Go with me, and help me in these hurried matters."

"Nay! father," answered Alice, "I would speak with him for a moment; go you, I pray you, and speak with Jeremy, and he shall join you in a minute. Now, Henry," she continued, as her father left the room — "now, Cousin Henry, show me the general's letter; tell me the worst at once, for this is not the worst that you have told me."

"It is, indeed, Alice," he answered very firmly. "Nay, it is something more than the worst; for Cromwell promises distinctly to grant your father a free pardon, if all go quiet for a year—his letter I would show you, but I can not. He has gained some intelligence on matters which he has misapprehended, and drawing false conclusions from false premises, has written that which you could be only pained to see, speaking with confidence of things, as soon about to happen, which we know can not be. On this I will soon disabuse him; and I feel sure, that I may even promise you a pardon likewise, when he shall know the truth."

The eyes of Alice fell, as Chaloner uttered these words, and a deep crimson flush covered the whole of her pale features, for she understood very clearly what he meant; and she was not merely pained by seeing that his mind still dwelt upon that which in bygone times had passed between them, and which she had been accustomed to hope was now forgotten, but was embarrassed likewise as to another question, which she was desirous of asking while it was still in her power to do so. Her cousin seeming, however, to misapprehend the cause of her agitation, took her affectionately by the hand, and said—

"Do not afflict yourself, I pray, sweet Alice—I would not have alluded to these things at all, could I have helped it. I would not have you misunderstand me for the world—it was necessary that you should know exactly how things stood; that, I assure you, was the only reason why I spoke, not to distress you or myself by waking any thoughts of what were better far forgotten."

"Oh, Henry!" answered Alice, "it is you that mistake now; it was not that at all which made me hesitate, but I was thinking how I should put a question to you, which it concerns me much to have directly answered."

"Put it directly, then," said Chaloner; "that is the wisest always; and, believe me, Alice, there is not a question in all the world that I would hesitate to answer you in the same spirit."

"I believe you, indeed I do, Henry; how could I do otherwise," replied Alice, "than believe the least asseveration from lips that, like yours, have uttered nothing in a lifetime but what is true and noble?—and I think, too, that you are right in this. Tell me, then, in these intercepted papers, was there no letter for my father, or myself?"

"None, Alice," answered the youth, "none at least that I heard of; and I can hardly doubt that, had there been such, the lord-general would have named it in his despatch, which is for him unusually long and copious."

"Strange," she said—"strange, indeed, and cruel;" and as she uttered the words, overpowered for the moment by her passionate feelings, and half forgetful of her cousin's presence, a tear or two stole silently down her soft cheek.

"And base, too, beyond measure!" exclaimed Henry Chaloner, yielding to that impulsive indignation, which it was ever difficult for him to control at the occurrence of injustice—"base it was in him, to write to a third party, things that, I fear, were revealed to him only under pledge of secrecy; but which, I am sure, no honorable man would have disclosed, even if such were not the case."

"Hush, Henry! hush!" she answered; "I may not hear such things spoken, and it becomes not you to speak them. Be that all as it may, it becomes not one so noble as Henry Chaloner to speak in aught harshly of one who might have, and most likely has, some good defence to offer were he present. But now, good Henry, go to my father, and assist him, I beseech you; and, above all, seek to amuse his mind, for I much fear this shock will fall on him even too heavily. I will make some few brief arrangements, and meet you at the noontide meal—till then, God bless you and farewell!"

CHAPTER XXIV.

Farewell! farewell! that is a sad word at the best, and full of dark associations. Even when in all fruition of the present, and high anticipation of the future, we leave some spot where we have passed glad days; which is linked to our hearts by golden memories; although perhaps we leave it at the suggestion of our own wishes, and for the furtherance of our own interests, even then there is a sense of indistinct and undefinable melancholy that will o'ershadow us, clouding our joys, as it were, in despite of our reason, and mingling our hopes with regret. Even when friends part, light-hearted, and care-free, after some pleasant merry-making, some spirit-stirring revel, part with the certainty—as if, alas! aught that pertains to poor humanity can be called certain—of meeting to renew that sweet communion, now for a little space dissevered—after a few brief months or weeks, or perhaps days, there is still in every sensitive and thoughtful soul, a tender and prophetic gloom, a mellowed sadness, a sprinkling* of that bitterness which, rising from the mid-fount of our pleasures, leaves a sting in the veriest flowers of existence. What is it, then, to say "farewell" to the place of our birth, to the home of our childhood, the cradle of our intellect, the shrine of our affections, the temple of our memories?—to say "farewell," when we go forth to cross wide seas, and visit foreign climes; to exchange all the sweet and magical associations, which belong not to any other word in our land's language as they do to that one—"home"—all the familiarity of friends, all the deep love of kindred, for the cold, heartless stare of the great world, the chilling intercourse of strangers?—what, when there is no term set to our reluctant wanderings, when there is no time named, when we may once again return to all we prize so far beyond all else that the earth circles—when Hope herself is silent of the

* Medio de fonte leporum
Surgit amare aliquid quod in ipsis floribus ungit.

future? I know not how it is, but it seems to me, to be something more than the mere work of fancy; something more real than the imagining of spirits depressed, and saddened, and rendered half poetical by sorrow — for sorrow is a mighty wakener into life of whatsoever gems of the ideal lurk unsuspected in the soul. I know not how it is — I say, that we never leave any place, which we have loved and should regret hereafter; but some chance circumstances will occur, some accidents, as painters call them, of light or shadow, or of the time of day, or of the ever-varying seasons, to clothe it with a new and fresher beauty than it has ever worn before, to make it put on a guise, rendering it far more difficult to quit without reluctance, or to think of without regretful memories. At such times it would be a relief, that the lovely scenes wherein our spirits have delighted, were veiled in the gray and ghostly mists of dark November; that the trees which have budded green and fresh, as our young hopes, were like them sere and cold and leafless; that the voice of the joyous streamlet were bridled by the ice of winter; the brilliant gardens flowerless, the happy warblers songless; but it is rarely so. We are for the most part torn from our pleasures, when they are the sweetest; exiled from our homes, when they are loveliest. And so it was now, to Mark Selby and his fair daughter. The gorgeous light of an unclouded afternoon, at midsummer, was clothing the rich woods and grassy lawns in a resplendent robe of golden glory — the air was alive and vocal with the hum of ten thousand glittering insects, the gardens were one glow of roses, with myriads of light butterflies round their perfumed petals — the streams were rippling with a soft melody like woman's laughter. Earth, water, air, were redolent of mirth and beauty; and as the slow and ponderous carriage which conveyed the old man and his daughter from the place of their birth, rolled, as it were, reluctantly over the smoothly-gravelled road, it seemed to Alice as if the grinding wheels were crushing out the joys, the hopes, the very life of her young heart; yet gloriously she bore up, and subdued the almost overwhelming sorrow; and though her sweet eyes swam with tears, and her voice faltered as she spoke, she yet compelled herself to talk hopefully and almost gayly to the depressed and spirit-broken man, who, utterly prostrated by the shock of this last great calamity, sat by her side, with his gray head bowed upon his knees, and all his senses for the moment paralyzed.

As they passed through the gates, and the old porter, with his long white hair uncovered, stood in the ivied porch of the brick lodge, his little grand-children, Alice's special favorites, smiling, and courtesying at his side, while they held back the leaves of the great gate; she almost thought that life could contain nothing more of pain or sorrow, than she experienced in that passing moment. For who of us, even the wisest, can so much as dream what is in store for him, save death alone, the one sure consequence — the sole, immutable, inevitable offspring of the future? The trifling shock occasioned by the turning of the cumbrous vehicle into the narrow lane, beyond the park-gates, aroused Mark Selby for a few seconds from his stupor; he looked about him with a long, wistful gaze, upon the calm green fields and fine old trees among which he had lived all his days, and grown up from the joyous, prattling child, to whom the whole world is but one happy present, to the frail-bowed octogenarian, looking from a sad past on to a sadder future. He gazed with a set, meaningless eye on the gray moss-grown roofs of his old home; he thought of her whom he had brought long years ago, a happy bride, to fill those dim and silent halls with merriment and glee; who, after a few little years, years that seemed in the retrospect as less than minutes, had left him more alone than ever: whose very grave he never should see any more — he gazed until a sudden angle of the park wall, with the thick leafy elms above it, shut off the well-known prospect; then, heaving a deep sigh, as if he was half refreshed—

"Alice," he said, "it may be that you will see these again; God grant it! but, as for me, I never shall behold them any more. I would have laid me down to my long sleep, this weary turmoil ended, on the same bed and under the same roof which witnessed the commencement of my pilgrimage—

I would have slept it out beside her. Nevertheless, not my will be done, but THINE," he added, looking reverentially upward, "who never chasteneth us but for our good—never forgettest any one, the humblest of thy flock."

But Alice could not answer him, nor speak at all, because in truth the very same thought was passing through her own mind; and when her father echoed it in that prophetic tone, which is so frequently adopted by the aged—especially they who have known many sorrows—she felt that it would be but a species of impiety to attempt any consolation, much more to feign a disbelief, which he must know she did not entertain. She looked up, however, with her soft, gentle smile into his face, and made an effort; but it was drowned instantly in an abundant flood of tears, the first to which she had given way, that burst forth hot and heavy, yet seemed to relieve the over-strained aching brain of some portion of its anguish.

"It must be so, my child," resumed the old man, taking her hand in his tremulous and withered fingers, "but do not weep for that. Sooner or later, it must still be so, my own sweet Alice; how painful it may be soever for you to contemplate, we must part, at some time or other, and in the course of nature. I shall set out the first upon that journey which in His own good time I wait for. The old must pass away, and leave their places to the young, even as the aged oak makes way for the fresh sapling, or the old year expires to give birth to the new. Therefore it is, my girl, that while I feel quite sure that I shall never again look upon these dear scenes, I have good trust that you may return hither; and pass happy days, where you have given so much happiness to others. Nevertheless, if it be ordered otherwise, we have, I trust, been too well schooled to murmur, or to repine at that which is before us. The world has many a varied scene, and every scene has its own beauty, every station its own phase of happiness. It may may be we shall find few landscapes in other lands, so lovely to our eyes as these green fields and quiet trees; it must be that we shall find none so endeared to our memories—but we shall yet have many joys and much contentment, and above all, the cheering confidence that we shall never be forsaken utterly, or burthened beyond our power to bear. Do not weep, Alice; there may yet be much happiness in store, much more, perhaps, than you have known heretofore. One thing is nearly certain, to which you must look forward with joyous expectation."

"Oh, say no more!" she exclaimed—"no more on that head, father, for I know but too well what you mean; and I have no hope at all, no expectation—how should I, when all is dark and bitter? and that the bitterest of all to which we might have looked for comfort. I mean that he, he of all men, should have betrayed us!"

"But *that* I do not in the least believe," answered her father instantly, and with much decision—"not in the least, Alice; it is against all probability, all nature. Marmaduke Wyvil may be light-minded, trivial, fickle; but he can not be—nay, I am sure he *is* not so heedless of the obligations of a most solemn oath—so wantonly base and dishonest as to betray us without cause or purpose. No! set your mind at ease on that score, Alice. I am an old man, and not wont to form opinions lightly, or when I have formed such, to be mistaken; and I am sure, I *was* sure from the first, that there is some mistake in this report of Henry's."

"You make me happy," answered poor Alice, "her whole face brightening up with newly-kindled hope and animation. "Oh, father, you make me very, very happy! And do you think that he is indeed true to us, faithful and loyal as we would wish him? Oh, if you do think so, surely it was most wrong in me to doubt him."

"Whether he love you as he ought to do, my child," replied the old man—"whether his fancy or his heart have ever swerved from you in absence—whether, in short, he is worthy of such virtues as yours, Alice, I can not tell. Although I do not clearly see why he should not, yet I am confident that he never wrote to Sir Edmund Vavasour—to any third party, disclosing what he swore never to reveal! All the rest, time will make certain; and in the meanwhile, I who am never sanguine, I tell you, my dear child, to be hopeful."

" But how can that be — how can that be?" exclaimed she, relapsing into doubt. " Oh, no! you *are* too sanguine, father — for how should they know else where he lay hid, much more the very trick and mode of his escape, when Henry searched the house — a trick of which none living, save you, and I, and he, are cognizant? No, father, no! Marmaduke Wyvil must have written — must have betrayed us! Wo is me! he must!"

" He must have written, Alice, but not to Vavasour. He must, as you say, have betrayed us; but it may very well be he wrote to one or the other of us two, and thus, through very reckless inadvertency, but without any guilt, betrayed us. Nay, but I am most sure that we shall find it to be thus.

" I fear me much you are wrong," answered the poor girl, " for I asked Henry Chaloner if there had been no letters found on Bartram, addressed to either of us, and he made answer, ' None! none at least that I heard of;' and he went on to say that, had there been such, he could hardly doubt that the lord-general would have named it in his despatches."

" Very like, Alice," said he, promptly; " but I do not believe that Cromwell himself had seen the letters. They were, it seems, immediately submitted to the council, and by them laid before the parliament, and he wrote instantly to Chaloner, so to anticipate the evil. For the whole world, my child, if I believed it possible that he should be the traitor this would make him, I would not lead you to form hopes which a few days would crush for ever; but I say, hope — hope, Alice, for the best; and sure I am you will not be deceived. But see, here we have reached the cross-roads inn, and our relay is waiting."

The horses were soon changed, and here, as the men who had brought them, came up to the coach-door, cap in hand, to make their last adieus to their young mistress before returning homeward, a fresh pang was awakened in a bosom that surely needed no new agonies to rack it. The carriage once again rolled onward, and the blunt, honest faces, shaded by sincere grief, of those domestic friends, were lost to the eyes of the mournful travellers, and no more words were spoken;

father and daughter both relapsing into gloomy silence. The sun soon set and darkness covered the skies, and by-and-by the stars came out on high, and the moon rose, and shed her pure, cold light over the lonely wastes through which they journeyed. All night long they drove on, slowly and wearily to spare their horses, pausing from time to time to water them at some lone wayside public house, but hurrying through the market towns and larger villages, as if unwilling to awaken the attention of the country. A little while before sunrise they reached a solitary inn, to which their second relay of horses had been directed to proceed; and here Henry Chaloner, who up to this time had ridden in the rear, avoiding to intrude upon the sorrows of his friends, came up to the carriage-window, and advised them to alight and repose themselves for some hours, as they were now distant but twenty miles from Bristol, whither there could be no advantage of arriving before nightfall. To this, Alice, who had at first objected, wishing to get over the whole journey at once, assented; when Henry pointed out to her that he wished, for the purpose of avoiding suspicion, to send an avant-courier to the commandant of the garrison and port, who was well known to him, announcing his arrival with two friends, who were about to sail for France under the sanction of the lord-general's sign-manual.

"By doing this," he said, "you will escape all disagreeable interference on the part of town officers, and, it is like enough, some painful and impertinent interrogation. Besides," he added, "you can not go on board before to-morrow night at all events, and you will, I think, be quieter and therefore more at ease in this little country-place, than in the bustling seaport."

This was unanswerable; and having once alighted, both Alice and her aged parent found themselves so fatigued and harassed both in mind and body, that, after all, they were not sorry to lie down and rest in the neat quiet bed-chambers of the little inn; nor did either of them make their appearance until late in the afternoon, after Chaloner's servant had returned from the town bearing the greetings of the commandant, and an invitation for his brother officer, with his friends to take up their abode in the castle, until the ship should sail. Then they were summoned, and after a slight meal, partaken of in almost breathless silence, with the exception of a short conversation respecting the propriety of accepting or declining Colonel Millanke's invitation, which was decided by a negative, they again set out upon their road; and the night falling shortly afterward, they entered the place of their destination before the moon was above the horizon, and consequently without seeing any of the romantic scenery which surrounds that prosperous city—a loss which did not seem, however, to be such to the anxious travellers, and which in truth never so much as occurred to the mind of either. That night they slept in Bristol, and oh! the anguish of awakening, in a strange place, from the forgetfulness of happy sleep—of gradually recovering the consciousness of sorrow, of that half-doubtful state, in which the reason seems to waver, unable to believe, and yet incapable of hope! Yet much has been written to no purpose, if any one, who has thus far pursued her fortunes, is not aware that Alice Selby had by this time so perfectly resigned herself to her lot, so far regained her self-possession and tranquillity, that she descended to the breakfast table and met her cousin, after one little struggle, arrayed in smiles and able to converse on all topics connected with their situation with absolute composure, and more, almost, than feminine decision. On her devolved all the arrangements of their voyage; for the excitement passed which had aroused her father for a little space, he had fallen back into something even heavier and duller than his usual abstraction; and it was sometimes not without difficulty that his attention could be called to the present, strongly enough to give an answer to an immediate question. Chaloner lent his aid, however; and before evening all their baggage, with the addition of their carriage and six horses—for these Henry advised her strenuously to take with her—were safely got on board; passports provided, sea-stores laid in, and all things put in train for their departure at an early hour on the morrow.

Once in France, it had been determined between Alice and her cousin, that they should remain at Boulogne-sur-Mer, writing thence to announce what had befallen them to all their friends in Paris, among whom was a certain Marquise de Gondi, a half-sister of Alice Selby's mother—born in a second marriage of her grandfather with a French lady—who had espoused a French nobleman, of wealth and distinction, and, early left a widow, had continued to reside in the metropolis of France, maintaining always a frequent and most cordial correspondence with her English relatives.

"Were I you, Alice," said Chaloner, continuing a conversation which had engaged them for the greater part of the evening, "for I can see that all arrangements will depend on your suggestions to your father, I would not move from Boulogne for some time, not certainly until you hear from me, and receive the amount of your father's autumn rental; the rest of your wardrobe, with the books you mentioned to me, and whatever else I may deem needful to you, I will remit forthwith; and when I can find aught to tell you, I will write, Alice, and you will answer me?"

"Surely I will," said Alice, "and I beseech you to write to me often; for I shall ever yearn to hear from Woolverton. But why should we not go at once to Paris? I am sure Madame de Gondi will be anxious to receive us."

"I am sure she will, Alice, too; yet I advise you strongly not to go as yet. The court is exiled from the city, living at present, as I learned by the last despatches at Pontoise; a furious civil war is raging in all the isle of France, in many parts of Champagne, in Bries, and all the country thence to the Flemish frontier. Monsieur Turenne, it is true, beat the princes in a great battle under the walls of Paris on the second of last month, and would have crushed their party utterly, but that the factious citizens admitted the rebels by the gate of St. Antoine, and played the cannon of the Bastile on the king's forces; but we hear that the Spaniards have retaken all the strong places they had lost in Flanders and elsewhere, and that the archduke of Lorraine has again entered France with five-and-twenty thousand men, and is in full march on the capital, hoping there to effect a junction with the prince of Condè. So you perceive, that were you to reach Paris now, you would be in the midst of hostile armies; and moreover, Madame de Gondi being of the royal party, and all the English cavaliers who have escaped since Worcester being engaged on the king's side, you might be possibly exposed to violence from the Frondists, who are strong in the metropolis; and what is worse, news would be likely to reach England, that your father was bestirring himself in French politics; and though *we* know that to be quite impossible, yet in such times as these, no rumors are too wild for credence."

"O Heaven!" said Alice, "and is our lot to be cast once more in the midst of warring armies? Is there to be no more place upon earth for ever, but civil wars, and blood, and parricidal slaughters?—kings trampling on the liberty of subjects, and subjects impiously armed against the majesty of kings, and sanguinary, selfish soldiers lashing both on to wilder madness, prompted by foul self-interest? Is this to be the history of the world henceforth, for ever, Henry? for if it be so, I care not how soon I may be where I shall see no more of it."

"He only can reply to you," said Henry, gravely, "to whom all things are known. It may not be denied, however, that matters do look strangely, the world over. The people, everywhere, having asserted and regained those rights, which of a certainty were threatened but a little while ago, seem set at present on pulling down the rights of others. How it may end, I know not; but I confess, for one, my confidence is shaken altogether in the self-governing power of the people—they do not possess equity, honesty, self-knowledge, self-respect, or self-control. I hope and pray, but I doubt, Alice, of the future. In France, I believe, however, this civil strife is nearly ended; and that soon, for a season, peace will be established. Turenne has marched against the archduke; and, as a soldier, I have little doubt he will beat him. The Cardinal Mazarin, whose favor with the queen-mother was the chief cause of disaffection, has withdrawn himself into voluntary exile; and altogether I am well of opinion, that before two months shall pass, all will again be quiet and the court firmly settled in the Louvre. By that time you will, if you adopt my plan of remaining at Boulogne, have secured all your remittances and wardrobe; you will have gained full information concerning this bad business, of which as yet we know so little; and then, if no change shall have occurred permitting you to return home, you can remove to Paris. Should the marquise solicit your immediate progress to the capital, I think the state of the countries and the vicinity of the armies will be excuse sufficient."

"Oh, yes, indeed it will," said Alice; "I would not be again within reach of such occurrences as followed Worcester, for all the wealth of France. I will persuade my father to adopt your plans implicitly, and shall hope to hear tidings of all my friends, both great and humble, at your hand very often."

"You shall, you shall indeed," he answered; "and you must not be very much surprised if you were to see me before very long. There is some talk of sending a fresh envoy to the Hague, and I have been entreated to accept the duty. As yet I know not how it will all end. But it is growing late already; and, as you must rise betimes to-morrow, I will now take my leave. Good rest to you, my gentle cousin."

The morning followed soon — the cold, gray, melancholy morning; and the sad exiles bade farewell to their last friend, and went on board the ship, with its foretopsail set, and sailing signals flying, but waited their arrival to get under weigh. To those who have parted from their native lands, words are unnecessary to recall the cold, dull, stunning agony which paralyzed their very souls, as those beloved shores, never perhaps to bless any more the straining eyes that watch them to the last, faded in the far distance; — to those who know not that dread trial, no words could paint it; but may they never know it! The wind, though fair, was fresh; and as the good ship left the harbor it freshened more and more, and the vessel rolled and pitched; and it was well perhaps for Alice, that for a time corporeal sufferings effaced the anguish of her spirit; and that no room was given her for contemplation of the past, or imagination for the future, until, a boisterous but rapid passage ended, they lay in safety at the pier-head of Boulogne — and then new scenes, new hopes, new fears, and all the keen excitement consequent on the first sight of a new country!

CHAPTER XXV.

THE current of events never stands still; the tide of cause and effect never ebbs; but still, advancing with a flood equally noiseless and invisible, whether it be slow or rapid, overtops the landmarks of the most sage experience, and shakes the bulwarks of the firmest resolution. Still, even in the most eventful periods of the most eventful lives, there will be many a pause, many a breathing space of seeming quiet, during which it not seldom happens, that when we deem ourselves most tranquil and secure in our ignorance of what is passing elsewhere, accidents are actually going on in places we never heard of, and among persons we have never seen, which are to alter the whole course and tenor of our lives, and work our happiness or wo. For well nigh two months after their disembarking at Boulogne, nothing apparently occurred, nothing assuredly transpired that could affect the Selbys either for good or evil. They soon, indeed, received replies from their Parisian friends, some kind and warm and cordial, others as cold and ungenial as a July hailstorm. The kindest from those persons on whom they had the slighter claims, who had least loudly tongued their protestations; the coldest from the most indebted, and the most prodigal of former offers. To this, there was but one exception — Madame de Gondi's letters were all that could be wished for or expected; so hospitably anxious to embrace her lovely niece — so strenuous in her delight at offering her a home in her heart of hearts — that she seemed positively to rejoice at the calamities which had enabled her to enjoy her society, and to give scope to all the largeness of her own generous spirit. After the first strong pressing invitation, she was induced, however, to admit the prudence of Henry Chaloner's advice, and to consent to their remaining tranquilly in private lodgings at Boulogne until the court should return to Paris, and the war be brought to a conclusion, which all the royalists now prophesied aloud must ere long be the consequence of Turenne's martial skill. Meanwhile, the life of Alice and her father passed on as stagnantly as can well be imagined. Letters came now and then from Chaloner, accompanying the promised bales of books and habiliments, but there was little in them of grand or stirring interest — relating as they did, for the most part, to local matters, to the tenantry, and poor, and household, at Woolverton, which had been formally sequestrated and granted in due course of law to Chaloner, who hastened to remit the proceeds of the rents; while all the charities of the late owners were still continued, and the establishment kept up almost upon its ancient footing. At times, long gossipping epistles would arrive from Madame Gondi, full of descriptions of the progress of the royal arms, of loyal hopes and exultations, and copious praises of the loyal leaders, among whom, more than once, poor Alice found enumerated the name of Major Wyvil, as one distinguished far above his fellows, for desperate valor and high conduct. Beyond this, nothing of any kind occurred to disturb the monotonous gloom of the life which they led, day after day, in the small uninteresting seaport. A solitary walk upon the cliffs, or on the strip of yellow sand below them, a wistful straining of the eyes toward the invisible shores beloved, and now and then a drive through the dull environs — these were her only occupations beyond the doors of their cheerless home. Her father, who now had fallen back completely into his ancient habits, seemed to be scarcely conscious of the change which had occurred in his fortunes; but a few of his favored authors being forwarded to him by Henry, he read, and wrote, mused, and methodized, in a small dingy chamber in Boulogne, with the same unremitting studiousness which kept him ensconsed for weeks together in his delightful library at Woolverton ; and seemed to be as happy now as he had been at any period of his life.

Two months passed, and the summer flowers had passed away, the harvest had been gathered in, the vintage had been pressed, and brown October was painting busily the woods with the rich hues of his autumnal pallet. From time to time they had learned that the Spaniards had retreated into Flanders ; that Monsieur de Lorraine was advancing a second time on Paris ; that Turenne had marched to intercept him, but having failed to prevent his junction with the princes, had taken up a strong position in the angle of the Seine and Heyère — the very same which had been occupied in June by the duke, and was too strong to be attacked with any probability of success, although the enemy were confident of speedily reducing him by want of forage and provision for his men. Soon afterward, news reached them that at the very moment when the princes imagined that the royal army must surrender within the space of a few days, the great French captain had bridged the Seine with boats in several places, and extricated all his troops without the loss of a single man, or the discovery by the enemy that he so much as meditated the evacuation of his lines Then came intelligence that the royalists had passed the Marne at Meaux, and, marching by Borest and Mont l'Evêque, had taken a position at Courteuil near Senlis ; and that the rebels utterly discouraged at finding themselves thus out-manœuvred. and left in a devastated region with all their work to do a second time — their foreign friends deserting them meanwhile, and their abettors, the most of the great cities, becoming weary of them — had fallen back into Champagne and Lorraine ; the Spanish leaders having engaged to meet them at Rathel on the Aisne, and aid them to reduce such fortresses and strongholds in those provinces as might be necessary to secure their winter-quarters. The consequence of these events, it was predicted strongly, would be the return of the court to Paris, and Alice was encouraged to expect a speedy summons thither.

Such was the state of affairs in the realm of France, when, on one bright, clear morning, it was announced with no small bustle throughout the streets of Boulogne, that an English bark had come into port a little after sunrise; and that a government courier was at that moment entering the town with despatches, it was supposed, of great moment. An hour or two afterward, the attention of Alice was attracted by the great concourse which began to pour through all the thoroughfares toward the market-place, where she soon learned, from the exclamations of the people, that the governor of the royal garrison was about to address the citizens, touching some news which had arrived from Paris. She had already risen from the window by which she had been sitting, with the intent of sending one of the men to learn what was passing, when the door opened, and her maid came in bearing two letters, with a face full of well-pleased smiles, exclaiming, "From England, Mistress Alice, from England! and from Paris, too! and all the town are mad, I think, for joy, for the great marshal, I forget his name, has beat the roundheads."

"The roundheads!" replied Alice, with a smile. "The rebels, you mean, Margaret; there are no roundheads here."

"Well, then, the rebels, Mistress Alice," answered the girl; "but I thought it was all one. Our roundheads, I am sure, were rebels. But beaten they are, and glad I am of it; and the king, and our good duke of York, and all the gentle cavaliers have been carried back in triumph to Paris."

"Well, that is good news, Margaret, if it be true," said Alice; "for in that case we can go at once to the city."

"Oh, I shall be so glad! oh, so glad!" exclaimed the country-girl, her whole face radiant with delight. "They say it is the finest in all the universal world. When shall we go, Mistress Alice? Oh, I am so glad!"

"I doubt it not," said Alice, laughing somewhat sadly; "but be not too quick in your gladness, Margaret, for many a thing which seems to us all joy in the beginning brings in the end much sadness; and it is well, if not repentance also. But, leave me now, my good girl, that I may read these letters, and you shall hear all in season." And as she spoke, she tore the cover off the English letter, which was addressed in the familiar hand of her cousin, and seemed, from its bulk, to contain several enclosures. The first on which her eye fell, as she broke the seal, was a small note directed separately to herself, with the word "private" added to the superscription. The writing was still Henry's, and her heart beat tumultuously, as she opened it, for she half feared that he might have procured her pardon from the lord-general, coupled with some conditions, which it would be painful for her to refuse, and to admit, impossible. But her heart smote her for the imperfect thought, even as she began to form it; and her fears were relieved at once when she began to read, as follows:—

"I know not, Cousin Alice, that I should have written at all by this present opportunity, the bark 'Good Providence,' about to sail this morning from Tower-Stairs, I being at this time in London; but that some matters came to my ear last night, which I judge all-important to be made known to you forthwith; and should it seem to you, that I am over-bold in touching on them, you will, I think, excuse me, seeing that I write only for your personal advantage; and further, that I once unwittingly misled you in relation to one of whom you have thought favorably. To be brief, Cousin Alice, I learned yesternight that the report which Cromwell sent to me at first was not the truth at all, he not as yet having perused the papers! There was, indeed, a letter to Sir Edmund Vavasour from Captain Wyvil: but it related solely to a projected rising in the north, which Wyvil, it would seem, discouraged; and contained not one word touching yourself, or his escape from Woolverton. All that affected you or Master Selby was written in a long epistle, addressed to yourself, and marked on the outside, 'to be delivered privately by Master Bartram.' What more it contained I know not, for it was burned by the lord-general at once, who rated, as I hear, the council very roundly for breaking private seals, and troubling their heads with women's matters. This I conceived it my duty to let you know forthwith, as you, I know, drew false conclusions from the rumor; and I, to my shame be it said, strengthened, so far as in me lay, instead of seeking to allay your indignation. I deem it therefore my bounden duty to let you know these facts; and that although it may have been indiscreet in Captain Wyvil to commit such things at all to writing, he certainly is quite exonerated from all charge of anything base or dishonorable. I am rejoiced to have it in my power to add, that something in the style and tenor of his letter had affected the lord-general so favorably, that I have been able to obtain his promise of a full pardon for yourself, and your father, within the space of six months, and a reversal of the decree of sequestration, so that, by the next spring at farthest, you may return to Woolverton. I have no doubt, moreover, so much was Cromwell gratified by the tone of Captain Wyvil's letter to Sir Edmund, deprecating any partial risings, which could but tend to bloodshed and fresh miseries, without effecting anything to aid the royal cause, and speaking with indignant condemnation of those infamous schemes which we hear of—that, if at any future period he should feel disposed to return to England, a ready abrogation of his outlawry could be obtained; he only binding himself on parole of honor, to take no hostile steps against the existing government. Should you meet with him, as you doubtless will in Paris, whither I fancy, by all we hear of Monsieur Turenne's successes, you will proceed ere long; pray say to him, should he entertain such views, he will at all times find in me, one anxious to assist him by all means in my power. I may add here, that every post that has reached us from the armies, speaks of his gallantry and conduct, as a partisan commander, in the highest terms of commendation. I have enclosed herewith bills on Parisian goldsmiths for one thousand pounds, made payable to your name; which you will endorse upon them on receiving their value, but not sooner, as in case of loss they are useless until your name is signed upon them. I have preferred this mode to sending them to my kind friend and cousin, Master Selby, fearing that his secluded habits and tastes for literary occupation, may render him averse, or at least indisposed, to the details of business. Praying you, my dear Mistress Alice, to hold me ever in your remembrance, and to commend me to your good father's friendship, I subscribe myself, with sincerity, your true friend and willing servant, " HENRY CHALONER.

" Post-scriptum.—When I was last at Woolverton, all your old protéges and tenantry were well in health, and earnest in inquiring after their bounteous lady, and most kind mistress.

" From my house in the Strand, this 15th day of October, 1652."

What were the thoughts of the sweet girl as she perused, line after line, the welcome letter which assured her that she had falsely blamed her lover—that he was true and stainless of every blot upon his honor—that so far from forgetting her, he had seized the first, as it seemed, safe opportunity of correspondence—can be more readily imagined than described. The tears gushed to her eyes before she had read one half of it, and blinded her for several minutes; yet they were pleasant tears, and as they flowed they soothed her restless and perturbed imagination. She dried them and read on, and wept again; and wept and read alternately, till she had run it over many times, and had its contents, as it were, by heart; then she sat for a long while immoveable and silent, communing with her own soul in secret; and then at last, as she yielded altogether to the conviction, that she had indeed been in error all the time; that all her hopes, when she had most believed them withering and blighted, were in fair progress toward fulfilment, she fell down on her knees and poured forth, to the great Giver of all human joy and sorrow, a flood of holy, heartfelt gratitude and humble adoration. She prayed for pardon of her past doubts and secret murmurings; for strength to bear this sudden change from the abyss of sorrow to happiness unspeakable, without undue and impious exultation; and having prayed, she rose refreshed and strengthened, and more like herself than she had felt for months. This duty finished, as soon as she felt sufficiently composed to betake herself to less exciting matters, she opened the other letter, which she saw at once was from her kind relation, Madame de Gondi. This confirmed fully the tidings which had been brought to Boulogne by the courier — the court was once more reinstated in the Louvre, the good Parisians having received their king, whom for many months they had banished from their capital, which they had even suffered to be filled with the red scarfs of the Spanish soldiers and the Burgundian standards of his most desperate enemies — with acclamations of enthusiastic joy, and such outbursts of joyous loyalty, that any one would have supposed that he absented himself for so long a time in opposition to the wishes of his subjects. The army of the princes had retreated into Champagne, and the king's troops under the indefatigable Turenne were in full pursuit of them, having already taken Château Porcien and Rethel on the Aisne. "Come, then, at once — come, dearest Alice!" ran the concluding sentences; "persuade your father to tear himself without delay from his dull books, and come to us while we are arrayed in smiles and merriment. There are more fêtes and balls, more masques and carousels, than we have seen for many a year; and as, to say the truth, we are the least in the world changeable and capricious — we good citizens of Paris — so that six months hence we may be again all rebels, and blockaded, and besieged, and famishing, and furious; it is best that you should come immediately, and see us *au plus beau!* But, seriously, the roads are all clear now, and there is nothing to hinder you, but everything on the contrary to make it wise that you should set out instantly. So order out your horses, and get into your carriage the very day you get this letter, and I will look for you within the week. Your English king is here; but the duke of York, who *entre nous* is much more to my taste, is absent with the army; so are the most part, and the best, of your countrymen, except a dozen noble buffoons and profligates, noisy without gayety and vicious without wit, who are King Charles's familiar friends. One of your braves is here, however, and we are all mad with admiration of him. He was a little wounded at Rethel on the Aisne, and invalided for a time, so they have given him a company in the Garde Royale. He wears his arm in a broidered scarf, but the ladies say it is but to render himself more interesting, which is needless, for by all accounts he is *beau comme un ange!* I suppose I need scarcely add that this *cavalier parfait* is no other than the Major Wyvil, concerning whom I have so often written to you. Adieu! a thousand remembrances to your dear father. Now, come at once; for, since I know that I can have you here so easily, *je me desole* without you.

"In the sweet hope of soon embracing you, yours ever, ever,

"HENRIETTE DE GONDI.

"Hotel de Gondi, Faubourg St. Germain, October 26."

She had scarcely finished reading these two, to her, most interesting letters, when, disturbed from his meditations and studies by the exclamations of the great loyal mob, which had been constantly increasing, ever since the arrival of the courier, her father entered the room in his sad-colored morning gown, carrying in his hand an open volume of Longinus, with an air of extreme dissatisfaction. "I wish, beyond all measure, that we could leave this odious town," he began, before Alice had an opportunity of addressing him; "I never have had a moment's quiet from sunrise to bedtime; what with *poissardes* yelling and howling through the streets at dawn—like the Eumenides of Orestes, and fifty thousand other trades and callings, all bellowing out their miserable wares: and now, since nine o'clock, there has been one continuous stream of madmen parading to and fro beneath my windows—I verily believe that this must be Babel; and that the confusion of tongues was nothing more than causing all the nations simultaneously to begin speaking French—for I am quite sure of this, that they can not understand one another. I would give anything in the world to quit this place, even if it was to go to the Bastile."

"I am sure, then—I am very glad, my dear father," replied Alice, almost laughing, when she thought of the long, protracted annoyance which he must have endured before his naturally calm and placid temper was worked into this fume and ferment—"very glad, to tell you that you can leave it when you please; within two hours if you think proper."

"How is that, Alice? I do not understand—what is it? I thought we could not go to Paris on account of this civil war—the people are mad, I believe, all the world over—for it seems to me that the only occupation of every nation, on the whole face of the globe, is cutting its own throat; as if there were not foreigners and strangers, or enemies as they call them, enough to kill—if they must be for ever killing."

"The war, however, is at an end, father—I have just received one letter from Madame de Gondi, telling me that the king and all the court have returned to Paris, and praying us to set forth this very day."

"Well! and have you not given orders?—have you not caused the carriage to be prepared?—have you not directed the horses to be harnessed? I am sure I can be ready in a quarter of an hour."

"I do not doubt it in the least," said Alice, laughing merrily; "you have only got to change your morning-gown for your black velvet doublet, and to shut up that volume of Sycophron, I suppose it is—for that's the hardest book in the world, they say—and then, you know, you would be ready to go to the top of Mount Caucasus."

"Now you are laughing at me, Alice—now you are laughing at me; and this is not Sycophron at all, but Longinus on the sublime and beautiful! But why can we not set forth in half an hour?"

"Oh! for a hundred reasons," she replied. "In the first place, because ladies can not prepare themselves for journeying with quite so much rapidity as you of the ruder sex—secondly, because we have got to send to the bankers for some money to pay our bills, and to pack our trunks and mails—and lastly, because it is necessary to have our passports *visés*, before we can proceed any further. All this, however, I will send Charles, who speaks French perfectly well, to arrange immediately; and, if you will but moderate your impatience a little, we will set off this afternoon. But you must listen to me now; for I have much to tell you that is of importance, though you have been too much excited hitherto to listen to me. I have another letter, from Cousin Henry! and he has obtained Cromwell's promise that we shall both receive a full pardon, and be at liberty to return to dear Woolverton, in the spring—is not that good news, dear father? And he goes on to say, that there was nothing in Captain Wyvil's letter to his kinsman relating in the least degree to any of us; and that the whole was discovered from his letter to myself; which the lord-general blamed the council exceedingly for opening, and burned, as soon as it came into his hands. He was pleased, too, with Captain Wyvil's style of sentiments and tone of writing, and will grant him a pardon likewise, if he ask for it, on parole not to act against the government. So everything, you see, is going to end happy."

"God grant it may," answered the old man solemnly; "I would fain once again see Woolverton, before I die; but there is on my mind a deep impression, I know not wherefore, that I shall not. It is, however, I doubt not, only an old man's fancy. And you see that I was right about your young cavalier. I was quite sure, it was not in the nature of things that he could be so base a villain as gratuitously to betray those who had risked their lives to save him. But I will go and arrange my books and papers, for I have something more to do, you saucy one, than to shut up this one volume of Longinus—and I beseech you make all haste you can with your preparations, for I do evidently desire to leave this noisy town."

"I will—I will indeed, dear father," answered Alice; "but upon my word, I am very much afraid, that in going to Paris you will only exchange a small tumult for a great one. The people, I fancy, from Madame de Gondi's letter, are madder there than anywhere else in the world."

"Ay! but I shall not be forced to live there out in the street, which I might as well be doing as occupying that miserable little room looking on that *place*, which seems to me to be the particular resort of all the market-women, and knaves, and swindlers, in Boulogne; but for that matter, I believe the whole population of the place is made up of the three species. Besides, there are some great Grecians in the Sorbonne, and I shall meet with some one fit to speak to upon reasonable subjects."

"That is to say, upon the most unreasonable subjects in the world," said she, laughing again; "but I am glad to hear that you anticipate pleasure, where I feared you would only find annoyance—but I will go now, and make my arrangements."

This was soon done; and immediately after dinner, which was served in those primitive days about noon, they set forth on their journey with their own horses and outriders, and a French courier in a half-military dress, with a short hanger at his side, and a gold-laced chapeau, perched on the box in front of the huge and cumbrous vehicle. The weather was lovely, with that pure blue sky which indicates the existence of a slight degree of frost; and the country, though not in itself very varied or attractive, looked beautiful to eyes which had been long confined to the dull range of dingy streets of the small seaport town; particularly as it was now decked with all the gay and various tints of autumn, and was enlivened by the glorious sunshine, which poured over it from the unclouded heaven. Those were times when journeys were not made with the lightning-speed of steam-carriages and railways, nor even with the less wonderful rapidity of post-horses and light chariots; and accordingly, many days elapsed before they reached the neighborhood of the metropolis. Nothing occurred, however, to impede their progress; no accident beyond the ordinary casualties, such as the casting of a leader's shoe, or the breaking of a wheeler's trace, befell them; but still they did not meet Madame de Gondi's expectations, if she indeed looked for them, as she said, within the week in which they started. The weather still continued fine, and though it was in some sort wearisome to be confined for so many days to the narrow compass of a carriage, there were still many intervals of rest, when they halted at noonday in some pleasant hamlet, or at some comfortable wayside hostelry to bait their jaded horses—there was still much to see that was new and strange to the English eyes of Alice; and on the whole, the time could not be said to pass unpleasantly. As for her father, he having taken the precaution of bringing along with him as travelling companions, four or five volumes of the most obscure and difficult Greek authors, it made very little difference to him whether he was rolling heavily over the deep and sandy roads in a tolerably roomy vehicle, or sitting in a small, close study. Indeed, he once or twice expressed his preference of the carriage to the lodging he had vacated at Boulogne. Making their way thus daily by gentle journeys, it was late in the afternoon of the ninth day, that the comparatively crowded state of the roads gave notice to the travellers that they were beginning to approach the suburbs of the gay metropolis. At every mile, the number of both carriages and passengers increased; now they would pass a rude ox-cart creaking and groaning under the weight of huge pipes of wine, and now they would in turn be passed by some gay equipage drawn by six stately horses covered with gilded trappings, with outriders in gorgeous liveries, glittering through the dust which they raised in their rapid transit — now it would be a group of jovial farmers jogging home after disposing of the produce of their fields or dairies, with heavy pockets and light hearts; now an old crone plodding along with her panniers full of eggs or chickens, on the slow, sober palfrey; and now a gang of hideous-looking beggars with loathsome sores displayed to excite compassion, or some keen-witted and sharp-visaged fry of youthful rogues and swindlers, with ever and anon a gay cavalier with waving plumes and jingling spurs, and lace and embroidery enough on their doublets to furnish forth a warehouse, dashing impetuously forward, and almost trampling the lower and more infirm of the pedestrians under foot — or gend'arme of the police, frowning from beneath the shade of his steel cap, on the known face of some incorrigible and notorious vagabond — or spurring furiously along with belted waist and leathern despatch-bag, some government courier, bearing unconsciously the fate of nations at his back. All was gay bustle and excitement, increasing more and more, as they drew nigher to the gates of Paris. At length, they came so near that they might see the huge square towers of Nôtre Dame looming up clear and massive above the house-tops, and hear the humming din which rises from the vast and busy throng that swarm in the dense streets of the great metropolis — and now the barrier was before them close at hand, and their courier was fumbling already in his portfolio for the passports, when a loud ringing laugh, distinctly audible above the clatter of several horses' feet in rapid motion, came to the ears of Alice ; and the next moment, as she leaned forward to the open window, several persons galloped past the carriage at an extremely rapid pace. The foremost was a tall and splendidly-formed girl, with large and rather bold black eyes, and a profusion of long jet ringlets falling from under the brim of her green velvet riding-hat ; she was superbly dressed in the magnificent fashion of the day, her velvet habit all laced and braided with gold cords, and slashed with satin, and the housings of her beautiful horse, which she sat fearlessly and managed with much skill, bedecked with embroidery and fringes of the same rich material. At her left hand, on the side furthest from the carriage, rode a fine military-looking man, of an erect and stately figure, with hair as white as snow, attired in a rich civil suit ; and beyond him a singularly handsome youth, of a dark complexion, with an expression of keen, vivid daring, clad in the complete uniform of the French *garde a cheval.* Three or four servants followed in scarlet liveries, and everything bespoke them persons of quality and distinction ; but Alice had not time to observe all these particulars before the young lady, whose eyes had encountered her own as she passed by, exclaimed, to her great surprise, in English — for her beauty was rather of an Italian or Spanish character — with a voice very musical and sweet, but pitched a little too high, " Oh, father, look — look what a lovely English girl is in that carriage !" and instantly directed the attention of the whole party to the object of her admiration. They passed so rapidly, however, that she had scarcely time to draw back, blushing and confused, before they had swept onward. The moment afterward another officer, in the same showy uniform, drove by the window, galloping even more rapidly than those who went before, as if trying to overtake them, and calling loudly after them to wait for him. He, too, spoke English, and there was something in the tones of his voice that induced Alice, who had shrunk back into the corner of the carriage, to look forth at the person. One glance was enough to show her the keen aquiline features, the bright blue eye, and the soft flowing hair of her affianced lover—for it was Wyvil—but he dashed onward without seeing her, or suspecting that the heavy travel-stained carriage contained any one with whom he was acquainted, and in a moment was riding by the side of the dark beauty.

"Oh!" Alice cried, while he was yet in sight—"oh! that was Captain Wyvil who rode by then."

"Was it? was it, indeed? why did you not call to him, Alice; you might have done so very fitly, for, of course, he did not see you, or he would certainly have stopped."

"Oh, no; he did not see me, I know that quite well," said she; "but he rode by so very fast that I had not time—I had but barely recognised him before he was gone; for he was galloping as hard as he could to overtake one of the most beautiful girls I ever saw in all my life, who had cantered on before. An English girl she was, too, for I heard her speak; but very dark, with coal-black hair and eyes. I wonder who she was; there was a noble-looking gray-haired man, whom she called father, by her side, and a handsome young French officer; and they had several servants in rich liveries: they must have been persons of distinction."

"Well, Alice, it will not, after all, make so much difference, for we will find out where he lives to-morrow, and send him word that we have come to Paris, and doubtless he will be at your feet in a minute. But, I declare, here we are at the gates already?"

A few minutes passed while the courier was parleying with the gen-d'arme on duty, and displaying the passports, which proved to be correct, and then they drove on slowly through the ill-paved and narrow streets for nearly half an hour, before they reached the faubourg wherein was situated the Hotel-de-Gondi; a noble pile of dark red brick with a courtyard in front, to which a stately *porte côchere* gave access, and a magnificent façade adorned with columns, all bearing witness of the wealth and dignity of the owner, who was, indeed, closely connected with the greatest families of France; the husband of the lady being the nephew of the duke of Retz, and cousin to the celebrated cardinal of that name, who, after having opposed the queen-regent and her favorite, Mazarin, by every factions means imaginable, had nevertheless, played his part with so much dexterity and skill, that now, on the banishment of that wily minister, he had contrived to ingratiate himself with Anne of Austria and her son, from whose hands he had recently received the cardinal's hat, which he had so long coveted in vain. The hall of the hotel was crowded with lacqueys in superb liveries; and a tall, gray-headed *maitre d'hôtel* hurrying out to assist Alice to descend from the carriage, and saying that he presumed he had the honor to address Mademoseille Selby, escorted her, bowing at every landing-place, up a magnificent staircase with gilded balustrades, and the walls finely painted with subjects of the Odyssey and Iliad—and through a suite of stately rooms, all furnished in a superbly massive style which has taken its name from the luxurious monarch in whose days it was introduced, with cabinets of buhl and marquetry, gigantic mirrors in huge sculptured frames, arm-chairs and ottomans of velvet and embroidery, fine pictures, tapestry, and curtains fringed with gold—into the boudoir of the marquise. But the marchioness de Gondi was, by far, too important a personage, in both her own estimation and the opinion of her friends, to be introduced thus at the fag-end of a chapter.

CHAPTER XXVI.

Henriette de Gondi, who rose from the deeply-cushioned chair in which she was reclining, with her hair fully dressed, and robed in a superb brocade, was a tall, delicately-formed fair-complexioned woman of something more than forty years, but showing few marks either in face or form of the time that had passed over her. Her manner was marked by much affectionate eagerness, as she embraced her youthful relative repeatedly and very warmly; seeming to be, and in truth actually being delighted, at having it in her power to receive her. Master Selby, whom she had seen many years ago, she also greeted very kindly and set him at his ease in a moment; but with Alice, whose extreme loveliness took her quite by surprise, she was evidently charmed, and felt that she was one whose perfect manners and rare beauty would reflect honor on the person who should introduce her to the court of that gay and voluptuous city.

"Now, my sweet friend," she cried, "how happy we shall all be here together. Upon my word, I think myself much obliged to this good Cromwell, whom all your English folks are cursing so unsparingly; for I suppose if it had not been for him, we should never have had any chance of seeing you here in France."

"But you will be, I am sure, much more obliged to him, when you know that he has promised in the spring, to pardon both my father and myself, and to give us back our estates; so that instead of looking upon this as a sad state of exile, it is indeed only a pleasant visit to a dear cousin, and a pleasant land."

"Of course, I am obliged to him for doing anything that is agreeable to you," answered Madame de Gondi; "but I assure you, I have no idea of parting with you in the spring. Who knows but some of our gay gallants may persuade you, as they did my dear mother, to stay here always and become a Frenchwoman? Nay! do not blush so deeply, Alice, for I was only jesting; but by my faith, I think that burning blush tells something farther than it was intended to reveal—tells something of an island lover. Well, well; if it must be so, I shall not repine, provided he be brave, and handsome, and well-born, and very graceful and accomplished. But, on my word! I had forgotten what I had intended to ask you the very moment you came in—what it was that you could possibly have done to enrage Cromwell and the government so much against you?"

"Oh, that is a long talk, Madame la Marquise," interrupted her father, who, deeming it incumbent on him to be unusually civil during this first interview with their kind hostess, had kept his faculties on the alert for a space that was quite wonderful to Alice; "but, to be brief, Alice brought to the house a young cavalier, whom she met flying from the battle-ground of Worcester, with a troop of rebels at his heels; and we sheltered him—though he was what they call a proclaimed rebel, whom all men were forbid, on pain of death, to harbor or assist—until he made good his escape to France. This was discovered by an accident, and we in consequence were forced to fly, and our estates were sequestered."

"To France, to France did he fly? then you will meet him—you *must* meet him here! Ah, now I understand that blush, *ma belle cousine*," she added, looking at Alice with an arch glance; "but I suppose he had a name, this cavalier?"

"He had indeed a name, madame," said Alice, rallying from her short confusion, and laughing gayly; "and it was one that you are well acquainted with already. It is lucky too for me, that you are a little premature in your conclusions; for if I had lost my heart to him, as you insinuate, it seems I should have had to dispute his with almost all your beauties here in France, perhaps with yourself, cousin?"

"With me! *fidonc!* with me, who am already an old woman! But I assure you that I do not understand at all. Who is he, pray explain, who is he?"

"He is no other than the Captain Wyvil, of whom, for some time, your letters have been so full!"

"The Captain Wyvil!" exclaimed Henriette de Gondi, and that, too, in no small astonishment; "the Captain Wyvil! and you have never even once mentioned that you knew him! nor has he said one word of your assisting him to fly!"

"In that, madame," the old man again interrupted, for he was unwilling that Alice should be too hardly pressed, "he did but act with common prudence. The slightest mention of it here might have led to the worst consequences; and the same reason of course justified Alice in keeping silent to you on the subject; since we know very well how often couriers are intercepted on the road, and robbed of their despatches."

But, although she said nothing more upon the subject, and appeared to be completely satisfied, Henriette de Gondi was neither deceived nor at ease. She had seen much of the world, and that too in its most polished and artificial phases; she had lived for years in the midst of that high and courtly society, wherein every man and woman learned to conceal, with the impenetrable mask of smiles, or nonchalance, or smooth tranquillity, the deepest feelings of their own hearts, and at the same time to peruse the thoughts and inmost sentiments of others, from the most trifling and superficial indications. Thus she was far from being misled, either by the unconcerned manner which Alice had assumed, or by the explanation given by her father; but, on the contrary, was confirmed in her first opinion, that her cousin did love the gay young officer whose life she had preserved, although her mind was crossed by many a suspicion as to his worthiness of her affection. She said nothing in reply, but sat for a few minutes quietly musing on what course she ought to pursue; for rumors had been spread broadly enough to reach her ears, concerning the attentions which were paid with so much assiduity by Marmaduke to the fair Isabella Oswald, and received by her with so evident pleasure, and she thought to herself and thought rightly, "This beautiful English girl, brought up from her childhood in the solitude of a country life, is just the being to conceive a romantic passion, and, that disappointed, to be a blighted and heart-broken thing for ever;" and doubting very much whether Wyvil cared anything for her, she began to think whether it was not her duty to caution her against him. But after a few moments of consideration, she felt as yet that it was too delicate a step to take lightly, and that it was not warranted by anything beyond a mere suspicion. She resolved, therefore, to let matters take their own course, reserving to herself the power of watching closely, and interfering the moment interference should seem necessary.

Meanwhile, for it was rapidly growing dark, candles were brought in, and the fine suite of rooms brilliantly lighted up. Then coffee, at that time a rare and exceedingly expensive luxury, was introduced; and Henriette de Gondi, telling her guests that she expected a few visiters in the evening, and consigning Master Selby to the care of her *maître d'hôtel* who, she said, would install him in a pleasant suite of chambers communicating with the library, proceeded to introduce Alice to the mysteries of a Parisian toilet; trifling and laughing merrily the while, and striving to entertain her fair cousin with all the gay and lively gossip, which formed the conversation of the court circles. Many things there were in those light anecdotes, that excited the unmitigated wonder, many that called forth the deep loathing, not all unmixed with indignation, of the sweet English girl: who, unsophisticated by the false sophistries of fashionable life, nurtured in grave and pure seclusion, whither the very name of unblushing sin had scarcely penetrated—brought up in perhaps the most moral age of the most moral country in the world, could not hear crimes, such as her uncontaminated soul had scarcely conceived possible, named as things of usual and every-day occurrence—chastity treated as a marvel, and virtue as a fiction or a jest. It was not that Henriette de Gondi was herself light, or frail, or vicious; nor yet that society had reached that abyss of infamy, into which it sank headlong in the days of Louis XV., and still more during the frantic horrors of the Revolution; but that already it had become no rare or extraordinary fact for married women to have favored lovers, and for married men to court girls of rank, and win them to become their mistresses, and that too without losing caste or station. Now, it is very true, that something of all this had penetrated even to the pure ears of Alice; for it had become somewhat common in puritanic England to rail loudly at the vices and the crimes of the neighboring kingdom, vices and crimes which she was about to imitate, even to exaggeration, under the third and basest of the unhappy and doomed Stewarts. But though she knew that such things were, it had never so much as entered her imagination that they could be matters of daily comment, laughed at, and jested over, and, if unapproved, at least uncondemned, by the lips of virtuous and noble ladies. It was not long, therefore, before Henriette perceived in the downcast eye raised suddenly and opened wide with wonder, in the averted head and crimson blushes of her innocent guest, how much she was dismayed, and it must be said, disgusted likewise, by the freedom of her anecdotes, and the whole tone of her conversation.

"You must not imagine, now," she said, as Alice turned away in irrepressible disapprobation at some tale of guilt and infamy, "that I think lightly of these shocking things, or speak of them because I find pleasure in the recital. Far from it, dearest cousin; for in mere truth I hate and loathe them, even as I can see that you do. Praise be to Heaven! the foulest and most ribald tongue in all France does not so much as breathe a whisper adverse to the fair fame of Henriette de Gondi, as maid, or wife, or widow. Oh no, dear girl, I only spoke to set you on your guard, for you will hear these things talked over freely, not only by the frail and the licentious, but by the good, and virtuous, and noble; by those who would die sooner than sink their souls to the degrading blight of sin; and spoken of by all in the same tone of gay and thoughtless raillery. I judge it best to make you know all this at once, that you may see at once how it behooves you to deal with it. Nay! do not interrupt me, do not interrupt me, cousin; I do not for a moment mean that you should think or speak of these things as we do here; but I would have you learn to repress that look of wonder mixed with hatred, to check that unsophisticated start, to keep down those bright blushes; for this is a wicked and ill-judging world in which we live, and by the people you will meet here on all sides, such indications will be considered only as the result of consciousness and prudery, or of a desire to attract notice and woo admiration for superior virtue. You must just hear such things, and hear them as if they had not been spoken, calmly and coldly, without smiling on the one side, or bridling or blushing on the other. I shall of course take care to keep aloof from you, so much as I can do so, those whom you would deem unfit associates, whether as gentlemen or ladies. None come to my poor house but persons of repute; still, as I said just now, you will hear much that will pain you, and that might cause you grave mortification, if you do not take my advice."

"Oh! dear Madame de Gondi," Alice replied, half crying, "I had so much, much rather live here with you in private, and in quiet while we remain in Paris. Consider I am nothing but a mere country-girl, perfectly unfit to associate with these people; I shall only commit some absurdity, and bring mortification upon you, and shame upon myself. Oh! no, no; I can never mix with such people as you talk of—I should be utterly, utterly wretched! in truth you must excuse me."

"Impossible, my dear girl, impossible indeed!" replied Henriette; "in every way it is quite impossible that I should excuse you. In the first place I do not, and I can not live in private or quiet—my birth, my station, and the state of the times forbid it. You see, Alice, though I am, as was my most excellent late lord, a zealous loyalist, all the rest of our house are more or less disaffected; and though the Cardinal de Retz has just received the hat from the young king, and is for the present in high favor with the court, there is no telling how long it may last; he is always plotting and conspiring for one thing or other, and just as like as not before six weeks* he may find

* It will be seen, by reference to history, that this opinion of the lady was justified in all respects except the place of his imprisonment. He was arrested and sent to Vincennes, on the 19th of December, 1652.

himself in the Bastile. It will be known, moreover — nay, I might say, it is known even now, that I have guests from England residing in my house. If, therefore, I should absent myself from court at present, or going thither fail to have you presented likewise, it would forthwith be suspected everywhere, and rumored that your father and yourself belonged to the rebel English party; since all your royalist countrymen are at the present time in high favor with the court, and affect to frequent it constantly, to show their gratitude for our king's kindness to the exiled majesty of England. It is impossible, therefore, that I can either shut my house up during your stay, or suffer you to remain in seclusion. The consequences of such a step might be of serious evil to me, Alice; and I am sure you would not subject me to that, and only to avoid a little temporary inconvenience!"

"That would I not, indeed," exclaimed Alice, eagerly— "that would I not for the whole world; but it seems to me, indeed, that there is a want of principle even in lending countenance to such things—besides, I am certain that I never could act as you bid me; it is so different from anything that I have ever been used to, so utterly abhorrent to the usages of England—"

"Oh, yes; that is quite true," answered Madame de Gondi; "but, believe me, my dear girl, it will not do for us to go about, like the knight-errantry of old, attempting to bully the world into reform; if we do that which is right ourselves, and set a good example, quietly, by our own conduct, we play the best, nay, the only part that is fit for women. As for the rest, mere difference of custom between two countries, by no means really implies that the usages of this are absolutely right, or of that absolutely wrong. And in the present instance, Alice, much as I deprecate the over-lightness, the real, and still more the affected depravity of France, I am not quite sure that the puritanical hypocrisy, the fierce fanaticism, the stern, untolerating hardness of religion, which is at present worn in England—I fear me, as a cloak to much secret vice—is not the worse and more dangerous evil. But we have not the time to discuss these grave and serious matters, for I perceive by the sound of wheels and the glare of flambeaux in the courtyard, that some of my guests have arrived—and your toilet is finished; really, YOU are *mise a ravir;* I had no idea that the English had attained so much skill in the science of dressing. Come, come, now, I will take care that you shall meet no annoyance."

With these words she took Alice Selby under her arm, and walking down the grand staircase, now splendidly illuminated, entered through several ante-chambers—so filled with liveried lacqueys, and magnificently-dressed upper-servants, that Alice fancied herself in some royal palace—a brilliant drawing-room, all glittering with marquetry, and buhl, and gorgeous mirrors, wherein were reflected fifty-fold from sconce and chandelier the gay and cheerful lights which made the great saloon almost as bright as day. The several guests had already gathered; and, with the easy and unformal grace which characterized then, as it does at the present day, the domestic *reunions* of French society, had fallen into various groups, chatting, and laughing, and pleasing each one the other, without effort or constraint or marked desire to please. The company assembled were not many in number, not exceeding a dozen or fifteen persons, all splendidly dressed, some in gay uniforms, others in gorgeous civil dresses, all fluttering with rich lace and bright ribands, and glittering with embroideries; and these were grouped in different seats upon the numerous ottomans and couches, which filled, according to the fashion of the day, the large saloon with their luxurious, though somewhat cumbersome variety. Among these there were but three ladies; one—to whom Madame de Gondi, sliding as it were imperceptibly into companionship with her visiters, made Alice known, as Madame de Maignelai—a singularly venerable-looking person, advanced considerably in years, but with a calm, beneficent placidity of feature that made her appear almost beautiful, was engaged in conversation with the good bishop of Lisieux; well suited to be, what indeed they were, intimate friends and associates, as being at that time, perhaps, the two most virtuous and unpretending and truly pious persons in the French king's dominions; and by her the young English girl was received with a tenderness of manner, a motherly air of unforced protection, that, while it set her completely at ease, went far to induce her to believe Madame de Gondi's late remarks upon society exaggerated and undue. After a few words had been interchanged, relative to the cause of her new friend's visit to the French metropolis, the length of time that had elapsed since her arrival, and such inductive topics— "I suppose, then," said the good old lady, "that you have but a few acquaintances here among us?"

"Very few, very few, indeed, madame," Alice replied; "or I might almost say none at all; for except my cousin Henriette and yourself, and Monsieur de Lisieux, I do not believe there is a person in all France whom I have ever seen, unless it be some of my countrymen who have been forced to take refuge here from the persecution of all these civil wars and conspiracies at home."

"Yes! you will see many of these here; they are all in great favor at the court, since your young duke of York has so distinguished himself with our own good maréchal. But, to say truly, I know but few of them; and, in the meantime, I must point out to you some of our great people, for we have here several celebrities. There, do you see that gentleman in purple velvet with a bright star, who wears a shade over both eyes? that is Monsieur de la Rochefoucault, one of the king's best officers. A very strange misfortune befell him in the terrible battle which was fought last July, under the very walls of Paris, and in the faubourg St. Antoine; while he was in the very act of carrying a barricade, a bullet entered at the corner of one eye and came out at the corner of the other; and what is more extraordinary yet, is that you see him there alive, and that he sees quite well, though for a time all the physicians declared that he would certainly be blind. That lady to whom he is talking so merrily, she with her hair dressed high—it is the new mode called *le tour*, but I must say I think vastly unbecoming—is the celebrated Madame de Lesdiguieres, a very great politician, and some people say as great an intriguer, but people are ill-natured; she is rising now to go and meet the cardinal — that is the cardinal de Retz who is entering now, who has been at the bottom of every plot and conspiracy since he was fifteen; the enemy of Richelieu and of Mazarin, the wittiest if not the wisest, and the most gallant man and the greatest favorite of the people in all Paris. He is the cousin, too, of your Madame de Gondi, so you will necessarily be presented to him; and that — that who is following the cardinal, he with the singularly-intellectual face, not handsome, but instinct with soul — that is the duke de Bouillon, the brother of the maréchal Turenne. De Retz said of him, the other day, that 'he was sure, by what he had seen of his conduct, those people did wrong to his reputation who decried it; but that he did not know if those did not do too much honor to his abilities who thought him capable of all the great things which he did not do;' so very shrewd and clever are his speeches, always pointed and terse, but cutting! But see, here comes your cousin to make you know, I am sure, the cardinal. He will answer you better far than I can; but, believe me, dear young lady, should you ever want a friend, which I hope you will not, you will find one in De Maignelai."

As she spoke, Henriette did indeed come up, and with the intent as the good dowager foresaw, of bringing her young relative somewhat more prominently before her guests, now that she judged her to be in some degree at least set at her ease, and superior to that timidity, which in those circles would have appeared an absurd affectation, and she was not disappointed; for so prepossessing was the peculiar style of Alice's young English beauty, so graceful and so quiet were her manners, and above all so fluently and well did she converse in the French tongue, that before long she found herself listening, and laughing at the jests and repartees of those whose names were history, and playing her part in the social circle, as if she had lived with them all her life. Presently supper was announced, and in a few minutes all were seated at a round table, then deemed the very mode, as bringing all the guests into one common circle, covered with all the choicest dainties of the French *cuisine* already famous the world over! Alice, supported on the one hand by the young comte de Bellefonds, celebrated as the handsomest cavalier in France, and on the other hand by the great cardinal himself. He, ever and anon, in the intervals of the stream of intrigue and finesse which he was pouring into the ears of Madame de Lesdiguieres, found leisure to indulge in some of his bright apothegms and quick-polished sarcasms, replete with knowledge of the human race, and intuitive perception of character, to the delight of Alice, whose ready appreciation had charmed in no less degree the politic and wily churchman. "Turenne?" he said suddenly, in answer to some question of the young English girl — "Turenne? what do you say about him? Great? yes, indeed — he has possessed from his youth every good quality, and at an early age acquired every great one. He wants, now, but those of which he is not aware. He has every virtue, but the glitter of none — however, people believe him abler at the head of an army than of a faction, and I believe so too, because he is not naturally enterprising — and yet," he added, somewhat thoughtfully — "and yet who knows?" and then after a little pause — "but enough of Turenne," he said, "*maintenant vive la bagatelle* — champagne, here give us champagne;" and filling his own and fair neighbor's glass, he bowed with the same gay, witty compliment, and turned away again to talk with the intriguing Frenchwoman, by whose means he was so soon afterward consigned to the dungeons of Vincennes. Just at this moment, while mirth was at the loudest, a noble-looking man dressed in the full uniform of the French guard, carrying his hat and unbuckled sword in his left hand, entered the saloon, and gliding up to the side of Madame de Gondi, began to apologize for the lateness of his visit; and then took possession with easy grace of the first vacant seat, and applied himself to entertain the third lady, who was no other than the famous marchioness of Villiers.

"Hold! Villequier," exclaimed the young count of Bellefonds. "What has kept you so late, you who are so great an adorer of bright eyes, and sparkling goblets?"

"Oh, we had a little fracas at the Louvre," answered the captain of the queen's guard, for such was the rank of the new comer; "and I, of course, was obliged to wait till everything was settled."

"A fracas!" exclaimed several voices, not without some astonishment, for in those days conspiracy trod so close on the heels of conspiracy, that the appetites of men were sharply set for novelties and horrors — "a fracas! what was it? tell us all — quick! quick! good Villequier; was it the duke of Orleans?" and loudest among the speakers was heard the voice of De Retz.

"My good lord cardinal," replied Villequier, laughing, "appears to be beside himself, at learning that there has been a fracas, and he not in it! No, no, my good lord," he continued, as the laugh, which his retort had created, again subsided; "it was not his grace of Orleans, nor was there any treason in the matter: nor, what is more surprising, even sedition. It was but a quarrel between two of these English bull-dogs, whom our young king so much affects just now. I thought they would have cut each other's throats in the palace-yard!"

"Who were they? — Villequier, what was it all about?"

"Oh! they are so ready with the sword that it is not easy to say even what it is about; small cause suffices, but in this case it was a woman."

"Of course — of course it was," replied La Rochefoucault, with a loud laugh; "there never was a quarrel yet but what there was a woman at the bottom of it; but come, expound — who was the woman?"

"A wondrous fair one," replied Villequier; "to my thinking, no other than the beautiful Oswald."

"Then I can name one of the combatants," exclaimed Bellefonds.

"And I," "and I," "and I," three other voices chorused him, the last adding, "one was your new made captain of the guards. But who was the other?"

"Whom do you guess? No! you will never guess at all; so I may just as well tell you — Sir Henry Oswald! what do you think of that now?"

A dozen of the fashionable oaths and exclamations of the day testified to the surprise of all who heard it; the ladies, who hitherto had taken but small share in the conversation, becoming all alive with the excitement of curiosity and envy. But, while all else were asking every kind of question, Madame de Gondi was employed in watching the pale and varying features of her cousin; who, though it was evident that she had not altogether understood what was passing, was not so dull but her suspicions were excited.

"I can not tell you all, or, indeed, much about it. I was called in to take them both in custody, after they had been parted by the men on duty on the grand staircase. Sir Henry was, it seems, coming down from the saloon, where there was a small court party, having heard something there which set his hasty temper in a blaze; and was, I fancy, going in search of the very man, when he fell in with him ascending; and, without waiting to get out of the palace, gave him hard words, called him a penniless adventurer, a swaggering sworder, and a presumptuous fool, for looking up to the peerless Isabella; and afterward, when the other would have turned aside his anger by mild words, he broke out into violence, and made as if he were about to strike him; but before it had come to that the guards seized both of them, so that neither of them had time to draw his sword. Then I was called in and took them both in charge; but, as no blow had been stricken, upon their pledging their words of honor that the thing should go no further, they were released, after they had been in the guardhouse nearly two hours!"

"But, after all you have not told us what it was all about, Villequier?" cried one.

"Because I do not know myself," answered he, laughing; "but I heard afterward that some of Isabella's other suitors told the old man, having found out that it would vex him, that Major Wyvil had been some time clandestinely accepted by the lady."

At the word, Alice, who had been listening all the time, with all her soul suspended on the tongue of the speaker, dreading to hear at every moment that the new-made captain of the guards was indeed Wyvil, turned pale as death itself, drew a long painful sigh, and would have fallen from her chair, had not Madame de Gondi, who had almost foreseen what was about to happen, sprang forward and caught her in her arms; crying out as she did so, "Oh, Alice, you are over-fatigued, and I was quite wrong to tease you into coming down to supper. Run, François, run and call my woman—thank you, thank you, lord-cardinal, a little water, if you please—oh, that is right, here comes Toinette and Vuleric—make haste now, but be careful—hold up her head—that's well—now carry her up stairs to her room; she is reviving even now. Excuse me for a few moments," she added, returning toward her guests; "Mademoiselle only arrived to-day, having come all the way from Boulogne without stopping—she wished to lie down at once, but I was wrong and persuaded her to come down stairs. Amuse yourselves, I pray you; I will return directly," and with the easy grace of their nation they promised that they would do so; and, until Madame de Gondi had retired, appeared to resume their conversation. But scarcely was she well up stairs, before leaving their compliments with the *maître d'hôtel*, they quietly and singly stole away, and long before their hostess knew it, the house was vacant except of its customary dwellers.

CHAPTER XXVII.

It was some time before poor Alice, despite all appliances, returned to her senses; and had it not been for the prudence of Madame de Gondi — who would not suffer Master Selby to be disturbed; and who, on one pretence or other, kept Margaret, Alice's faithful girl, out of the room, retaining her own woman who could not speak or understand one word of English, in which tongue she was well assured her cousin would speak, when she recovered — there would have been a terrible confusion, and the whole matter would have been bruited to the household. At length, when her beautiful form had been released from all the ligatures that confined it, her temples bathed with cold water, and stimulating essences applied, she stretched out her arms, heaved a long breath, and opened her fair eyes, but with that bewildered and unconscious expression which shows the senses to be absent, although the life may have returned. In a moment or two, indeed, they reclosed for a little space; but, when she opened them again, it was with a calm and more intelligent glance; and she pressed her cousin's hand, saying —

"I shall be better in a little while — do not be frightened — and pray do not tell my father."

"Oh, no, indeed!" replied Madame de Gondi; "he has been long in bed, and all our guests have gone, and the house is quite quiet. He need not know anything about the matter; why should he? It was only the fatigue of travelling and the heat of the room."

A faint and sickly smile crossed the pale lips of Alice, and she half shook her head; but her cousin, although she well knew what she meant, was resolved not to understand her; and after remaining with her till the night was far advanced toward morning, and seeing her fall into a natural and quiet sleep, she left her to the care of Margaret, saying, "She doubted not she would be quite well to-morrow."

The following morning rose bright and joyous; and Alice, as Madame de Gondi had foretold, was perfectly well as regards the mere health of the body, and was astir before the earliest. For when Henriette, who herself had risen some hours before her wonted time, anxious about her lovely guest, entered the chamber, she found her sitting fully dressed by the window, with her head leaning on her hand in a disconsolate mood; the maiden Margaret, quite overdone with watching, outstretched in deep sleep on a sofa by the bed which her mistress had so long deserted.

"Oh, my dear Alice, I am so glad to see you up, and well again!" exclaimed her cousin, as she entered; "I was afraid you might still feel some remains of your indisposition."

"No! oh, no!" answered poor Alice; "but I am sure I need not tell you that I was not indisposed at all."

"You love him, then?" said Henriette, but rather in a tone of question, than of positive affirmation—"you do then love this Captain Wyvil? I feared so from the first!"

"I saw you had my secret, cousin, and I am but a poor dissembler; besides, I am sure you will never speak of what I tell you; and in good truth I want the support of a female adviser. I *do* love him."

"And he?" asked Henriette.

"Is my affianced husband; troth-plighted, in the presence of my father!" Alice replied.

Madame de Gondi started in vehement surprise; for she had, until that moment, no possible idea that matters had gone on to such a length—and she paused a little while before she made any answer; but at last said, "I would be loath, my sweet Alice, to raise hopes—or, I should rather say, *renew* hopes—in your mind, which may but lead in the end to disappointment; but it appears to me that this makes all the difference. At first I fancied this was but a girlish preference of yours—I did not even know that he returned it."

"Madame de Gondi!" interrupted Alice, her pale face, and

her whole neck and bosom, suffused with burning blushes, as she spoke in a tone of grave disappointment; "and did you think so meanly of poor Alice Selby, as to deem that she would give her love unsought?"

"Indeed, indeed!" answered Henriette, "I never thought at all of Alice Selby, but as one who was all maidenly modesty and virtue; but, trust me, dearest one, our love is not always our own to give—nor does it always wait for asking. But suffer me to finish what I was about to say; that, fancying this to be only a girlish fancy, I doubted much the wisdom of that fancy, seeing, beyond doubt, that this Captain Wyvil is somewhat famous for gallantry, and has been paying much attention to this Mademoiselle Oswald. But since you tell me that it is gone so far, I begin to believe we have been too hasty. It is extremely likely that all this has been mere levity; that flattered and amused by the evident liking of a very pretty woman, he has allowed himself to be led, as a sort of fashionable victim, both parties well understanding one another; for I need not tell you, dear Alice, that although there may be the same depth, there is by no means the same singleness of love in the men as in us women; and that full many a man who really is in love, and that constantly and truly with one woman, deems it no flaw in his allegiance to make love to another—merely to pass the time, or to amuse himself in the absence of his mistress. Therefore we must not be too quick in judging—this Paris is a great place for flirting and scandal; and it is very likely that there may be no truth in this at all. But if there were—if he should prove so vile and infamous a traitor, you do not love him so much, Alice, that your pride would not come to your rescue, and that you would not shake him off as a thing too worthless for a moment's lamentation?"

"Alas! dear lady," answered poor Alice, with a sigh, "should it be so, indeed, he would have robbed me of all the friendship of my soul; he would have heaped my heart with the ashes of consumed hope and happiness; he would have covered my young days with desolation; he would have taken from me that best boon of nature — confidence in the truth of our fellows — but, lady, but —" and she paused, unable to complete the sentence, and Henriette took it up —

"But you would love him no more — is it not so, dear Alice?"

"As woman loves but once," she answered, clasping her hands together; "I love him, and that for ever!"

"A very, very woman!" replied Madame de Gondi, with a smile; "neither is our task an easy one; we have to learn, in the first place, whether this be not all a mere evanescent fancy; and, in the second, if the wild bird's wings have been lured from its true owner by honeyed words, to win him back again to his allegiance. My life on it! and these bright sunny locks, and soft blue eyes, will wake him to his senses in a moment, if he have strayed somewhat in your absence. Gratitude, honor, faith, all bind him to your footstool. Besides, you are fairer by one half than she, and twenty times more feminine; then think what the proverb says of old — '*On revient toujours a ses premiers amours.*' Oh, be sure, Alice, if this bright Isabella Oswald has won him for a moment, you shall retrieve him yet more easily than you have lost him."

"I would die sooner than attempt it," answered Alice, coloring high, and speaking loud with the energy of indignation. I win him back? I stoop to win that which is mine already? I humble myself to receive back a pledge which he has forfeited? No! Henriette de Gondi, no! whom Alice Selby marries she must not only love, but respect, and esteem, and honor! Love him? alas, for me! I shall, and oh! how deeply — even to my dying day — pray for his happiness, and well-being, and honor; but never could I respect, or esteem, or honor, one whose heart *could* swerve, or whose faith falter!"

"What would you do then, Alice," asked her cousin, almost crying between sympathy and excitement — "what would you do, my sweet Alice?"

"Pray God to give me strength to bear my sorrows meekly — and bear them, and, perhaps — die, Henriette!"

She raised her voice with the last words so loudly, that

Margaret was aroused; and starting up from the sofa, she exclaimed, as she rubbed her eyes, "Coming—I'm coming, Mistress Alice. Did you call?"

So near are the founts of tears and laughter, that, sad although she was, and grieved at heart, Madame de Gondi could not refrain from smiling at the air half-bewildered, half-terrified, half-stupid, of the English maiden, when she beheld her mistress risen from her bed and dressed without her assistance; and in a moment Alice joined in the mirth which her quaint excuses and apologies called forth, although it was but for a second, when she relapsed into her usual repose of air and manner.

"We will talk more of this hereafter, Alice," said the other. "Meanwhile, let Margaret arrange your hair, and hurry down to breakfast; for Master Selby, I doubt not, is even now awaiting us." And with a word she left the bedchamber; and Alice, with that strong mastery of her passions that formed so prominent a feature in her character, composed herself so thoroughly, that no one could have dreamed that a few short minutes before her heart had been rent by the most violent emotions. It was not long before she joined her friends at the breakfast table; and when she did so, although she certainly was a little pale, she conversed cheerfully and even gayly, and that too without any expression of the forced merriment, which it is so painful even to witness. Old Selby was in one of his brightest moods, having quite shaken off his abstraction, and talking with much real interest about some of the great scholars of the day, with whom he was desirous of becoming intimate, and with whom Madame de Gondi promised to make him speedily acquainted. "Indeed," she said, in conclusion of some little offer of the kind, "I had thought of this already. We had a little supper here last night, of which I did not speak to you, fearing that you would be so ceremonious as to do what I knew would be disagreeable to your health; and I engaged the good old bishop of Lisieux, who is himself a man of talent, to call on you to-day, and take you to see our famous Pierre Huet, and several others of the academicians."

"You are, indeed, most kind and thoughtful," he replied. "I myself know Pierre Huet; at least, we have corresponded on subjects of mutual interest, and I feel quite as if we were old friends."

"Yes, indeed," interposed Alice, laughing so naturally that Henriette gazed at her with amazement, "my father used to write him long letters, and a work beginning, '*Mon cher Huet* — Lycophron, in the 367th line of his Cassandra, has the word so and so, the mystic sense of which,' and so on — whole pages full of stuff that no one in the world could understand, without one intelligible word, till you came to *serviteur tres humble.* And Monsieur Huet used to reply; '*Mon Ami Selby* — Camillus and Decius Junius Brutus were not as foolish people have imagined, men, but merely fresh developments of the mythic personage variously represented as Ulysses and Agamemnon and Prometheus; just in the same manner as Tarquinia, Medea, Helen, Semiramis, Omphale, and, in short, all the women mentioned in mythologies, are new types of the witch of Endor.' These are exactly the kind of letters they used to write, upon my honor. And now my dear father talks about his knowing the man; and he can not tell whether he is rich or poor, old or young, well-intentioned, or the worst of men."

"Well, that is true; that is true, at least," answered Selby, smiling; "although all that stuff about the letters is an exaggeration of Alice's, and quite untrue, moreover; for Huet never could have made such blunders as to say Ulysses and Prometheus were one person — although it may be very clearly shown that the mystic personage, Orion —"

"For Heaven's sake, dearest father," Alice interrupted him, "do not waste these most excellent and, I have no doubt, valuable discoveries, on minds so incapable and ignorant as mine and Madame de Gondi's."

"Upon my word! I do think you were wiser to reserve them for the good bishop, or Pierre Huet," Henriette chimed in, with a silvery laugh; and the old student was compelled to join in the merriment, excited by his own eccentricity.

Soon afterward, almost indeed before the covers had been removed, and while they were yet lingering in the breakfast room, the worthy bishop was announced; and after a short conversation with the ladies, carried off the high-minded and unworldly scholar, apparently delighted at finding a person, of pursuits and a spirit so congenial. Then, quietly resuming their previous conversation, Madame de Gondi advised her young friend, very wisely, neither to do or resolve anything hastily.

"I think I can see," she said, "already, though I have known you for so short a time, enough of your character to be sure that the happiness of your whole life is at stake; and that is not to be cast away on slight or mistaken causes. Moreover, to you, who are I know so fraught with conscious and religious scruples, it should be no small inducement to calm and deliberate judgment, that the happiness of another is probably involved equally with your own; and, above all things, I entreat you to remember, what I have learned by a life's experience, that the constancy of men and of women are very different things. A man may act—nay, often does act—while he is perfectly true to his first love, exactly as it would argue a woman utterly false to do."

"Oh, yes," said Alice, "I know that; and I have too much cause for wishing all to go on well, to suffer myself to be rash or indiscreet in this case, even if I were naturally inclined to do so, which, I think, I am not."

"I am sure not," said Henriette; "and you will have abundant opportunities of judging, for you will meet him everywhere, and that, too, in company with this lady, who is considered very beautiful. And now that I begin to recollect, I think still more that there is nothing in this; for I remember hearing that Major Wyvil and Monsieur de Bellechassaigne performed a very valiant exploit, in saving this girl and her father from some of the duke of Lorraine's soldiers; I fancy it will only prove to be gratitude and friendship. But here is the carriage, I perceive, at the door; I want to take you around to some of our gay shops, to the perfumer's, and the jeweller's, and fifty other pleasant places, excellent for getting rid of superfluous money; and after dinner we will go and walk in the gardens of the Tuileries, which is quite the mode now-a-days, and I dare say the king will be there, and the queen-mother likewise."

The morning passed pleasantly away, although, to say the truth, the heart of Alice was far away from the gay scenes through which she passed; nor were her thoughts to be diverted by the rich laces of the low countries, the silver-fringed gloves of Bruges, the silks already famous of Lyons and Tours, and the thousand other gay and splendid wares, which, irrisistible to female eyes, were everywhere displayed to tempt her.

The noonday meal was ended; and happy ever at witnessing the happiness of those dear to her, Alice was gayer when she witnessed the delight of her father, at the mode in which he had spent the morning, and at an engagement he had made to pass the afternoon in visiting some library, full of rare manuscripts, and dim, illegible papyri, than she had fancied she could ever be again; for, though she would not suffer herself to despond, she had by no means succeeded in persuading herself, as Madame de Gondi had half done, that Marmaduke was true and faithful; but, on the contrary, there was a heavy cloud continually overcasting her brighter anticipations; one of those almost causeless shadows, which all of us, even the least imaginative, at times have experienced, and which even the least superstitious half believe to be ominous of coming evil. Soon after dinner, the carriage was again announced; and splendidly dressed in the superb and stately fashion of the day, with the small hoop, or *vertugardin*, as it was sometimes called—not the absurd monstrosity of later days—lending a graceful contour to the hips, and setting off the slender waist, displayed to advantage by the long corsage, with satin robes looped up with knots of gold or silver ribands, to show the petticoat of some rich tissue, and long brocaded trains gracefully carried over the left arms, with their long soft hair trained to fall in luxuriant ringlets over the neck and shoulders, the ladies set forth to walk in the palace gardens. Those gardens, sumptuous though they were and beautiful, were by no means what they are now; for at that time the changes which sprang from the exquisite taste of the great Colbert had not as yet been made, although they were commenced only a few years later; and, in the days of which I write, the gardens were divided by a small narrow street—not cleaner than streets usually were in Paris—from the palace to which they belonged; and were flanked on the river side by a range of mean and insignificant houses, which appeared to belong to the royal residence, and detracted sadly from the dignity of the view. The magnificent terrace, on the water's side, had not then been constructed, nor the great basins and superb waterworks, which now form so great a portion of the attractions of the place. They were, however, even then, the finest gardens in the world; and Alice, who had been accustomed only to the natural and inartificial shrubberies and parks of her native land, eould not but be struck by the superb and shadowed avenues, the long rows of pleached hedges, solid and high as walls of yew, or box, or hornbeam; by the secluded mazes cut in the massive greenery, the sheltered seats, and pleasant arbors, the urns and vases, columns and statues, which decorated every open place; and by the fountains which, though far less noble than the jets which now adorn those princely gardens, sparkled and flashed with bright, prismatic colors, unrivalled in the clear autumn sunshine. The gardens were already crowded with the fair, and great, and noble, when Henriette de Gondi and Alice, leaving their carriage at the splendid gates of gilded iron-work, guarded by two tall sentinels in the magnificent and gaudy costume of the Swiss guard, entered the principal avenue. Hundreds of gentlemen in gay court-dresses, or rich uniforms sparkling with gold and gems, and fluttering with scarfs and ribands, and broad laces, were strolling to and fro, in groups or singly, perfuming all the air with the rich scents which were scattered from their waving locks; for the abominable fashion of perukes had not as yet been introduced, and all their heads were bare, as well in compliment to the ladies, many of whom enlivened the bright scene yet further by their graceful presence, as in deference to the young king, who was known to be within the precincts of the garden. Scarcely had they made a dozen steps into the garden, before they were recognised and joined by several of the gentlemen who had supped with them on the previous evening, and who appeared determined to lose no opportunity of attaching themselves to the train of one, whose beauty, they foresaw, would elevate her to the rank of a reigning belle in the court of the young and beauty-loving monarch. Light, gay, and sparkling, was the conversation of the gay youths, mingled with many a jest and racy anecdote of this or that great personage, who passed or repassed constantly. This was the splendid and voluptuous Fouquet, the celebrated minister of the finance, who, though his fall was not far distant, still basked in the meridian favor of the boy-monarch—that was Count Anthony Hamilton, the wittiest man, where almost all were witty—and that superb and gallant cavalier, who walked beside him jesting and laughing noisily, all blazing with inestimable diamonds, that was the count de Grammont; and his appearance recalled some recent bon-mot, which was of course retailed—and thus, almost despite herself, between the interest of seeing so many noted persons, and the gay repartees and *jeux de mot* which were continually flowing round her, Alice was rapidly forgetting her griefs, when she was suddenly called back to them by a group of persons of both sexes, which met them and swept onward in a moment, scarce noticing if they saw the young English beauty. The first person, who walked a step or two in advance of the rest, and was covered, was a young man, well made and not ungraceful, and with a natural air of dignity, which was not altogether destroyed by the unpleasant expression and hard features of his dark-complexioned, strongly-lined, and saturnine countenance. His hair was harsh and coarse, of a deep black, and his eyes, which were quick and expressive, were of the same color. It was remarkable, that the son of two among the handsomest persons in Europe, should have been so ungainly, yet so it was; for it was Charles the Second, an exile from the land of his fathers, and a pensioner on the French king's bounty, who passed by, laughing indecently and boisterously at some licentious joke, which had just fallen from the lips of Buckingham or Wilmot, both of whom walked almost beside him, although a step or two behind. Several other English gentlemen accompanied the thankless master, for whom they had bled and were now in banishment, and three or four ladies; but it was on the last of these, a tall and very beautiful girl, with a high and perhaps somewhat bold style of loveliness, a profusion of magnificent black ringlets, a shape of exquisite voluptuous symmetry, and the unrivalled gait, springy yet slow, and blithe and graceful, of a Castilian lady, that the quick eye of Alice rested. It was the same girl who had ridden past the carriage just as they reached the gates of Paris on the preceding day, and her heart told her in a moment that it was Isabella Oswald—and it was she; superbly habited in a rich robe of emerald velvet slashed with white satin, and decorated with slight chainwork of wrought gold, with diamonds in her bosom, and in her splendid hair—nothing could be more queenly than the whole air and carriage of the proud beauty, as she passed along leaning upon the arm of the tall gray-haired soldier, whom she had addressed the previous day as her father.

"See, see; Mademoiselle de Selby," exclaimed the young count de Bellefonds in a loud whisper, as she swept along. "That is the heroine of Villequier's tale last evening, that handsome black-haired girl."

"Indeed!" said Alice quietly, "she *is* extremely handsome certainly; I do not wonder that the gentlemen should be somewhat bold to win her."

"Nor I, nor I," replied Bellefonds; "but as I thought at the time, there was a good deal of romance in our worthy captain's story; the quarrel had nothing to do in the world with the lady, it was merely about some military duty or other. The old man is a very rigid disciplinarian, and is blest with a fiery temper; and was intemperate and violent in his language. Wyvil—what singular names, by-the-by, you English people have;

it is almost impossible to speak them—behaved extremely well and coolly; and all is well arranged, and they are friends again!"

"Oh! I am glad to hear that," replied Alice, as if she had been quite unconcerned; "I am very glad to hear that Major Wyvil conducted himself so well. He is an old friend of ours, although I have not seen him since I have been in Paris."

"Ah! you will see him very soon; he is a great favorite at court, one of the bravest and most noble of our young officers; I dare say he is in the garden now; but ha! what have we here?" he added, as a considerable bustle might be observed a little farther up the walk, the people hurrying to and fro, and arranging themselves in lines on either hand, "there is a movement." As if in answer to the count's question, there came a cry, "The king! the king! room for the king!" and bowing courteously to all his subjects, and pausing now and then to speak to some one of the more distinguished, the young and splendid prince came slowly down the avenue, attended by a band of courtiers as gallantly attired as can be fancied. Louis, who was at this time little advanced beyond the ripening term of boyhood, was singularly, ay, wonderfully handsome, not very tall, but splendidly proportioned, with a fine brilliant countenance of somewhat Roman outline; a forehead all bland expanse, yet broad and massive, an eye bright, penetrating and undaunted as an eagle's; a lip which could express an empire's proud authority, but which was now wreathed in a sweet and fascinating smile; a gait, at the same time easy and majestic; an air, so wonderfully winning, that when he chose it, no one on earth could resist its imperative seduction; such, at that period, was the youth, whose name was to be coupled for all ages with everything that relates to magnificence and grandeur, whether of war and glory, or of pleasure and ostentation; who certainly possessed beyond all others the regal power of winning hearts as it were by a word, of gaining almost by a glance man's adoration—woman's deep devotion. Of all the court, there was no man so plainly dressed as the young monarch; he wore his own rich chestnut hair in flowing ringlets, a coat of black velvet, lined with white satin, with vest and breeches of the same material, without a particle of lace, or embroidery, or chain of gold, or jewelry, or any other decoration, except a single star of superb brilliants on the left breast of the doublet, a pair of diamond buckles in his shoes, and a diamond hilt to his court rapier. His eye glanced rapidly from side to side, as he came up the walk, dwelling for a few moments complacently upon any face of more than ordinary beauty; and when he had come to the spot where Madame de Gondi stood, he came to a dead stop, looking full at Alice Selby. "Ha!" he said, "our fair lady of Gondi, methinks you have a new face there! one that we have not seen at our court—one of the fair daughters of the noble house of Retz?"

"Not so, sire," answered Henriette de Gondi, courtesying very low at this unexpected civility; "a young English lady, a cousin of my dear mother's, who had been forced to fly from her country in consequence of loyalty to her king; Mademoiselle Selby, I had proposed to ask permission to present her to your majesty on your next reception-day; she only arrived in your majesty's capital last evening."

"We shall be happy always to receive so loyal and so fair a lady," answered Louis, very gracefully; "our lady mother also, will be glad to see Mistress Selby;" and he was already moving onward, when he appeared to recollect something, and turning short round, "I presume," he said, "you have received our commands, madame, through our lord chamberlain, to attend our ball this evening at the Louvre?"

"I have not heard of it, sire," she replied, when he interrupted her—

"Artagnac, then, must have forgotten; well, now you comprehend, and your fair cousin will accompany you;" and with these words, the ladies courtesying low in token of assent, the monarch and his train swept onward, the former saying so loud that his words reached the ears of Alice, "Ma foi! Beaugen, these English girls eclipse the brightest of our beauties; I thought the Oswald the handsomest woman I had ever seen, but this fair-haired girl is twenty times more lovely."

A well-pleased smile came over the face of Henriette, as she heard the flattering comment of the king, well knowing that so open an expression of his admiration, would send the whole world of the court to worship at the feet of Alice; and hoping that a reception so distinguished would go far to reclaim the recreant lover. Alice smiled likewise, but it was with a sad and calm expression that spoke of anything rather than gratified vanity or pride. The gentlemen around did not, however, seem to notice either the smile, or the feelings that gave birth to it; but continued their attentions for some time, strolling the while along the shadowy walks, and pausing now and then by the basin of some brilliant fountain, until, having remained as long as politeness would permit, one by one, all of them dropped off, pleading some business or engagement as an excuse, and only Bellefonds, who was indeed related to the house of Gondi, felt it his duty to await their pleasure. After a while, "Well, Alice," said her cousin, "I think we have had enough of this; if Monsieur de Bellefonds will be so good as to inquire for my carriage at the gate, we will sit down and wait for his return in this quiet arbor." The place of which she spoke, was no more than a nook, or green recess, hollowed out of the massive thickness of a great yew hedge, with a seat capable of accommodating two, or at the most, three persons, overlooking the principal jet d'êau, and the great *carré four*, or common centre from which the several avenues diverged. The gentleman bowed, and walked quickly off toward the gate of the Tuileries, and the two ladies sat down in the shade, neither of them for the moment much inclined to talk, for there is a reaction which follows the excitement of very forced and brilliant conversation, as surely as it does the excitement of any other kind; and a sort of vague lassitude had crept over them, inclining them rather to think within themselves, than to speak of what had been passing. It happened to be the case, however, that the same hedge in which the sylvan seat was framed where they were sitting, was the external boundary of a maze or labyrinth, laid out with rare skill and many intricate and doubtful windings; and exactly behind the spot where Alice sat, another similar recess had been cut, in the thickness of the same hedge, opening to the walk behind; and only separated from the bower in front by a few inches of thick evergreen foliage, sufficient indeed to prevent the eye from discerning anything beyond, but suffering every word that was spoken to pass through its leafy screen. This seat, the existence of which had been suspected by neither of the ladies, was unoccupied when they first sat down; but scarcely had they been there a minute when they distinguished the footsteps of two persons, one evidently a lady, coming along the walk behind them, and immediately afterward became aware that they had paused almost beside them. A moment afterward the sweet and low-toned voice of a woman was heard saying, "Oh! this is very wrong—I fear that this is very wrong indeed—what will my father say when he misses me, and finds that you have come off with me?"

"Say! why, what should he say, sweet Isabella?" answered a man, in tones each note of which struck to the very heart of Alice, "but that you are a wild one ever, and ran away into the maze, and that I came to seek for you, lest you should lose your way. But Isabel, it is not you, but I, that have indeed strayed from my road; and if you will not deign to lead me back, I fear me I am lost for ever. Beautiful, beautiful Isabella—listen one moment—nay! do not turn your head away, nor beat the earth so proudly angry with that small foot—listen, for I must speak. I can not be confined, and cribbed and fettered by their confounded rules of *convenance;* and I must speak and be answered. I adore you! words can not speak my adoration, and you know it! Yes! well you know it, Isabella! and you have smiled on me, and seemed not wholly to despise my suit. Speak, then—speak, Isabella, and say—can you not love me?—will you not be mine?"

The moment she had recognised the voice, Alice grasped Henriette by the arm so rigidly, that instantly she comprehended what was passing; and when her cousin would have risen, detained her quietly, yet by a hold so firm that she could not escape from it without creating so much noise as would have reached the ears of the others. A second or two followed, before any answer was returned by the girl; and there was a sound, that might have been either that of weeping or of suppressed laughter; but when she spoke, her voice was clear and silvery, and, if anything, pitched higher than before.

"Yes," she said, "Major Wyvil, I will be quite frank with you. I *have* perceived your attentions—nay, chafe not! your love, if you will—and I will not say that I have perceived them altogether with indifference; but, ere I give my love, I must be certain, and I am not quite certain. Sir, I have heard something whispered of love passages in England—something of a fair girl who rescued Captain Wyvil from strange peril, and loved and was loved in return. Methinks—"

"Mere talk," Marmaduke answered, interrupting her; "mere empty, idle slander; uttered by fools who know not, or knaves who care not what they publish. Nay, dearest, loveliest Isabella, I swear to you that my whole heart is yours—yours only—and for ever! Why, she—she was the merest country-girl! I never so much even as thought of her—"

"Enough!" whispered Alice, vehemently—"I will hear no more!" and, starting to her feet, she hurried out of the little arbor before Henriette had time to hinder her, and went on speaking, when she joined her, not without manifesting strong indignation—"I am astonished at you—ay, astonished, Madame de Gondi—that you should wish me to remain and hear things not intended for my ears; it is unprincipled and base."

"Alice," interposed Henriette—"Alice, you are now angry, and very naturally so. The time will come, however, when you will do me justice. I am the last, the very last person, Alice, who would encourage any one to listen meanly to the words of another; but in this case you had unwittingly heard so much, that it was absolutely necessary that you should hear more. But you are right in this—you have heard all that it behooved you to hear; you *have* detected and *shall* foil a villain! And, as you say, we had no right to wait or listen for the lady's answer. Now take my arm—here comes De Bellefonds to announce the carriage—and see, the gardens are already almost empty."

CHAPTER XXVIII.

THE Louvre, although it had not, at this time, been rebuilt and decorated by Claude Perrault, De Vau, and Dorbay, as it was a few years later, was a magnificent and stately pile, well worthy to be the residence of a line of great and powerful kings; it contained many vast saloons and stately halls, splendidly furnished according to the taste of the times. It must not, indeed, be imagined that now — when the revenues of the country had been exhausted, the court impoverished, and the treasury emptied, by the long and terrible civil wars which had been raging throughout France, and before the master-hand of Colbert had revived the credit and refilled the coffers of the state — its furniture, and other appliances of luxury, were so extravagantly sumptuous and grand, as they became in after-years, when France had learned to manufacture for herself the mirrors, and the tapestries, the carpets, and the laces and velvet, which she was now content to purchase, at not far short of their weight in gold, from Venice, the Low Countries, Turkey, and Italy, and Flanders; all was, however, rich, and gorgeous, and magnificent, and certainly far more luxurious than had ever met the eyes of fair Alice Selby.

The court was filled by a detachment of the horse body-guard, and their fine band was playing, at short intervals, to the great delight of an immense multitude of people who were collected without the gates, the popular and stirring tunes peculiar to the house of Bourbon: "Vive Henri Quatre," "La belle Gabrielle," "O Richard!" and the like, which were received now with tumultuous applause by the same wild and fickle multitude, that had but a few months before fired the cannon of the Bastile on the troops of the very king whom they now affected to adore. In the hall, at the foot of the great staircase, were stationed a small party of officers and gentlemen pensioners, with burnished breastplates and broad-bladed partisans ; and on every landing-place up to the royal antechamber was stationed a subaltern of the guard in full uniform, with casque and breastplate, sword and musketoon. Many of the old *haut-noblesse* had arrived already, and all the officers, civil and military, of the royal household, had come together. When Madame de Gondi entered the palace with her young guest, the ante-chamber was filled with gayly-dressed, flippant pages, whose long curled hair and blooming cheeks, and dresses vivid with light, brilliant colors, made them resemble girls rather than effeminate youths of the ruder sex, one of whom started forward instantly to receive their names, and pass them onward to an usher who stood, leaning on a long gold rod, at the door of the principal saloon. Another moment, and the whole gorgeous scene burst, like a fairy-vision, on the dazzled senses of the young English girl. The long suite of splendid halls, illuminated by vast pendant chandeliers of gold and crystal, the hangings of brocade and velvet, the giant mirrors of Venetian fabric, reflecting every object fifty-fold, the very atmosphere rendered voluptuous by the breath of the softest perfumes, and vocal with the dying fall of sweetest instruments. Such was the first impression, a sort of vague bewilderment, that made the head swim and the heart flutter, and the breath come thick, unmingled with any very clear consciousness or distinct perception of the things that met her eyes. The second thing that struck her was the apparent fewness of the guests, the effect of numbers being in a great measure lost, owing to the vastness of the apartments, and to the distribution of the company throughout the whole length of the suite ; so that, although at the further end of the long vista she could discover by the blazing lustres which rendered all the rooms as light as day, a crowd of gay forms wheeling in the slow and graceful dances of the time, she passed in the intermediate halls only a group or two of gentlemen playing at games of hazard on tables laid out for the purpose ; and a few pairs seemingly busied in matters of love or intrigue, seated apart in the luxurious alcoves, or partaking of the delicate refreshments which were displayed in such profusion. Madame de Gondi, therefore, hurried her somewhat quickly toward the ball-room, making no pause at all, except to return the salutations of the gentlemen who recognised her. Scarcely, however, had they reached the ball-room, where, as they entered, the dance was gayly circling, when a gentleman in a rich court-dress stepped forward from the crowd to meet them, exclaiming—

"At last, Madame de Gondi! at last you come to rejoice our eyes, which we have been straining all the evening in the hope of discovering you. His majesty has inquired thrice, if you had yet arrived; and has commanded Artagnac and myself to bring you to him the moment you should make your entrée!"

"I hope we have not been accused of treason, Monsieur de Broglie," replied Henriette, smiling, "that we should be thus made prisoners by to so *preux chevaliers* as Monsieur d'Artagnac and the Count Charles de Broglie!"

"Oh, by no means—by no means, madame," answered De Broglie, laughing, "unless to pierce the hearts of kings with the shafts of Cupid may be deemed a species of *lese majesté.* But if we understand the matter rightly, his majesty has no thought of making prisoners of you; but rather, I believe, of offering himself a willing captive to the *beaux yeaux* of this fair lady, whom I have never," he added, half hesitating as he said it, "enjoyed the happiness of seeing here before."

"I should think not," said madame, "for she never was in Paris until yesterday afternoon. Alice, my dear, let me make you know the Count Charles de Broglie; in his own estimation, the wittiest and best-dressed man in France, except the Grammont! Monsieur le Count, Mademoiselle de Selby. After bowing and murmuring his compliments, the young lord led them again forward, saying as he did so, "Upon my word! if we stay talking here, I shall get sent myself to the Bastile; for his majesty was all impatience when he sent me."

By this time, they had reached the upper end of the saloon, where, under a sort of a canopy of cloth of gold and velvet, the king was standing with a number of his lords about him, and the queen-mother, Anne of Austria, seated in a rich chair of state, with a bevy of court beauties ranged behind her—and nothing can be imagined more flattering or courteous than the reception of the two ladies, by the young monarch and his stately mother; a favor, which was perhaps as much to be ascribed to a piece of policy in honoring one branch of a family so powerful as the house of De Retz—when it had been almost determined to put an end to the ambitious career of another, in the person of the celebrated cardinal—as it was to the king's admiration of a fair face and handsome figure. Be this, however, as it may, the king, after commending the young guest of Madame de Gondi to the attention of his mother, and desiring his lord-chamberlain to place her on the list of those to be invited to all the court festivities, actually led her out to dance as his own partner; rendering her thereby a mark for the envy of every woman, and the admiration of every man in the room.

There was, perhaps, never a woman less afflicted with the vice of vanity, than Alice Selby. Sprung herself from a family of so ancient distinction as to consider herself naturally equal to the highest of her own land, she was not one to be dazzled beyond the bounds of reason even by the condescension of a great king; and she was too intrinsically proud and high-minded to fancy for a moment, that she could gain anything of real elevation from a circumstance so purely adventitious. But, notwithstanding all this, there is, and must be a gratification, and, even to the best-balanced mind, a sort of pleasurable excitement, in being selected for any honor by the high and noble; and although Alice Selby was, as I have said, as little likely to imagine herself magnified by this contact with a king, as to deem herself disgraced by collision with a beggar—although she was unhappy, and so sick at heart that, but for a little touch of feminine pride, she would assuredly have preferred the seclusion of her own chamber to the glare of a court ball—she was yet, beyond doubt, both pleased and gratified at finding herself the partner of the most distinguished and magnificent prince, the handsomest man, and most accomplished cavalier of the day; and it was owing perhaps no less to this pleasure and excitement, than to the natural self-reliance of a high and well-tutored mind, accustomed from its childhood upward to no thoughts but what were noble and distinguished, that she displayed neither bashfulness nor vanity, neither timidity nor exultation, in circumstances which might well have turned the head of one so unused to society. Never, perhaps, in her life, had Alice looked more lovely. Gratification, and the slight excitement of the dance, had called up to her cheeks a brighter tinge of the carnation than was natural to her pale, pure complexion—her eyes sparkled more brightly, and as her long fair ringlets waved about in the breath created by her own motion, and her beautiful, rounded figure swayed gracefully in the varied attitudes of the slow and measured dance, nothing could well be fancied more exquisitely beautiful than she, who, at that very moment, was rejected and deserted for one as much inferior to herself in personal charms, as in those higher attributes that constitute the beauties of the soul.

It was not long before the royal dance was finished; and then, although the king, when he had led her back to the court circle, where her cousin waited her return, noticed her no more during that evening except by a passing bow and smile, the proudest and the noblest lords of that proud court vied with each other for the hand of a girl whom they would have scarcely deigned to see, had not the monarch's approbation stamped her indelibly a reigning beauty. Ladies, although they envied her in secret, sought the acquaintance of one who, they foresaw, must rank with them in all future parties. Madame de Montbagor, known as the *belle des belles*, and the bright duchess of Longueville, for one glance from whose fair eyes courtiers foreswore their fealty to kings, and Grammont, peerless in beauty as was her lord in wit, and Mademoiselle d'Espinasse, and Madame de Chatelet, and twenty others, some famous for their present loveliness, some for the reputation of their bygone charms, asked the familiarity and friendship of one whose name they never knew, and of whose claims to their esteem they were completely ignorant. Thus passed the night; and, to speak truly, if all the cares of Alice Selby were not forgotten, they were at least lost, once and again, in the whirl and tumult of the gay sights and merry sounds that were around her—for such is human nature; and it is by no means incompatible with the pervading sense of a deep, real, ever-present grief, to laugh, to enjoy wit, and to admire beauty—in short, to be temporarily gay, if not, in truth, happy—and such was now the case with Alice. The stunning blows of the morning had, as it were, passed away, leaving a dizzy and bewildered sense of ill, which she had not as yet had time fully to comprehend, or to realize to her own feelings; and now, plunged, as if by magic, into the vortex of all that was most gay and witty, most dazzling and seductive in the gayest city of the world, she could not but yield to the contagion of example; and though at times the question would rise to her mind, "What have I now to do with happiness?"—though the sense of betrayal and desertion would intrude, like a ghastly phantom in the midst of revelry and mirth—yet was the question speedily, if not satisfactorily answered—yet was the phantom quickly banished by the first happy laugh or sparkling bon-mot. It is always the first blow only, that pains or shocks the mind or body deeply; the after-things are more easily endured, and the pangs they create readily concealed, even although they may be felt keenly. The first and stunning blow had been dealt at the supper-table on the previous night—it had been heavily repeated in the gardens; yet although Alice felt it—oh, how bitterly! she was nerved to bear, like the Spartan boy, in silence, the pangs that might be gnawing at her vitals. Several times during that night of triumph—as it would have been considered by every woman in the room, except her who had enjoyed it—the thought had crossed her mind whether her faithless lover was a witness; and what would be the effect upon his mind, which, she could no longer conceal from herself, was worldly, frail, and fickle. An indistinct and floating hope did occur to her more than once, that his allegiance might be reclaimed by the mere sight of the effect wrought by her beauty upon others; and though, whenever such hopes did arise, she asked herself scornfully and half-indignantly,—"and could I—ought I to pardon him such baseness, if even he were to return?" she never fairly answered herself in the negative. The evening was waxing late, however, and she had, as yet, seen nothing of either Wyvil or of Isabella; although she fancied once that she caught a glimpse of the tall form and dignified movement of the lady amid a crowd of courtiers, but before she could distinguish it, she was hurried onward and lost sight of her completely. The evening was waxing late, and the hour of supper was approaching, when, just as she had promised her hand for the following dance to the young count de Bellefonds, she heard the sound of a well-known footstep close behind her; and a voice, every note of which went directly to her heart, exclaimed—

"And has not Mistress Selby one glance of recognition—one word of welcome for an old friend?"

She turned her head round quickly—and not now pale and haggard from long and close confinement, as when he plighted her his faith, but full of health and vigor and high manly beauty, sumptuously attired, and seemingly in the highest spirits, Marmaduke stood before her! Her cheek, indeed, and brow—nay, more, her neck and bosom, and all the smooth expanse of her fair shoulders were suffused for a moment with a deep crimson blush; but her clear eye retained its natural calmness, and her melodious voice did not falter, as she extended her hand to him frankly, and replied in French, to the words which he had spoken in their own language, in order that De Bellefonds, who was standing by her side, might not conceive himself excluded—"Indeed, I have," she said; "I am sincerely glad to see you; and Monsieur de Bellefonds here can tell you, that I asked after you from him, and expressed my joy at your well-doing."

"Well, you will dance with me," he added, "will you not? for I have very much to say to you, and more to ask—I can not guess what brought you hither; come, they are standing even now."

"I would with pleasure," she replied, "and I will, if you wish it, by-and-by; but for this time I am engaged to the count here."

He looked at her steadfastly for a moment, and then said in English, in a low voice, "You are changed, Alice, you are changed; you have been flirting here with kings, and dukes, and barons, until you think an English gentleman below your notice." She gave him one look — *one!* fraught with the whole of her deep mind — so mild, so tender, yet at the same time so ineffably reproachful, that his eye sank beneath it.

'Those," she said, "sir, who are the first to suspect change in others, are often wont to change the first themselves." This time she spoke in English; and then turning to Bellefonds, "*Allons!*" she said — "*Monsieur le Comte*, the dancers are arranged in their places," and with the words, she gave him her gloved hand, and passed onward.

"Beautiful creature!" muttered Wyvil to himself — "more beautiful, ten-fold!" and then he followed quickly after them, and said in French, as he overtook them, "The next dance, then — the next dance, Mistress Alice, will be mine."

"Certainly, if you wish it," she replied; and then the instruments burst forth with a lond symphony, and all the graceful forms started at once into quick motion; and all the while, with his eyes following the figure of the sweet girl whom he had so treacherously abandoned, thinking in his heart how far more lovely she was, whether in motion or repose, than the gay, artificial beauties of the court, and drawing comparisons not very favorable to Isabella Oswald, stood Marmaduke, until the measure was concluded, and, more than half-regretting his base fickleness, he received her from the hand of the young French nobleman.

"Now, tell me," he said — "tell me what can have possibly occurred, to bring you to Paris? where are you staying? and is your father with you?"

"Your letters were intercepted by the government," she answered, "and we are banished England, and all our property sequestrated, for sheltering you after the Worcester fight.

We only came last night to Paris; my father is with me, and we are staying with my cousin, Madame de Gondi, at her hotel in the faubourg St. Germain, where we shall be all glad to see you. There now, do not look so tremendously alarmed and wo-begone, for there is not much harm done after all—except that poor Bartram, or Colonel Penruddock rather, is desperately hurt and taken prisoner, and, I fear, dead ere this—for Cromwell has been very kind, and has made our cousin, Chaloner, a promise that he will grant us all a full pardon in the spring, and restore all our property. So, you perceive, that all we have lost is really a gain, for we have had a trip to Paris, and I expect to pass a very pleasant winter. How very gay the court is—and how many lovely women! By the way," she continued, running on very rapidly, for she was, in truth, afraid of his getting upon subjects too delicate for the time and place—subjects on which she knew she could not speak without betraying that agitation which she was most anxious to conceal—"by the way, although this is the first time you have seen me since I have been in France, I have been much more fortunate, for you were the very first person I beheld as we were entering the barriers. You galloped past the carriage without seeing us, at which I did not wonder very much, for you were in pursuit of a very pretty lady—one of the prettiest ladies I ever saw. I met her again in the garden of the Tuileries this morning, magnificently dressed in green velvet—who is she? I should like to know, she is so very handsome."

Shrewd as he was, and deeply versed in all the wiles of the artificial world, Wyvil was fairly foiled and puzzled. The perfect coolness of Alice Selby's manner, the lack of any seeming consciousness, such as a girl must naturally feel and show in the presence of her betrothed lover—the evident, yet quiet cordiality with which she met him as an old friend, so perfectly unloverlike and free from agitation, were all beyond his comprehension; while, at the same time, the very ease and freedom of her conversation forbade him to believe it possible that she could have discovered his disloyalty. He paused a moment, therefore, ere he answered, and, when he did so, it was with an air of confusion, that did not escape the observation of the interested questioner.

"Do you think her so very handsome? rather too dark, perhaps! Her name is Isabella Oswald, the daughter of Sir Henry Oswald, a cavalier who left England many years ago, at the first outbreak of the troubles, and has risen to the rank of major-general in the French army."

"Ah! English, is she?" replied Alice; "she is certainly very dark to be English; she looks more like a Spaniard or an Italian. Is she as agreeable as she is pretty? I do not see her here to-night."

"How strangely you run on; you are most strangely altered since I last saw you," exclaimed Marmaduke, unable any longer to conceal his astonishment.

"Am I, indeed?" she said. "Well, if I am, it is the way of the world, you know, to alter; but I hope it is not for the worse that I am altered. See, they are going to dance again. Let us begin."

There were, in those days, in the course of the dance, none of those opportunities for conversation which are afforded now by the intervals of the waltz or quadrille; and, therefore, Marmaduke could press no further his examination into the meaning of Alice Selby's changed and peculiar manner. Once, as they met and interchanged hands in the mazes of the graceful measure, he pressed her fingers so closely that she could not have failed to perceive it; yet, neither did she return the gentle pressure in the least degree, nor did she seek to withdraw her hand from his grasp. A slight blush crossed her pale cheek for a moment, but except that, she gave no sign that she understood his meaning.

The music ceased—the pastime of the evening was at an end—all but the splendid banquet, which closed the regal entertainment; and, as the guests filed off in order, Alice presented Marmaduke to her cousin, so that, although he attended them during the supper, and handed them to their carriage afterward, he got no opportunity of again speaking to her.

privately; although before they parted he asked permission, which was granted readily, to visit her on the morrow.

"Well, Alice, well," exclaimed Madame de Gondi, the moment they were left alone, "what do you think about it now?"

"That he was false, and has half repented of his falsehood," replied the fair girl.

"And what then?" asked her cousin eagerly. "Will you forgive the penitent? Say you will, dearest, say you will, in pity to yourself; for I declare I never saw a girl more desperately in love — every look, every movement shows it."

"I must not promise," answered Alice, with a faint smile; "I must not bind myself, for I do not know — I must learn — I must learn how far this has gone. But I fear — I can only say, I fear very greatly."

"Oh, you should never fear. I always hope, always expect the best —"

"And are always disappointed — that follows as a thing of course," said Alice.

"Not always; no, not always," replied Henriette; "for I fully expected to find a very sweet girl in my cousin Alice, and that she would win the heart of every one who saw her; and there, you see, I was not at all disappointed, but was quite right. But here we are at home, and, I declare, it is already almost morning."

CHAPTER XXIX.

In one of the by-streets of Paris, not very far distant from the palace of the Louvre, there was a large old-fashioned house, standing a little way back, with a narrow yard before it surrounded by an iron railing. The outer door stood open, but just within it there was another scarcely less strong than the first, having a grated wicket in its upper panel, by which the porter, an old invalided soldier, might reconnoitre the faces of all visiters, before admitting them. In this large house, as is so much the custom at the present day on the continent, there was one common staircase, with several strong doors, one or more on each landing; the several floors being let separately as suites of apartments to travellers, or those natives who had neither houses of their own nor the means of maintaining them. On the third floor of this building there was a handsome suite of rooms, consisting of an antechamber, with a small closet opening from it for a servant, a large saloon, a spacious and luxurious bedchamber, and several small apartments for the attendants of a gentleman of consequence; and, at a late hour of the night, or it would be, perhaps, more correct to say, early in the morning, that succeeded the royal ball, the principal room of the suite was brightly illuminated, and occupied by a person who appeared in no wise inclined to sleep, though all the rest of the inhabitants of the great city were buried in deep slumber. The room, as I have said, was large and airy, with windows reaching to the ground, and was well furnished with a rich carpet on the floor, and hangings on the walls. Two or three slabs and tables of various forms were ranged against the panels, or occupied the central space, covered with Persian carpets, and littered with a variety of articles for use and show — some ornamental vases and other specimens of the antique that might have charmed a virtuoso; papers, and books, and instruments of music, two or three swords with their embroidered baldrics, a plumed hat, gloves with silver fringes, a scarlet mantle heavily laced with gold, and many other things which seemed to designate the occupant for a man of elegant and intellectual tastes, a soldier and a gentleman. Over the mantel-piece was hung a richly-chased and inlaid musketoon, and a pair of long horseman's pistols with Spanish barrels, at that time the most famous in the world; and, upon hooks, along the wall facing the windows, were several cuirasses of steel, two polished head-pieces, and several pairs of gauntlets, and below them three of the long, straight, double-edged swords peculiar to the cavalry of the period. A little fire of wood was burning on the hearth, for though the autumn was not far advanced, and the days were yet warm, the nights were chilly; and, near the fire, there had been placed a small round table, with a silver lamp, a writing-desk bestrewn with notes and letters, most of them written in a feminine hand, and among these a miniature portrait, in enamel, of an exceedingly beautiful girl with dark hair and eyes, and a marked aspect of voluptuous boldness. A large arm-chair stood close to the table, as if some one had just occupied it, but it had been pushed a little way back, and Marmaduke Wyvil, for it was to him these rooms belonged, was walking to and fro the floor, with rapid and irregular strides; his face all pale and bloodless, his eye full of a wild and anxious restlessness, and his arms folded on his breast with the hands tightly clenched. Several times he walked up and down the saloon, pausing at each turn, and standing still beside the table for a little while, gazing upon the letters and the miniature, although there was but little speculation in the fixed stare with which he regarded them; and, although he seemed hardly conscious how he was occupied, at last he caught the picture up, and gazed upon it earnestly.

'Lovely!" he said, "ay, it is very lovely! but, after all, it is the loveliness of a *bona roba*, rather than of a wife; and when you see them both together, she is not half so truly beautiful. I marvel how I could have so forgotten!" He paused again for a moment or two, and casting down the portrait half disdainfully — "Curses!" he muttered between his teeth — "curses upon it! This comes of playing double. Both won — ay, both; and now, I trow, both lost! And then, and then?" and he resumed his hurried strides, smiting his forehead with his hand as he did so, and muttering stifled imprecations.

He soon, however, became tired of pacing and repacing the apartment; and again threw himself into the chair, covering his face with both his hands. After a little while he again started up, and nothing could more thoroughly display the perturbation and the agony of his mind, than did the sharp, and keen, and haggard look which had come over his smooth features; changing him in the space of a few hours, from a fresh-looking, fair young man, to a pale, conscience-stricken, spectral-looking personage. "Let me think," he said, as he did so; "I must think, for there is everything to gain, and more than all to lose. Let me think!" and he did think, very long and deeply; and though he spoke no more aloud, he muttered to himself often; and his thoughts shaped and arranged themselves in words and sentences, almost as definite as those which he had just before enunciated.

"This girl," so ran his anxious meditation, "this artless and unsophisticated girl! what can it mean? I do not understand. By Heaven! no regular town beauty, accustomed for long years to all the homage, all the gay flattery of courts, could carry it more easily. So calm, so self-possessed, so graceful! Can she have heard? can she suspect? No, no! it is not possible; there would have been wrath, indignation, jealousy. No, no! she could not so have met me, could not have so conversed with me, and that, too, touching Isabella, had she dreamed only that she was her rival, her successful rival! And yet in what, in what is there comparison, or rivalry? In what? in nothing. She must! she shall be mine!" and, with the thought, he sprang up from his chair, and began once more to stride with heavy and irregular steps, to and fro the saloon, till he stopped once again, and said aloud, "And what then, what with Isabella? her fiery Spanish temper, when she shall find herself deserted! There will be no restraint, no curb upon its fury! no corselet that could ward off her sharp vengeance! And it was but to-day; this cursed, ay, doubly cursed to-day! that I committed myself to her, beyond all retraction; and if I could retract, would Alice hear me? There was no love in her cool eye, no consciousness, either of injury endured, or of reanimating tenderness, or of premeditated wrong. All calm, as if we had been ever friends, more than friends ever! Oh! I am hedged about with toils on every side, beset, betrayed—thousands of devils! ruined, ay, ruined beyond hope! My estates forfeited! ay, and the very hope of their restoration gone—sold to the pestilent Jews—lost! lost! beyond redemption! Ha!" as a sudden thought, as if by inspiration flashed on his soul—"ha! but Sir Henry might refuse—might? *would!* By Heaven! I have observed it in his eye, his voice, his manner! and, till this night, that was my terror—that which shall be my preservation. He knows, too, or suspects, I fancy, that I am given to those infernal cubes of bone—those devilish dice! but if I once succeed, I have done with them for ever! Ay, that is it, seek out a quarrel with Sir Henry, and find in that a cause for rupture with this bold beauty—had I but known this somewhat sooner, I might have won her without marriage! but that is too late now! She is the richer, though—tush! Woolverton is worth three thousand, every pound of it, in yearly rent; and the old gray-beard scholar, simple as any child, and unsuspicious—it is the better, the better every way! And Alice, ay, sweet Alice! in good truth, she is the only woman I ever looked upon, that was worth love—love! ay, I do love her, have loved her always, although necessity, and opportunity, and this girl's beauty, blinded me for a while; there needed but one tone of her soft voice, one glance of those sweet eyes, to argue me of guilt! of madness! But it shall soon be ended! This morning I will see her, this morning seal my recantation, and the rest will be soon managed."

He took a few more turns about the room, then entered his bedchamber hastily, and pulling off his boots, threw himself down without undressing further; and wearied in both mind and body, soon forgot all his plots and cares in profound slumber. The sun was high in the heavens, and the streets of Paris had been filled for several hours, with all their dissonant and ceaseless din, before he summoned his attendants, and dressing himself with unusual care, ordered out his horses, and sat down to amuse himself during their preparation, by dallying with his morning meal.

Alice, meantime, on her return from the ball, had been met by a strange and glad surprise; for, scarcely had she reached the head of the great staircase, before her girl Margaret came running out, full of wild and eager joy, with her eyes sparkling.

"Oh! Mistress Alice, they have come. I am so glad—so glad, they have all come!"

"Who have come, Margaret? what in the world ails you?" asked Alice, greatly astonished and half-frightened.

"Why, General Henry, Mistress Alice; and Master Fletcher, the steward, and Anthony, and Matthew Harland, and Frank Norman, who used to live with the Lord Fairfax. The general was up stairs with Master Selby for an hour or better, soon after you went hence."

"Well! this *is* good news, Margaret," Alice replied; "did you see General Henry?"

"Oh yes! I saw him, and he knew me instantly, and left word with me that he would call and see you very early, at nine o'clock. So you had better go to bed directly, or you will never be afoot in time to see him. And all the folks are well at Woolverton except poor old Dame Rainsford, who has been dead some time, and good John Sherlock is striving hard to get Marian—but Marian never will wed any more, I think."

"Never, indeed," said Alice with a sigh, "she has loved once too deeply!" and, without saying more, she suffered the girl to undress her, and lay down. But she continued sleepless until within an hour of the time when Margaret had been ordered to awaken her, and when she slept at last, her sleep was restless and uneasy; and when she rose her face was extremely pale, and its expression painful, and exceedingly unlike its usually calm and serene character. The glance of her eye, too, as her maid observed, was uncommonly bright and glassy;

and ere she had been long up, a round defined spot of hectic crimson settling on either cheek, remained there throughout the day—an evidence of the strong conflict that was at work within. Chaloner arrived, as he had promised to do, at an early hour; and was, as ever, all that was kind, affectionate, and noble. He was, he told her, on his way to the Hague, whither he had been appointed as a special envoy to their high mightinesses, for the purpose of demanding reparation of wrongs and outrages done to the British commissioners by certain royal refugees; and had been induced to take Paris on his route, partly on business of the state, and partly from the wish of seeing her, and communicating to her in person, the agreeable tidings, that a full pardon had been made in due form to herself and Master Selby, accompanied by a reversal of the decree of sequestration; "so that your property is all restored to you," he said, "after a very brief alienation, during which you will find that it has suffered no diminution, or detriment whatever. I have likewise obtained a full indemnity, and permission to return to England at his pleasure, for your friend, Major Wyvil, whom I shall endeavor to see to-day, in order that I may congratulate him on his fortune—for your good father, my dear Alice, has told me everything; and I know that he is to be the owner of that hand and heart, to which I once so foolishly aspired. But it is the best as it is. Even as all the things of the Great Maker's planning are better than the fitful dreams of mortals! and I thank HIM that it is so—that I can freely and fully wish you all that happiness which you so merit, without one feeling of base envy, or weak repining, at the success of another; who, I can well believe, is better fitted far than I, to make you happy. I feel, that had I won that heart and hand, they would have all unfitted me for the vocation to which I am unerringly devoted—my country's service! There is naught now to distract me from my single line of duties, and I believe and feel, that I shall be as happy in following out what I know to be the right course, as you, I trust, will be in that sphere to which God has called you."

"O Henry!" replied Alice, affected almost to tears; "ever

the same—the same pure, noble, excellent! I thank our God most fervently and truly that you *are* happy, and, I doubt not, you will be happier tenfold in your high course, than any being, so poor and frail as I, could have made you by love, had it been mine to give; but," and her voice faltered for a moment, till with a little effort she recovered herself, and spoke quite firmly; "I think you are mistaken, I do not believe that I shall ever be the bride of Major Wyvil."

"How!" exclaimed Chaloner; "how! not the bride of Wyvil? why, it was but last night your father told me that it should be so! How, Alice!" and his whole grand and noble face brightened with glorious indignation; "this man, whom you rescued from destruction, well-nigh at the price of your own ruin—this man has not—can not have dared to slight you?"

"Cousin," said Alice quietly, "dear cousin Henry, you must now ask me nothing. Be sure that should poor Alice Selby require defence or aid, there is no arm on earth from which she would so gladly seek it as from his who did once save her! But there is no cause now, not even why I should ask advice, and trust me, I know well how to provide for my own dignity, and happiness, and honor."

"Indeed you do," Chaloner answered, his wonted calmness conquering the brief passion; "I never doubted it, so far as dignity or honor—the way of these is clear and not to be mistaken by an eye which takes, like yours, truth for its only lamp. But happiness! happiness, Alice! men often toil to win what they deem happiness, and when won, find it anguish! But this I can not understand, you loved him once."

"You can not, Henry, you can not," she replied. But I *did* love him, or perchance I had loved a better man, if not a brighter—and I *do* love him yet, and I *shall* love him while I live. But, Henry, do you remember how my mother died! Look at my cheek, and eye, and see if you can not therein read the signs of the same sure destroyer?"

He started; for, with these words, a terror almost amounting to conviction flashed on his soul, and he almost believed that her foreboding was prophetic. He tried, for a little space, to conquer this depression, to give the conversation a more cheerful tone ; but it was useless all, and ere long he departed, with a promise to revisit her in the evening.

" When," he added, as he left the room, " I trust I shall find you with better and more cheerful spirits ; for I feel sure that you are over-tired, and you had better take some rest." But, as he descended the great stairs, he muttered to himself, " There is more — there is something more in this ! I fear he is a villain ! I will watch — I will watch ! It is providential that I came here. I will see St. Eloy ; I fancy he can tell me, or find out — I will see St. Eloy forthwith !" Thus saying, he reached the door, and was just going down the steps into the yard, where his horses waited for him, when a young cavalier, gorgeously dressed, but rather in the English than in the French fashion, and mounted on a superior charger, entered the *porte cochère*, and throwing his rein to one of his attendants, leaped to the ground, came quickly up to the door — and face to face stood Chaloner and the very man on whom his thoughts were running at the moment.

" Ha ! Major Wyvil, I believe," said Chaloner, raising his hand quietly to his hat ; " the last time we met was in a hotter place."

" I do not recollect at all," Marmaduke answered ; " I *am* Major Wyvil, very much at your service ; but I do not recollect when we have met before, nor have I even now the happiness of knowing whom I am addressing."

" We met last, sir," Chaloner answered, " upon Worcester field — on different sides, it is true — and I had the honor of exchanging two thrust and a cut with you, till we were parted by the melée — but all this is ended now happily. My name is Henry Chaloner, and as I understand we are soon to be cousins, I hope we may be good friends. I believe I speak to my fair kinswoman, Alice Selby's destined husband. I had a cause for speaking to you now, sir — since, in consideration of what I heard and believed true, I was induced to apply to the person who now virtually governs England ; and, having some weight with him, I am very happy to say that I succeeded in obtaining from him the full pardon of Major Marmaduke Wyvil, with permission to return home at his own will and pleasure. If you will do me the favor to call at my lodging — General Chaloner's lodging in the Rue Royale — I will give you the document, formally sealed and witnessed. In the meantime, I will not detain you from more fair society. Give you good day, sir," and bowing, in reply to Wyvil's profuse thanks and acknowledgments, he mounted his horse and rode silently away. The face of the other brightened with exultation.

"Free pardon!" he exclaimed aloud, "and full permission to return! And Woolverton, and Alice Selby!" he added in a lower tone — "Fortune, thou *art* a goddess!" He entered the house, and giving his name to a servant, was immediately ushered into the presence of Alice, who was waiting alone to receive the visit that was to determine her fate for ever. The meeting of the lovers was not as such are, or should be; both were confused, embarrassed, almost cold; but Alice was the first to recover herself, and she spoke, as was usual to her frank and open disposition, freely at once and to the point—

"I am glad you have come here to-day," she said, "Major Wyvil, for I have much to say to you, and hear from you; and I will pray you—"

"But why so cold," he vehemently interrupted — "why so calmly and bitterly cold, Alice? Why '*Major* Wyvil?' time was when I was Marmaduke. Is it, can it be possible, that Alice Selby — the pure, and true, and tender Alice Selby — can have so fallen off from her plighted faith, so utterly forgot the vows she swore, not one year past — so totally overcome the love she once professed!"

"Professed!" exclaimed Alice, her beautiful eyes flashing fire — "professed! No, Marmaduke, it is not — it is not possible; no word of it is possible or true — and *that* no man more surely knows than you do! I did, as you say, plight my faith, and from that faith my soul has never swerved — no! not so much as a hair's breadth! and never will swerve while the life quivers in my veins! Nay, hear me out, for I must speak! I did, as you say, *profess* to love you — for, as you know too well, I did — *did* love you! oh, man, man! you *can not* know how deeply! But let me ask you now, and I adjure you answer me frankly, truly, freely — so may all yet be well God is my gracious judge, that I ask it in no mean spirit of suspicion or vain jealousy; but in that I have heard things that must, *will* be heard, and must be answered. Have *you*, Marmaduke Wyvil — have *you* not fallen from the faith you pledged to me at Woolverton? Have you not so forgotten the vows you then swore, as — I say not to flirt, or toy, or trifle — but to pledge solemn vows to another? Have you not so overcome the love which you once felt for me — for I believe that you *did* feel it — as to lose sight of me in absence, and give your heart up to another? Pause, pause! I beseech you, and answer truly; and above all, fear not too harsh a judge in your poor Alice — for my heart yearns toward you, Marmaduke, with an undying love; and I would fain be yours, if yours I may be honorably, in this life and for ever!'

He did pause — he did reflect — and the better spirit that was for the time awakened in him, half-prompted, half-persuaded him to own the truth — to confess his brief hallucination, to throw himself at her feet, and implore her pardon. But no! he thought no! woman can not forgive such errors — and then he proudly raised his head, and though his soul quailed in him with the dread sickening sensation of conscious guilt and baseness, he proudly answered — with a lie!

"Never!" he said — "never! so help me He, who looks on all things — no, never!" and he went on so rapidly, heaping asseveration on asseveration, that she could not, although she wished it, interrupt or check him. "I may, as you say, have laughed, and danced, and whispered tender nonsense in ears that believed it not; but never! on my salvation, Alice, never has my faith ever wavered — never has vow been plighted — or love felt by me, for any girl or woman, saving you only, Alice!"

"Have you done?" she exclaimed fiercely — "have you

done now? Never to Isabella Oswald? Oh! think — think, Wyvil, ere you speak — think and beware! for I have heard, and seen, and know!"

"Never! oh, Alice, I *swear* never! I will swear —"

"Swear NOTHING!" she looked at him, with an air of majesty so perfect and so grand, that he could not brook it, but cowed before her like a whipped and whimpering hound — "you have already sworn too deeply, and too falsely! A traitor, traitor, traitor! Oh, man! that I should so have loved you — that I should even now, knowing you base and false beyond conception, still love — almost adore you! No words! no words! Listen — I sat yestreen in a green bower of the Tuileries — there is another unseen bower just behind it — and thither, while I sat — thither came Isabella Oswald, and there to her did Marmaduke Wyvil — ay, you pale now and tremble! — swear, as he swore to-day to me, that he never did love, did never even *think* of, Alice Selby! *her* answer I heard not. Oh, Wyvil, Wyvil! you know not what a heart you have cast off from you for ever! Even to-day, had you frankly owned your error — had you convinced me that it was but a temporary and involuntary treason; had you showed me that her happiness was not jeoparded — even to-day, I had taken you to my bosom; I had said, 'All is forgotten, all is forgiven — let us be happy, Marmaduke!' but now —"

"Oh! say so — say so now!" exclaimed Wyvil, falling upon his knees before her.

"Kneel not to me," she said — "kneel not to me, but to the great God, whom you have so grievously insulted!"

But he went on, quite disregarding her interruption —

"For it is all as you have said, it was mere frenzy — the wild frenzy of a moment."

"Degrade yourself no more," she said, in a voice wherein no touch of passion, anger, or pity, or contempt, was audible; but slow and even and majestic, as one might imagine the voice to have sounded from the oracular tripod — "degrade yourself no more but leave me — strive not, speak not — your case is hopeless! Not for the empire of the universe, would Alice

Selby marry a man whom she thoroughly despises. And I — Marmaduke Wyvil, the words must be spoken — I love you still, I shall for ever love you. I shall rejoice to hear of your well-being, of your well-doing, of your repenting, of your becoming what I fear too deeply you never will — an upright and honorable man! but I thoroughly — ay, utterly despise you! A cowardly, base LIE! sworn to two trusting women! Oh, you have filled my heart with fire! — oh, you have heaped my head with ashes, blighted my young, fresh life — left me no hope, nor aim, nor object; but only a long, solitary waste of weary days to traverse — a long, sad pilgrimage to travel, unlightened by a gleam of hope, unaided and forsaken, before I may find rest in the grave! All this have you done to me; yet I forgive, I love, and I will pray for you. Begone! begone! and commune with your own soul in silence, repent, and prosper! No word of what has passed between us will I breathe to any mortal ear, so long as you insult me not with your addresses. Speak one word more to shake my resolution, presume to persecute me with your love hereafter, and I will blazon forth your infamy to the broad world, if my heart break in uttering it. Begone! — farewell! farewell for ever!"

And, goaded by the stings of that dread conscience, more terrible avenger than the blood-hunting, serpent-locked Eumenides, he rushed forth from her presence with the undying worm already gnawing at the heart-strings; while she, deserted by the strength that had so nerved her in his presence, drew a long sob, and fell to the ground senseless — and lay there till she was found, cold and unconsious, by Madame de Gondi, who, seeing the precipitate departure of the false lover, and therefrom foreboding evil, came hurriedly to see her, barely in time to bring her back once more to that long act of agony, which is called life by mortals.

CHAPTER XXX.

Many days passed, before Alice Selby sufficiently recovered to leave her chamber. A fever had attacked her, produced by anxiety and undue excitement, and for a considerable time she had been quite delirious ; but she had partially recovered, and was enabled now to rise and return to her ordinary avocations and amusements, although it was still considered improper that she should leave the house. It could not fail, moreover, to be seen by every person who was the least interested, that she had been indeed fearfully shaken by the brief illness she had undergone, or perhaps by the causes which had produced it. Her slight but rounded figure had lost much of it graceful contour, her lovely eyes were sunken ; but, at the same time, there was a clear and glassy glitter in their orbs, a cold, transparent lustre, that tells too surely the presence in the vitals of that dread minister of death, fatal consumption ! All healthy color had deserted her pale face, and in its place glared the fell hectic spots, now permanently fixed, as though they had been branded upon each cheek-bone — she was extremely weak, moreover, and a slight husky cough would at times shake her for a moment, and those profuse night perspirations, most fatal signs of all that mark the progress of the insidious slayer, reduced her, as it might be said, to a shadow of her former self. Every one noted the sad change, even the meditative unobservant scholar ; and, though he spoke not on the subject, it might be seen by the wistful gaze which he would rivet for hours together on her face, as she sat reading or employed in some feminine occupation near him, and by the sad and hopeless air with which he would shake his thin, gray locks, and mutter half-heard words — "It was thus with her mother." Madame de Gondi saw at once, and appreciated fully, the whole extent of the evil ; and she alone, it may be said, knew really the secret cause — for, although Selby himself much suspected that Wyvil had betrayed and deceived her, he did not know at all the circumstances which had occurred, nor was he aware even, that she and Marmaduke had met since their arrival in the French capital. Chaloner, who was yet more suspicious, and who had ascertained beyond doubt from his friend, the old marquis de St. Eloy — himself the father of a very lovely child, who was sought in marriage by Wyvil's friend, Bellechassaigne — that Marmaduke had been paying very undue attentions to Isabella Oswald, and who knew that he had been with Alice immediately before her seizure, was yet unable to make up his mind as to the exact truth ; and till he could do so, was perfectly determined neither to take any action, nor even to speak on the subject. Meantime, driven to desperation by his detection, goaded by poverty and threatening creditors, and maddened by the cool contempt of Alice, Wyvil had pressed his suit more eagerly with Isabella Oswald, and had indeed succeeded in winning her consent, although her father, suspecting somewhat the necessities and addiction to play of the young soldier, had as yet refused his permission. The report, notwithstanding, had been spread abroad, and gained strength every day, that they were actually betrothed, and that the wedding would take place almost immediately.

Aroused at length by this hourly growing rumor, Chaloner made his mind up fully to a task, to which he naturally felt the strongest possible repugnance. But he was satisfied that Alice, whom he still loved with more than a brother's love, was slowly dying, and that the only hope of saving her lay in the compassing her union with the man whose perfidy was slaying her, as surely as the mortal sword ; and therefore he resolved, if possible, to fathom the cause of their alienation ; and, having fathomed, to strive with all the powers of his mind for the removal of those causes. Nothing, perhaps, could be conceived more morally heroical, than the self-sacrificing and disinterested resolution of this pure-minded, upright man, to defeat for ever all his own chances of domestic happiness, and to bestow the idol of his own affections, so to secure her ultimate felicity, upon another. But few men have lived in any age, less selfish, or more careful of the feelings of all his fellow-creatures, than Henry Chaloner; and it would as easily have entered his mind to prefer the transitory bliss of mortal life to the beatitude of immortality, as to hesitate between securing his own happiness or that of the woman he so truly loved and honored.

In his first efforts he was foiled utterly; for with his customary, frank straight-forwardness, he went one morning to visit Wyvil in his lodgings, which he readily discovered, taking with him the pardon he had procured for him which Marmaduke had never called to receive. Wyvil received him courteously, and displayed much gratitude for the obligation under which Chaloner had placed him; and, during a brief conversation on various subjects which ensued, continued to impress his rival with a far higher estimate of his qualities, of both heart and head, than he had before entertained. But when, at last, Chaloner asked him plainly whether he had been misinformed concerning the fact, that there existed an engagement between him and Mistress Alice Selby, he replied instantly, with a grave and somewhat altered air, but not without a show of frankness: "Indeed, General Chaloner, that is a question which, to any person but yourself, I should decline to answer, even if I did not look on it as a rudeness; but, taking it into consideration that you have lately done me no small favor, and that you are a near connection of a lady to whom it is owing altogether that I am alive at this moment to acknowledge all her excellence, I shall not hesitate to reply to you frankly. You were not misinformed, that such an engagement *did once* exist; but if you were told that it does so at present, you were assuredly deceived, for it was annulled some time ago, by the lady's own act. More than this, you can not, I think, ask of me to declare."

"Not under ordinary cases," answered Chaloner, after a moment's thought, "could I do so, nor, I admit, can I *demand* it of you now; but you must allow me to point out two or three reasons, why I may ask some further information. In the first place, with the exception of her father, I am her nearest blood relation—I may say her only one—and he, as you know, from age and infirmities, and from his own peculiar habits, is hardly capable of her guardianship. In the second place, I know that she did love you very deeply, and I am well assured, that even now she has not lost that sentiment. I can not, therefore, but regret deeply this alienation; and I am very anxious to ascertain the cause, in order that, if possible, I may remove all misunderstanding between two persons, one of whom I love very dearly, and the other I am disposed to think well of, and befriend so far as lies in my power. Therefore I am frank with you, and request you to afford me any insight into this perplexed matter, which you can do with honor."

"You push me hard," replied Wyvil, rather warmly—"too hard, I think, General Chaloner. Most men would hesitate to admit at all, that they had been rejected suitors of any lady, how beautiful soever. But this, it seems, is not enough for you—and you expect me to disclose to you circumstances of the most private nature, and to explain things, which, for aught you know, may depend on mere womanish caprice—"

"Do you mean, sir," Chaloner sternly interrupted him, "to cast the shadow of a shade upon my cousin's reputation? Do you mean to accuse her of what you choose to call 'mere womanish caprice,' but the right name of which is base, unwomanly dishonesty and faithlessness? or did I misapprehend you?"

"Again! again!" Wyvil answered, very haughtily, and something with the air of one not indisposed to seek a quarrel. "What if I did mean so? I am not to be questioned as to my terms, particularly when such terms are given in answer to a question of your own, which, give me leave to say, was warranted neither by courtesy, nor by the length or intimacy of our acquaintance! I am not in the least accountable to you, sir; and if I should refuse to reply altogether, I should but do rightly. But I do not refuse," he added—for a deep sense of the baseness of his conduct came across him, and he felt that he could not add to his villany the guilt of laying any imputation on the faith of one whom he knew to be all purity and truth—"no! I do not refuse, for I esteem the lady's character, and honor her too highly, to wish to cast the slightest blame on her. Besides, I could not do so truly; for she is not in any way to blame, unless it be in undervaluing the love and devotion of a person who was once most sincerely attached to her."

"ONCE!" replied Chaloner—"then I am to understand that you are so no longer?"

"You are to understand, sir, precisely whatsoever it pleases you; for, by Heaven! I will be plagued no further, or, I might say, insulted! Another question I shall look upon as a direct affront! On other topics I shall ever be willing to converse with General Chaloner; but, upon this, let it be understood, we speak no more."

Beyond this, of course, Henry could not urge him; and he almost immediately departed, saying to himself, "Ay, ay! he has behaved ill to her in some way or other, and would not now be sorry to undo the Gordian knot, like Alexander, with the sword; but how can he so have injured her, as to have made her so determined in her wrath against him?"

To apply to the aged father, who now appeared to be more broken down than ever, both in spirits and in perception of external things, would have been worse than useless, and therefore, as a last resort, he once more went to Alice, and with the greatest tenderness and caution approached the delicate subject, and with an air so kind and so considerate, that she felt no shock to her senses, torn as they had been, and wounded by the discovery she had made of that man's complete worthlessness, on whom she had set all her hopes.

"Henry," she said deliberately, "I can not tell you—I can not tell any person all—but this much I can say, in justice to both myself and Wyvil. He is not so to blame as you imagine. He made no pledge to me, which he was not ready—nay, eager to redeem. He would, I have no doubt or question, be more delighted than words can express, if I would recall him to my feet to-morrow. But, although I regret to say it, I love him still, and shall love him to the last; I would not be his wife—no! not to compass everything of happiness that gratified love could afford! I would not! If I would, I could do so to-morrow. Him I neither blame nor acquit — if he have wronged me, in his own heart and conscience lives my avenger! If I do him injustice in my thoughts, I will do him none with my tongue; and, sure I am, I shall find pardon for all the evil I have ever thought or done to him, both here and hereafter!"

"The evil you have done! the evil!" exclaimed Chaloner; "*you*, who have never wronged a worm! *you*, whose life has been but one scene of kindnesses, and charities, toward all men! *you*, who preserved his life at peril of your own — sheltered him, when his own next of kin would have abandoned or betrayed him! *you*, whom his treachery — for I can not be hoodwinked or deceived — is hourly killing!"

"Peace! Henry, peace!" replied the sweet girl; "you who are so calm ever, and so gentle, must not be rash now, or excited. We must not talk of this again; and, I beseech you, do not you speak of it, or lay aught to his charge, or seek to punish any imagined faults. This I entreat of you, as, perhaps, the last prayer of one whom you love, and who would, if she could, have given you love for love. But hearts are stubborn things, dear Henry, and deceitful. I could not love, whom I esteem and honor above all men — I could not honor whom I love the best, I say not of all men, but of all beings, except my God and my Redeemer. I love him still, and I can not but love him, although I may have little cause — but Alice Selby names not whom she may not esteem and honor, nor never, while she lives, will sacrifice one jot of principle, to a whole world of passion! The struggle *may* — *will* — for I feel that I am already within the shadows that float over the dark vale of death — *will* be too much for this weak frame. The seeds of hereditary disease, latent till now, but still existing at the core, are springing into weeds baneful to human life — a few more weeks, perchance a few more days, and this corruptible will be with the worm, its sister! this incorruptible with its Creator! Yet, Henry Chaloner, mourn not for me, when I shall have gone hence. My life has been, it is true, but a brief one—but oh, how calm and happy! Except this one short storm, it has been like one summer's day of breathless innocent delight. I have lived very happily—I have no consciousness of any very flagrant wrong—I live in all humility and knowledge of my own unworthiness, yet in all confidence in the illimitable mercies of my judge and Savior. I shall die in tranquil hope, fearless and calm, and go, I trust, unto my God rejoicing!"

"Most happy, and most holy!" answered Chaloner, amid his tears, for the sweet resignation of the dear, dying girl had called forth from their springs the hot tears of the self-restrained and philosophic man. "God grant, that I too may so meet his summons—and God forbid that I, by word, or deed, or thought, or sign, or motion, should recall one embittering thought into a spirit, from which the bitterness of life and death would seem already to have passed away. Trust me, dear Alice."

"I do, indeed," she said—"most confidently I do trust you. But let us speak of this a little further. I know and feel that I am dying; I know and feel, as surely as that we are speaking here together, that I shall no more see my country—no more tread the free soil of glorious England—no more revisit the dear scenes of my childhood—the cradle of my happy infancy! The leaves that are now rustling on those sere boughs, will not have fallen before I shall have departed to the long last home of mortals. When I—and he, who will not long survive me—shall have gone hence, our race, our very name, will be ended; and you, dear Henry, will succeed to our inheritance and dwelling-place. I need not say to you, be kind to the old man; I need not say, cherish my old pensioners—watch over those who will then have lost their only earthly friends and supporters. These things I need not ask, knowing, right certainly, that unasked you will do them. But there are two things that I would fain request; first, Henry—it is in truth a vain and foolish wish, but yet it is heart-fixed, and daily it grows stronger as my term draws more nigh—I would, when all is over, lie in my native land. There is in the church-yard at Woolverton, a large and lovely linden, covering many a yard with the canopy of its umbrageous foliage, and under it a little grassy knoll, where many a day I have sat when I was a merry, careless child; and even then I used to think it would be sweet to lie in that pleasant spot. Here, Henry, if it can be accomplished, I would wish my bones to rest. My second prayer is, though perhaps more difficult, less whimsical, and has a reason for its base. It is, that you will live some portion of each year at Woolverton, that you may learn to know the tenantry and lowly neighbors, who have been wont in our day to look up to their landlords as to trusted and familiar friends. I do not ask you to make any promise; I do not wish to bind or fetter you at all; but telling you what I desire, I am quite sure that you will do it, if it be right and compatible with graver duties, and if it be not, then would I not have it done at all. And now that we have finished this unpleasant topic, let it be finished altogether, and for ever; let us no more think or speak of it, but talk of pleasanter and gayer matters. I would not have my last days spent in sadness or repining, nor the last thoughts of me connected, in the minds of those I love, with dark and gloomy images. So tell me, now, when do you think of departing for the Hague?"

"Oh, not for some time, Alice," he replied. "I have to wait instructions, and receive answers to the despatches which I have sent home." And for some time the conversation flowed on, Madame de Gondi having come in, turning on topics of general and varied interest; till just as Chaloner was about to depart, and had actually taken up his hat, the sound of a carriage was heard entering the *porte cochère*, and in a moment the door was thrown open by a servant, who, to the surprise of all parties, announced Mademoiselle Oswald. Though wondering not a little what had procured for her the honor of this visit, Madame de Gondi advanced courteously to meet her, welcoming her with a polished ease peculiar to herself.

"You must think me exceedingly odd, not to say impertinent," she began, as if aware that her coming needed some explanation, "but the truth is, that I heard you had a countrywoman of my own living with you; and I consider it a sort of duty among English ladies to seek out one another when abroad, and offer any little courtesies in their power. And so, being the older resident in Paris, and almost an *habitué*, I took the liberty to call, in the hope to gain Mistress Selby's friendship. There, the whole secret's out now! I always do things in my own way—and do whatever I choose, too," she added, tossing back the luxuriant ringlets which had fallen forward over her face, with a saucy air; "and in the present case I choose, Mistress Alice Selby, that we should become great friends instantly and without ceremony."

Abrupt and even rough as was Isabella Oswald's manner, there was yet a sort of gay and open frankness, a directness of purpose, and an apparent singleness of heart, that, coupled to her exceeding beauty, and to the peculiar richness of her silvery voice, was anything rather than unattractive. It had, perhaps, scarcely so powerful an effect on women as on the other sex, who were almost always singularly struck and fascinated by her manner, but it was still far from lacking its due weight. Alice, particularly feminine herself and gentle, was very much moved by an air so exactly the reverse of her own; and although she by no means admired that dashing independence, which she considered, and considered justly, to be no attribute of woman, she saw and felt at once that her great beauty, with its bold and striking style, and her wild, fearless manners, were just the thing to seize on a mind like Wyvil's, which had, perhaps, less of resolute firmness, than of any other quality needful to give it tone and power. She thought, moreover, that her visiter was a person whose impulses, whether of good or evil, were so perceptible and unconcealed, and whose fearlessness led to so great a degree of candor and simplicity, that she could not be, on the whole, other than an amiable and estimable woman. She replied, therefore, not only courteously, but even warmly; expressed her sense of obligation at the civility, which had produced this visit to a stranger, said that she had no doubt they should be very great friends, and remarked with a smile upon their former meeting at the gates of Paris. This led to some mention of Major Wyvil; and Alice, ever remarkable for the strength and coolness of her resolution, spoke of her former lover with an air so entirely calm and unembarrassed, as would have rendered it impossible for any stranger to suspect that a feeling warmer than mere friendship ever had existed, if even that were not more than was warranted by her manner. Meantime, Chaloner took his leave—and, laughing merrily, and jesting in a wild, light-hearted style about all sorts of things, now rattling on with some strange, witty nonsense; now uttering deeper thoughts and sentiments more powerful than one would have expected her to entertain, Isabella still remained; and Alice, half-amused, half-tired, but with a sad and burning heart, was compelled to entertain her, wondering how long this strange interview would continue. At length, Madame de Gondi was summoned out of the apartment on business of a pressing nature; and then, starting up from her chair, Isabella crossed the room to the sofa on which Alice sat, exclaiming—

"Oh! I am very glad that she has gone away, for now I can tell you what I want. I was afraid she would not have gone at all. You think me, I see, a strange, bold girl, and are, I fancy, half afraid of me; and I don't wonder at it. I never had a mother, that is within my recollection; and I have been a spoiled child all my life, and have been rambling about always among camps and garrisons, and battle-fields, and doing just what suited me, till I have grown up to be what I am. But, I assure you, I am not so bad as you think me. My manner is the worst part of me, indeed; and you will find that if I am wild, and free, and fearless, I am true and honest. I would not tell a lie to be the queen of all France! and the truth is, that I have come to see you because I want to be resolved of something, of which nobody can resolve me but yourself. So I shall go to the point at once—this Major Wyvil, whom you know so well, and whom you saved, I understand, from death, by your presence of mind and courage—who could have thought that so quiet and gentle a little thing as you could be so brave?—this Major Wyvil, I say, swears that he loves me very dearly; and as I love him very well—that is to say, a great deal more than I ever loved anything; more than my beautiful black horse Roland, and twenty times as much as my dear Persian greyhound, I think it quite probable we shall be married some day. Now, I can not exactly tell you why it is but I have taken it into my head that you and he were going to be married once, and that he has used you ill—and me, too, if I am right; and I would sooner marry old Monsieur de Grandpré, who is the ugliest man in all France, or what is still worse, remain all my life an old maid, than take a man on whom another woman had a claim of honor. So I came straight to you to ask you all about it."

It can not be denied, that this speech tried poor Alice deeply—tried her in many ways. It probed her own deep love-wound to the very quick—it sorely shook the constancy and endurance of her principles; but so deep was the root of that fixed principle, that it resisted the assault, and yielded not a whit to the fierce, passionate tempest that was awakened for a moment in that calm breast. She blushed very deeply, and paused a little while to frame her reply before she uttered it—for in truth, she found it no easy matter to answer as she would. Her firm decision never herself to countenance him as a lover, her strong and still enduring love for him, and her desire to make him happy in his own way, united to render her willing to promote his union with her rival—so perfectly pure and disinterested was her passion for this unworthy object—while, at the same time, her native truthfulness made it impossible for her to deceive even by implication. She was, however, fully impressed with the idea, that such a union would be well for both—that it would reclaim, or rather fix the vacillating character of Wyvil, and satisfy the ardent love which, she could readily perceive, existed in the bosom of this high-souled, though wild and erratic being—and she began to think that really a girl of Isabella's marked and masculine decision was better suited than herself to insure the happiness of a man, whose greatest fault appeared to be the want of a resolute and energetic will. She paused, therefore, a moment or two before she answered, and then said—

"I would not reply to your question too suddenly, for I must justify the frank and open confidence which you have placed in me — and for the world I would not deceive you. To be frank, then, we were once engaged; and that engagement might have been binding still, but that I, of my own will, annulled it. I can not, therefore, accuse him of any breach of faith toward me — for he was not willing only, but actually anxious, to make good his promise. I had, however, my own views on the subject, and rejected him."

"Rejected him!" exclaimed Isabella, staring out of her great black eyes in astonishment, not all unmixed with indignation. "Rejected Marmaduke Wyvil!"

"I did, indeed," Alice replied, with a sad smile; "does that seem so strange to you?"

"It does — it does!" answered Isabella, with a sad smile — "it does seem strange to me, that any woman should reject him — so brave! so noble! and so handsome! Oh, had you seen him, as I have, rushing into the deadly fray, as if he were hurrying to a banqnet — heard his clear voice pealing above the din of battle — you never, never could have done so! Why, he is fit to be the husband of the stateliest queen that wears a crown or wields a sceptre!"

"I doubt not that you think so," answered Alice. "Perhaps I once thought so myself — perhaps I think so even now; but I do not think him fit to be the husband of Alice Selby, or Alice Selby to be the wife of him."

"You are playing at enigmas with me — you are making game of me," said Isabella. "I did not look for this from you!"

"Indeed, I am not — I would not mislead you unintentionally for half a hemisphere, much less would I jest with you, on so grave a subject. I say to you simply the truth, when I say that Major Wyvil has never broken any promise to me — for he has never made me one which he would not have performed, had I been willing; and further, I have no claim on him whatsoever, whether in law or honor; and further yet, I should be more glad to learn, than I think I ever shall be, that *you* have become his wife! Upon my word! and that is what I do not, I hope, say lightly — I think that you are suited excellently well to one another, and that his character will take a tone from your decision; and, once more, upon my honor! I know no cause why you should not wed him — our views of these things, as are our characters, are very different."

"He did not, then, break his word to you?" asked Isabella.

"He did not!" Alice answered, very firmly; "so far from that, the first time, after he plighted me his word, he was exceeding urgent on the subject; and, as I told you, even now the weight of this breach of contract rests upon my head only. Now, are you satisfied?"

"Not quite," replied Isabella. "No, I am not quite satisfied. Why did you reject him? and when was it? I must know all about it."

"Not from me! I have informed you of all that I can reveal honorably. My reasons for rejecting him are between myself, him, and my God! They might have arisen — perhaps they may have — from false views or prejudices; and therefore I have no right at all to influence you by telling them. I hold the confidence of love matters between man and woman to be the holiest and most binding that exists on earth; and I think that no true girl ever discloses the overture which she has been forced to reject, even to mother, sister, husband, unless there be some cause, such as this present, which makes it, not justifiable only, but right, for all parties to declare it. You must excuse me, therefore, if I decline to say anything further. This only I can add more — he would have kept his word to me, but I would hear him not."

"But he told me," answered Isabella, very quickly, "that he had never known or even thought of you — that was not true!"

"No! it was not — but I presume he was afraid to tell you that he had ever loved before, lest you should esteem that a reason for discarding him; for many girls are so foolish, Isabella, as not to be satisfied with knowing that a man loves them truly, but they must needs insist on being told that they are the first and only object he has ever loved at all; which, if he be over eighteen years, and not an idiot, or as cold as snow, can hardly be true anywise. I am quite sure that he loves you truly now; and I have no doubt in my mind that he will prove a very true and loving lord. So, trust me, the best thing you can do is just to marry him directly, that is to say, if your family consent."

"Family, indeed!" answered Isabella; "what have my family to do with it? My great grandmother or my tenth cousin are not going to marry the man, but I. But I suppose it is my father that you mean — and I am not at all sure that he will consent, for he expects that my husband should be rich, I fancy — though what it signifies, when we have such quantities of money, I can not guess; and Marmaduke, poor fellow, has not a franc beyond his pay."

"Ah! is it so?" asked Alice; "well, if it be so, and you should really find any difficulty on that score, I must insist that you let me know it. I may — nay, I can almost say — I shall be able to avert that, if it be the sole objection!"

"You! you!" exclaimed Isabella, very much astonished — "you are able to avert it! How can that be? and will you, if you can?"

"I can not tell you how," said Alice Selby, "but be sure that, if I can, I will — and gladly! gladly! Does that satisfy you?"

"Indeed, it does, dear lady," replied the other, rising as she spoke, to go; "I should be bitterly ungrateful else — and I can not well tell you how sensible I am of all your goodness, and how sincerely grateful I shall be to you for ever! I am not very ready at professions, but, as I told you before, I am honest. No, no; dear Alice — may I not call you Alice? — you must let me kiss that pale cheek of yours — we must be friends hereafter. Now, I will say farewell! Excuse me to Madame de Gondi."

CHAPTER XXXI.

The afternoon of that day passed away very quietly; no other visiters arrived, and the evening meal was served to Madame de Gondi, Alice, and her old father, only, who was far less abstracted than his wont, as indeed he had been ever since his arrival in Paris, observing the occurrences that were going on about him, and appearing at times even to take an interest in them. They had been conversing for some hours, as gayly as it was possible for persons to do, all three of whom had something heavy at the heart, and each one something to conceal or keep back from the others, when suddenly, without the least apparent cause or excitement, Alice was seized with another of those terrible fainting fits, which had so much alarmed her friends on their occurrence twice before, and remained longer under its influence, and continued weakness, and more indisposed after it had passed, than she had done in either of the preceding cases. Her cousin, as usual, had her removed to her own chamber, and did all that personal kindness and attention could effect, to hasten her recovery; but it was very much to her astonishment that, on her return to the saloon, she found the old man walking up and down the room with long and steady steps, holding a billet, which he had written, in his hand, and seeming to expect the presence of a servant, who had probably been summoned.

"My dear Madame de Gondi," said the old scholar, as she entered, "we never can thank you sufficiently for your great kindness — but you can add even to the vastness of that debt by being quite frank with me. My sweet child — my own Alice! think you not that she is fearfully — dangerously ill?"

"Indeed! indeed! I fear so — and I have thought it right to send over now for old Monsieur Pallie, the best esteemed of all our leeches."

"Ay," replied Selby, gravely, with a half doubtful shake of his thin locks — "ay, if it be not all too late — if it have not its root deeper. Her mother faded even thus — faded and fleeted out of sight, like a brief meteor, before one has even time to fear that it is passing. Think you not that her heart — her affections, I should say — have much to do with this? Has she not told you of her love for Captain Wyvil, and their troth-plighting?"

"She has, indeed." answered Henriette, not without many a tear — "she has, indeed — and my fears point too truly, even as yours do. You know, I presume, that she has met this gentleman, that he has visited her even here, and that but yesterday she declined, as she told me, positively and for ever the completion of that contract?"

"I did not — no, I did not," said the old man. "Are you quite sure? — declined? — is it possible that she declined? That is exceeding strange, for I am almost sure that she still loves him."

"Most certainly she does so," answered Henriette, "but she will never marry him, and I am afraid that it is the conflict between principle and passion, although the first has prevailed grandly and will maintain its victory — her health, nay, her life itself, is endangered!" and without any further hesitancy, she told him everything that had occurred since their arrival in Paris — what had taken place in the garden of the Tuileries — what at the ball in the palace — and what in the first interview between Alice and Marmaduke, so far as she had informed her.

"Oh, villain! villain!" exclaimed the old man bitterly — "weak, vacillating knave and villain! and fool yet more than either! Had she but had a brother, and this had never happened, or had been bitterly avenged! But I — I — God be gracious to me! I have not wisdom to deal with the veriest fool in worldly craft — nor strength to be avenged upon a froward child!" and with the words he flung himself into a chair, and burst into an agony of tears so terribly convulsive, sobbing and choking so with the effects of anguish and rage blended, and that in their most appalling crisis, that Henriette actually dreaded for the endurance of his reason, if not of his life; yet dared not call a witness to break in upon the sacred and most solemn privacy of that paternal passion. As suddenly, however, as it had broken out, the transport of his grief subsided.

"Pardon me," he said, slowly and even calmly—"you will pardon me—she is my own, my only one—the very image of her, who was the best of women, and now is an ever-living spirit of God's kingdom—my only hope's support and treasure! And he has slain her—speak not of consolation! the young may be consoled, but not the old who have grown old in sorrow! But it is not for us to judge, but to submit us to His judgments. We will not trouble her; she has decided wisely now—although she loved not wisely but too well! Had she forgiven, and accepted him to be her lord, it is too likely that the vile earthly temper of his soul would have clogged and weighed down to earth the spiritual essence of her pure and heaven-soaring mind. He who knows all things hath so ordered this, that it must be the better—although to us blind worms it seems the worst conclusion. We will name this no more, but wait, and watch, and pray; with this one comfort, that whom He chasteneth, he loveth."

He left the room as he ceased speaking, but he retired not to his own lonely chamber. He entered the still and sad apartment, where, all unconscious of her cares and sorrows, his lovely child lay sleeping, as calm, as motionless, and only not as cold, as though she had already passed the portals of the tomb. He stood there long, and gazed in silence—not a tear soothed the hot anguish of his burning eyeballs—not a sigh came from his pale lips—he gazed till he was satisfied that there was no hope left to him, turned on his heel, and passed with a step very slow, but firm, to his own bed-chamber—there was no more abstraction, no more vacillation, no more weakness, in the old scholar's eyes or manner. Before he laid him down to sleep, he called the faithful servant who had followed him from Woolverton, the oldest and most attached of his attendants; gave him the letter he had written, telling him to carry it the first thing to-morrow—that he whom it concerned should have it early; "He will come hither shortly afterward," he added, "wait for him there, and bring him to me hither as quietly as may be; I wish that as few as possible of this household know of it." The man read the superscription with much ease, bowed, and retired; and Selby, after kneeling long in fervent and heartfelt communion with HIM, from whom alone strength cometh, stretched himself on his bed, and sad although he was and stricken, slept with the undisturbed repose that springs from a sound conscience.

It had not long been daylight on the following morning, before a startling and stubbornly-sustained knocking awoke the ancient porter of the house, wherein were Marmaduke's apartments; and though the crusty and ill-tempered veteran declared that Major Wyvil had scarcely been abed an hour, and would not be seen by any one before noon, the messenger, a hale, broad-shouldered, rosy-cheeked Englishman of some forty years, persisted, with so much of the dogged pertinacity of his Saxon race, that he made his way per force to Wyvil's antechamber, where he made such a din that Marmaduke was aroused thoroughly, and calling sharply to his valet, inquired, "What in the fiend's name means that racket?"

"It is a billet, sir, only a trifling billet," answered the fellow; "which this rude knave in a green jerkin insists upon it he must give into your own hands."

"Let him do so then, Clement," replied Wyvil, "if it be only to get rid of his insolent din. Your master, fellow," he went on, as the servant came in, and delivered the note, "should know more of gentle courtesy, than to disturb people in the night thus."

"My master," answered the hardy yeoman, nothing abashed, "knew more of gentle courtesy, forty years before thou wert in the cradle, than thou and all thy kindred—and that wilt know, I warrant me, when thou hast read his letter."

And it would seem, indeed, that there was in that brief epistle some spell of strange puissance; for though he tore the paper open with an impatient gesture, and with a heightened color, and a flashing eye, his whole air altered as he read the few words which it contained; and he appeared crest-fallen and abashed, when he again spoke.

"Ha! it is well," he said, though with a very visible effort to maintain his composure. "Go! tell thy master, I will be with him presently—forthwith! Clement, my dressing robe—so! hurry! hurry! death to my soul, man! dost not see I am in haste?"

And within far less time than the valet had ever seen his master devote to the arrangement of his love-locks only, he was completely dressed, and went forth unattended, leaving his household in strange wonder and excitement, to which the perusal of the mysterious billet—for in his haste he left it on the coverlid—brought no alleviation; for it contained but these words—

"MARMADUKE WYVIL: I charge thee come to me, on the very instant. "Thine,

"MARK SELBY."

A short walk through the quiet streets, which lay outstretched all silent and deserted in the gray morning twilight, with nothing moving over their noiseless pavements but some poor houseless dog, searching the kennels for a thrice-gnawed bone, or rarer still, some early artisan hastening to his daily toil, Marmaduke Wyvil reached the *porte cochère* of the Hotel de Gondi; and, though anxiety, and something that was like a fiery hope, and much that was like harrowing terror, were busy at his heart; it was still almost a relief to him to feel that he was soon to be plunged into excitement, even of a painful nature; so terribly reproachful had the calm coolness of the June morning air, and the unusual solitude of the slumbering city seemed to his guilty and perturbed imagination. Of all the numerous and gayly-dressed attendants, who were wont to fill the courtyard of that lordly mansion, no one was moving, even in the porter's lodge, with the exception of the English servant,, who had summoned him; and he stood leaning carelessly against the wicket, which alone was open, whistling the burden of some old border-ballad with a true air of listless independence. As Marmaduke drew near, however, he made way for him with a sort of surly civility, touching his bonnet; but it was evident that he looked with no good-will upon the courtly gallant, and very probably he had something more than a vague suspicion that he was in some sort connected with the illness of his beloved mistress. He led the young cavalier immediately into the house, though not by the grand entrance, and up a dark and narrow staircase, and so by several intricate corridors and passages into a little antechamber; and pausing there, the sound of a regular and heavy footstep fell on the ear of Wyvil, and the deep groan of a man, apparently in acute pain, or deep affliction; the next instant, the servant knocked gently at a door, and a voice but too well remembered, cried, "Is it he? Let him enter!" and he walked with a faltering step and a fearful eye into the presence of Mark Selby. The old man said, "It is well, Charles; now begone and wait for him at the head of the staircase beyond earshot; let no one come to us, unless I ring my bell, or call to you. Be seated, Major Wyvil, it is some time since we have met."

"It is, indeed," said Wyvil, exceedingly confused, and not in the least knowing how to conduct himself toward the old man.

"It is, indeed," he repeated, with a bitter sneer; his voice though feeble, trembling not in the least, and his gray eye piercing the shrinking wretch, as the falcon's overpowers the craven gaze of all meaner fowls; "It is, indeed, some time, and I suppose it might have been full longer. What does this mean, sir? what does this mean, I say? what were you thinking of when you dared do this thing?"

"I know not what you mean, Master Selby," replied Marmaduke, rallying all his courage; "I know not anything that I have done."

"Nor left undone?" the old man answered, in a tone so piercing, yet so stern, that he dared not reply for a moment or two, till *feeling* that dread gaze still fixed upon him, for his own eyes were downcast, and no more could brook the glance of the injured father, than could the carrion vulture face the meridian sun, he forced himself to say—

"Nor left undone, sir—for I would fain have fulfilled my pledge and married your fair daughter, whom I love beyond every woman upon earth, but she rejected me—rejected me as doubtless you well know, with bitter scorn and contumely; and that is what may not be borne by any man of honor!"

"And have you, have you really the daring to call yourself a man of honor? Look you, I know you, poor, vain, vacillating fool, I know you! Answer me not, I say—answer me not—sit there till I rehearse to you your honorable exploits. Some thirteen months ago, there lived in Worcestershire a very happy aged man—exceedingly happy, for he was blessed with as beautiful, and innocent, and sweet, and good a child as ever lived on earth, or died and went to heaven!" The old man was now thoroughly aroused, and his cheek, thin as it was and withered, was kindled with a glow of noble indignation; and his voice, though it quivered with excitement, seemed to his panic-stricken auditor to thrill, trumpet-like, to his heart's core. "Thither were *you* sent—there, at your utmost need, were you preserved by that girl's more than heroic constancy and courage; by that old man's untimely pity, and fool confidence! Liar and traitor! you won her innocent heart, plighted false vows, escaped, forgot, forswore her!"

"Not so! not so! by heaven and Him that made it—not so! I would have claimed her hand, would claim it now, out of ten thousand, as I would prize her heart."

"Liar again! Her heart which thou hast broken, her hand which thou didst set aside as a thing lighter than thistle-down, and far less worthy! thou fool! thou fool! Oh! trivial, wretched and most miserable fool! All this thou has done in the pride of thine earthly wisdom. Her didst thou win in the mere idleness of a frivolous and fitful fancy—didst win such an angel as had been too high a boon for the best man that ever trod the soil of this bad world—was fool enough to forget—liar enough to forswear—and then traitor, and knave, and fool enough, all three in one—to fancy you could win her back to look upon a thing so vile and vicious!"

"Have you done yet?" exclaimed Wyvil, whose spirit, naturally high and fiery, was at length kindled, and aroused beyond all its self-control by the reproaches which the old man poured so vehemently, and so deservedly upon his head; "have you done yet? For I will hear no further—"

"Done yet?" cried Selby, even more fiercely than before, "not well begun! Dog, I will blazon out your villany to the broad world! your crime shall not succeed, your baseness shall not screen you! Two victims have you slain already; the third I will rescue from your clutches. Listen—now listen: a short life shall you drag out here! a short life and a wretched; scorned and despised of all men, abandoned by your God! For when your soul shall turn toward him, the spirit of my Alice—my Alice, whom you have so foully murdered, shall stand between you, and screen the light of his forgiveness, and shut you out from mercy, condemned by your own conscience, the basest and the blackest thing that crawls. And, when you die, the very fiends shall cast you out from among them, too vile, and villanous for their companionship. Now then, begone! For the first time you have heard, this morning, what henceforth you shall hear for ever; begone, I say, villain and slave! Make me rid of the contamination of your presence!"

"It is well for you," exclaimed Wyvil, as savagely as the sense of guilt detected, and despair and frenzy, can drive a man to exclaim even against his conscience—"It is well for you that you are an old man, and *her* father, else—" and he clenched his fist, and shook it in the air, as he turned to leave the room.

"Ha, dog!" shouted the old man—"Ha, dog! dost thou dare threaten? Then, old man as I am, I will put thee to shame! Ha! ha! the old man will strike thee! Without there—Gregory, Charles, Martin—come all! come all! I say, and see me strike him!" and he rushed fiercely forward as if to clutch him. But there was still enough of grace and manhood left in Wyvil, that he awaited not the onslaught of the aged mourner, but darted quickly through the door, closed it behind him, and rushing down the passage, met the man Charles, who, fancying that he was called only to show him forth, did so in scorn and silence. As soon, however, as he had seen Wyvil out of the gates, and had satisfied himself that no one of the household had observed him, he hurried back to his master's room, for he had heard his voice raised so far above its natural pitch, and had caught words of passion so unusual, that he almost feared some catastrophe. He reached the door, and as he was about to knock for admission, his worst apprehensions were confirmed by the appearance of a thin, narrow stream of some dark fluid, trickling slowly over the sill and dabbling the rich carpet. Without a moment's pause he rushed in, half beside himself with terror — under his feet there was a pool — a veritable pool of blood; and in a large armed-chair, half-seated and half lying on the table — as if he had fallen, and with an effort struggled up again — was the good, gentle scholar; his thin white hair, splashed with the gory witness, and his pale lips crimsoned with the tide, which in that ecstacy of anger, had flowed from his vitals.

At first, the servant believed that he was already dead; but as he raised him gently to an erect position, he perceived that the rush of blood had for the most part ceased, and that, though very weak and faint, he was still alive and sensible; for, as he met his eye, a faint smile played over his wan face, and he seemed about to speak.

"Hush, hush! my master, my dear honored master! Hush thee till I call help, and all shall yet be well."

"No, Charles," the dying man said very feebly, and at each word a little blood again oozed from the corners of his mouth — "no, do not go; I shall be dead directly — and I have much — much that I would say!"

"Curse on him — curse on him!" exclaimed the servant; "he hath done this, the villain, and I not near to aid thee, my master!"

"No, you are wrong; no, Charles!" Selby gasped even more faintly than before, "not he, not he — my own rash, wicked passion. Remember this — promise me that you speak no word of his being here to any one but General Henry — and tell him what I say. Promise, Charles — promise me — you did not use to disobey."

"And will not now — I promise thee," cried the man, as distinctly as he could, in the intervals of his tears.

A gleam of satisfaction brightened across the face of his dying master.

"Let Alice never know it — remember! Oh, Lord, receive my spirit!" His speech now came in gasps, and the blood gushed out constantly, so as almost to choke him. "Tell — tell —" he hiccoughed with a mighty effort — "tell her — that I died — blessing her!" The last two words he enunciated clearly, as though he no longer felt either pain or weakness; and, with them, he rose to his feet, stretched his arms upward, and, as if answering some summons heard by his ears alone, "I come!" he cried, and fell gently backward on the breast of his faithful follower. The good man had gone to his account!

CHAPTER XXXII.

Those were the days when servants waited on their masters, not with lip-loyalty alone, but with heart-service; when the dependant was not looked upon as a mere hireling, to be considered only with reference to the work done and the wages paid; nor the employer regarded solely as the dispenser of food and raiment, to be cheated as much, and obeyed as little, as practicable; which, I fear will be found the case too often, despite the much vaunted superiority and intelligence of these modern times. Charles, who had lived in the household of Mark Selby from his boyhood, did not, therefore, immediately rush down to tell every member of the family, from the maître d'hôtel and housekeeper down to the *marmiton* and scullery-maid, how Major Wyvil had slain old Master Selby; but taking into consideration the extremely delicate situation of Alice, and her entirely unprotected situation — having first laid the body decently on a couch and covered it with the long red-colored cloak which the good gentleman had worn while living — he went down stairs and called up his fellow-servant, who, like himself, had been born at Woolverton, and had never known any other master. Desiring him to remain with the body and suffer nobody to enter, lest Mistress Alice should learn what had passed too soon, he went off instantly to Henry Chaloner's lodgings in the Rue Royal, and, telling him all that had occurred, precisely as it *had* occurred, alike without exaggeration or diminution of the truth, entreated him to come up forthwith to the Hôtel de Gondi. Shocked as he was and pained by this intelligence, there needed no entreaty to hurry Chaloner's proceedings; he was already up and dressed, when the man was admitted to his presence, haggard, and pale, and panic-stricken — for the excitement which had nerved him to his duty, in the first instance, had wholly passed away — and after hearing his sad tale, and asking him a few pertinent questions, he put on his cloak and high-crowned hat, and bidding two or three of his own most trusty men to buckle on their swords and follow him, took his way to the scene of the terrible catastrophe.

"You have done well — very well," he said, "Charles, exceeding well; had you not strictly obeyed what my poor cousin told you, much evil would have come of it. You are quite sure that you have not mentioned it to any one that Major Wyvil was in your master's room this morning?"

"I promised master that I would not, General Henry," said the man, tears streaming down his face — "promised him just before he went to heaven; and do you think I would break my word to him, and he looking down and hearing me?"

"Indeed, Charles, I do you not so much wrong; I only feared that in the haste and terror of the moment, you might have let it out incautiously to some of your fellow-servants."

"No, General Henry, no; I did nothing in haste, and I have

seen no one this morning but Anthony, who is now with the body, and he knows nothing of it."

"And you are certain that no one saw him enter?"

"No one at all; nor go out either, general."

"So far, at least, all is well. Then, mark me, Charles — poor Master Selby was quite right, it would go near to kill Mistress Alice did she ever know what hand Major Wyvil had to do in your master's death. Therefore, my good fellow, hold steadily to your story — tell the truth only — add nothing, but quietly omit all mention of the cavalier. Say you called Master Selby at his usual hour, and saw him arise and begin to dress himself, left him to do some other work, and upon your return found him as you have told me. Now, do you understand me perfectly?"

"Perfectly, general," the man replied; "and you may trust me — I will do as you desire."

They had by this time reached the house, and all the servants of the establishment being at length on foot, Chaloner sent a message to Madame de Gondi, saying he would like to speak with her, as soon as might be convenient; and then bidding his servants wait for him in the great hall, took his way, quietly and sadly, to the chamber of his departed kinsman. It is a bitter and heart-chilling scene at all times, and under circumstances the most favorable — the dwelling-room of a dead person! tenanted only by the cold and senseless clay of him who, but a little while ago, rendered it gay and lightsome by his living presence. The chair whereon he sat — the pen with which he wrote yet standing in the ink, as he perhaps left it — the favorite book with its leaf turned down at the favorite passage — the garments — the very gloves, perhaps, which he so lately wore, retaining still the mould of the recent hand that never more may fill them! all these, and fifty other little accessories too trivial to be noted or remembered, contribute to make up at all times a dark and frightful picture. But it was a far sadder and more terrible array of circumstances that met the eye of Chaloner — all, all those were there; the book — the very Epictetus — treating of restraint and patience under wrong — which he had probably been reading, to school his spirit for that fatal meeting — lay on the board, with all the other well-known volumes that employed the good scholar's studious leisure; but, there among his books, and on the tapestried wall, and on the Persian carpet, glared the dark clots of life-blood! while, outstretched, pale and livid on the couch, with the stout serving-man holding the cold, stiff hand, and weeping over it with all but woman's fondness, lay all the mortal part of the wise and gentle student!

"This is a sad sight!" said Chaloner, with difficulty restraining his own tears. "He was a good man; we will trust he is now with the blessed. Now, leave me, honest friends; I would be here alone with him for the last time. Do not go down, but wait beside the door till I come forth to ye." His words were instantly obeyed; and then, kneeling beside the body — "Thou art gone from us," he exclaimed, "my more than friend — my father! thou art gone from us, happy to go at this time!" and burying his head in the vestments of his dead kinsman, he prayed long and fervently; and when he arose, although his air was sorrowful and chastened, it was composed and firm. "Heaven give me strength," he said, "to go through with this painful duty." With these words he left the chamber; and telling the two men to watch, and alter nothing in the position of the furniture or the body, until the police-judge should be called with the physicians to survey it, he went to break the heavy tidings to Madame de Gondi, and to concert with her the means of disclosing them to Alice. The former he found almost prepared for what he had to tell her; for she declared to him, while mentioning the conversation that had passed between them the last evening, that there had been so strange an alteration in the whole manner, tone, and appearance of Mark Selby, as almost to satisfy her that his mortal term was rapidly approaching; and it was with a feeling almost amounting to pleasure, that he heard her express her conviction that Alice, after the first sudden grief, would bear the blow with resignation, and even look on it as a release for her dear father from worse and far more grievous suffering.

"It was but last night she said to me — speaking of her own coming dissolution, which she foresees as certainly as we do — that she should go hence with the regret alone, to leave the old man her survivor; so I am sure, good friend, that she will not be grieved by this beyond her power to bear. Now, general," she added, "I will write forthwith to my kind friend, the bishop de Lisieux, and pray him to see his majesty, and procure the remission of the odious *droits d'aubain*, by which you know all personal properties of any foreigner who dies here becomes forfeit to the crown. Do you send for the judge of the *Quartier* and Monsieur Pallie, the great surgeon, and let us have the investigation over before she knows aught of it. Remember, she has no suspicion that her father knows anything of what passed in Paris. It will be better far to leave her in ignorance — think you not so?"

"Oh! surely," replied Chaloner, "she must not for the world know that he died in the agony of grief and passion, nor that her recreant lover had any hand in it. I have already written to England to resign my public duties, and when the funeral is over I will persuade her to return home to Woolverton. New scenes may give new tone to her mind, and she may recover."

"Never!" said Henriette — "never! her end is nearer than we think for. She never will see England, and she knows it."

"Think you so?" he said, "indeed, think you so? Oh! this is very terrible, — God's judgments, of a truth, are all inscrutable — how else should this one villain work all this agony and ruin, and go unwhipped of justice!"

Nothing more was said at that time — both parties hastening away to perform their sad duties; and, for awhile, the necessity of occupation and exertion overpowered the keenness of their present grief. Before noon, however, all was arranged; the investigation had been held; and nothing material or suspicious having been elicited from the servants, it was decided by the judge that he had died, as we should now say, by the visitation of God, and accordingly, the permission for the funeral was issued in due form. The king returned a gracious message, remitting instantly the forfeiture, accompanied by kind inquiries. The scene of death was cleansed of its fearful attributes; the corpse laid out and robed in the vesture of the grave; the chamber darkened from without, and an old English clergyman—many episcopal dignitaries having been forced to fly the presbyterian persecutions of their own land—summoned to do the last sad offices of his religion—to render "ashes to ashes, dust to dust," the mortal part of his respected countryman. The day was far advanced, however, before Madame de Gondi again met Chaloner; and when she did so, it was to request his presence in the sick-room of Alice.

"She bore it, as I told you I believed she would, most Christianly—most nobly; there was a burst of acute grief at the first, but soon she became quite calm and contented. 'I shall be with him,' she said, 'very soon; I am happy that it is so—he would have pined and been very wretched had I gone before him. We shall soon meet—I feel it—yea! with a humble confidence, I know it—in blessed habitations, never again to sorrow or be severed.' She wishes now exceedingly to see the body, and confer with you respecting the funeral. There is, you know, some difficulty. Our people—our *canaille* I mean of this good city—are by no means too tolerant; and I fear if we should seek to bury him with pomp, there might be rioting and insults."

"Oh, that is easily arranged," said Chaloner—"nothing more easily. Good De Granville will perform the rites here privately, with none to witness them except ourselves and his servants. The coffin—I have ordered one of lead, for he will be removed to England shortly—can be conveyed in your carriage to your private vault at midnight—can that not be managed?"

"Oh, yes," she replied; "I will give orders for it now—but would you let her see the body?"

"Assuredly," said Chaloner; "why not, I pray you? she would never be contented if she did not. If you will take me to her chamber, I will support her thither; it is but a step"

"Oh, she is strong enough to walk; I only feared its effect on her mind."

"You do not know her mind as I do, dear lady," said Henry; "no hero has a firmer or a higher! Come, let us go to her."

Alice was seated in a large easy chair, when they went in to see her, dressed in a close gown of white muslin, which scarcely showed more delicately pure than her transparent skin, with the redundant tresses of her beautiful brown hair concealed by a plain cap of lawn. Upon a little table at her elbow, there lay a flask of some stimulating perfume, and an open bible; and near to these stood a glass pitcher full of water, with a Venetian goblet. She had been weeping, as could be readily perceived, for her eyelids were inflamed and slightly swollen, and all her features, even to the lips, were as pale as living flesh can be, but perfectly resigned, and calm, and gentle. She stood up as they entered and put out her hand to Chaloner, who raised it quietly to his lips; and she could feel, as his mouth pressed it, a warm large tear drop upon its tender surface. For a moment she was quite overcome, and sinking back into her chair, covered her face with her handkerchief; but in less time than could have been expected, she removed it from her features, and spoke in her natural voice.

"Oh! Henry, this is very sad — this is very sad and terrible! That he should have gone hence, whose whole life has been nothing but one act of kindness and attention to others — with no one to allay his sufferings — no one to hold his dying head — to listen to his last word!" and she again burst into tears, even at the images she had herself conjured up.

Chaloner waited till the paroxysm was over, and then said — "It is very sad, Alice — quite sad enough without our conjuring up additions to make it sadder and more terrible. You may be sure he suffered little or nothing of mere pain, for he was quite well a little time before, and all was over in ten minutes. Besides, he had some one to hold his head, and mark his dying words, and save them for his fond survivors; for, although you or I were not there, as doubtless would have been sweetest to him, his faithful servant Charles was with him, and tells us of so Christian and so calm a parting as few, the best of men, may hope for. His last thought, except one, was of you; his last message, 'that he died blessing you;' and then it seemed to Charles that he received, or fancied he received, some heavenly summons, for, starting to his feet, with eyes, and arms, and hopes all heavenward, he cried aloud — "I come!" — and I think that, without presumption or impiety, we may believe him even now to be with Him who called him from this scene of trial and of sorrow. There was the sweetest and most placid smile I ever witnessed on that benevolent, pale face — such smiles mark not the faces of the dead who die not just and happy!"

She listened calmly and with profound attention while he spoke, and seemed to muse deeply after he had finished, but she still wept, though there was nothing violent or passionate in the character of her grief; and Chaloner again said —

"I do not tell you not to weep, Alice, for that would be irrational, and I should therefore be sorry that it were the case; but I do tell you not to mourn as one who has no consolation, for you must recollect that your dear father had already long passed the ordinary term of human life — that he retained all his faculties, all his enjoyments to the last — and that, had he lived much longer, he must in the course of events, have been subject soon to those sad ailments and afflictions which are peculiar to extreme old age. There is, therefore, perhaps as much cause to rejoice as to mourn for him, who has only exchanged doubt for certainty — mortality for everlasting bliss!"

"I know it, Henry — I know it," she replied; "sorrow is selfish ever, perhaps more selfish than joy even; and though I know that by his easy and not untimely death, he has escaped not only these things which you have enumerated, but much acute and poignant sorrow, that must ere long have broken on him, and of which he passed away in happy ignorance; still it is hard, very hard and bitter, to part from one who has so loved and cherished us from our birth upward; on whose face we have never seen a frown — from whose dear voice we have never heard a tone that was not all benignity and kindness," and with the words her eyes again overflowed, and she continued for some little time incapable of speaking; while Henry and her kind hostess kept silence in reverence and regard for her feelings. "I am better — I shall be better now," she said, after a while, as if relieved by her tears — "and firmer. Come with me, Henry — I would look upon him — would take leave of him here; soon, I trust — soon again to meet him where there be no more partings."

"You are strong enough, Alice?" he said, in a tone of inquiry; "if so, I am quite ready to attend you — but nerve yourself, dear girl, for it is as you say, a sad and painful sight!"

"No, Henry!" she made answer, "the sight of a dear father can in no case be painful — let us go!"

Chaloner gave her his arm immediately, and conducted her to the little study where the event had taken place, and where the body lay, clothed in the habiliments of the tomb — the face covered with a linen napkin — the two serving men, who had followed him from his distant house, watching in tears beside the dead. They rose up gently as their young mistress entered, and stole with noiseless steps out of the room, feeling, with a delicacy rare to their rude though honest natures, that grief such as Alice's should have its vent in solitude. She entered with a step so steady, and a mien so composed and tranquil, that Chaloner gazed on her in amazement — one little shudder shook her slight figure for a moment, as her eye fell upon the motionless and rigid outlines of that dear form; but she made no pause, nor did the transient shiver again move her, but she walked straight forward to the couch whereon he lay, and there stood still, gazing on him with a tearless eye, but with the shadows of many memories fleeting across her eloquent features. Chaloner stood beside her in deep silence, not all unmixed with awe; for there was something almost terrible in the appearance of the fair, pale girl — so slight, so frail, so spiritual, in her evanescent beauty — so still and passionless, that she seemed scarcely more alive than that on which her eyes were fixed immovably, until she made a gesture as if she would have the face uncovered, when he stretched forth his hand and removed the napkin from the countenance of the dead. It was indeed as he had said, perfectly calm and placid, and withal, it possessed an air of bland and benignant majesty, which gave an air of almost supernatural beauty to the white lips, and their aquiline features. There was a sweet smile still lingering round the mouth, and it indeed seemed impossible that anything of pain or passion should have disturbed the last moments of one, whose expression was so lovely. And this was probably the case—that in the little space that intervened between the gust of wrath that proved too violent for the fragile body, and the actual dissolution, the permanent and real character of the man had overcome the temporary conflict, and that he had indeed died happy.

"Yes," said Alice, after she had gazed upon him quietly till her eyes were so dimmed by the moisture which welled into them constantly, that she could no more see the features—"yes, it is beautiful—almost divine! Dear, dearest father! happy, indeed, and blameless was thy life—if anything of mortal mould can be called blameless; and, God be praised for it! thy death was happy. Farewell—farewell! and if, as I believe, thy spirit looks down from above on her whom thou so truly and so tenderly didst love, and hears the words I utter, pardon—oh, pardon me the many cares and troubles I have given thee! Farewell—farewell," and she stooped over him, and pressed her lips to the clay-cold brow. "Farewell! My moan is made—my tears shall no more flow. I shall go to thee, my father, and that right soon; but thou shalt not return to me." And with the words, she took the napkin from the hands of Chaloner, and fixing one more long and wistful look on the unconscious lineaments—one more last kiss upon the icy brow—she spread it gently over him, turned away suddenly, as if she could not trust herself to look again, took Henry's arm, and glided from the darkened chamber.

Beyond the threshold of the door, she passed the servants who had been watching, and raising her eyes to their faces, she said, with a melancholy smile, "I thank you very truly, my good friends; and God, who forgets no good or grateful deed, will certainly reward you, for that you have not forgotten him who was kind to us all, and a father while he was yet here. Go in and watch with him; this last sad duty will ere long be over."

That very evening, all was over — that very evening, in the same small room where he had passed the most of his days since he had lived in Paris, and where he had met his end, his body was consigned to its last tabernacle — the cold coffin; and there, with some of those about him, whom, through a long and innocent life, his presence had filled ever with a sentiment of joy — none, indeed, who had known him truly, save Chaloner and Alice, and the servants who had followed him across the sea; although Madame de Gondi and all her household were assembled, the meek old clergyman performed the exquisite and touching service appointed by the church of England, and thence at the dead of night was he conveyed by Henry, only with the sacristan and the two English servitors, to the vault where he was to rest, until the time should come when he might be removed to his native land, and gathered to the long home of his fathers.

CHAPTER XXXIII.

Several days elapsed after the funeral of her father, and Alice gradually, as it appeared to those about her, regained not only her cheerfulness, but health. Her step was firmer, her eye less wildly brilliant, and her complexion more natural in its hues, and showing less of the hectic flush, which tells of latent fever. So much, indeed, did she seem to amend, that a delusive hope had already begun to grow up in the bosom of Madame de Gondi, and even, though to a less extent, of

Henry Chaloner; yet, when they hinted this to her, and spoke to her of pleasant projects for the winter, and of her return to Woolverton with the early spring, she would only shake her head and smile — but since the death of her father, it was remarkable that the smile had lost its grave, if not melancholy character; and that although she was never joyous, or even gay, nothing could be more remote from hopeless grief, or permanent yet uncomplaining sorrow, than was the air of that lovely girl. She appeared, indeed, though she avoided speaking on the subject, to be looking forward to her approaching dissolution with a quiet confidence, and to regard it not as a thing to be deplored, but rather as a joyous consummation. To the visits of the worthy surgeon she acceded readily, and to all his medical measures she assented willingly; but, one day, when Chaloner, deceived by one of those singular turns to which this terrible malady is subject, which was consuming her, expressed his conviction that she was recovering —

"Do not," she said, "deceive yourself, truest and best of friends; I never shall recover — nor, indeed, do I wish it. I take all proper remedies — I submit to the precautions of the leech, because I know it is my duty to await, not hasten, His appointed time. But these matters do not deceive me; let them not mislead you, Henry. Moreover, as I tell you, it is my earnest prayer evening and morning to Him, that when his time is come, he will permit me to depart in peace, and join those that await me. Pray, therefore, Henry, if you pray for me at all, that he will not give me life, but death — which, for them that die in the Lord, is a boon far more blessed."

After this conversation, no illusions more were made to the subject. Chaloner, now admitted as an *habitué* of the family, passed much of his time at the Hotel de Gondi, and things were falling gradually into the old routine, except, that as yet, no strangers were admitted to the house of mourning; when late one evening, when Henry was reading aloud to the ladies a tragedy of Corneille, a servant entered with a small note, upon a silver salver, addressed in a feminine hand to Mistress Alice Selby. She opened it without emotion, observing, as she did so, "I knew not that I had a correspondent in this great city." But, as she read it, she was a little agitated, and blushed deeply; and then, asking for the pens and standish, she wrote a few lines in reply, sealed it, and carefully handed it to the man, with instructions to give it to the messenger who had brought the letter. This done, she rose from her seat, and twisting up the note she had received, lighted it at the candle, and then threw it among the hot wood ashes on the hearth. "It was a note," she said, as if imagining some explanation might be necessary, "from Isabella Oswald, asking permission to come and see me soon."

"And what did you say in reply?" asked Henriette.

"I told her to come as early as she could to-morrow. What little I saw of her the other day pleased me very much, I confess, and that against my preconceived opinion; for, though she is beyond doubt extremely handsome, there is something not altogether pleasing in the style of her beauty, and her manners are at first extremely rough and masculine. But she has clearly a fine heart and a noble spirit, and is as true and upright as the heart of truth!"

"I have heard also," said Chaloner, in reply, "and that, too, from one who knows her very well — the excellent old Marquis de St. Eloy — that she is a most noble girl, the very soul of honor. His expression touching her was, that she would not say a word that was not true, or do a thing that she did not feel to be right, to win a world to her feet; but what she considered true, and judged right, that she would do, in despite of the whole world!"

"It is a fine character, truly," said Madame de Gondi; "though not a woman's character — at least, what I think a woman's character should be."

"Not, perhaps, altogether," replied Henry; "yet it is the distinction barely, the shadow of a shade. The first part of his sentence is, of course, pure praise — no man or woman either ought to say or do anything which they believe false, or evil, to win a universe; and every woman ought to do, no less than every man, that which she knows right, against a world's opinion. As to the saying all that she knows true, that is a different thing — for many things may be true, and yet exceeding untimely — and most untimely things, even untimely truths, do evil more than good. Still, perhaps, Mistress Oswald's fault is more in the manner, than the matter, and, as Madame de Gondi says, it is a very fine and noble character. I have heard some exceedingly great traits and actions of her doing."

"Pray tell me; I should like much to hear them," exclaimed Alice.

And without any hesitation, Chaloner proceeded to relate the adventure of Isabella near Villeneuve St. George, and her spirited conduct in interposing between Marmaduke, and the punishment he had incurred in her behalf; and several other anecdotes, displaying the same fearless generosity, and disregard of consequences, in the prosecution of whatever she believed it right to carry out. Thus the night passed, until they retired; and, the next morning, when Henriette descended to the breakfast-room, she was informed that Mademoiselle Oswald had been engaged in private with Mistress Alice for nearly two hours space, and had not yet departed. Almost at the same instant the two girls entered; and, at once, Madame de Gondi perçeived a peculiar air of flashing joy and triumph on the dark fiery eye and proud features of Isabella, contrasted by a calmer glow of happy satisfaction, that seemed to warm up the tranquil face of Alice into more animation than it was generally seen to wear. Isabella tarried at her request, to partake the first, and perhaps most thoroughly social meal of the day; and everything passed very pleasantly till Henry entered; soon after which, with an excuse for having made so long a stay, the fair visiter withdrew.

"Now, Cousin Henry," said Alice, before the other could have reached the hall door, "I want to have some talk with you on matters of grave business — about estates, and rent-rolls, and life-tenures, and I know not what; and so, as these things are not very entertaining to most people, we will leave our dear Henriette a while, and go to settle these matters in the library."

The library was a large and somewhat gloomy room, the last of the suite of great apartments, and opened by a side-door into the little chamber, which had been occupied by her father; and it so happened, that except the servants, who had been especially directed since the arrival of Mark Selby to alter the arrangement of nothing in the library, no person had entered it since his death. As they went in, therefore, the first thing that met their eyes was a pair of library-steps standing against one of the tall book-cases, with a large folio volume lying open on the topmost ledge, where it had been unquestionably left by the old scholar; and, as if to render this fact even more certain, one of his gloves had dropped upon the floor, and still remained where it had fallen, probably on the very morning of his decease.

"Alas! alas! my father!" exclaimed Alice, as she saw it; and darting forward she caught it up, and pressed it to her lips, and bathed it with her tears, and remained for some time in great and speechless agitation. By degrees she recovered, however, her self-composure, and sitting down by the great velvet-covered table—"This is no time," she said, "for weakness; and I have much to say to you and to do, Cousin Henry, and I require your assistance and advice. Therefore, without apology, I shall go to the point at once. I am now, if I understand it rightly, since the event that we so much deplore"—and her voice faltered as she spoke—"sole and last heiress of Woolverton Manor, Low Barnsley, and Thorpe Regis—Oakdale and Thorney Burn falling to you, as next male heir; pray interrupt me, if I am wrong."

"No," he said, "you are perfectly right, Alice; all these are yours, in your own right, and at your own sole disposal—you being last heir entail of the three manors first mentioned."

"And can I, by will, give the reversion of these three to any one I choose, Henry?"

"Surely you can, and could even, if you had children."

"And if I were to die without any will?"

"Then Alice—but may God long avert the day—would they revert to me, as next of kin and heir at law."

"I thought so—I thought so," she replied; "then, so far there is no will needed. Now tell me, what are each of these three manors worth in annual rent? you used to assist my poor father—tell me the value of the three."

"Woolverton is the most valuable, yielding clear eighteen hundred pounds; Low Barnsley is called twelve hundred, and Thorpe Regis nine; together, they are worth at least three thousand.'

"Now tell me, Henry, can I, without assigning away the ownership of the soil, the right of the land, the fee simple I believe they call it, order a sum to be paid annually to any one I will, from the rents for a term of years, or for ever?"

"Surely, you can a rent charge for a term of years, or in perpetuity—that is quite easy, but why not bequeath the estates at once, if you are resolved to do this now?"

"Because I do not wish it, I will not remove the ownership of one foot of land, or the right of protecting one of the poor tenantry from him to whom it rightfully belongs. Now listen to me, Henry, take up a pen and make notes of what I tell you. Find me a good and honest lawyer, an English one he should be; can you do this?"

"Easily, my dear Alice, there are, I regret to say, too many English of all ranks and professions here in Paris, banished from home by these sad civil wars, to make it difficult to find soldier, or priest, or counsellor. I know a man who will do your bidding truly, and I myself was long enough a templar, to see that he did so. Now then, proceed."

"Let him then draw up, with the least possible delay, my last will and testament. It will be but a short and easy one. I wish to bequeath all the lands, all the books, and furniture, and plate, in short *everything* to yourself: thinking you would rather receive them as the affectionate bequest of a woman you love, than as the award of the law. All the old servants of the family and pensioners, I likewise bequeath to your charity; charging you never to permit them to want homes, or food, or raiment. To my dear cousin Madame de Gondi, five hundred pounds to buy a diamond solitaire in memory of her poor Alice!

And now—now, dear Henry, comes the point of all! I fear that you may not approve it, but still it must be so, and if I grieve you by it, you will forgive me, for that it is the first grief that poor Alice Selby ever caused you *knowingly*—the second she *ever* caused you! Is it not so, dear Henry?"

"In the first place," answered Chaloner, "I have no right either to approve or disapprove, dearest Alice; and in the second, I do not see why you should suppose me likely to disapprove, but, at all events, be quite sure, that as far as in me lies, I will do your wishes."

"This it is, then," she went on quietly; "I wish to settle one thousand pounds per annum upon Major Marmaduke Wyvil," and again her voice failed her, so much that she could hardly utter the words, "provided he marry Mistress Isabella Oswald within one year from the date of the bequest; that thousand pounds to be chargeable on the rents of Low Barnsley and Thorpe Regis; but if that sum can not be raised, without trenching on the revenues of Woolverton, then so much as the rents of the said manors will produce; during the time and to the end of his natural life, or to his widow if she should survive him, until the end of her life, that widow being the said Mistress Oswald, the whole, after the death of both of them, to return to yourself, Henry. I will not ask you whether you think well or ill of this application of my property, for I know that you can not think well of it; and I will not put you to pain by compelling you to say so. But I have thought much and deeply about it; and I have so many reasons for devising it, and reasons which I can not explain to you, but which are altogether satisfactory to myself—which are based on a good motive—which will, I think, produce a good end—and which, whatever be the consequences, will at least make me happy in the contemplation of what I have done, while I remain here."

"For me, Alice," answered Chaloner, "the last reason is sufficient; beyond this I will say nothing, except that I will go forthwith, and have your wish placed in train of execution. Is there aught more that I can do?"

"Yes!" replied she, "there is! I wish a rent charge, or

whatever you call it, of the same amount, and on the same conditions, and chargeable upon the same estates to be made, so as to be binding during my life-time, from this very date; for my object is to give him that sum now, and secure it to him during his life, so as to bring about his alliance with Isabella, whose father has refused to consent until Wyvil can show that he has an income of the amount named. This deed I wish to give him, and it must be so worded, as to leave it doubtful by what means it was obtained, or upon what consideration."

"Do you feel sure that you are doing well, Alice, in bringing these two persons together, after all that has passed?"

"I think I do," she answered, "I feel sure that I do; and I trust that I am not mistaken. At all events, my intents are pure—the end of them is with Him who only knows and governs all things. Will you assist me, and that presently?"

"Be sure I will!" said he, "I will go look to it directly."

"And how soon can it be effected?"

"I think this very evening; but to-morrow at the latest."

"Pray, then, let it be done at once; and when it is done, let your lawyer bring both documents up hither forthwith to be signed. You and Madame de Gondi will, I doubt not, be my witnesses. I thank you, Henry, for this is very kind."

"Not kind at all," said he, "it is a simple duty;" and with these words he left the room, taking the notes, which he had made, along with him; but she continued some little time in deep and solemn meditation.

"How very noble ever, and generous, and good, and gentle!" she exclaimed at length: "It is wonderful that I could not, that I can not love him, wonderful, truly. Oh Wyvil!" and with a deep sigh she too arose, and leaving the deserted library, went to join her cousin Henriette.

CHAPTER XXXIV.

It was already evening of the day that succeeded to the conversation between Chaloner and Alice; but the sun had not yet sunk below the horizon, and his slant rays were pouring a flood of lurid ruddy light into the western windows of the library, where there were gathered, in that stately room, a little group consisting of five persons; Madame de Gondi and her young English cousin; Chaloner and the lawyer, a fine bald-headed man, with a high prominent forehead, and an expression of intellect and benevolence, rather than of craft or shrewdness; and lastly, the lawyer's clerk or scrivener, carrying a leather case which contained the documents. All these, with the exception of the personage last named, were seated at the board, while he was reading aloud, in a clear, cold, and extremely unpleasant tone of voice, the will which had been drawn up strictly in accordance with the dictates of Alice; and it would have been no uninteresting study, whether for a painter, or a searcher into the minds of his fellow-men, the several expressions of the four faces of those who listened to that unimpressive reading. The countenance of the fair girl, whose will it was that occupied all ears, was perfectly intent on every clause and phrase as she sat still, assenting now and then by an easy motion of the head, and evidently pleased and gratified at the luminous style in which her bequests were detailed. Chaloner's noble head expressed no more than earnest and undivided attention; while Henriette de Gondi, although attentive to a degree, was restless and impatient; and so dissatisfied with the tenor of the whole testament, that it could not fail to be observed by every one in the library. The counsellor, by whose opinion the testament had been planned, while he took in the whole sense of every word, even the most trivial, which his clerk recited, had at the same time leisure to let his eyes, and one faculty at least, if not more than one of his capacious mind, wander over the other actors, and form an estimate, if not an opinion of their motives. At length the reading was brought to a conclusion; and when the clerk had ceased, and the document was laid upon the table—

"Now, Cousin Alice," said Chaloner, "does this which you have heard, embody all you intend? and is there any error in our understanding of your bequests? For the rest, having carefully perused it, I can be answerable that this man has read it correctly."

"It is precisely what I wish—precisely to the letter," answered Alice; "what now remains to make it binding and complete?"

"Your signature and seal," answered Chaloner, "but—"

"Well then, give me the pen, and I will sign it now," said she, "and you two can witness it."

"I was about to say," interrupted Chaloner, "that I should strongly recommend your taking it yourself, and reading it in private."

"No, no!" she replied, "oh, no! my mind is perfectly made up, and I shall not change it, so give me the pen."

"As you will," he replied; "but it concerns myself too nearly, that I should witness it—but our good friend here, Counsellor Mansfield, will be a very fitting person."

"Is Mistress Selby of the requisite age, to make her signature to this valid?" asked Mansfield.

"Oh, yes indeed!" said she, with a smile; "I have been of age some months, as the parish register at Woolverton, and this book," producing, with the word, her father's bible, wherein the date of her birth was recorded; "will quite sufficiently testify."

"I had not thought you had spent so many summers, my dear young lady," answered the lawyer; "but though you have, you are still very young to be the sole proprietor of so fine a landed fortune!"

"Too young!" she said, with a deep sigh, her eyes again filling with tears, for her loss was still too recent that she could bear to hear it spoken of by a stranger; "far, far too young! But come, give me the pen, I would fain have this over; besides, there is the other paper, which must be read afterward."

"But, Alice, my dear girl," exclaimed Madame de Gondi, who had evidently been anxious for some time to speak, "I can not sign this will as a witness; and I hope that you will consent to alter it, for—"

"Oh, no!" interrupted Henry Chaloner, so decidedly that it was impossible for Henriette to proceed. "That legacy of five hundred pounds can not unfit you for a witness;" and, as he spoke, he fixed his clear gray eye upon her with a glance so meaning that she understood, immediately, that he wished her to comprehend more than his words expressed. "At all events," he added, "if you are not convinced, permit me to say three words to you in private, when I doubt not I can remove your scruples. Alice, excuse us for one moment—your pardon, counsellor," and he led her out into the next saloon and closed the door behind them.

"It was not that! it was not that at all," said she, in great agitation. "You quite misunderstood me."

"No, my dear lady, I did not; it is the bequest of the rent charge."

"Oh, yes, yes, yes!" she replied. "It is quite, quite too horrible! quite too unnatural! to see her thus endow the man who slew her father; for he did slay him, as much as if he had smitten him with his sword!"

"I know it," he replied, gloomily, "*I* know it, and *she* must not; and therefore we must let this pass. Believe me, I regret it, loathe it, as much as you can do; but yet, believe me, it must be, unless indeed we reveal to her the part the villain played in her father's death-scene; and—"

"By so doing, you would say, *we* should *slay* her!" interrupted Henriette, greatly moved. "Is it not so, General Henry?"

"Even so," he replied, "and gain nothing by it. No other argument can avail, save to annoy and lacerate her feelings. So fixed is she, so high, and so full of her good and great intent, that it were an easier feat for some new Archimedes to unsphere this puissant globe, than to warp her or turn her from the path of what she truly believes right. Besides, although Alice mean it not, bethink you, lady, didst ever hear or read of a more grand and noble—I had well nigh said, Godlike—vengeance? If this be not to heap coals of fire on his head, I know not what it is. That—that is half the cause why I consent. Think you the recreant and dastard knave will not writhe like the wretch upon the mortal rack, and sweat blood in his agonies, even as he receives—for, mark my words, the craven will receive—these alms from her whom he has murdered? Lady, we must consent to this; but think not that this base wretch shall go scathless, or his crimes unavenged. Surely there sitteth One above, without whose knowledge not so much as a sparrow falleth from heaven."

His eloquent and fervent manner—the splendid tones of his deep, rich voice, suppressed, that it might not reach the ears of whom he spoke—and above all, something almost prophetic in his confident divination—had its full weight on the mind of his companion, so that she grasped his hand and answered only—

"You are the wiser—now let us return," and, as they entered the library, she addressed Alice in a tone far more subdued and grave than usual, saying, "Your cousin has convinced me, as he promised he would: I am ready to witness."

"I thank you; it is all right now," said Alice, smiling, as she affixed her seal and signature to the testament, and went through the legal forms, witnessed by Mansfield and Henriette de Gondi.

The reading of the deed followed; and as it was much shorter than the other, and as no opposition followed, this was accomplished speedily, and all was finished. The will was delivered instantly to Chaloner, in whose custody Alice insisted that it should remain; but the deed she retained herself, saying, that she knew how to dispose of it. Duplicate copies of either deed, unsigned, but with the date of signature, and the names of the witnesses endorsed thereon, were also handed over by the lawyer to his fair client, and then, after refreshments had been offered, and refused, he declared that his business was at an end, and courteously withdrew. He had not been long gone, however, before Alice, whose manner throughout the evening had denoted much excitement, made an excuse to her friends, and retired at an early hour to her own chamber, leaving the others sitting together in the large library. For several minutes after her departure, they both kept silence, pondering in their own minds the things which they had heard and witnessed. At last, Madame de Gondi spoke —

"Surely, this is the most strange and fearful tragedy that ever I heard of. It is one of those things that happen at times here on earth, that almost make men doubt Heaven's justice. As excellent and pious an old man — as innocent and pure a girl, as ever bowed in prayer — brought down to the grave in sorrow by one villain's baseness — and that villain rewarded for his very crime and treason!"

"Rewarded *here!*" answered Chaloner; "but who shall tell of that which shall come hereafter? No, no! dear lady, this ought to make no man doubt Heaven's justice. Heaven's Lord professeth not to reward or punish here, but suffereth these contradictions to exist here — this crime triumphant, and this virtue persecuted — only to teach us where to fix our treasures and to build our hopes — not in the perishable present, but in the everlasting future. Besides, who shall pretend to know or to mete the judgments of the Everlasting? Who shall presume to style this mortal miserable, or that one happy? Truly, it is not gratified ambition, or love satisfied, nor gorged avarice, but a pure soul and blameless conscience that gives happiness. Think you that Wyvil, in all the fervor of his passion for this new beauty — in all the pride of winning, the rapture of possessing her — conscious, within himself, of his own vileness — think you that he will be more happy? — or the deserted girl, that seems to us so wretched?"

"Doubtless, within herself, she will," replied Madame de Gondi; "indeed, I believe that in the midst of her very wretchedess, she might be called happy now."

"And he," said Henry Chaloner, sternly, "in the midst of his triumph! Nay, more! which one of us can tell how long this triumph will last? Perchance, even now the Lord has raised up for himself a temporal avenger! For surely I believe that, with the crimes as with the virtues of mankind, he worketh as with tools his own great ends! Most surely I believe that he hath put it many times into the souls of men, that they should do this thing or that, and lo! they have done it straightway, not knowing wherefore; and very like imagining they were accomplishing some small and selfish object, when of a truth they were God's ministers of vengeance!"

"And think you, then, that it is lawful for a man to avenge his own wrong?" asked Henriette, almost awed by the deep voice and flashing eye of the enthusiast, "or those of his friends and kindred?"

"I know that God hath said 'vengeance is mine!' and, therefore, I do not think man at his own fancy may usurp Heaven's prerogative. That men have felt themselves commissioned unto vengeance, so that they could not in anywise resist the bidding from on high, though they have watched, and fasted, and prayed earnestly, that that cup might be removed from them, I well know, for I have seen it. Sure am I that they were ministers of punishment; how far so justified, I dare not even conjecture."

A wild and painful thought crossed Henriette's mind, and caused her to look up intently into the earnest face of the speaker; but there was nothing fanatical or ecstatic in the noble, thoughtful forehead, or meditative eye—and after a moment she continued:—

"And how should a man know whether indeed he is commissioned, or if it be but a vain delusion, fed by his own resentment, and fostered by the instigation of the evil one?"

"Ay! how, indeed?" said Chaloner in reply, very thoughtfully; "there is the question, in that how? If it were not for that—" and he fell for a time into a fit of gloomy musing. Madame de Gondi watched with an anxious and half-fearful expression, every variation of his features; but by-and-by, he said—"a man should greatly doubt all such suggestions, and examine himself carefully, and pray; and even then, I fear, he would be very often misled—such thoughts are dangerous at best; I am sorry that we spoke of them. But see, we have worn the time away with our conversation, and the night is already far advanced. Good rest to you to-night; I shall call to-morrow, and shall hope, as we talked of, to persuade our dear invalid to take the air, either on horseback or in your carriage."

"Oh, not on horseback, that would be quite impossible; she is too weak by far. You do not at all dream how weak she is, when not aroused by circumstances; but we will talk of this to-morrow."

In the meantime, Alice Selby had not, as her friends imagined, retired to rest; but when she reached her chamber had sent her waiting-maid, Margaret, for writing implements and paper, and had continued constantly occupied until this late hour of the night. For a considerable time it seemed, as if she could not satisfy herself with the style and tone of that which she was desirous of composing, for she commenced a dozen times, and after writing a few lines, laid down her pen and read what she had written, and tore it up and committed it to the flames, as if in disgust. At length, however, she seemed to have hit upon the right vein, for she continued to move her pen very rapidly for many minutes, her thoughts appearing to flow from her mind more swiftly than her hand could commit them to paper; and, all the while, the big, round tears were plashing down upon the sheet, she perfectly unconscious that it was so, until the words were obliterated almost as fast as she formed them; and, when she had finished one side of the sheet, and was about to read it before turning it, she discovered that her labor had been absolutely lost. "Oh!" she exclaimed aloud, as she saw what she had been doing—"this is extremely weak and foolish, and I will do so no more," and she rose up and walked across the room, and bathed her brows and eyes in water from the ewer, and returned seemingly quite composed, and sat down again to her task—and this time she kept her word; for she was no more affected in like sort, but wrote with a clear eye and a steady hand, till she had done what she desired.

"Marmaduke"—thus ran the letter which cost her so much pains—"or, for the first and last time, *dear* Marmaduke, I have thought much and deeply on our last meeting; and if I can not quite acquit you of having sinned against me, I must confess that in some sort I have wronged you; this—for we two shall never meet again in this world—I wish to repair. I do not believe that you have wilfully, or with a preconceived determination, wronged me as you have done. Your constancy was not of that enduring quality, your mind not of that vigorous and resolute stamp, to resist absence and brave temptation. This, perhaps, was not, and should not be esteemed your fault, but the misfortune rather, and frailty of your nature. I have, moreover, seen and learned to know, since we two parted, her who has been happier than I in gaining your affections—may she be happier, likewise, in retaining them! and having seen and known her, I recognise in her free soul and fearless spirit, a spell more potent than any I possess to hold dominion over the love of a mind like yours; to bring out your excellences—for you have many such—to their brightest lustre, and to inhibit and restrain your foibles. That you should love her, therefore, and that your love for her should surpass that—perhaps but a fancy, born of circumstances and gratitude—which you once entertained for me, I do not marvel. Had you dealt uprightly by me, and candidly, all had been well. Now, mark me, if I have anything for which to forgive, I do so, how freely and how happily! and if my words, wrung from me by passion, have wronged you anything, forgive me likewise. But do not, Marmaduke, from this that I write, deceive yourself, or vainly fancy that I repent of my late decision. No! I am fixed—and fixed for ever! Nay! but a thousand times more firmly since I have learned to love that beautiful and noble creature whom I give to you for your wife. Yes—start not as you read—*I* give to you! Cherish her, love her, honor her! for she is worthy of all cherishing, all love, all honor! Treasure her as the apple of your eye — cleave to her as your sweetest stay in time of trouble. Thus, and thus only, can you now show the love that once you felt — the kindness that I hope you will feel for ever — to poor, poor Alice Selby. Yes, Marmaduke, I give her to you! may you be happy! and to be so, you must be virtuous and true! I send you, herewith, what will enable you to perform the conditions of Henry Oswald. It is my own to bestow, and with my whole soul do I bestow it. Do not shrink back, do not refuse my gift, Marmaduke — do not, I beseech you. If your proud heart disdain it, think and remember I am proud likewise; yet I humble myself to entreat you, if ever I have done you aught of unkindness — if you now owe me anything of love, or gratitude, or reparation — refuse not my poor boon! It is now the only thing that can make her, who was once *your* Alice, happy! By the life which I gave you! by the love which I bore you! by the affections squandered on you! the hopes blighted by you! by your own happiness, and hers to whom the gift shall unite you! I adjure you — hard though the task be to your haughty soul — refuse me not! No, Marmaduke, you will not! The old man, the good old man, who loved you — he is dead! I tell you not this to grieve you, for he knew nothing which had passed from me, nor, I believe, suspected anything. His last words were a blessing upon me, and, I doubt not, upon you likewise; and in this knowledge I rejoice daily. I would not for the world, that he had thought me wronged, for that would bitterly have grieved him; and, perhaps, good and forgiving as he was, he would not have then blessed you. He is gone, Marmaduke, and I shall, ere long, follow him! and you will give us both a tear and a green spot in your memory! And you, too, Marmaduke — you must one day go hence, and your bright Isabella; and we shall one day meet and know each other, not as now, through a glass darkly, but face to face. And then — then, Marmaduke, let Isabella thank me for having made her yours, and tell me you have made her happy; and that will well repay me for all my transient sorrows. Fear not then — scruple not to accept this my parting gift; two persons only in the wide world besides myself know of it, and trust me, their mouths will be for ever silent. Farewell, then, my beloved! for so in this last parting — so I must call you. Peace, and prosperity, and love, and blessings be about you! Farewell! and when you think of Alice Selby, think of her as one who loved you to the very last, and prayed for you, and blessed you, and will bless you dying!

"For the last time, YOUR ALICE.

"Hotel de Gondi, Nov. 20, 1652."

CHAPTER XXXV.

A WEEK had passed since Alice despatched her letter, to which she had received no answer, save in the report that shortly reached her ears, and the positive announcement that soon followed the report, of the approaching marriage of Major Wyvil and the fair Isabella Oswald. Soon after this announcement had become public, and the busy world had ceased to marvel at the less than nine-days wonder, she had received a visit from the grateful girl herself; who, full as she was of her own hopes, and fears, and happiness, and gratitude, could not but notice and deplore the ravages which the few days, since they had met, had made upon her lovely benefactress. The cough was now almost incessant, and visibly painful to the sufferer; the hectic glow was fixed and constant; the ghastly glitter of the eyes, once so soft and tender, was now unnatural and terrible; and the emaciation of her whole frame frightful to look upon, the light seeming almost to shine through the delicate and slender hands. Yet was she kind, as she had ever been, and thoughtful, and more attentive to the feelings of any one than to her own. She received Isabella with an evident and unfeigned joy; congratulated her upon the prospect of her future bliss; wept over her, and kissed her fondly as a sister;

and ere they parted, she called her maiden, and sent for a little case of morocco, containing a small set of beautiful and costly diamonds, which she put into her hands, saying, "They were my dear mother's, Isabella; and though the setting is old-fashioned, the stones are of a good water, and the devices have been much admired. I shall never wear them, and I have none dear to me to whom to leave them; do me the kindness, then, to take them and wear them at your bridal — when you look on them, they will serve, at least, to remind you of one who will be far from this world, long before you have awakened from your first dream of married bliss."

"As if, by any means, or ever, I could forget you — forget one to whom I owe everything."

And with the words they embraced each other, and wept burning tears each on the other's bosom, until Madame de Gondi entered, and insisted that Alice should not be so agitated any longer; and with one last embrace, those strangely-made friends parted.

A week had passed, and the morning had arrived on which they two were to be made one. It was a clear and lovely sunrise as ever shone out of the heavens; there had been a slight touch of frost on the preceding night, and the atmosphere was clear and limpid, and the sky blue, as though it had been the month of June instead of November, and yet the air was from the westward, soft and balmy — for the warmth of the sunbeams had already touched the earth, and dispelled the hoary rime; and a few birds, the last of autumn's songsters, were chirping merrily, forgetful that the genial days had indeed flown, and that this, which wore their semblance, was but a loiterer in the lap of winter. Everything wore a bright and cheery aspect; the very sparrows in the gutters and on the housetops, little smoked-dried and dingy effigies of birds, were twittering their hymns of rejoicing, at the pleasant time, and appeared more than half inclined to anticipate the season, and commence their loves and courtships.

There were few hearts, perhaps, in that great city, even of the neediest and most unhappy, but derived some gratification from the uncommon beauty of the weather; but there was one to which neither that cause, nor many others, which would have been the sources of much joy to most men, brought anything that could be properly called pleasure, much less content or happiness. That one was Wyvil. Young, handsome, ardent, brilliant of intellect; endowed with that nervous temperament whence springs the keenest appetite for excitement; well esteemed by his comrades, rapidly rising in his profession, the envied bridegroom of the richest and the fairest girl in Paris — Marmaduke Wyvil was not happy; and that, too, on his bridal morning. Alone he sat in his large chamber — alone and in that chamber, as he surely thought, for the last time. His morning meal lay on the board scarcely touched, although it had consisted of the choicest delicacies of the French kitchen; but a large flask of Burgundy stood nearly emptied at his elbow, with a tall drinking-glass drained to the very dregs — while, in an easy chair beside the hearth, a rich furred dressing-robe cast carelessly about him, and his unstockinged feet thrust into his embroidered slippers, with a sad, listless, wandering expression in his eye, and his whole air uncommonly depressed and altered, sat the young cavalier. Several times during the morning, his favorite servant had come in with various articles of splendid clothing, which, after somewhat ostentatiously displaying, as if in the hope to catch his master's eye, he had arranged upon the chairs and sofa. But, if such were his motive, he had failed utterly — although, in good sooth, the articles which he from time to time arranged and disarranged, only, as it would appear, for the pleasure of arranging them again, were of a beauty and richness that might have fixed the gaze of a colder and a wiser man than the young soldier, who so listlessly surveyed them. There was the shirt of the finest cambric, with frills and ruffles of Mechlin lace, such as a duchess now would envy; there was the long cravat, with its deep edge of *point d'Espagne;* the snow-white silken hose, with their embroidered clocks of silver; the *hauts de chausse* and jerkin of white watered taffeta, laid down upon the seams with silver cords; the short cloak of blue velvet, lined with white satin and dusted with seed pearls; the court sword, with its hilt, and sheath, and baldric, all white to match the dress, and studded, like the cloak, with pearls. The very hat and plume, and shoes, with their huge satin roses, were in accordance with the rest of the habit, and composed as magnificent an apparel as could be worn by the most splendid cavalier in those days of profuse expenditure and gorgeous decoration. Yet, though by no means indisposed to splendor, or inaccessible to the vanity of personal appearance, much to the wonder of his assiduous valet, Wyvil took no note of the glittering raiment, nor seemed to be aware that the hours were passing rapidly. Three different times Clement addressed him with entreaties that he would suffer him to arrange his hair, and that he would begin to dress; but each time he was repulsed sharply, until, at last, getting quite out of patience—

"Well, Master Marmaduke," said the man, "I have been praying you to array yourself these two hours and better; and there, the clock of St. Germain l'Auxerrois is chiming ten of the morning — and here comes Monsieur de Bellechassaigne. Now, if you mean to be married to-day, after all, you must needs get up and dress you — and little time enough left you to do it."

And while he was yet speaking, a hasty, firm footstep came up the staircase, and the clash of a rapier jingling against the steps, mixed with the burthen of a light French love-song, chanted in a rich manly voice. As if ashamed of his delay, and not wishing to be caught in so disconsolate a mood, Marmaduke now resigned his head to the care of his experienced valet, enduing, at the same time, his comely limbs with the almost transparent hose which he had so neglected till this moment. Now, however, he made some passing comment on the fineness of their texture; but it was all too late to appease the offended dignity of his servant, who maintained a stately silence — when the door flew open and in rushed Bellechassaigne, full dressed, as became the friend and supporter of the bridegroom.

"Bon Dieu!" exclaimed the partisan, as his eye fell on

Wyvil—"only beginning now to dress! Ten thousand thunders! we shall be all too late. And, my life on it! if you are half a minute behind hand, the marriage is at an end for ever—and for that matter, I should not wonder if that old Amadis, Sir Henry, were to insist on running us both through the body!"

"Nor I, upon my honor," answered Wyvil gloomily, "even if we are in good time. I can not tell wherefore it is, but there is a strange shadow over me this morning, and I am certain some ill will befall me before nightfall!"

"Tush! man, cheer up your love-sick wits! You, Marmaduke Wyvil—you desponding! You, at whose luck all Paris is wild with astonishment, and green with envy!"

"I wish to God all Paris had my luck then!" answered Wyvil: "they are quite welcome to it, I am sure."

"What, in the devil's name, does your master mean, sirrah?" exclaimed Bellechassaigne, turning short round upon Clement.

"Master has been this way, sir, all the morning; but for my soul, I can not divine wherefore," answered the man, shrugging his shoulders.

"You can not—ay! a pretty fellow you are to call yourself a gentleman's gentleman; God-'a'-mercy!" cried the gay young man, with a laugh. "So, as I shall cut both your ears off in five minutes, if he is not better, I advise you to bring out instantly two flasks of his very best champagne, and two of his biggest goblets—do you hear? for we must try to cure him."

"Yes, sir, I hear," replied the man, without desisting from his sedulous attention to Wyvil's flowing curls. "Are you without there, Peter? bring two flasks of the dry sillery and the large beakers!"

The order was obeyed immediately, and, twisting the wire off the neck, Bellechassaigne uncorked one bottle, and at once decanted the whole of its creaming contents into the two large beakers, and forcing one upon Wyvil, drained his own at a draught.

"Very passable wine that, on my honor," said he, laughing. "Ah! you feel better, I perceive, already; there is a twinkle beginning to steal into the corner of your eye—by the time you have quaffed the other, you will be all right. Oh, none of your remonstrances! here, down with it—it is not altogether so very difficult to swallow. Now, tell me honestly—do you not think yourself the most ungrateful dog in Europe, to be railing thus at your bad fortune, when you have won the heart of the finest and most difficult girl in all France, and gained, by witchcraft people say—and by the Lord I half believe it!—her father's leave to wed her? I wish—wish, did I say?—I would give ten years of my life, if I could prosper in my wooing—and yet my sweet little Annette, God bless her! loves me as truly as I do her; and her good father, the excellent old marquis of St. Eloy, affects me well enough; and all would do very well, I fancy, if it were not for that infernal old she-dragon—whom, for his own sins, and mine too I suppose, he took to wife when Annette's mother had been dead some six years. Poor devil! he is sorry enough for it now—but little good that does me, or will do me, unless she will make a stolen match of it; and that she never will, I am certain."

By this time Marmaduke—between the effects of the wine he had drank and his friend's lively raillery—had partially recovered his natural character and spirits, and began to talk in a gay strain, though it might be seen that it was not without an effort, while Bellechassaigne, whose buoyance of manner, springing from a free heart and a mind unconscious of any serious wrong, nothing could check, continued rattling on in a style that soon delivered Wyvil's mind from the gloomy notions which had possessed it during all the morning.

"By Heaven!" he said, as Marmaduke, who was now fully dressed, with the exception of his hat and short cloak, was knotting on the baldric of his rapier—"by Heaven! that is an exquisite device—that pure white suit; and admirably will the rich mazarine blue of the cloak relieve it. So, Clement, so! a little more this way, more over the left shoulder; that is it. Now, the hat and the gloves; ay! that is it. A very perfect cavalier in faith! I do not think the fair Isabella hath any right to complain. Faugh!" he added, looking contemptuously down upon his own gay and tasteful garb — "Faugh! my knave tailor has decked me out like one of your English May-day mummers, whom you talk about, and yet, I thought it not so much amiss, before I saw yours. There is something singular, original, and most appropriate about that plain white silk."

"You do yourself and your tailor wrong, Bellechassaigne," replied Wyvil, smiling; "the peach-colored linings of your trunk-hose and doublet suit admirably well with the deep violet; and the embroideries of your cloak and baldrick are, to my taste, of an absolute fancy. Here, Clement," he continued, tossing a full purse to a man, "divide that with your fellows, keeping the lion's share yours; and hark ye, when the wedding's over, see all my mails, and armors, and the like, removed to Sir Henry Oswald's; and then I would advise you to come hither, and get as drunk as possible with all that is left in the cellar, before the landlord pounces on it. The furniture I give to you, for yourself. You go to church with me."

"Surely, sir, surely," replied the servant with a low bow; "I am all dressed except my coat, and Gregory and Peter are in their new liveries with favors; we will be ready in a moment — Sir Henry's coach has not come yet."

They had not long to wait, however; for, before many minutes had elapsed, the state-coach of the wealthy baronet, all crimson velvet, and rich gilding, and plate glass, drove up at the door; and Marmaduke with his friend instantly entered, and proceeded to their destination, with twenty or more of their body servants, gallantly arrayed and mounted, following close behind. They were not long in reaching, although they drove but slowly, the house of the English baronet; before the door of which thirty or forty carriages, and at least three hundred mounted servants, with led horses for their masters, were assembled. A great crowd had collected, even before the arrival of the bridegroom, and a still larger had come up with the carriage that conveyed him; all the innumerable loiterers and idlers of the streets having fallen into a sort of rude procession, partly from curiosity, and partly in the hopes of coming in for a share of the largesse, which was still in some cases distributed; although, like other usages of the feudal times, this custom was fast falling into desuetude. The persons of both these young officers were familiar to the people; and the high character which they bore, as daring partisans, continuedly courting peril, had rendered them especial favorites; so that as they descended from the vehicle, a loud shout arose from the multitude, and was repeated several times, even after they had passed out of sight into the vestibule of the mansion—until a strong body of mounted police came up at a trot, and dispersed the people—the government being, at that period, extremely jealous of any gathering concourse, as well they might, from their experience of Parisian mobs at the barricades, and other tumults of the Fronde.

The whole suite of apartments was thrown open, and many guests of dignity and rank were assembled of both sexes, to witness the signing of the contract, and partake, as was the custom of the day, a splendid banquet or collation previous to the performance of the sacred rite, which was to render that contract indissoluble; and which, in this case, was to take place in the magnificent cathedral of Nôtre Dame de Paris. Many there were in that gay crowd, of splendid form and stately presence; nor did these forms lack setting off by all that can be fancied of sumptuous and rich in garb and garniture; but so near were the two young men, who now entered as principals in that which was about to happen—the bridegroom, namely, and his friend—to the perfection of high manly beauty, that there was a brief pause in the conversation, followed by a low hum of admiration. They had scarce entered the saloon, however, and interchanged a few words with some personal acquaintances, when Sir Henry advanced from an inner room to meet them, and shaking his intended son-in-law cordially by the hand, conducted him with his friend to the with-drawing room, where the fair bride awaited them.

Having no mother, on whose care and tenderness to rely at this trying moment, Isabella Oswald was supported only by a bevy of young and lovely girls; but among these were numbered several, whose names stood highest among the high-born daughters of her adopted land; yet young and lovely as they were, they only seemed to act as foils to the superior beauty of the bride. Either in form or face, it would be scarcely possible to fancy anything that could have surpassed the splendor of her whole appearance on that eventful morning. All that at other times had seemed objectionable in her peculiar style was so subdued and softened down, that no one, how severely critical soever, could have demurred to her air, her carriage, or her aspect. The full black eyes, that could at times so boldly and so brightly lighten on beholders, were now suffused with a soft languor, and half seen through their long dark lashes, expressed no sentiments but those of maiden modesty, not all unmixed with tenderness, and awe at her new situation. The haughty curve of her imperial mouth, was melted down to a slight dimple—the proud elevation of her queenly neck was meekly lowered. All seemed to betoken the sweet conscious love, and gentle bashfulness of a young, happy maiden. Her black luxuriant ringlets fell down in a rich maze on either side of her face, until their longest curls rested in beauteous contrast on her snowy bosom; but at the back of her head the hair was collected into a thick classical knot, encircled by a wreath of orange flowers, from which the bridal veil, of Brussels point, flowed down in ample draperies to her feet. Above her fair and regal brow, she wore a small tiara of splendid diamonds in a rare antique setting, the gift of Alice Selby; and all the body of her dress, from the downward curve of her sweet bosom to the girdle which encompassed her slender waist, gleamed like a cuirass of the same inestimable gems—for so thickly were they strown upon it that not half an inch of the material could be discovered; although that material, of which the robe was formed likewise, was a superb brocade of silver and white damask, with a long train above it of snow-white velvet, bordered with cloth of silver, and looped with knots of pearl. The falling sleeves exposed the whole of her exquisitely moulded arms and fairy hands, ungloved, and glittering with the choicest gems. She was, indeed, for beauty, one in ten thousand.

What wonder, then, that Wyvil—fickle and most impulsive ever—should once again forget the less commanding charms of Alice, and yield himself a willing slave, and dream of endless bliss in the possession of so rare a being; when even Bellechassaigne, the bold, light-hearted, reckless, and unimaginative soldier of the day, was so deeply struck, not by her gorgeous beauty only—for that he had seen many a day unmoved before—but by the whole tone and style of her subdued and chastened loveliness, that he bowed his knee to her as he approached, and hesitated, and was embarrassed like an awkward, inexperienced youth, on his first presentation to some mighty monarch; and scarcely could find words to express his sincere congratulations and kind wishes.

Much time, however, was not given to him for consideration; for the ceremony of reading, signing, and witnessing the marriage contract in due form, was instantly commenced; and, as this duty for the most part lay with him, until it became necessary for the parties to affix their signatures, he was withdrawn from the vicinity, and Marmaduke eagerly seized the occasion offered him of whispering some words of passion, and of tender encouragement into the ears of her, whom, for the moment, he did really believe he loved beyond all others of her sex. The time arrived, and each in turn took up the pen, and applied it to that powerful and binding document. But here it was observed by Bellechassaigne, that while the signature of Isabella was affixed in a clear, beautiful Italian hand, perfectly steady and unbroken, the name of Wyvil was scarcely legible; but feeble, blotted, uncertain, and betraying singularly, as he thought afterward, a mind embarrassed and uneasy; although his ordinary signature was in a bold and dashing style.

This ceremony finished, the bride was led out to the banqueting-room by her father, Wyvil giving his hand to the first, and Bellechassaigne taking charge of the second of her bridemaidens. The rest followed as they might—and all were marshalled to the splendid board, and the feast was spread, and the rare wines were filled out into brimming bumpers, and toasts were quaffed, and all was mirth and joy. But when that mirth began to wax uproarious, and the attention of the guests was diverted somewhat from the bride, her father gently withdrew her from the table; her bridemaids and a few of the more immediate friends of the family rising and following, with Marmaduke and Bellechassaigne, and handed her to the carriage in waiting to convey them to the church.

The lamps were burning at the high altar in the superb cathedral of Nôtre Dame, and near it, in his grand sacerdotal robes, with his inferior clergy round him, stood the archbishop of Paris himself, to perform the sacred rite, and administer the sacrament, one of the holiest in the Roman ritual. A few spectators had assembled in the body of the building; and, as is ever the custom in Roman catholic churches, several groups were kneeling here and there, at the various shrines, quietly and devoutly praying in their own hearts, and observing nothing of the gay party that came up the chancel, with rustling robes, and waving plumes, and all the pomp of this world's blithest pageantry. Among the spectators was a tall young man, with a fine brow and very intellectual face, to whom, she knew not why, the eyes of Isabella were attracted as by a species of fascination. He was dressed very plainly, in a suit of dark brown velvet, slashed in a few places with black satin, and embroidered with black lace—a taffeta scarf, of the same color with his pourpoint, supported his long horseman's sword, and he had boots and spurs upon his feet, as if he had just dismounted from his horse. It was nothing, therefore, in his garb that riveted Isabella's notice, for that was nothing but the habit of an ordinary gentleman; nor, to say truly, was it his personal appearance either; for, though a very handsome man, he was not to compare with Wyvil in beauty of face or feature; while his figure, although perfectly well-made and symmetrical, was more athletic, and certainly less graceful. There was, however, something in his countenance which both attracted and disturbed her; an air of calm and majestic dignity, with a character of benevolence and goodness palpably breathing out from every feature; but as her eye met his, she fancied, at the moment, that there was in it likewise an expression of interest and pity for herself, which she could not at all comprehend or fathom. All this passed in an instant, for Isabella withdrew her glance as soon as she saw that the stranger noticed it; and still more to her astonishment, on looking round to Wyvil, she perceived that he also seemed to recognise that calm and grave spectator, and to be discomposed and embarrassed by his presence. Meantime the services commenced; and as they did so, a carriage stopped at the great door, attended by one or two servants in liveries of green and gold. Two female figures one a lady evidently, and the other as it seemed, a soubrette or attendant, issued from it; and the former, leaning on the other's arm, came up a side-aisle quickly but silently, to a spot whence they could command a view of the proceedings—near to the stranger who stood there, but separated from him by the base of a great clustured column, which hindered either party from discovering the presence of the other. Meantime the ceremony went on; and still, strange as it may appear, the eyes of Isabella, guided by some unaccountable and irresistible impulse, were drawn furtively toward that grave spectator; and still she saw that his clear, passionless glance was fixed upon her, full of a soft compassion; and above all, she perceived that he who was soon to be her lord and husband, was overawed and crestfallen, and actually trembled under the observant gaze of that mysterious person—and well he might, for it was Henry Chaloner!

So heavily did this strange sense grow on her mind, with a dim presentiment of evil, that she too was very greatly troubled; and half repented the irrevocable step which she was taking, and half began to wish that something might occur to hinder it—a thousand things which she had barely noticed when they happened, now coming vividly upon her memory, and filling her with strong doubts and suspicions as to the faith of Wyvil. Still she mechanically knelt, and rose, and knelt again, and made the due responses, until she was yet more distracted by the sounds of suppressed sobs and stifled weeping, which was now heard by all the party, and that so sensibly, that every eye was turned to the quarter whence it came. The service had now reached the point after which there can be no change — no retraction more, for ever, unless death shall divide whom God hath joined together; and the tremendous adjuration was even now upon the lips of the archbishop, when the veiled lady sank with a deep sob forward on the pavement, the black gauze falling off which had concealed her features, and disclosing the pale inanimate face of sweet Alice Selby! and at the same time, the girl who had accompanied her uttered a piercing shriek, and cried aloud —

"Help! oh, help my dear young lady — she is dying!"

All in a moment was confusion. At such a sight Wyvil's first, truest — only true passion returned with all its ancient force; and leaving his fair bride, forgetful of all else but that dear, fainting girl, he darted forward to assist her whom he had so shamefully deserted, exclaiming —

"Look up! look up once again, MY Alice!"

But as he stooped to raise her, his shoulder was seized by a stout, heavy grip, and the deep, rich voice of Chaloner rang in his ear —

"Back, villain! it is thou that hast done this thing! Back, I say! tempt me no further!"

At this moment the archbishop closed his missal, seeing at once the cause of what had happened. But Wyvil, as he felt himself thrust firmly backward, remembered himself a little, and shaking off the grasp of Henry, said fiercely —

"You shall answer me for this, General Chaloner."

"Begone!" said the other, with an expression the most bitterly contemptuous; and turning round, he beheld Alice Selby supported in the arms of the noble Isabella, her face literally watered with the burning tears that fell from the eyes of her late rival, and covered with eager kisses from that fair mouth, no longer haughty or imperious, but tender and affectionate as that of a young mother.

"Thanks! gentle lady," exclaimed Chaloner — "thanks for myself, and my poor cousin; a thousand thanks for your kindness. But suffer me to bear her to the carriage. I knew not that she would come hither, but fearing that she might, I ventured to intrude upon your ceremonial, which we have interrupted so inopportunely!"

"So opportunely rather, you should say, sir," answered Isabella, as she rose to her full height, resigning the unhappy girl to her protector. "I thank God for it! most opportunely, in order to preserve me from a fate too dreadful."

At this moment, Marmaduke, who heard not the words which were passing between Chaloner and Isabella, advanced and offered her his hand, as if to lead her back again toward the altar.

"No!" she said, bright indignation flashing from her eyes, and her beautiful lips curling with utter scorn — "No! sir — I am no longer blinded — I can see all now! Ay, all! everything! Well may you quail and cower! Begone! out of my sight! begone! How dared you imagine that Isabella Oswald would brook baseness? How dared you hope even, that Isabella Oswald would build up her happiness upon a sister's sorrow? What fooled you to the fancy, that Isabella Oswald could entertain a feeling save of disgust, and scorn, and loathing for a knave! a liar! and a traitor!"

"Brave heart!" said Henry Chaloner, looking admiringly on her fine form, dilated as it was with generous ire, and her face glorious with the best heroisms of her sex — "Brave heart, and noble! how could I so misapprehend thee?" and with these words, he bore away the still unconscious girl in his strong arms to her carriage — but Isabella heard him not, nor paused, but turning from the baffled bridegroom continued—

"Your pardon, Lord Archbishop! God, of his gracious mercy, has this day interposed to save me from a doom, to which the most abhorred death were a luxury! Unto him, therefore, endless praise is due; and when I shall have schooled my heart by solitude and prayer, most gratefully and humbly shall that praise be rendered. Meantime, my lord, your pardon! Nay! father, nay!" she continued, seeing that angry feelings were aroused, and angry words were bandied to and fro among the martial audience — "nay, father, I insist — Monsieur de Bellechassaigne, I do intreat — De Rochefort,

I command you! This is my own deed, my own ground—and none but I shall answer it. Father, you will not do your daughter—nor you your cousin, De Rochefort—so foul and shameful wrong, as to make her the theme of the vile world's scurril comments, the cause of broil or duel! Besides, you must not do *him* so much honor! The swords of brave men are for the brave and honorable! nor must they be degraded by the punishing of so low knavery and treason! The world's scorn is the only whip for such men, and to that," she added, casting a look upon him, which, if looks could scathe, would have consumed him where he stood—"to that, and his own guilty soul, I leave him!"

"By St. George! Isabella is in the right of it," exclaimed Sir Henry, "and I will have it so; and if I choose to overlook this insult in very scorn of the insulter, I think no one will deem it wise to take up my quarrel, or hint that I know not what best to consult for mine own honor!"

Not a word more was spoken, for Bellechassaigne and De Rochefort bowed in silence; and with a haughty toss of her head, shaking off every thought of tenderness or weakness, she swept on, unblighted by the brief gust of passion which had passed over her and vanished into air—heart-whole and fancy-free. While, with the agonies of hell itself alive at his heart's core—finding himself shunned equally by all, forsaken even by his stanch friend, Bellechassaigne, and loathed by the very servants who attended him—Marmaduke Wyvil threw a dark mantle over his wedding bravery, and hurried back on foot, sullen and dogged, to his cheerless home.

CHAPTER XXXVI.

Night had already fallen misty and dim over the great city, and all the evil things that prowl the streets during the hours of darkness, were up and stirring. No lights were seen in those days, even in the most public thoroughfares, except from the lamps in the shop-windows, or the lanterns which hung over the gates of the better mansions, save where some proud hotel or royal residence cast from its long range of illuminated casements a lustre, as of day, into the gloom without. At ordinary times, one of the brightest of these stately palaces was the Hôtel de Gondi, but, on the night in question, all its façade was steeped in darkness; even the lantern at the port cochère had been left unlighted, in the great sorrow and disturbance which had fallen on the household when Alice was brought home by Chaloner, and conveyed to the chamber whence she was never more to issue living. It was, indeed, not a little singular, to what a degree, during her short residence in Paris, the young English girl had won the affections of all who came within the sphere of her attraction; there was not in the Hôtel de Gondi a menial, from the highest to the lowest, who did not mourn as if about to lose a dear friend, when it was rumored in the household that she was surely stricken beyond the power of man to save — beyond the hope of recovery. Yet so, in truth, it was; for, as is oftentimes the case with the terrible disease that was destroying her, it had worked secretly and silently, sapping and undermining the very throne of life, scarcely suspected until the last moment. That morning when she set forth to the church, though any eye could have discovered that she was dangerously, perhaps incurably, ill, no one could have doubted that there were weeks, perhaps months, or even years of life, in that delicate, attenuated frame; nor, although well aware that she was dying, had she herself entertained the least suspicion that her hour was so near at hand. But, when she had been brought home, and recovered from her death-like swoon, it needed not the sentence of the leech to prepare the minds of the beholders; for the seal of approaching dissolution was stamped on her brow visibly, and she herself declared that she knew certainly, and felt that her days were numbered, and her hours fast dwindling into minutes. Much has been written to no purpose, if it is necessary now to say that, for her, death had no terrors; that he came on her, not in the guise of the cold and terrible destroyer, but of the mild consoler—the healer of all mortal sorrows—the guide destined to introduce her to a holier and happier land. Her worldly business had been all arranged—she had no cases to vex her parting moments, no earthly passions, no strong mortal ties to render her pure spirit reluctant to depart; she had lived always as one who was assured that this night her soul might be required of her, and now that the hour had arrived for her, whose coming no man knoweth, she was filled not with dread, anxiety, or doubt, but with an humble joy—a confidence of hope that rested on the rock of ages. As soon as she had recovered the full mastery of her senses, after the shock which scattered them so rudely, she asked for the venerable clergyman who had officiated at her dear father's funeral; and when he came, stretching out her hand, with a tranquil smile, she said—

"I have to trouble you again, good Doctor Markham, a little sooner than I had dared to hope. I have sent for you to pray with me, and if you find me in a fitting state, to administer the holy sacrament before I go hence."

And, while he stayed with her, so fully satisfied was he with her condition, that he was wont, so long as he lived, to refer to that Christian death-bed, as, out of many terrible and awful scenes which he had witnessed, the one which, by its bright and tranquil lustre, sufficed almost to efface from his memory the combined horrors of the rest. After about two hours, during which she remained alone with the good man, she requested to see her friends—Madame de Gondi and Henry Chaloner especially; and on their coming, she told them in a few brief and touching words, that knowing her own hour near at hand she wished that they should know it likewise; and not sorrow, but rejoice as she did.

"And now," she said, when with a voice unfaltering, and a clear eye, she had made this announcement; "let us talk pleasantly and calmly, as it befits friends to do, who have many things to say to each other before parting — one, to set forth on a long and distant journey; the others to await, yet a while, the day and hour set for their departure. My own mind is made up fully to the change, and, though it may be hard to part from some we love, exceeding great is the reward. I am sure, therefore, that you will restrain your griefs, that you may not disturb that serenity which, I thank Him who gives it, now reigns in all my spirit."

Madame de Gondi strove to speak, but she could only press her hand in silence. Yet her tears, though they could not be restrained, flowed silently; and she maintained, at least, an outward semblance of composure, aided by the extraordinary self-command of Alice, and by the almost stoical philosophy of Chaloner — who begged her to speak on, and tell him all her wishes, which, to the very least, she might rest sure shonld be obeyed, even to the letter.

"First, then," she said, "tell me what passed in the church, after I fainted — that one thing disturbs me — for I fear I did wrongly to go thither; and that I have frustrated all my schemes. Is it so, Henry?"

"Remember, Alice," answered Chaloner, "before I tell you anything — remember that we can but propose schemes here, and that it is He who disposes them, as it may seem good to his wisdom, which is omniscience. Remember also, that from the first I disapproved of your plans, although I yielded to your wishes."

"I do remember — I do," replied Alice. "Now, tell me — in any event I shall not now repine — as far as concerns myself, I have done with the earth and its idols."

"I will tell you. When you fainted, that man, whose name

I will not trust myself to mention, left his place by the side of Isabella, and rushed toward you, with words on his lips, that proved to all who heard them, that he had been in the very act of deliberate perjury! When your fall, and the discovery of your face, saved him from that dread consummation of his crimes, the archbishop refused to proceed with the ceremonial; and Isabella Oswald so cast him off from her, when he fain would have led her back to the altar, as shows that her heart is whole, and that no weak regrets will make her duty painful."

Alice listened attentively to every word he spoke; and, as he ceased, she drew a deep breath, and then paused for some time, her lips moving slightly as if she syllabled a prayer.

"Amen!" she said, at last, "His will be done! yet I had hoped it might be otherwise. What were the words he spoke?"

"Words, Alice," Chaloner replied, "which clearly showed that, while he was standing at God's altar to wed one woman, his heart was with another. He called you *his* — *his* Alice!"

A faint, brief flush came over the pale face of the dying girl; but like the summer lightning, ere you could say — look! look! how beautiful! 't was fled.

"Is it, indeed, so?" she said, thoughtfully; "then is it for the best; for she is not the woman to brook divided love. Frail creatures! how frail are we all, and easily misled even in our best interests, and purest motives! There, in the wish of doing good, was I near making one noble creature wretched, and one most guilty! Alas! alas! and perhaps even then, when I thought myself most passionless, it was the most of earthly passion that dimmed my mental vision, and clouded my more sober reason."

"If it had not been so, dear Alice," Chaloner soothingly replied, "you had been more than mortal."

She was again silent, and remained so for very many minutes, with her eyes closed, and her hands folded on her bosom; and when she spoke again, her voice was considerably weaker than before.

"It is gone," she said, "it is past and over — it was the

last! Now, let us speak of other things. That deed is worthless now — and the will, likewise. Is it not so?"

"Unless you wish to renew them without the conditions," answered Chaloner, "which, if you desire it, can be done."

"No," she said, "I will not. Have you the will here, Henry?"

"I thought you might wish for it, therefore, I have."

"That is well — let me see you burn it — my eyes are clear now, and, I believe, I see the path of duty straight before me."

She was obeyed immediately; and after she had looked at the document, it was consigned to the flames and destroyed. Then she requested Henriette to bring pens and paper, and dictated a few words, brief and explicit, bequeathing everything to Chaloner, with the exception of the one legacy. Having herself read them, she signed the paper with a firm hand, and having seen it witnessed by Madame de Gondi and the good clergyman, she handed it to Chaloner, with these words —

"May you enjoy it, as you will use it, well — and take care of my poor, for they will miss me. I have, you know, left everything to your discretion, but there are many things that I will pray you to do, as if I had named them in my will. You will keep up the old house, Henry; and retain all the old servants for my sake — when they became too old, we even gave them little pensions, and if they wished it, a small farm or cottage — you will do likewise. Poor Jeremy is growing old, likewise; you will look to him. I have heard say that good John Sherlock would wed our little Marian Rainsford; if it be so, you will give her a dowry — at all events, the Stag's Head rent free, so long as she will dwell there. I think she will not marry. There are more things — but there comes a faintness over me at times, and I begin to grow forgetful — but your own feelings will tell you what I would wish done."

"I think so, dearest Alice," he replied; "I know all your old clients, and you may be quite sure that, so long as I live, they shall want nothing, but shall ever find a friend and protector in their landlord; and, when I die, I will provide for their welfare."

"Oh, you must leave them, as a sacred trust, as I do," answered she, rallying again a little — "as a sacred trust, *to your son*, Henry! For, when this grief is over-passed, you must marry."

But he shook his head sadly, and a grave shadow, as if of displeasure, settled down on his features, and he turned his face to the wall, and answered nothing.

"Give me to drink," said the sufferer — "give me to drink, Henriette, I am athirst and faint. I would fain stay a few minutes longer here, if so it may be — I expect to see one here, anon!"

"Give her some wine and water, lady," said the clergyman, "it can not hurt her now, and may yield her some support," and in a lower voice he added, "whom does she think to see?"

"No one!" said Henriette, with great difficulty choking her tears; "her mind wanders."

"I think not," replied the good man; "I never saw one clearer, or more conscious to the last — God grant us all such death-beds!"

She drank, and seemed refreshed and strengthened; and, after lying tranquilly for a few minutes, she raised herself a little up, and said —

"Now, it will be a painful scene for me to bear, and you to witness; but I should not like to go hence without speaking to my poor English servants, and bidding them farewell. They might well think unkindly of it, if I were to leave them in a foreign land, without a word at parting. Henry, will you call my poor girl Margaret, and the two men, Charles and Anthony — tell them to be as calm as possible, for noisy lamentation would afflict me."

He rose at once, and left the chamber, and in a minute or two he returned again, leading himself the girl Margaret, who was pale as death, and seemingly upon the point of fainting, yet kept her sobs down, and controlled her tears wonderfully, through the great love she bore her mistress; while the two men — stout, hardy, and athletic yeomen, either of whom could have felled an ox with but slight effort — followed, their knees knocking together, and the big tears rolling down their cheeks, and moistening their close curled beards.

"I have sent for you, my good friends," she said, in a tolerably firm voice, "to take you by the hand, and thank you for the good service you have done me — and done better far than I — and to bid you farewell before I leave you! for I must leave you, and that very shortly — I pray you, Charles, control yourself, or your grief will unsettle me. I am sorry, my friends, to leave you; but I leave you in kind and familiar hands — for General Chaloner will be the master of all my estates, and, of his love for me, will provide well for all of you who deserve well of him; and I doubt not that will be all of you. God bless you, my good friends, and keep you! may you be good and happy. And now, before I say farewell, I would pray you, if ever I have been fretful, or over-urgent, or unkind to you, as I have doubtless been many times, that you will forgive!"

"Oh, no! oh, never! never!" exclaimed all three at once, as well as they could speak for the tears and sobs, which now burst out all uncontrollable. "God bless you — God preserve you, Mistress Alice! You fretful! unkind! you over-urgent! you, whom no one of us, for all we have been greedy, lazy, unthankful knaves, had ever heard say one harsh word!" cried Charles.

"No! not unthankful, Charles," said Anthony, "all else is true, but we are not unthankful!"

"Indeed, you are not," replied Alice, now moved herself to tears; "nor lazy, nor aught else but true and honest; but shake hands with me, and then say, farewell! for this is almost too much for me. God bless you, and farewell! Good General Henry will be soon your master."

And the men grasped the two small feverish hands, and bedewed them with their tears, and left the room in an agony of grief. Then she said —

"Kiss me, Margaret: you are a very good girl, and have been so to me, ever. I love you very much, and I thank you very truly for all your goodness, especially in these late days, since grief and trouble have lain heavy on me. Kiss me — farewell! Whatever Henry Chaloner *can* do to make you happy, I promise you he *will* do. Now, if you wish to stay to the last with me, sit down there — I can trust you to control yourself; can not I, Margaret?"

"Yes, Mistress Alice," the girl answered, with a great effort, "I will be very quiet, if you will let me stay with you," and she walked with a tottering step to the further corner of the room, and sitting down, covered her face with her apron; and, though her whole frame shook with the violence of her emotions, she uttered no sound that was heard by Alice, or by any one of the watchers. After this agitating scene, Alice again took a little wine and water, and soon afterward sank into a calm and gentle sleep, breathing as regularly as an infant, with a sweet smile on her lips, and an expression, almost angelical, pervading all her features. More than once, each of those who watched beside her, stole with a noiseless step up to the pillow, half-doubting, so quiet was that slumber, whether she had not already passed away — but it was not so; and after she had been asleep above an hour, and it was now drawing near to morning, a light footstep was heard at the door, and a gentle hand touched the latch, but seemed afraid to raise it. Madame de Gondi rose, and stole to the door, and opened it very quietly — and there, to the astonishment of every one, stood Isabella Oswald, in all her superb bridal attire, but with the trace of many tears upon her beautiful cheeks.

"I have been without," she whispered, "these five hours and more, and can no longer bear it. Let me stay here — I will not disturb you!"

Henriette led her in without a moment's hesitation, answering —

"I am glad you have come hither — I think she wished to see you, and had a sort of prescient hope that you would come!"

"And is she, indeed, dying?" asked the agitated girl; "Oh! but this is too fearful! Never! never shall I forgive myself!"

"Forgive yourself for what?" asked Chaloner, in the same low tone.

"For having ever seen him—for having ever listened to him. Had I not, she had now been well and happy."

"God knows," said Chaloner, "and he only. But I think no one could have been happy with that man; and I am quite sure no one could be happier than she. At all events, it can be no blame to you, who never heard or dreamed of her existence. But, hush! hush! she is waking," and, as he said the words, she opened her eyes and looked around her, but without seeming to notice any one.

"Oh!" she said, "I have slept so sweetly, and heard such heavenly strains, and seen such glorious forms—all gold and azure," and she seemed to ponder for a moment, and then said, "It was a dream, but most delightful. All these things, too, ere long, will be as a dream likewise. Dear Henriette—dear Chaloner, I am very shortly going. I had hoped to see Isabella; but—"

"I am here, Alice," whispered the lovely girl, rising from her seat, which was screened by the draperies of the bed. "I have been here all the time!" and kneeling down beside the pillow, she buried her face in the clothes, and clasping her friend's hand, wept bitterly.

"You do not weep for me, Isabella," said Alice, "or if you do, truly you waste your tears. I would not have it otherwise than it now is—no! not for anything that human hopes can compass. I am happy! perfectly happy! and if aught was wanting, now that you are here with me, that want is removed—for I wished, dearest Isabella, before I died, to ask your pardon for the pain I have given you unwillingly. I meant, indeed, to do well, and to sacrifice myself only; and lo! I have sacrificed you!"

"Sacrificed *me!*" cried Isabella, excited beyond all control; "say, rescued me! say, saved me from perdition! If you had not done as you have, I should have either pined for his love, and so been wretched, or wedded him, and perished! Pardon me, pardon me, Alice; my feelings are too strong for me. Oh, God! oh, God! what have I done, that this burden of your death should rest upon me! You! whom I saw so fresh and lovely, not six weeks gone, entering the gates of Paris—you, whom I now see dying!" and with the words she burst into a fit of violent and agonizing sorrow, so loud and convulsive that the old clergyman arose, and signing to the others to sit still, half led, half lifted her out of the chamber—but Alice looked at Chaloner, and said—

"Is she not noble—is she not noble?"

"Yes!" he replied: "very noble!"

"And so are you," she answered, very quickly, as if afraid that he would interrupt her. "You two are the two noblest beings on the face of the earth. The noble should mate with the noble—she in her great, brave impulses, you in your grand composure! Nay, do not interrupt me, Henry, nor shake your head so sadly. I do not say now, nor to-morrow, but when this sorrow shall have passed away. It is my last wish—my last earthly hope! I know she would make you happy—I know I would rather see her mistress of my Woolverton than any woman living. There, do not answer me. Forgive me if I have hurt you—think of it, and Heaven bless you!"

Chaloner did not answer her, but he sat and mused deeply: and though, at the time, he thought of it as a wild fancy, and impossible, years brought to pass a change in his feelings. Alice, whose strength had been failing rapidly, was quite exhausted by the vehemence of her own late utterance, and, feeling that she was almost gone, cried—

"Henriette, Henriette—come to me quick—quick! quick!" and as she came, she drew her down close to her bosom, and kissed her eyes and lips. "Thank you," she said—"may God deal with you as you have dealt with us! Bless you—farewell! Now, Henry, kiss me—dear, dearest Henry! and Isabella—call her—where is Isabella?"

"Here," she replied, as, having calmed herself, she again returned—"I am here, Alice."

"Where—where? I do not see you—my eyes are growing dim—your faces all are leaving me! Where are you, Isabella?"

"Here, dearest," she replied, taking her by the hand; "do you not feel me?"

"Yes; kiss me," and as she stooped to do so, she tried to whisper, but spoke quite loud, for her numbed ear had lost its sense: "If ever he ask aught of you, for my sake grant it, Isabella."

The beautiful girl had no clue whereby to guess her meaning, and fancied that her mind was wandering, and that she thought of Wyvil; she made, therefore, no reply, but pressed her hand in silence. Alice sank back at once upon the pillow; and though for nearly half an hour she continued to breathe, she did not speak, or move, or unclose her eyes any more—till suddenly she sat erect, and looking upward with a sublime and rapt expression, cried out in a clear and musical voice—"Hush! listen! Do you not hear the harp and the seraphic strains? Glory—glory be to God in the highest! Hush! hush!" and with her arms extended, and her eyes radiant with a vision that, perhaps, in that dread moment, pierced into realms beyond mortality, her pure soul passed away, and the old clergyman saw that she was no more; and as she fell down on the bed, he said in a high, sonorous tone, as if of triumph, "I heard a voice from heaven, saying unto me, Write: from henceforth blessed are the dead who die in the Lord; even so saith the Spirit, for they rest from their labors."

CHAPTER XXXVII.

The morning had already broken, when Alice Selby passed into another world; and the cold, gray light of the early dawn was mingled in the chamber of the dead with that of the waning lamps, which had burned all night long unheeded; and pale and haggard with the excitement and the agitation of those trying scenes, were the countenances of the weary watchers, and their hearts faint with care and sorrow. But now, when all was over, they withdrew — the women to seek some repose, for they were absolutely wearied out, and Chaloner to brood over the things that had passed, and to devour his own heart in silence. For, self-subdued though he was, by a habit which had grown upon him until it was now almost a second nature, his character had been originally fiery and vehement, and prone to bursts of sudden passion, and it had cost him no small labor or exertion to bring his temper under subjection to his reason. It was not his passions only against which he had at this time to contend, although there was very much to excite these in what had taken place, in the villanous, and, as he believed, cold-blooded treachery of Wyvil, by which the man he most esteemed in the world, and the only woman he had ever loved, had been brought, almost before his very eyes, the one to an unnatural, the other to a most cruel and untimely death; and many times his spirit had been strangely tempted to inflict summary and instant punishment upon the traitor. But this was not all; for although Henry Chaloner was by no means a fanatic, nor, in embracing the political creed of the puritans, had adopted their intolerant and bigoted religious tenets, it must be remembered that a species of wild superstition was a strong characteristic of the age, the country, and especially of the faction to which he was attached. His own mind was naturally of an imaginative turn, and how excellent soever, as related to fine arts and poetry, imagination may be deemed, it is assuredly, when applied to religious matters, the most deceitful and dangerous of attributes. Thus, though by no means a fanatic, neither a bigot nor a canter — neither deluded by the jargon of the day nor a deluder of others, he had imbibed some strange sentiments, and pondered over them till they had almost become opinions. No character of mortal man can be perfect, and this was the darkest blot on Chaloner's — a fancy had possessed his mind, long before the occurrence of the events which seemed to stir that fancy into action, that men, their passions, and their very crimes, were instruments of the Almighty to punish the faults and avenge the sufferings of others; and further, that there was a species of dark inspiration, a divine destiny, inborn and felt within, compelling him who was its subject to the performance of whatever it suggested.

In his more calm and reasonable moments, when no extraneous influence was brought to bear upon this perilous creed, he was wont to half doubt the nature of this inspiration, and altogether to dispute, if not deny, its operation as justifying the deeds of the individual. But now, with his passions all excited to the utmost, and all bearing with concentrated power upon this weak point in his judgment, he was fearfully disturbed, and strongly goaded forward to the perpetration of a deed which, had he been one whit less strong in his religious creed, he would have surely considered it his bounden duty to perform — the avenging, namely, with the sword the deaths of his friends and kindred. That was an age when the duel was resorted to on the most slight and trivial grounds — when no honorable man of the world would have dreamed for an instant of omitting to call out a rival, on the most venial provocation, to the arbitrament of blood — when no man whatever, unless a cripple or infirm by years, would have admitted the possibility of refusing such an invitation.

Not one of these, however, was Henry Chaloner — his notions of religious duty were by far too severe, his mind too firmly balanced, and his whole character too strictly conscientious, to be deterred from doing that which he considered right, or to be led into doing that which he thought wrong, by all the sophistry of the world united. Wronging or insulting none, there was no risk that he should ever be called to account himself; and proved as he was to be the bravest of the brave — tried in some six pitched battles, and skirmishes almost innumerable — bearing the scars of eight wounds on his body, he could well afford to overlook the arrogance of foppish courtiers, or the presumption of boy-braggarts — and many a time he had done so; and, for a wonder, the world's opinion had sustained him: and though he had treated with scorn only, more than one petty insult, suffering the authors to creep off unpunished — not a doubt, not a shadow of a shade, hung over Chaloner's unblemished courage. This was a different case, however, and far different did it work on his strong mind — strong even in its weakness. He had seen his dear friend, the man to whom he had ever looked up as his father, slain almost by the hand, indisputably by the deed, of this base person; whose treachery had blighted also the best and brightest hopes of his existence. He saw the murderer of both — escaped, at large, beyond the reach of any earthly punishment! His morbid fancy pictured him, perchance, laughing in his secret soul over the ruin he had wrought, and making mockery, with his wild companions, of her whom he had slaughtered by the sword of her own best affections. He set his teeth hard, as the thought occurred to him, and walked, grasping his sword-hilt, to and fro the room in fearful perturbation. For, although when conversing with Madame de Gondi, his clear mind had rejected the idea as absurd, of judging mortal happiness by the scale of mortal success — although he could then distinctly see that this same man, this very Wyvil, must of necessity be wretched even here; he could no longer satisfy himself with the same reasoning — he could no longer obtain the same end. Wyvil seemed to him now the proud, triumphant, and exulting villain — the wretch escaped from all the whips of justice, beyond all reach of mortal punishment. His mind was clear no longer — the cloud of passion had dimmed its perception, and through that cloud, loomed up gigantically the monstrous combinations of fantasy and superstition.

All that day long he fasted — no food had passed his lips since breakfast on the previous morning, nor any drink save water; nor had he closed his eyes in sleep — but without sitting, or even pausing, he walked up and down the floor, with uneven and irregular steps, lashing himself — while he believed even that he was pondering gravely — into a species of solemn fury. The shadows changed upon the dial, and noon succeeded morning, and the evening twilight darkened upon the afternoon, and still he strode backward and forward, the rafters cracking under his heavy foot, and the old servants, who had never witnessed such a move before since they had served him, marvelling what should next be. Watching, and fasting, and the terrible excitement, when added to the agony of grief, had for the time completely overmastered him. His better mind was utterly obscured and hidden. He had at first striven, and for a little while successfully, with the dark fantasy that crept upon him, whispering that he was the chosen instrument, appointed from above, to wreak the vengeance of the Lord upon the secret criminal. Had there been any human voice to speak to him, to back the small, still voice within —which, though half drowned by the trumpet-tongued suggestions of pride, and wrath, and superstition, and the overwhelming sense of wrong, still feebly warned him — he had come off victorious. As it was, more and more as hour succeeded hour, and darkness came at last to add its gloomy influence to the sad colors that already steeped his soul, the heavy superstition grew upon him, till he convinced himself at last — sad truth! that it should be so easy, even for a good man, to convince himself that wrong is right, and passion principle — till he convinced himself at last that it was a solemn and a holy duty, enjoined upon him by a supernatural will, which he had neither right nor power to resist, to call this murderer forth to the field of arms, and there to slay him as a great sin-offering and sacrifice.

It may seem strange that a mind so well balanced as that

which I have represented Chaloner to possess, should have been mastered by so vain and absurd a superstition. But we must recollect, that the age wherein these things occurred was an age of anomalies and wonders; that men and women — wise men and virtuous women! — in those days did things, undoubtingly, unblushingly, which now would stamp them fools and harlots; that mortal passions had the widest scope, and common sense and reason the least sway; that fifty things were admitted and believed as truths, which the wisest schoolboy of the nineteenth century could prove to be fallacies; and, above all, that the minds of men were greatly agitated and disturbed on matters both of politics and religion, as generally is the case in the commencement of what may be termed an era of transition. That Henry Chaloner was a wise man and a good man, according to the wisdom and the virtue of the day in which he lived, is an unquestionable truth; but he was neither better nor wiser than the best of the children of his generation. He was not that monster of a poetic fancy, a being of unerring instincts, and unblemished virtue. Many things combined to bring about this hallucination — for it was clearly an hallucination, and one of a very dangerous character; and had it been indulged, or carried much beyond the point which it had now attained, it speedily might have degenerated into a religious frenzy — but that they did so combine is certain. At many moments of his life, he would unquestionably have denounced the very part which he was about to play, as the highest insanity, or laughed at as the height of folly. Nevertheless, he now yielded to the impulses that were hot within him, and, fancying himself the instrument of a great, superior will, became the dupe and tool of his own little passions. He had prayed several times in the course of the day, and to his fervid and imaginative temperament, the very act of prayer, by stimulating the religious sentiment, had increased rather than diminished the morbid action of his mind, and rendered him more confident in the right — more resolute to the performance of his self-imposed solemn duty. And now that his determination was once taken, all the disturbance and anxiety of his manner vanished. He washed and dressed himself with care, arranging his locks, which he wore long and waving, though not exactly after the curled and flowing fashion of the cavaliers, with much attention; clad himself in a full suit of the deepest mourning, black broadcloth faced with silk, with neither velvet nor embroidery nor lace, but only a broad band of cambric round his neck, and plain ruffles of the same at his wrists; and summoning Frank Norman, desired him to be in attendance in an hour with three horses and another servant. Then he caused supper to be served; and, although alone, he sat down to his meat with a good appetite, and ate, and drank his wine — more than one kind of which was set before him, with evident appreciation. He even spoke a few words cheerfully to the old steward who attended him, saying that he had resigned his office, as envoy to the Hague, and should return to England within a few days, more or less. With him, the strife was to make up his mind — the anxiety, to decipher the right law of conduct; that once done, all else was a mere thing of course. No weak irresolution ever marred his action — no paltry fear of consequences, or doubt of results, so much as once occurred to him. Resolved to do a thing, he ever went right on and did it! and that had been the one great secret of his success in life — that, acting ever upon principles which he knew, or conscientiously believed to be right and true, he always brought a clear head, unencumbered by any doubt or hesitancy, to the execution; and while other men were planning, he was doing. Thus, in the present instance, though it cost him much anxiety and thought before he could resolve upon his principle of conduct, and though it must be admitted that he had reasoned himself into a false conviction and an evil resolution; yet once determined, he never cast another thought to the execution! It never once so much as entered his mind, that Wyvil, whom he knew to be a brave man and a master of his weapon, might chance to be the victor. It never appeared possible to him that he could fail. He was the destined and appointed instrument, the unconcerned avenger of his kindred, the weapon in the hands of the Almighty! He had no wrath, no angry feelings against the wretch whom he was about to slay as a sacrifice, not to the vain punctilio of a code, but to a jealous God! Nay, at that very moment he would have unsheathed his sword to rescue him from peril at any other hand — he would have braved the fiery conflagration, or rushed into the molten torrent, to save his life this minute, that he himself might take it in the next. Had he been one iota more a fanatic, or less a gentleman and soldier, he would have stabbed him to the heart, and deemed assassination virtue! As it was, such an idea came not near him, nor any other, except to call him to the field with equal arms, and slay him there in solemn combat. And, with that end in view, he took the measure of his sword with a strip of paper, and when his horses were announced, buckled his riding-cloak about him, and went forth as tranquilly to meet his mortal foe as if he had been preparing for a banquet.

CHAPTER XXXVIII.

A MAN, more thoroughly and utterly wretched than Marmaduke Wyvil, existed not perhaps on the whole face of the world, peopled although it is with wretches. There was not in his heart one spark of consolation, one gleam of hope; not even that last stay and resource of the miserable — the consciousness of right, the sense of self-respect. His schemes had failed, deep laid as they appeared, even in the moment of their consummation. He was completely ruined; and, to his own soul he could not deny it, ruined entirely by his own knavery and folly. He had destroyed the man who had preserved his own life, at the risk of all most dear to him; for, though he knew not all the circumstances of Mark Selby's death, and though he strove to palliate it to his own accusing conscience, he was yet perfectly aware that he was the cause of his decease. He had broken the heart of the woman he loved best, and to whom he owed the deepest gratitude; who loved him with a love almost surpassing that of woman; who might—who *would* have rendered him the happiest of men, but for his own inconstancy and treasonable falsehood! He knew not, it is true, that she was dead; but, like all others who beheld her fainting in the cathedral, he had seen that the seal of death was on her brow already; and, had he not seen it, he felt but too surely, amid the dread condemnation of his own inner heart, that Alice Selby was a plant of too frail growth, and of too slight a tenure on this mortal soil, to endure such a shock, so rude and sudden as that which he had given to her most vital sensibilities! And what had been the consequence of all this crime and falsehood? what, but the very demolition of all his own hopes and prospects? This present means all lost already, his chances of recovering them in France, or of returning home with honor—either of which alternative was in his reach three little days ago—cast to the winds! His very reputation questioned! his name for chivalry and honor blighted! It might have been, had success crowned his wickedness; had he gained by his treason the lovely bride and the vast wealth for which he had played so foully—it might have been then, in the exultation of his retrieved fortunes, the fruition of present pleasure, and the anticipation of a proud and ambitious future, that he could have drowned the voice of conscience—have blotted from his memory the thoughts of those who had so nobly succored him in his hour of need, and whom he had so repaid.

But now, when everything was lost—when, pressed and persecuted by his creditors, forsaken by all those who had consorted with him in his better days, looked upon coldly by the king, scorned and despised by those who would, a week before, have courted him—the memory of his past sins, enhanced by his present misery, was constantly before him; conjuring up dread remorseful phantoms, that threw a fixed and moody gloom, not far removed from settled melancholy, alike over his waking and his sleeping hours. He had not left his apartment, and, in truth, he dared not leave it, since the moment when he hurried homeward, baffled and despairing, from the very ceremonial to which he had so long looked forward as to the consummation of his triumph. His servants, all recent hirelings, except the valet Clement, and his groom, a Yorkshireman, from the North-Riding — for both whom he had sent to England immediately after his arrival in Paris — had deserted him so soon as they discovered that his fortunes were no more in the ascendant; and these two remained stanch to their employer, from ancient habit, and from a downright instinctive fidelity — more like that of the canine species than of the human race — which rendered them reluctant to desert a falling man, rather than from any real love or esteem for a master, whose faults were tainted with that mean and truckling falsehood so odious to the English character. His doors had been besieged by angry and impatient creditors; and he had passed the night following that fatal ceremonial, and the day which succeeded it, in an alternation of despondent fits, and violent bursts of nervous irritable restlessness, that bordered closely upon downright madness — now sitting with his head propped upon his hands, gazing before him into vacancy, with a dim, lack-lustre eye, as though the atmosphere were peopled with dread forms, for ever present — now hurrying to and fro the spacious room, raving aloud, and uttering strange imprecations, till, worn-out and exhausted by his own violence, he would again sink down into his chair and resume his moody meditations. His meals had been prepared for him with sedulous care, by his faithful servant, who had ventured even to press him to his meat, and to argue with him on the foolishness of such impotent and child-like passion. But it was all in vain — the man's remonstrances were received either with an apathy that left it doubtful whether he comprehended what was said to him, or with rejoinders so impatient and ill-tempered, that they soon quieted all interference. He had, it is true, tried to force his appetite — had compelled himself to swallow one or two morsels — but the meat would not go down; and the man, who had often devoured with zest and real appetite a hard crust of bread, washed down with wretched brandy, while within point-blank range of hostile cannon-shot — which, although falling thick around him, had not the power to spoil his stomach — now loathed the most delicious *consommés* and *ragouts*, cowed and disheartened by the creatures of his own conscience. But in proportion as he felt no hunger, so had a fiery and incessant thirst tormented him; and though he had drunk vastly more of the strongest and most generous wines, than at another time would have sufficed to lay him senseless, the liquor seemed to possess no power at all upon his system, so thoroughly was its effects superseded by the terrific and unnatural excitement of his brain and nerves.

It was a cold, raw, gusty evening, and a fire had been burning on the hearth all day; but it had for some time become very low, and only a few half-dying embers cast a red waning light over the deep jaws of the large arched chimney. The evening had set in quite darkly, and it was growing very cold; yet so great was the heat and fire within him, that when Clement brought lights, and would have replenished the fire, Wyvil insisted that the room was stifling hot, and the air thick and murky; and positively forbade his heaping on the wood which he had fetched for that purpose. The man shrugged in his shoulders, but said nothing; and continued fidgeting about the room for some time, as if unwilling to leave Marmaduke alone in that fearful mood; lowering the heavy curtains over the long windows, which reached quite down to the floor, opening with casements upon the narrow ledge of projecting stone-work, unguarded by any balcony or balustrade — setting the chairs in order, and arranging the various articles which lay scattered on the tables, until a sharp and peremptory order forced him, although evidently anxious and unwilling, to quit the apartment. As soon as he had shut the door, Wyvil arose from his chair again, and began traversing the room with a fretful, hasty gait, not unlike that of the caged hyena; muttering the while about the heat and closeness of the air; gasping as if for breath, and pausing more than once to drain a goblet of the racy Burgundy, which stood on the table. At last he stopped before the window farthest from the hearth, and pushing back the curtain, threw the tall casement open, and then stood for some minutes gazing out into the quiet night; for the weather was so unpromising and cheerless that the streets were almost deserted, and so few sounds were abroad, that from the ear alone it would have been difficult to imagine that he was in the heart of a great city.

"Ay!" he said, "this is calm—this is refreshing—the cool, tranquil night air! That closed room's atmosphere is like the vapor of a seven-times heated furnace. Strange that the air should be so sultry in November! Yet it may be," he added, after a minute's thought—"it may be that this heat, like the quenchless thirst that consumes me, has its seat in my own bosom! I am sick—sick of this world—and aweary!" and leaving the window, he let the curtain once more fall across the opening; but forgot, or perhaps intentionally omitted, to close the casement. "Sick of it," he continued, in a doubtful, meditating tone: "then why not leave it? It were but one little thrust—one gasp—one moment's struggle! Nay; I have seen hundreds of men die without so much as one struggle! There was that roundhead fellow I shot through the head at Edgehill—one moment he was charging his pike at my horse's poitrel, and the next he was as motionless upon his back, as if he had been dead a week! I do not think his eyelids winked after the ball sunk into his forehead—I think I can see him now—*he* felt nothing! Then why not? why not?" and, as he spoke, he took down one of the horseman's pistols that hung above the mantel-piece; tried it with the ramrod, and finding that it was loaded, opened the pan and shook the priming out, and freshened it from a small powder-flask; and then cocked the weapon. "It were the better way—one pang!—perchance not one! and then peace!" and, with the word, he raised the muzzle slowly, till it was level with his temples, and held it there quite steadily for nearly half a minute—but then he raised the left hand to his brow, and clasped it tightly with his fingers as if to still the throbbing; while the right, holding the murderous implement, sank gradually to his side.

"Peace? peace?" he murmured next, in a tone of indecision —"that is it—is it peace? that which cometh after—or are this heat, and thirst, and agony, but foretastes of the things that shall be? There is, methinks, a fearful scripture that tells of the tongue of one so scathed and tormented, that he craved but a drop, such as should trickle from the tip of a finger dipped in water! Strange that this should now cross my mind, that has not heard or thought of it for years! I would I knew—I would I knew if I should see these faces, that look at me always—that pale, mild, studious countenance of the old man, with his gray locks all blood-sprinkled — and why should they be bloody? There was not so much blood in all his veins, if I had smitten him. But I shed not his blood — nay! but it was not shed at all! Tush! this is mere dreaming! Shame on thee! courage, Marmaduke! courage! Ha! cowardice? Fear of the present! fear of the future! cowardice — rank cowardice both ways: No! I—I dare not do it!" and he let down the hammer of the pistol, and hung it up again beside its fellow; and, still grasping his fevered brow with his left hand, resumed his oft-repeated walk, but with a slower step, and an air more contemplative and less nervous than before.

"I dare not!" he repeated; "yet when before did it ever fail me? and what now? what else is left to me?"

Before, however, he had time to answer that question, even to his own mind, the trampling of horses came loudly to his ear from the courtyard below, and he heard a clear, sonorous voice inquiring for Major Wyvil. He went and looked out of the window, but so dark was the night, and so dim the lantern over the door, that he could only distinguish the outlines of three figures, all on horseback. An answer was given by the old porter, whose mumbling tones reached not so high as to be audible; but that it was affirmative, was evident by the leaping of the principal person to the ground as soon as he had the reply—and, at the same time, the jingling of the spurs and the clash of his steel scabbard on the pavement, assured Marmaduke that he was a gentleman, and possibly a soldier, who sought for him.

"Ha!" he said, "this is well. Now would I wager my best horse against a mule of Arragon, that that is the bearer of a cartel, either from that misproud old doting baronet, or, better yet, from some one of those prating popinjays of France. Heaven send it may!" and his eye flashed, as it had not done for many an hour. The spurred step mounted the staircase, and paused at the door, and in a moment Clement came into the room, announcing that a gentleman was without, asking to speak with Major Wyvil.

"Who is it, Clement?" inquired Marmaduke, half-doubtfully.

"I don't know, sir—he refused to give his name. Yet I have heard his voice before: though when, I can not just now recollect."

"Are you sure, that it is a gentleman, at all; and not an archer, or a sergeaut in disguise?"

"Oh, no! it is a gentleman, and a soldier—I saw his hand, with a fine diamond ring upon his finger, although he hid his face from me. But it was not the diamond: no sergeant of police or archer ever had such a hand."

"Admit him then at once," said Wyvil; and the next minute a tall man entered, wearing a slouched black hat with a falling feather, dressed in deep mourning, and holding a lap of his cloak over the lower part of his face, until Clement had left the room and closed the door after him—then he withdrew the mantle; and Wyvil, whose eyes had been fixed on him with eager expectation, started back exclaiming—

"General Chaloner!"

"Even so, Major Wyvil!" replied Henry, uncovering himself as he spoke.

"And to what?" asked Marmaduke, recovering himself with a little effort, for he had been surprised; and moreover, though he knew not why, he never felt entirely at his ease in the presence of that man—"to what circumstances do I owe the honor of again seeing General Chalonor in my poor lodging? I trow, it is not as a visit of courtesy, or a call of pleasure?" and he endeavored to veil his discomposure under a sneer.

"It is not, sir," Chaloner answered coolly, "except so far

as courtesy must ever have a share in these matters. In truth, I have little pleasure in your company—"

"You might have spared yourself the trouble then, and me the annoyance of this untimely interruption," returned Wyvil, haughtily; "sending your wishes by a more proper messenger."

"You are wrong, sir; I could not do so, or I would," said Henry, perfectly calm and unmoved by his insulting manner; "for my purpose being to hand you this, the measure of my sword, and demand a meeting from you at the *Pres aux Clercs*, or whatever other place you may appoint, at the dawn of day to-morrow; and as I propose, that we should meet without seconds, save only a servant on each side to see fair play—for where is the use of involving others, who have no share in our quarrel, in its consequences—I could not send a gentleman to bear my cartel; and of course would not send it by a menial."

Scarcely ten minutes had passed, since Wyvil, in the pride and fierceness of his heart, expressed a wish that his visiter might be the bearer of a cartel—and when he so spoke, he really did wish it; and, perhaps, had it been any other man on earth than he who it was that summoned him to fight, he would have felt something akin to rapture at the opportunity of banishing, by so vital an excitement, the conscience-conjured phantoms that made his solitude dreadfully populous. But as it was, he liked it not, and he hesitated as he answered. It was not that he feared—no! all deficient, despicably deficient as he was in moral courage—there was no braver animal on earth; no one more full of that high, dashing, and impulsive gallantry, that makes it a far harder thing to sit by a mere spectator, than to rush as a leading actor into the fiercest fray. He had no dread of death at all, unless from his own hand. It was not long before that, by his own hand actually, he had thought to die; and perhaps, but for the timely interruption, might so have died, in his greater dread of life. Yet now, now, when the very circumstance had come to pass, for which he had been wishing, he shrunk from it.

"I knew not," he replied, with a tongue that almost faltered, "that we had any quarrel. I do not comprehend the meaning of your claim; and, though I am the last man living who would refuse an invitation founded upon cause, I may say, without boasting, that I have proved myself so often to fear nothing, that I can well afford to decline a causeless challenge!"

"I thought," replied Chaloner, "from all I have ever heard, that Major Wyvil was less scrupulous! But since his conscience is so strict, I can assure him I *have* cause, deep cause, for this proceeding. Nay, farther, that it is forced upon me by no will of my own, and even, in some sort, against my principle. But so it is! meet me, you must; by my hand you must fall to-morrow!"

"Are you, then, the disposer of events?" asked Wyvil, almost with a shudder, and so tamely that he himself was astonished at his humbleness; "or how can you foretell the fate of battles? My sword is as keen as yours! my hand—"

"Trembles!" said Henry Chaloner, "and how should it not tremble, steeped as it is knuckle-deep in innocent and friendly gore! heaped as it is, with foul and festering sin; weighed down by conscious treason; loaded with the pure life of one who loved you, saved you, sacrificed all for you! and for her love, you—slew her!"

"There is no blood on my hand save what was shed in battle, and for a righteous cause," Wyvil began, but Henry fiercely interrupted him.

"Was it then for a righteous cause—was it then from a battle-field that Mark Selby's blood cried out to God for vengeance? And lo! he has appointed his avenger!"

"Mark Selby's blood! What mean you! I shed no blood of his—no blood of his *was* shed—"

"If not with the strong hand, with the murderous heart, thou didst slay him! and his blood *was* shed! Man! man! with these eyes—with these abhorrent eyes, I saw the walls, the floor bedabbled with the thick gore where he fell! I saw the mild benevolent face, the venerable hairs smeared with the witness of thy crime—and wilt thou dare deny it? Fool! fool! the servant had a tongue who called thee to his chamber!

had ears, which heard the words which passed between ye — the shameful words that slew him! had eyes, which saw the master he adored, steeped in the life-blood oozing from his aged veins — ay! dying — dying by your deed! when he returned, and you had gone forth from the house which you had plunged in sorrow. Now, then — now, then — did you not slay him? Is not his blood upon your head — upon your soul?"

Wyvil made no reply, but cast himself into a chair, and covering his face with both his hands, fell into a fit of convulsive sobbings, though not a tear flowed from his stony eyes, while all his sinewy frame shook with the terrible intensity of his passionate remorse — but not for that did the accuser cease from his dread appeal.

"Is not this murder? and if it were not so, how died sweet Alice Selby? How, I say, died she, that her blood is not on your soul. Was it a natural decay that bore her off, whom I saw not three months ago as lovely as the morning, as blithe as the summer wind which wooed her tresses? Was it a casual stroke — a sudden fever — that cut her off, before whose beauty, I have heard say, a king bowed scarce a week past? or was it — was it, I say, the canker planted in the heart of the rose, by the vile worm that crawled into that sanctuary, and marred the beauty that preserved it? Man! If you be indeed a man, that do such things and yet live — man! at the risk of her own, and what she valued more, her father's life, did she preserve you from the Ironsides — who never yet did so righteous deed, as they had then performed, if they had trod your human clay beneath their horses' hoofs into the mire that had been so polluted. Man! for your sake, she rejected one who would have died or made her happy. She gave you her invaluable love — the whole and single adoration of that angelic heart! and you betrayed — rejected — murdered her! Yet more! yet more! when she well knew your villany, your loathsome baseness, she gave you, from the highness of her own heart, the means to win her rival — and you — most miserable beast! — nay, but I will not shame the honest beasts of God's creation by so naming you! — and you, base, Judaslike betrayer, profited by her own bounty to destroy her! Have I yet said enough—or must I more? Have I not cause? will you now fight? or are you coward also?"

"You have said enough," replied Wyvil, withdrawing his hands, and showing his face paler than monumental marble, "and you have caused—yet spare me, spare me the misery—the guilt of further bloodshed."

"Of further bloodshed?" said Chaloner, in an inquiring tone. "The wretch is distraught with abject terror—what bloodshed?"

"Force me not—force me not, for the love of Heaven! to shed thine likewise."

"Mine? my blood? thou shed my blood?" exclaimed Chaloner; "thou? Thou fool! miserable fool! Know you not that I call you out to slay you—chosen—appointed—yea! inspired, to do this judgment? and think you, that your sword can harm one hair of me, thrice armed in innocence and virtue, and thrice-threefold, as the predestined instrument of His great vengeance? I call thee not to fight, but to die! to give blood for blood! to make atonement, with thy sinful life, for the lives that thou hast taken! Think not to shield thyself, therefore by that subterfuge. I shall not, can not die by your hand; and lo! I tell you, not of myself, but of the spirit that possesses me—even the spirit of Him, who alone can not lie—you die the death to-morrow! Will you fight now? or must I brand you first, and proclaim you slave and coward, till every corner in all Europe shall ring with your shame—till 'dastardly as Wyvil' shall be a byword and a proverb! and then batoon you in the public streets, wheresoever I may find you, till you die like a slave and villain under the bastinado. Will you fight now?"

"Yon leave me no choice," answered Wyvil, gloomily; "but I take Heaven to witness, that this encounter is of your seeking, and the guilt of it yours! If you fall, on your own head be it!"

"Amen!" said Chaloner. "But fear not on that account, for I shall *not* fall! At five o'clock, on foot, and with one servant, will I call for you, here at this house! There lies the measure of my blade — at five! Remember!"

He said no more, nor awaited for an answer, but bowed his head, left the room, strode down the creaking staircase, and mounting his horse, rode deliberately to his lodgings; and within half an hour was buried in the tranquillity of calm and dreamless slëep.

CHAPTER XXXIX.

No words can describe the state of Marmaduke, when he again found himself alone. Even while Chaloner was there, taunting and lashing him with his indignant eloquence, he had been dreadfully shocked and horror-stricken by the tidings he had brought him; and it was his pride only, that even then prevented him from yielding to the full agonies of his remorse and despair. For he was very far, indeed, from being in his character all evil — few men indeed are so — and Wyvil, had there been one or two traits in his mind which were wanting, might have been as conspicuous for good, as he now had become for ill. The great want, the great weakness of his character, was a lack of resolute, energetic will — of an established principle. His impulses were, for the most part, good and noble, and the resolves founded on those impulses right in the main, and honorable — but the misfortune was, that the impulse was immediately succeeded by another, and the first resolve supplanted by a new determination; so that from the one radical defect of vacillation, there grew up with the growth of his mind inconstancy, and inconsistency, and falsehood. He never, perhaps, in his life, had committed any crime with deliberate premeditation; but suffering his passions of the moment to sweep him into difficulty after difficulty, he was brought constantly into positions from which he only could be extricated by a falsehood or a crime; and then he would say and do things the very possibility of which he would have ridiculed an hour before, and the commission of which he repented, perhaps, before they were concluded. He was, in short, a man whose intentions were ever better than his actions; as must be the case always with those who act from impulse not from principle. Had he been, strange as it may seem to say, a greater villain, he would not have committed one of the offences which rendered him so mean a wretch in the eyes of others, so miserable in his own — and when he had committed them, he would have smiled upon the ruin he had wrought and lapped himself in his own security. A thorough villain, acting with a bad view, would never have been guilty of the strange inconsistent folly by which, while really as much in love as he could possibly be with one woman, he had been induced to flutter and disport himself about another, till gratifying neither passion nor ambition, he betrayed both, and finally lost both, and himself likewise. That he could never have been an originally and radically vicious man — that nature had not, in his composition, mixed the ingredients necessary to make up a thorough villain — was now evident enough, from the tremulous paroxysm of remorseful torture into which he was thrown. He flung himself upon his knees, and strove to pray, but the words seemed to choke him.

"I can not — I can not!" he exclaimed; "how should I? Oh, my God! how should I pray to thee? Repentance! how can *I* repent, whose deeds are done and registered already? I can believe — I can believe right easily — that, for the thief upon the cross — that, for Cain even, there might be pardon! but for me, no! no! It is impossible! and I must on! on! on! deeper, yet deeper, into blood and murder!" and he sat down and buried his head for a while in his palms, and then rose up, muttering, "No! I will not — I dare not meet him! Truly, he said, there was already too much blood upon my soul! I will fly — fly! but whither? Wretch! wretch! there is no spot, no foot of the wide world, to which I can escape; where my own name, my own black deeds will not ring in my ears, and drown my soul with their eternal condemnation! And how fly — how? with but one rouleau left of all my princely fortune? No! here am I fettered down — meshed as completely as the fly in the devouring spider's toil — hemmed in, as the stag at bay, with the whole world hooting for the savage pack that bay about me! Well! it is best so! It is fate! destiny! What fools we are — what fools! to dream ourselves free agents — we, whose whole course of life, from the cradle to the grave, is but one chain of chances, circumstances over which we have no control, binding us in their adamantine links, dragging us onward, where they will, now with the speed of the tornado, now slow and scarcely felt, but still omnipotent — inevitable! Why struggle, then? why flutter our weak wings, where every new convulsion but cumbers us with a new chain? Be it so! I, at least, will strive no longer — I, at least, will go, henceforth, where fate leads and fortune. If they have driven me to bay, let them beware the horn! I will die, now that all is over, bravely! And yet why die at all? why should my spirit sink, or my heart falter, at meeting this mad fanatic — for mad he must be, thus to play prophet and avenger? Pshaw! have I not crossed swords with Fairfax, and come off unscathed? and unhorsed the butcher Harrison — both better men, I trow, than this precise and preaching Puritan? Ho! Clement! without there! bring me more wine, and heap the fire! it is cold, and I am still athirst!" And as the man came, he addressed him, speaking hastily — "Clement," he said, "thou art a faithful fellow, and hast well served me. Now, I have one more service for thee —perchance it may be the last. I stand pledged to give General Chaloner the meeting, at five o'clock to-morrow, for mortal combat in *Près aux Clercs*. We are to be attended each but by one servant, as a witness. You will go with me, Clement? If I should chance to fall, you shall be my executor; and to secure your escape in case of trouble, here are a hundred louis — the last my purse holds at present — if I survive, there are bright days before us. You will go with me?"

"Surely I will, sir," answered the servant; "else were I a

poor Englishman, to leave my master at a pinch like that. What weapons shall I take — my sword and buckler."

"No weapons, Clement," replied his master, "you go but as a witness — not to fight. Now, my good fellow, heap up the fire, leave me good store of wood, and let me not lack wine — and then begone to bed, for you must be on foot by five at the latest. And now good night — get thee away to bed!"

His orders were performed immediately; the fire blazed up on the old hearth, and several flasks of wine stood ready on the board, strangely contrasted with some six or seven swords of different lengths and sizes, the steel blades glittering blue and cold, beside the crimson wine, which Wyvil was engaged in measuring. "Ay! this will do," he exclaimed at last, as he found one which matched exactly the strip of paper that Chaloner had left. "I am very glad of it — it is my best blade — and a good omen too — I never used it, save when our arms prevailed!" and as he spoke, he tried its temper on the floor, bending it nearly double, and suffering it to spring back at once, which it did, brilliantly clear and elastic. He then wiped it carefully with his cambric kerchief, before he consigned it to the velvet-covered scabbard, and made two or three graceful thrusts in carte and tierce with the sheathed weapon; and as he laid it on the side-table, "This, and my art to boot," he said, in a tone of exultation — "and may the Lord have mercy on his soul" — but after a moment's pause, he amended the sentence, by adding the words — "who falls to-morrow! And yet — what right have I to call on Him for mercy?" he continued, relapsing again into his fearful and despondent gloom. "For me he has no mercy, else would he not haunt me with these faces! They were gone but a while ago, and now they are everywhere around me! pale, wan, reproachful faces! Tush! I will not be thus the fool of my own fancies! Let us see, if this will not banish them!" He poured out, and quaffed four or five glasses in succession of the strong, rich Burgundy, and stirred the logs on the hearth into a hot, fierce blaze, which filled every corner of the room with cheerful light; then he looked around him with a half-fearful gaze, and said, "They have vanished—they never brook a steady and determined eye—yet it is passing strange how they return for ever! and passing strange it was, that I should see blood on his face and locks, when I knew not that any blood had been spilt—that looks not like mere fancy! the empty phantoms of a guilty conscience! And yet why guilty?" he went on, sometimes conversing with himself in a low, smothered tone, and sometimes merely meditating and arguing with his own mind in silence: "Surely it was all fate—all fate or chance! I sought her not—it was not my fault, that she sat there in the fish-house, as I rode down the hill; it was not my fault that she called to me in her tenderness of heart, and saved me from the Puritans, and hid me in her father's house, and tended me, till love grew upon us both, and has at last made both so wretched! No! it was fate—all fate! and I am guiltless." Meanwhile, he continued to apply himself continually to the wine, which now appeared to take some hold on him, for his face began to get strangely flushed, though it had been before as pale as marble; and the veins on his brow were fearfully disturbed, and his eyes had a wild and almost insane glare, as they wandered through the vacancy of the large room. Never was a more fearful spectacle, of a mind harassed and tormented by the stings of a conscience, which, despite all his attempts at self-delusion, persisted in pronouncing him miserably guilty! He spoke no more, however, but sat quite still, fixing his eyes steadily upon the blazing embers, while past events came to his memory so palpably, that he almost believed he saw them with his bodily vision. The last words he had uttered, struck a new chord; and a long, long array of pictures came crowding one by one upon his soul with terrible distinctness. The gray and misty evening when he first saw her—the sandy road winding down the steep hill—the clump of shadowy beeches on the right hand—the swampy woodland on the left—the sudden angle, and the scene that then flashed upon his eyes—the ivy-covered bridge, and the small fishing-house, and the fair, lovely creature standing upon the platform, and beckoning him the road of safety! All! everything was clear and tangible as when it happened—every word that she spoke, every graceful gesture with which she led him along the tangled deer-path; the very tones of her soft silvery voice, the very touch of her warm hand, was present to him. The scene changed, and he lay in the rude loft of the boat-house, with the harsh threats of the Puritans echoing under the low vault, and the glare of their torches filling the nook in which he lay with smoky radiance, while ever and anon he seemed to hear her gentle notes, inspired with calm readiness of mind, diverting the suspicion of the vengeful searchers! Again, he was in the secret vault, with that young innocent face bending compassionately over him, soothing his weary hours by all that her simple skill in song, or music, or artless conversation could effect; ministering to his wants, anticipating every wish, whispering hope and consolation. He saw her, as the first deep blush irradiated her pale cheeks, as her soft eyes swam in a softer tenderness, as her sweet bosom heaved as though it would have burst, and her slight figure shook with the strong emotion, when he first whispered love, and her soul—though not yet her tongue—confessed it mutual! He heard her faint and interrupted words—like gentle music, half lost amid the breeze that wafts it—plighting her troth, and promising eternal confidence, and love, and fidelity! He saw her again in the hall of princes, resplendent in her unmatched beauty, worshipped by all that looked upon her, moving a star of a milder yet more glorious lustre amid that galaxy of queenly beauty. And once—once more—outstretched, pale, faint, and in the shadow of the grave, where she fell by an arrow from his quiver—that quiver whence the shaft was drawn that had slain her father! a witness of his wedding with another! And how had her troth been kept—how had her love been proved, and her fidelity? Betrayed—wronged—outraged—slighted, and scorned, and trampled on, how had she borne her burden? How been avenged upon the traitor? Betrayed, she had but the more trusted—wronged, she had but loved more—slighted, scorned, trampled on, she had been still—still faithful—till death had swallowed up fidelity! To sacrifice her all — to win at any price his happiness — to pardon, and to love, and to load with benefits — that was the sole revenge of Alice Selby! And all these things rushed in at once upon his guilty soul, like to an entering flood-tide — and more than all these things! For he could see the places, which she had made glad by her gentle presence — lonely, and desolate, and sad! He could see her chair, vacant in her wonted chamber; and her lute, hanging on the wall, never to sound again beneath her fairy touch; and her old favorite bloodhound, stalking among the deserted haunts of his beloved mistress, and filling the courts with his vain lamentations, and pining for her love daily. He could see the merry villagers upon the May-day green, despoiled of half their mirth by her absence, at whose coming all hearts bounded. He could see the old poor, crouching round their fireless hearths, deprived of more than half their scanty comforts by the loss of their benefactress. Now he could hear their mingled voices — the stern and angry tones of manhood, the feeble mutterings of old age, and the shrill babbling tongue of childhood — all swelling one great chorus of dread imprecation against him, her slayer! Yet more! — he saw yet more! His frenzied, fury-haunted conscience seemed to draw back the curtains of the grave — to dissipate the gloom of the death-vault — to lift the coffin-lid — and he saw — horror of horrors! the worm revelling, and corruption, the worm's sister, creeping! It was too horrible, even for his imagination, full fed as it had been with terror. As the dread image came before him, he sprang up — his hair bristling — his flesh quivering with a cold awe — his eyes fixed and glaring — his hand pointing —

"Ha!" he cried aloud, with a wild and frightful sound, half shriek, half laughter — "Ha! ha! who says that it is fancy? who says that she is dead! Lies! lies! Ye fool me not! I see her — there, with her mild eyes full of love and radiant tenderness — her sweet lips parted with a smile! Alice, my Alice — mine! I come — I come! Nay, leave me not — fly not! She beckons, I will follow — I am here, love — here! I will follow, if it were to the pit of ——"

As he uttered this wild rhapsody, he had rushed from the hearth by which he was sitting, as if in pursuit of something visible to his eyes only, to the further end of the room; and, as the last word left his lips — the most awful word that human lips can syllable — he plunged headlong, with arms outstretched, to grasp the fancied fugitive, against the curtain of the furthest window; it yielded to his furious impulse — there was no casement there to check his impetus — no balustrade to save him — one moment he was staggering in the vacant air — the next, he plunged, sheer downward, upon the granite pavement! It was but, indeed, as he said himself, one pang — perhaps not one! for his head smote the stones first, that he never moved, nor even groaned. He was dead — he had made no sign!

CHAPTER XL.

It was already morning, but not daylight, for a thick, heavy mist had come up from the Seine, and blotted the stars long before they set, and mustered in the narrow streets so densely, that even at noonday the sun would have had scarce power to make a dim and cloudy twilight through its dense fog-wreaths. So dark was it when Chaloner set forth from his lodging in the Rue Royale, that he was forced to desire Norman, whom he had chosen to accompany him, to take a lantern in his hand, in order to thread the murky lanes through which his course lay, unobstructed. The clocks were already striking five; and yet so dark and dismal was the morning, that not so much as a chance passenger was moving in the streets — the latest revellers were abed — the earliest artisan had not stirred forth. Not a chimney, as yet, sent up its smoke; not a window-shutter was unbarred, or a shop opened. Only at rare and distant intervals the light, just flickering ere it died, in the lantern of some *port cochère*, gave token that the hand of man had not long since been moving. Such was the morning, and such the aspect of the town, when Henry Chaloner arrived at the little court which separated the house wherein dwelt his destined victim, from the open street. He was dressed in his ordinary garb, except that he was wrapped closely in a thick mantle, to guard against the inclemency of the weather, and carried his sheathed rapier in his hand, Frank Norman moving a pace or two in advance of him with his lantern. Chaloner had not spoken a word since he left his lodging, so heavily was his mind burdened by the tremendous thoughts engendered of his present purpose; but as he entered the little gateway in the iron palisades —

"Lower your light," he said — "lower your light, Frank. There is a strange shadow on the pavement, there before you — if it be a shadow."

The man did as he was directed; and, as he did so, let fall the lantern, and started back with an exclamation of horror, for the first gleam had fallen full on the ghastly face and mutilated form of the dead man!

"What ails thee now?" cried Chaloner, entirely undaunted by the alarm of his servant, allthough he knew him to be as brave and true as steel against any mortal peril. "The light will be put out," and, as he spoke, he sprang forward and caught up the lantern, just in time to preserve the flickering candle it contained from extinction. "And now," he said, "what is it that so terrified thee? Ha!" he continued, as the reviving beam showed him the fearful object, all crushed, and maimed, and gory, that lay at his very feet; "there hath been murder here! who can it be?"

And stooping down over the grim and ghastly corpse, which lay upon its back, with the head toward him and the arms extended — for it had turned quite over in the fall — he recognised the features of the man whom he had left his home on that cheerless morning, to send to his account unhouseled and unshriven! One glance was enough for him — his work was anticipated — his crime prevented! for the cloud instantly was swept away from his mind, and in its true light he saw the deed which, to that very moment, he had been bent on doing. He understood the arrogance — the bold, presumptuous impiety of daring so much as to judge, much less to meddle with, the execution of the Lord's vengeance! He rose from his knee an abashed and altered man.

"This is the deed of the Most High," he said, "who hath preserved me from blood-guiltiness! I bow my knee, O Lord, humbly and thankfully — even the knee of my heart — in gratitude for thy great mercy; for thou hast saved me, thou only, from deadly and presumptuons sin. For what am I, O Lord, that I should judge — weak sinner that I am — of thine eternal judgment? or what am I, that I should think to execute thy vengeance on my brother? Alas! alas! that I have so much gone astray — so far forgotten that which, in the foolishness and vainglory of my heart, I thought I knew so well — even thy holy scripture! For what have I, or any man, to do, but to await thy time, as thou hast spoken —

"VENGEANCE IS MINE; I WILL REPAY, SAITH THE LORD!"

It was long ere the horror and the awe which these events — these terrible events! treading so quickly as they did each on the heel of the other, spread even through the volatile and gay society of Paris — passed away; but it was longer yet before the shadow and the gloom were banished from the mind of Chaloner. From that day forth he was a wiser, and, good as he had ever been, a better man; for never — from the hour when he shrank back in dread at finding his wish done by Him who needs no earthly minister to execute his judgment — did he again suffer his imagination to crush his better judgment; and in the place of confidence, he took humility and hope, to be the guides of his feet in the journey through this vale of shadows.

Years passed before his mind could bear to contemplate a second love. But in after-years, he did love again, and if not as ardently, certainly not less fondly nor less truly. And when, in after-days, he asked a favor at the hands of Isabella Oswald, she understood the meaning of the last words of Alice Selby; and partly for her sake, and partly at her own heart's bidding, she did not say him nay — and she became the mistress of Alice Selby's Woolverton, and never did she any wrong to the dying maiden's preference; for her high, noble, and brave impulses, and Chaloner's grand, calm, composure, did temper one another well — and they lived honorably, honored, and happy; and when their time was come, Chaloner did bequeath his tenantry and poor, as a solemn trust and sacred, to a noble and brave son.

There are but few more of the personages to be accounted for, who mingled in the thread of events which made the life of Alice Selby worthy this passing record.

John Sherlock, the stout yeoman, when he found after many a month of courtship, that Marian Rainsford would indeed never again marry, took to himself a buxom wife, and rode his hunter with the earl's hounds as boldly as the blithest knight of the shire, till his hair was as white as December's snow, while his frame was as stout, still, and as hardy, as the oak of his native country. A mossy grave-stone in the church-yard at Woolverton, tells the men of this generation, that "John Sherlock, farmer, died, anno Domini, 1711, having for 90 years loved God, honored the king, and injured no man."

Frank Norman, soon after Chaloner's return to England, wedded fair Cicely, the maid of the inn; and for full many a year maintained the credit of the Stag's Head, the representative of Marian Rainsford, its tranquil and respected hostess.

Madame de Gondi, though she continued all her life an arbitress of the great world of Paris, never entirely recovered the gayety which had been her chief characteristic before the eventful visit of the Selbys; and from that time she associated more with the good bishop of Lisieux, and Madame de Maignelai, and less with the Count Hamiltons and the Preux Grammonts of the day.

Sir Henry Oswald lived long enough to see Charles the Second reseated on his father's throne, but lived *not* long enough to see him sink that throne lower than ever it had ever sunk before, or — so the Almighty still extend to it his favor and protection — shall sink for ever! aud never, till he died in the arms of his dear children, did he cease to rejoice at the escape of Isabella from the wretched and guilty Wyvil, or to bless the day when she made Henry Chaloner his son.

Saving alone the kings, and cardinals, and generals, who have scarce figured for a moment in our passing pageant, whose fates and follies may be read in solid history, one person only now remains of any note — the sieur de Bellechassaigne; and he, as constancy and valor ever should find their reward at last, overcame the opposition of his fair Annette's kindred, and won a fair and gentle bride, to partake the fortunes of as brilliant and as brave a partisan, as ever drew sword for his lady or his king.

THE END.

PHILOSOPHERS AND ACTRESSES

By Arsene Houssaye. With beautifully-engraved Portraits of Voltaire and Mad. Parabère. Two vols., 12mo, price $2.50.

"We have here the most charming book we have read these many days,—so powerful in its fascination that we have been held for hours from our imperious labors, or needful slumbers, by the entrancing influence of its pages. One of the most desirable fruits of the prolific field of literature of the present season."—*Portland Eclectic.*

"Two brilliant and fascinating—we had almost said, bewitching—volumes, combining information and amusement, the lightest gossip, with solid and serviceable wisdom."—*Yankee Blade.*

"It is a most admirable book, full of originality, wit, information and philosophy Indeed, the vividness of the book is extraordinary. The scenes and descriptions are absolutely life-like."—*Southern Literary Gazette.*

"The works of the present writer are the only ones the spirit of whose rhetoric does justice to those times, and in fascination of description and style equal the fascinations they descant upon."—*New Orleans Commercial Bulletin.*

"The author is a brilliant writer, and serves up his sketches in a sparkling manner." *Christian Freeman.*

ANCIENT EGYPT UNDER THE PHARAOHS.

By John Kendrick, M. A. In 2 vols., 12mo, price $2.50.

"No work has heretofore appeared suited to the wants of the historical student, which combined the labors of artists, travellers, interpreters and critics, during the periods from the earliest records of the monarchy to its final absorption in the empire of Alexander. This work supplies this deficiency."—*Olive Branch.*

"Not only the geography and political history of Egypt under the Pharaohs are given, but we are furnished with a minute account of the domestic manners and customs of the inhabitants, their language, laws, science, religion, agriculture, navigation and commerce."—*Commercial Advertiser.*

"These volumes present a comprehensive view of the results of the combined labors of travellers, artists, and scientific explorers, which have effected so much during the present century toward the development of Egyptian archæology and history."—*Journal of Commerce.*

"The descriptions are very vivid and one wanders, delighted with the author, through the land of Egypt, gathering at every step, new phases of her wondrous history, and ends with a more intelligent knowledge than he ever before had, of the land of the Pharaohs."—*American Spectator.*

COMPARATIVE PHYSIOGNOMY;

Or Resemblances between Men and Animals. By J. W. Redfield, M. D. In one vol., 8vo, with several hundred illustrations. price, $2.00.

"Dr. Redfield has produced a very curious, amusing, and instructive book, curious in its originality and illustrations, amusing in the comparisons and analyses, and instructive because it contains very much useful information on a too much neglected subject. It will be eagerly read and quickly appreciated."—*National Ægis.*

"The whole work exhibits a good deal of scientific research, intelligent observation, and ingenuity."—*Daily Union.*

"Highly entertaining even to those who have little time to study the science."—*Detroit Daily Advertiser.*

"This is a remarkable volume and will be read by two classes, those who study for information, and those who read for amusement. For its originality and entertaining character, we commend it to our readers."—*Albany Express.*

"It is overflowing with wit, humor, and originality, and profusely illustrated. The whole work is distinguished by vast research and knowledge."—*Knickerbocker.*

"The plan is a novel one; the proofs striking, and must challenge the attention of the curious."—*Daily Advertiser*

MACAULAY'S SPEECHES.

Speeches by the Right Hon. T. B. MACAULAY, M. P., Author of "The History of England," "Lays of Ancient Rome," &c., &c. Two vols., 12mo, price $2.00.

"It is hard to say whether his poetry, his speeches in parliament, or his brilliant essays, are the most charming; each has raised him to very great eminence, and would be sufficient to constitute the reputation of any ordinary man."—*Sir Archibald Alison.*

"It may be said that Great Britain has produced no statesman since Burke, who has united in so eminent a degree as Macaulay the lofty and cultivated genius, the eloquent orator, and the sagacious and far-reaching politician."—*Albany Argus.*

"We do not know of any living English orator, whose eloquence comes so near the ancient ideal—close, rapid, powerful, *practical* reasoning, animated by an intense earnestness of feeling."—*Courier & Enquirer.*

"Mr. Macaulay has lately acquired as great a reputation as an orator, as he had formerly won as an essayist and historian. He takes in his speeches the same wide and comprehensive grasp of his subject that he does in his essays, and treats it in the same elegant style."—*Philadelphia Evening Bulletin.*

"The same elaborate finish, sparkling antithesis, full sweep and copious flow of thought, and transparency of style, which made his essays so attractive, are found in his speeches. They are so perspicuous, so brilliantly studded with ornament and illustration, and so resistless in their current, that they appear at the time to be the wisest and greatest of human compositions."—*New York Evangelist.*

TRENCH ON PROVERBS.

On the Lessons in Proverbs, by RICHARD CHENEVIX TRENCH, B. D., Professor of Divinity in King's College, London, Author of the "Study of Words." 12mo, cloth, 50 cents.

"Another charming book by the author of the "Study of Words," on a subject which is so ingeniously treated, that we wonder no one has treated it before."—*Yankee Blade.*

"It is a book at once profoundly instructive, and at the same time deprived of all approach to dryness, by the charming manner in which the subject is treated."—*Arthur's Home Gazette.*

"It is a wide field, and one which the author has well cultivated, adding not only to his own reputation, but a valuable work to our literature."—*Albany Evening Transcript.*

"The work shows an acute perception, a genial appreciation of wit, and great research. It is a very rare and agreeable production, which may be read with profit and delight."—*New York Evangelist.*

"The style of the author is terse and vigorous—almost a model in its kind."—*Portland Eclectic.*

THE LION SKIN

And the Lover Hunt; by CHARLES DE BERNARD. 12mo, $1.00.

"It is not often the novel-reader can find on his bookseller's shelf a publication so full of incidents and good humor, and at the same time so provocative of honest thought."—*National* (Worcester, Mass.) *Ægis.*

"It is full of incidents; and the reader becomes so interested in the principal personages in the work, that he is unwilling to lay the book down until he has learned their whole history."—*Boston Olive Branch.*

"It is refreshing to meet occasionally with a well-published story which is written for a story, and for nothing else—which is not tipped with the snapper of a moral, or loaded in the handle with a pound of philanthropy, or an equal quantity of leaden philosophy."—*Springfield Republican.*

A STRAY YANKEE IN TEXAS.

A Stray Yankee in Texas. By PHILIP PAXTON. With Illustrations by Darley. Second Edition, 12mo., cloth. $1 25.

"The work is a *chef d'œuvre* in a style of literature in which our country has no rival, and we commend it to all who are afflicted with the blues or *ennui*, as an effectual means of tickling their diaphragms, and giving their cheeks a holyday."—*Boston Yankee Blade.*

"We find, on a perusal of it, that Mr. Paxton has not only produced a readable, but a valuable book, as regards reliable information on Texan affairs.—*Hartford Christian Secretary.*

"The book is strange, wild, humorous, and yet truthful. It will be found admirably descriptive of a state of society which is fast losing its distinctive peculiarities in the rapid increase of population."—*Arthur's Home Gazette.*

"One of the richest, most entertaining, and, at the same time, instructive works one could well desire."—*Syracuse Daily Journal.*

"The book is a perfect picture of western manners and Texan adventures, and will occasion many a hearty laugh in the reader."—*Albany Daily State Register.*

NICK OF THE WOODS.

Nick of the Woods, or the Jibbenainosay; a Tale of Kentucky. By ROBERT M. BIRD, M. D., Author of "Calavar," "The Infidel," &c. New and Revised Edition, with Illustrations by Darley. 1 volume, 12mo., cloth, $1 25.

"One of those singular tales which impress themselves in ineradicable characters upon the memory of every imaginative reader."—*Arthur's Home Gazette.*

"Notwithstanding it takes the form of a novel, it is understood to be substantial truth in the dress of fiction; and nothing is related but which has its prototype in actual reality."—*Albany Argus.*

"It is a tale of frontier life and Indian warfare, written by a masterly pen, with its scenes so graphically depicted that they amount to a well-executed painting, at once striking and thrilling."—*Buffalo Express.*

WHITE, RED, AND BLACK.

Sketches of American Society, during the Visits of their Guests, by FRANCIS and THERESA PULSZKY. Two vols., 12mo., cloth, $2.

"Mr. Pulszky and his accomplished wife have produced an eminently candid and judicious book, which will be read with pleasure and profit on both sides of the Atlantic."—*New York Daily Times.*

"The authors have here furnished a narrative of decided interest and value. They have given us a view of the Hungarian war, a description of the Hungarian passage to this country, and a sketch of Hungarian travels over the country."—*Philad. Christian Chronicle.*

"Of all the recent books on America by foreign travellers, this is at once the most fair and the most correct."—*Philad. Saturday Gazette.*

"Unlike most foreign tourists in the United States, they speak of our institutions, manners, customs, &c., with marked candor, and at the same time evince a pretty thorough knowledge of our history."—*Hartford Christian Secretary.*

"This is a valuable book, when we consider the amount and variety of the information it contains, and when we estimate the accuracy with which the facts are detailed." —*Worcester Spy.*

DISCOVERY AND EXPLORATION

Of the Mississippi Valley. With the Original Narratives of Marquette, Allouez, Membré, Hennepin, and Anastase Douay. By JOHN GILMARY SHEA. With a fac-simile of the Original Map of Marquette. 1 vol., 8vo,; Cloth. Antique. $2.00.

"A volume of great and curious interest to all concerned to know the early history of this great Western land."—*Cincinnati Christian Herald.*

"We believe that this is altogether the most thorough work that has appeared on the subject to which it relates. It is the result of long-continued and diligent research, and no legitimate source of information has been left unexplored. The work combines the interest of romance with the authenticity of history."—*Puritan Recorder.*

"Mr. Shea has rendered a service to the cause of historical literature worthy of all praise by the excellent manner in which he has prepared this important publication for the press."—*Boston Traveller.*

NEWMAN'S REGAL ROME.

An Introduction to Roman History. By FRANCIS W. NEWMAN, Professor of Latin in the University College, London. 12mo, Cloth. 63 cents.

"The book, though small in compass, is evidently the work of great research and reflection, and is a valuable acquisition to historical literature."—*Courier and Enquirer.*

"A work of great erudition and power, vividly reproducing the wonderful era of Roman history under the kings. We greet it as a work of profound scholarship, genial art, and eminent interest—a work that will attract the scholar and please the general reader."—*N. Y. Evangelist.*

"Nearly all the histories in the schools should be banished, and such as this should take their places."—*Boston Journal.*

"Professor Newman's work will be found full of interest, from the light it throws on the formation of the language, the races, and the history, of ancient Rome."—*Wall-street Journal.*

THE CHEVALIERS OF FRANCE,

From the Crusaders to the Mareschals of Louis XIV. By HENRY W. HERBERT, author of "The Cavaliers of England," "Cromwell," "The Brothers," &c., &c. 1 vol. 12mo. $1.25.

"Mr. Herbert is one of the best writers of historical tales and legends in this or any other country."—*Christian Freeman.*

"This is a work of great power of thought and vividness of picturing. It is a moving panorama of the inner life of the French empire in the days of chivalry."—*Albany Spec*

"The series of works by this author, illustrative of the romance of history, is deservedly popular. They serve, indeed, to impart and impress on the mind a great deal of valuable information; for the facts of history are impartially exhibited, and the fiction presents a vivid picture of the manners and sentiments of the times."—*Journal of Commerce.*

"The work contains four historical tales or novelettes, marked by that vigor of style and beauty of description which have found so many admirers among the readers of the author's numerous romanaes."—*Lowell Journal.*

NAPOLEON IN EXILE;

Or, a Voice from St. Helena. Being the opinions and reflections of Napoleon, on the most important events in his Life and Government, in his own words. By BARRY E. O'MEARA, his late Surgeon, with a Portrait of Napoleon, after the celebrated picture of Delaroche, and a view of St. Helena, both beautifully engraved on steel. 2 vols. 12mo, cloth, $2.

"Nothing can exceed the graphic truthfulness with which these volumes record the words and habits of Napoleon at St. Helena, and its pages are endowed with a charm far transcending that of romance."—*Albany State Register.*

"Every one who desires to obtain a thorough knowledge of the character of Napoleon, should possess himself of this book of O'Meara's."—*Arthur's Home Gazette.*

"It is something indeed to know Napoleon's opinion of the men and events of the thirty years preceding his fall, and his comments throw more light upon history than anything we have read."—*Albany Express.*

"The two volumes before us are worthy supplements to any history of France."—*Boston Evening Gazette.*

MEAGHER'S SPEECHES.

Speeches on the Legislative Independence of Ireland, with Introductory Notes. By FRANCIS THOMAS MEAGHER. 1 vol. 12mo, Cloth. Portrait. $1.

"The volume before us embodies some of the noblest specimens of Irish eloquence; not florid, bombastic, nor acrimonious, but direct, manly, and convincing."—*New York Tribune.*

"There is a glowing, a burning eloquence, in these speeches, which prove the author a man of extraordinary intellect."—*Boston Olive Branch.*

"As a brilliant and effective orator, Meagher stands unrivalled."—*Portland Eclectic.*

"All desiring to obtain a good idea of the political history of Ireland and the movements of her people, will be greatly assisted by reading these speeches."—*Syracuse Daily Star.*

"It is copiously illustrated by explanatory notes, so that the reader will have no difficulty in understanding the exact state of affairs when each speech was delivered."—*Boston Traveller.*

THE PRETTY PLATE,

A new and beautiful juvenile. By JOHN VINCENT. Illustrated by DARLEY. 1 vol. 16mo, Cloth, gilt, 63 cts. Extra gilt edges, 88 cts.

"We venture to say that no reader, great or small, who takes up this book, will lay it down unfinished."—*Courier and Enquirer.*

"This is an elegant little volume for a juvenile gift-book. The story is one of peculiar instruction and interest to the young, and is illustrated with beautiful engravings."—*Boston Christian Freeman.*

"One of the very best told and sweetest juvenile stories that has been issued from the press this season. It has a most excellent moral."—*Detroit Daily Advertiser.*

"A nice little book for a holyday present. Our little girl has read it through, and pronounces it first rate."—*Hartford Christian Secretary.*

"It is a pleasant child's book, well told, handsomely published, and illustrated in Darley's best style."—*Albany Express.*

POETICAL WORKS OF FITZ-GREENE HALLECK.

New and only Complete Edition, containing several New Poems, together with many now first collected. One vol., 12mo., price one dollar.

"Halleck is one of the brightest stars in our American literature, and his name is like a household word wherever the English language is spoken."—*Albany Express.*

"There are few poems to be found, in any language, that surpass, in beauty of thought and structure, some of these."—*Boston Commonwealth.*

"To the numerous admirers of Mr. Halleck, this will be a welcome book; for it is a characteristic desire in human nature to have the productions of our favorite authors in an elegant and substantial form."—*Christian Freeman.*

"Mr. Halleck never appeared in a better dress, and few poets ever deserved a better one."—*Christian Intelligencer.*

THE STUDY OF WORDS.

By Archdeacon R. C. Trench. One vol., 12mo., price 75 cts.

"He discourses in a truly learned and lively manner upon the original unity of language, and the origin, derivation, and history of words, with their morality and separate spheres of meaning."—*Evening Post*

"This is a noble tribute to the divine faculty of speech. Popularly written, for use as lectures, exact in its learning, and poetic in its vision, it is a book at once for the scholar and the general reader."—*New York Evangelist.*

"It is one of the most striking and original publications of the day, with nothing of hardness, dullness, or dryness about it, but altogether fresh, lively, and entertaining." —*Boston Evening Traveller.*

BRONCHITIS, AND KINDRED DISEASES.

In language adapted to common readers. By W. W. Hall, M. D. One vol., 12 mo, price $1.00.

"It is written in a plain, direct, common-sense style, and is free from the quackery which marks many of the popular medical books of the day. It will prove useful to those who need it."—*Central Ch. Herald.*

"Those who are clergymen, or who are preparing for the sacred calling, and public speakers generally, should not fail of securing this work."—*Ch. Ambassador.*

"It is full of hints on the nature of the vital organs, and does away with much superstitious dread in regard to consumption."—*Greene County Whig.*

"This work gives some valuable instruction in regard to food and hygienic influences."—*Nashua Oasis.*

KNIGHTS OF ENGLAND, FRANCE, AND SCOTLAND.

By Henry William Herbert. One vol., 12mo., price $1.25.

"They are partly the romance of history and partly fiction, forming, when blended, portraitures, valuable from the correct drawing of the times they illustrate, and interesting from their romance."—*Albany Knickerbocker.*

"They are spirit-stirring productions, which will be read and admired by all who are pleased with historical tales written in a vigorous, bold, and dashing style."—*Boston Journal.*

"These legends of love and chivalry contain some of the finest tales which the graphic and powerful pen of Herbert has yet given to the lighter literature of the day." —*Detroit Free Press.*

THE CHILDREN OF LIGHT.

By CAROLINE CHESEBRO', Author of "Isa, a Pilgrimage," "Dream-Land by Daylight," &c., &c. 12mo., Cloth. $1.00.

"It is truly an attractive gallery of portraits, vivid pictures of human beings wrought by human hands. The work is admirably conceived, and in every page bears the clear impress of Miss CHESEBRO's keen perceptions, her powerful and original intellect, and a depth of sentiment and feeling that are only developed and made useful by the highly gifted and the pure in heart."—*Albany State Register.*

"To those of our readers who desire a good book—one for the most part not filled with the common trash of the times, and which is the production of 'a perfect woman nobly planned'—we would recommend the 'Children of Light.'"—*N. Y. Truth-Teller.*

"The work is characterized by great boldness of thought, elegant diction, and vigorous tone."—*Greene County Whig.*

THE FOREST.

By W. HUNTINGTON, author of "Lady Alice," "Alban," &c., &c. 1 vol. 12mo, Cloth. $1.25.

"The author gives us an exceedingly vivid description of forest-life, and has worked up the incidents of his story so happily, that the interest of the reader is sustained unflagging to the close."—*Portland Eclectic.*

"The author is a passionate lover of Nature, and is distinguished for the philosophic beauty and accuracy of his descriptions. The tone of thought pervading the book is quite elevated and healthy."—*Cincinnati Journal and Messenger.*

"For dramatic effect the plot and incidents are well managed, the narrative is sustained with spirit, and several of the characters are sketched with a vigorous hand."—*Protestant Churchman.*

"The work abounds in graphic portraitures of our glorious forest scenery, and in sharp delineations of character."—*N. Y. Evangelist.*

"The style of the work throughout is one which can not fail to claim the attention of the reader, and win for him an unreserved approval."—*Syracuse Daily Journal.*

CAP-SHEAF,

A Fresh Bundle. By LEWIS MYRTLE. 1 vol. 12mo, cloth. $1.00.

"If one wants a book to read when he goes home and sits down by his fireside at night, wearied and careworn with the toils and buffetings of life, this is just the one for him."—*Syracuse Daily Journal.*

"It is a book for a minute, an hour, or a day. Throughout its pages are distributed chaste and tender thoughts, glowing imagery, and high moral influences."—*Philadelphia City Item.*

"There is a rich vein of simplicity, and naturalness, and true feeling, running through this volume. The author evidently carries a well-practised pen, and speaks from a gifted and well-furnished mind and a full heart."—*Albany Argus.*

"In fact, it is a delightful book—hearty in tone and healthy in morality, and we bespeak for it the favor which its merits wherever it goes will be sure to command."—*Temperance Courier.*

"This is a collection of light stories and graceful sketches, which must have proceeded from a warm and affectionate heart. The volume is earnestly commended to the perusal of the reader."—*Lowell Journal and Courier.*

CLOVERNOOK;

Or, Recollections of our Neighborhood in the West. By ALICE CAREY. Illustrated by DARLEY. One vol., 12mo., price $1.00. (Fourth edition.)

"In this volume there is a freshness which perpetually charms the reader. You seem to be made free of western homes at once."—*Old Colony Memorial.*

"They bear the true stamp of genius—simple, natural, truthful—and evince a keen sense of the humor and pathos, of the comedy and tragedy, of life in the country."—*J G Whittier.*

DREAM-LAND BY DAY-LIGHT:

A Panorama of Romance. By CAROLINE CHESEBRO'. Illustrated by DARLEY. One vol., 12mo., price $1.25. (Second edition.)

"These simple and beautiful stories are all highly endued with an exquisite perception of natural beauty, with which is combined an appreciative sense of its relation to the highest moral emotions."—*Albany State Register.*

"Gladly do we greet this floweret in the field of our literature, for it is fragrant with sweet and bright with hues that mark it to be of Heaven's own planting."—*Courier and Enquirer.*

"There is a depth of sentiment and feeling not ordinarily met with, and some of the noblest faculties and affections of man's nature are depicted and illustrated by the skilful pen of the authoress."—*Churchman.*

LAYS OF THE SCOTTISH CAVALIERS.

By WILLIAM E. AYTOUN, Professor of Literature and Belles-Lettres in the University of Edinburgh and Editor of Blackwood's Magazine. One vol., 12mo. cloth, price $1.00.

"Since Lockhart and Macaulay's ballads, we have had no metrical work to be compared in spirit, vigor, and rhythm with this. These ballads embody and embalm the chief historical incidents of Scottish history—literally in 'thoughts that breathe and words that burn.' They are full of lyric energy, graphic description, and genuine feeling."—*Home Journal.*

"The fine ballad of 'Montrose' in this collection is alone worth the price of the book.' *Boston Transcript.*

THE BOOK OF BALLADS.

By BON GAULTIER. One volume, 12mo., cloth, price 75 cents.

"Here is a book for everybody who loves classic fun. It is made up of ballads of all sorts, each a capital parody upon the style of some one of the best lyric writers of the time, from the thundering versification of Lockhart and Macaulay to the sweetest and simplest strains of Wordsworth and Tennyson. The author is one of the first scholars, and one of the most finished writers of the day, and this production is but the frolic of his genius in play-time"—*Courier and Enquirer.*

"We do not know to whom belongs this *nom de plume,* but he is certainly a humorist of no common power."—*Providence Journal.*

CHARACTERS IN THE GOSPEL,

Illustrating Phases of Character at the Present Day. By Rev. E. H. CHAPIN. One vol., 12mo., price 50 cents. (Second edition.)

"As we read his pages, the reformer, the sensualist, the skeptic, the man of the world, the seeker, the sister of charity and of faith, stand out from the Scriptures, and join themselves with our own living world."—*Christian Enquirer.*

"Mr. Chapin has an easy, graceful style, neatly touching the outlines of his pictures, and giving great consistency and beauty to the whole. The reader will find admirable descriptions, some most wholesome lessons, and a fine spirit."—*N. Y. Evangelist.*

"Its brilliant vivacity of style forms an admirable combination with its soundness of thought and depth of feeling."—*Tribune.*

LADIES OF THE COVENANT:

Memoirs of Distinguished Scottish Females, embracing the Period of the Covenant and the Persecution. By Rev. JAMES ANDERSON. One vol., 12mo., price $1.25.

"It is a record which, while it confers honor on the sex, will elevate the heart, and strengthen it to the better performance of every duty."—*Religious Herald. (Va.)*

"It is a book of great attractiveness, having not only the freshness of novelty, but every element of historical interest."—*Courier and Enquirer.*

"It is written with great spirit and a hearty sympathy, and abounds in incidents of more than a romantic interest, while the type of piety it discloses is the noblest and most elevated."—*N. Y. Evangelist.*

TALES AND TRADITIONS OF HUNGARY.

By THERESA PULSZKY, with a Portrait of the Author. One vol., price $1.25.

THE above contains, in addition to the English publication, a NEW PREFACE, and TALES, now first printed from the manuscript of the Author, who has a direct interest in the publication.

"This work claims more attention than is ordinarily given to books of its class. Such is the fluency and correctness—nay, even the nicety and felicity of style—with which Madame Pulszky writes the English language, that merely in this respect the tales here collected form a curious study. But they contain also highly suggestive illustrations of national literature and character."—*London Examiner.*

"Freshness of subject is invaluable in literature—Hungary is still fresh ground. It has been trodden, but it is not yet a common highway. The tales and legends are very various, from the mere traditional anecdote to the regular legend, and they have the sort of interest which all national traditions excite."—*London Leader.*

SORCERY AND MAGIC.

Narratives of Sorcery and Magic, from the most Authentic Sources. By THOMAS WRIGHT, A.M., &c. One vol. 12mo., price $1.25.

"We have no hesitation in pronouncing this one of the most interesting works which has for a long time issued from the press."—*Albany Express.*

"The narratives are intensely interesting, and the more so, as they are evidently written by a man whose object is simply to tell the truth, and who is not himself bewitched by any favorite theory."—*N. Y. Recorder*

www.ingramcontent.com/pod-product-compliance
Lightning Source LLC
LaVergne TN
LVHW020934110826
845150LV00004B/857

* 9 7 8 1 4 2 5 5 5 2 3 5 0 *